DEFEAT

CE SHORLAND

CHAPTER 1

The heavy scent of aged paper and mahogany enveloped Austin as he stepped into the grand library of Biltmore, the echo of his footsteps a whisper against the silence. Jacob's presence faded away as Abraham waved a dismissive hand without lifting his gaze from the documents sprawled across the desk. Alone now with only the towering shelves for company, Austin's eyes roved over the spines of countless books, their titles etched in gold and embossed letters that promised knowledge and escape. It was an oasis of calm he had barely savoured since his arrival.

"I am truly sorry about your friend," Abraham's voice sliced through the tranquility, devoid of warmth, "but I feel that at least now you will have justice." Austin's jaw tensed, and he forced down the indignant retort bubbling up his throat. His gaze flicked to the man who might as well have been a stranger to empathy, then back to the rows of literary sentinels that seemed to stand at attention.
"Thank you." When he began to speak, he had to summon all his self-control to offer a polite remark instead of a snide or sarcastic response.
"By this afternoon, things will be as they were," Abraham's words were slow and deliberate, the underlying steel in them couldn't be mistaken, "you know the rules, Austin. We all have our parts to play."

"Of course," Austin muttered, the taste of the words like ash on his tongue, "if that's all, may I be excused? There's work to be done in the storehouses to further prepare for winter." He shifted his weight from one foot to the other, keen to distance himself from the cloying atmosphere of obligation that filled the library. Abraham leaned back against the desk, fingers interlaced in front of him as he surveyed Austin with an air of detached amusement.

"Indeed," he drawled, eyes narrowing slightly, "anyone who has been stealing must steal no longer, but must work, doing something useful with their own hands, that they may have something to share with those in need." His words hung heavily in the air, a veiled reminder of past transgressions and the thin ice upon which Austin now tread.

"Which one's that one?" Austin questioned cautiously, meeting Abraham's gaze with a questioning brow.

"Ephesians," Abraham eyed him gingerly in return, "chapter four, verse 28."

"Ahh, one of my favourites." A hint of sarcasm laced Austin's tone as his eyes wandered around the room again, noting the cast iron poker next to the fireplace.

"I don't tolerate insolence, Austin." Abraham's words were short and sharp, mirroring his frustration.

"Understood," Austin replied curtly, resisting the urge to clench his fists, "my apologies for my *insolence*." With a curt nod, he turned on his heel and strode out of the library, the echo of his boots against the hardwood floor punctuating his departure. Once Austin's footsteps had faded into the vastness of the Biltmore, Jacob slipped silently back into the room like a shadow reclaiming its space.

"I don't trust him," he murmured, eyeing Abraham with a mix of respect and unease, "or any of his lot. Not after what Rocky shared about them."

"Jacob." Abraham began, his tone taking on the quality of chastisement laced with patience.

"Sir." Jacob's body became rigid, his stance solid and affirming. Abraham stood and approached the window. Where light filtered in, it cast long shadows across the polished floor.

"John chapter one verse nine tells us, 'if we confess our sins, he is faithful and just and will forgive us our sins and purify us from all unrighteousness'," he paused, allowing the scripture to settle between them like dust, "Austin has shown himself useful since his arrival, wouldn't you agree?"

"I suppose." Jacob conceded reluctantly, his gaze dropping to the floor.

"Are you questioning my judgment, then?" Abraham's voice was soft, almost a whisper, yet it carried the weight of command that left little room for argument.

"No, sir." Jacob replied quickly, too quickly perhaps. The words were automatic, but his nervous glance betrayed the conflict within.

"Good," Abraham nodded with satisfaction, his attention returning to the imposing desk and the papers and decisions that awaited him like loyal subjects awaiting their king, "leave me now, Jacob. I have much to consider." Jacob bowed his head in acquiescence and made for the exit, pausing to linger by the door, his posture rigid with unvoiced apprehensions. The echo of his footsteps had long since faded into the cavernous silence of the library, yet he remained a statue, hesitant to retrace his path back to the world outside Abraham's domain.

"Sir," Jacob began, the word barely a whisper, "can I ask for your forgiveness? My concerns were not meant as disrespect." Abraham peered over the rim of his spectacles, eyes locking onto Jacob's with a tranquility that belied the intensity of his gaze.

"Of course Jacob," he said, his voice as measured as the ticking of the grandfather clock by the wall, "your vigilance is noted, but let it not cloud your trust in my decisions."

"You have my utmost faith and respect, sir." Jacob's praise was meant as a compliment, yet the subservience was beginning to frustrate Abraham.

"Good. Now, please leave me. There's much work to be done, and peace is a scarce commodity these days." His hand waved gently, almost as a king dismissing his subject. Jacob nodded, a flush of relief warming his cheeks as he turned and slipped out, the heavy door closing behind him with a soft click that sealed him away from the sanctum of power and plotting, leaving Abraham alone once more in the grand library surrounded by silent tomes and the weight of his own authority.

Julia lay still upon the narrow bed, her gaze tracking the grotesque dance of shadows cast by the flickering lights. Each picture, each painting on the walls, seemed to pulse with an eerie life of its own, the eyes of painted figures following her every breath.

"Why do they call it the Halloween Room?" She asked, the words floating up to the ceiling where darkness clung like cobwebs. Standing at the foot of the bed with her arms folded, Anne glanced around with a clinical detachment.

"I don't know," she replied, her tone devoid of curiosity for such trivial mysteries, "how are you feeling?"

"Fine." Julia answered without shifting her gaze, the single word hanging between them, hollow and insubstantial.

"Physically you may be. But mentally?" Anne prodded, her expression unreadable in the dim light.

"I'm fine." Julia repeated, turning to meet Anne's probing stare. Her eyes echoed the void left by loss, windows to a soul grappling with the unseen wounds that cut deeper than flesh. Anne observed her in silence, sensing the layers of armour Julia had wrapped herself in, an invisible shield against the world's cruelty. But even steel could bend and break, and in the quiet of the Halloween Room surrounded by silent sentinels from the walls, both women understood that some scars were carved far beyond the surface.

"Any follow-up cramping? Bleeding?" Anne's hand, steady and reassuring, rested on Julia's shoulder, urging her gently into a sitting position. Her voice was calm, the practiced neutrality of a doctor who has seen too much yet still hoped for healing. Julia shook her head, a shiver running down her spine as she pulled her gaze from the macabre artistry around her.

"It's quite creepy down here." She murmured, wrapping her arms around herself as if to ward off the chill that seemed to emanate from the very walls. Anne's lips pressed into a thin line.

"I had no say in where they put the infirmary." A trace of frustration seeped through her usually controlled demeanour, a rare crack in her professional facade.

"Have you spoken to Austin lately?" Julia asked, the name like a stone dropped into the still waters of their conversation.

"Only when we cross paths in the halls." Anne answered, her eyes not meeting Julia's. There was something final in her tone, a chapter closed and shelved away.

"Can't believe he cheated on you." Julia said, her voice faltering, disbelief and hurt vying for dominance. Anne's face hardened for a moment before settling back into indifference.

"I don't care about it. Not anymore." She turned away, ostensibly to tidy some equipment, but there was an air of dismissal around her that suggested she'd rather leave certain stones unturned. Julia let out a sigh and cast her eyes once more across the room, the unsettling decor making her feel even more isolated. Sensing a need to change the topic, Julia opened her mouth to speak but her inquiry was abruptly cut short by approaching footsteps in the corridor outside and the sudden appearance of Austin, as if he had been summoned by her mention of him. His figure was momentarily framed by the threshold as he stepped into the dimness of the infirmary carrying a box that seemed too small to justify the strain on his face.

"Sorry to interrupt." He murmured, almost breathless as if the words were an afterthought, his presence an unwelcome ripple across the calm surface of their solitude. Austin set the box down with a thud and dust motes dancing in the slanted light as they were disturbed from their rest. Anne barely glanced up from her clipboard but gestured absently to the back wall where provisions had been stacked with methodical precision.

"Looks like we're preparing for a siege." Julia muttered, her eyes scanning the cans and bandages that had transformed the corner into a makeshift storehouse.

"Abraham makes sure we're never short on necessities." Austin replied, trying to sound casual though his gaze didn't quite meet hers.

"I wasn't talking to you." Julia snapped, her tone sharp enough to slice through the chill air of the room. The words hung between them, heavy with unspoken grievances.

"Sorry." Austin murmured, chastened. He turned on his heel, ready to escape the undercurrents of tension but Anne's voice halted him.

"Austin, wait," her voice was softer now, tinged with concern, "how's your back?" He paused, the memory of the whip's bite searing across his skin as fresh as if it had happened moments ago. Ten lashes that had stripped away more than just flesh, leaving behind a stark reminder of his place in this new world order at Biltmore.

"Phillip says it's healing fine." Austin answered after a moment, avoiding divulging the nights when the pain made sleep an elusive spectre. Anne nodded, her expression unreadable, but there was an acknowledgment in her eyes that spoke of shared hardships. She turned back to Julia who was still surveying the room with a detached sort of curiosity. Austin took that as his cue to leave, stepping out into the corridor where the shadows seemed less oppressive than the weight of history and heartbreak that clung to the stones of the walls.

"You don't have to be so angry." Anne said softly, the nonchalance in her voice belied the weight of her words. Julia's fingers curled into fists, the fabric of the bedspread bunching beneath her grip.

"And you don't have to be so calm," she chastised, her voice strained like a wire pulled too tight, "you should be furious." Anne paused and turned, facing Julia with an impassive expression.

"Anger doesn't keep you alive here," she shrugged, a ghost of resignation flickering across her features, "I'm done. You can leave if you want to."

"I'd rather stay a bit longer," Julia's eyes fell away, seeking refuge in the shadows that clung to the corners of the room, "I hate it upstairs."

"Why?" Anne asked, her curiosity piqued despite herself.

"Something feels wrong," Julia confessed, her gaze still evading Anne's, "there's a, a heaviness." Anne sighed, placing a gentle hand on Julia's shoulder.

"There's a lot wrong with this place," she said, her voice a quiet echo of truth, "we have to accept it, or it'll consume us."

Austin gripped another box of supplies tightly as he navigated the dim corridor near the kitchens. The weight of the contents was nothing compared to the heaviness in his chest, the latter borne from more than just physical scars. Luis appeared from the shadows, his smirk sharp as a knife's edge as he taunted, laughter lacing his words like poison. Austin passed him, every muscle coiled, ready to strike. He clenched his jaw, his voice low and steady.

"How does it feel being at the bottom of the food chain?"

"Be careful, Luis," he warned, "or you might end up with more than just a black eye this time." Luis's smirk widened into a grin, all teeth and malice.

"Threatening me again? You'll get double the lashes next time." He jeered, his eyes alight with a sadist's glee. Austin's knuckles whitened around the edges of the cardboard box, the words festering like a wound.

"Luis, there'll come a day when you're the one needing help," Austin's voice was edged with steel, fixing Luis with a look cold enough to freeze the marrow, "and I'll be there making sure you feel every bit of the abandonment you've earned."

"Sure Austin. But until that fateful day, make yourself useful and keep those kitchens stocked. We wouldn't want anyone going hungry because of your negligence," Luis's laughter echoed hollowly in the corridor, bouncing off the stone walls with mocking resonance as he backed away with exaggerated caution, "and by the way, I'm sorry to hear about Beth. Such a shame. But at least now maybe we'll have some peace and quiet." The taunting words clung to Austin while he stood motionless as Luis walked away from him down the dimly lit corridor. The false sympathy in his voice grated against Austin's ears. The words hung heavy in the air, a poisonous miasma that seemed to seep into the very stone. Austin watched Luis's retreating figure, a silent vow hardening within him like a stone. Without a word, he turned and continued his solitary march towards the kitchens, each step echoing the rhythm of his pulse - a silent drumbeat of suppressed rage and simmering defiance. Luis slinked up the stairs with an air of authority he felt entitled to but had not earned. He stepped into the library with a sense of purpose that filled the space, his boots barely whispering against the richly carpeted floor.

"Someone in your position has not yet earned an entrance without knocking," Abraham, who had been engrossed in his papers at his massive oak desk, looked up and fixed Luis with a measured gaze, "is there something you need?"

"Everything is set for the afternoon." Luis announced, his voice holding an edge of pride.

"Thank you Rocky. Or is it Luis?" Abraham asked with a wry tilt of his head, acknowledging the duality that Luis had crafted around himself.

"Call me what you will," Luis responded, the corners of his mouth lifting slightly, "but yes, the platform is ready." Abraham nodded, his eyes reflecting satisfaction.

"Good. I'm pleased with how swiftly we've managed to organise it. Efficiency is a rare commodity these days," his pause was lengthy and ominous, as though the burden of countless questions and duties weighed heavily on the king's mind, "why did you provide a false name?" Abraham raised a questioning brow before standing straight, turning his full attention to Luis.

"Given my history with that group, I thought it best to avoid any unnecessary attention," Luis replied, his hands clasped behind his back as he maintained an easy stance, "I knew I'd run into them again, or someone from Prescott would. I didn't want my real name thrown around."

"Deceit is something I find distasteful." Abraham criticised, his voice dropping an octave, a subtle undercurrent of threat weaving through his words.

"It wasn't deceit, Abraham," Luis countered smoothly, "merely caution."

"Be that as it may," Abraham conceded after a brief pause, "let's not make a habit of it." His eyes flickered back to the stack of papers on his desk, signalling that he was ready to move on from the topic.

"Noted. My apologies, sir." Luis nodded once, a sign of his obedience yet his expression held an undertone of repugnance from being chastised. Abraham sifted through the documents with meticulous care, each page turn a deliberate act. Among them, detailed medical records stood out, their contents revealing more than just physical well-being.

"The young Doctor Major has been thorough." Abraham mused aloud, his fingers tracing the lines of text as if committing them to memory. Luis remained silent, his posture relaxed yet attentive. He understood the weight of the information those papers held, and the power they bestowed upon Abraham. The future of many hinged on the decisions that would be drawn from the ink-stained pages, and Luis knew better than to interfere. Abraham plucked a single sheet from the stack with a gentle tug and held it up to the light as if to divine hidden truths from the script.

"Shame," Abraham finally said without looking up, his eyes scanning the neat handwriting, "she could have made an excellent wife and mother, were her circumstances and morality different." His voice carried a note of genuine regret that lingered in the air before he strode across the room. With a flick of his wrist, he sent the paper twisting through the air to meet the flames of the fireplace. It curled and blackened at the edges, the secrets it held turning to ash and smoke. Abraham watched the embers consume the paper entirely, his expression unreadable.

"Have you settled on one?" Luis's voice was tentative, probing the edges of Abraham's decision-making like a cautious intruder. Abraham barely glanced up from the desk where he had returned, his fingers sorting through the remaining documents with authority. A grunt escaped him, neither affirmative nor dismissive as he methodically organised the papers into a pristine pile on the corner of the desk.

"Even if I had," he finally answered, his tone flat and final, "you wouldn't be the first to know." Luis offered a nod, not daring to press further, and took his leave. He knew the line between useful ally and expendable nuisance was thin under Abraham's command. Alone now, Abraham turned back towards the fire, its glow reflecting in the depths of his calculating gaze. The warmth did little to soften his austere features as he stood there, steeped in thought. His mind wandered through the profiles of potential mates, weighing their virtues and vices, their strengths and their weaknesses. The future demanded a bearer of his legacy - a wife to sculpt, to shape into the matriarch this new world required. The answer remained elusive, dancing just beyond reach like the shadows cast by the licking flames. Abraham's eyes narrowed slightly, a silent vow to bend fate to his will as he contemplated his decision about a wife to bear his child. The door to the library creaked open, breaking the silence that had settled in the room like dust on an old book. Abraham glanced up from his contemplation at the fire to see one of his soldiers standing rigid at attention.

"Sir," Brian began, a sense of urgency in his voice, "it's time to start ushering everyone outside." Abraham considered the man for a moment, his eyes lingering on the soldier's eager face. He then looked back towards the window where the snow lay thick upon the grounds of Biltmore, a pristine white blanket that seemed untouched by the troubles within its walls.

"See to it that everyone is collected," Abraham instructed, his voice carrying the weight of command, "and make sure *she* has a front row seat." Brian hesitated, confusion flickering across his features. With a look that could curdle milk, Abraham shot Brian an aggravated glance. The soldier quickly composed himself, his posture stiffening as he recognised his misstep.

"Of course, my apologies," Brian bowed his head slightly, "I'll find Jacob right away."

"See that you do." Abraham said curtly, dismissing him with a wave of his hand. As Brian exited, the quiet returned, but Abraham's focus was already shifting back to the dance of the flames before him - a reflection of the control he held over those who dwelled within these walls.

Beth sat motionless in her room, her gaze fixed on the world outside. The winter landscape was deceptively calm, the snow glittering under the caress of the afternoon sun as if beckoning her to forget the darkness that lurked behind the beauty. But there was no forgetting the sharp pain that once radiated from her jaw, now only a dull ache - a constant reminder of Luis's brutality. Her fingers traced the line of her jaw gently, the memory of his grip still vivid in her mind. She winced at the recollection, not from the physical pain which had since subsided, but from the betrayal and the fear that had come with it. The wind whispered through the barren trees outside, a soft rustling that might have been soothing in another life, in another world. But for Beth each gust was a harbinger, a prelude to the gathering that would soon unfold beneath their skeletal boughs. She knew what was expected of her, what ominous performance awaited her participation. With a heavy heart she watched as the breeze played with the powdery snow, each flake dancing its own silent ballet before settling once again into cold stillness - a stark contrast to the turmoil that churned inside her. Beth's gaze drifted from the frosted pane to the ice pack, its shape distorted and softened by a thin layer of melted water. It lay abandoned on the sill, a relic of pain that no longer served its temporary purpose. Pushing herself up from her perch, she moved away from the window with a grace that belied the weight in her chest. Her footsteps were silent on the plush carpet as she paused in the centre of the room. The opulence of the Hoppner Room surrounded her - a testament to a grandeur that felt misplaced amid the current turmoil. The rich tapestries hung heavy on the walls, their threads woven into patterns as intricate as the lies and deceit that filled the halls of Biltmore. Gilded frames boasted paintings of tranquil landscapes, cruel mockeries of freedom to those trapped within these stone confines. Even the air seemed to hold its breath, thick with the scent of aged wood and the faintest hint of lavender, a lingering ghost of serenity. Beth closed her eyes for a moment, allowing the silence to envelop her, before the rustling from the hallway clawed at her solitude. With a slow exhale, she opened her eyes and crossed the few steps to her bed. The edges of her bedspread were perfectly aligned, untouched since the morning's making, but now she perched on the edge, disturbing the pristine order. Her hands rested in her lap, fingers intertwined to still their trembling. She didn't need to look at the ornate clock to know the appointed hour was upon her - the muted sounds of doors opening and closing, footsteps, and muffled voices heralded the gathering that awaited outside. Beth's heart thudded against her ribs, each beat a countdown to an event she wished she could flee. But there was nowhere to run, no corner of Biltmore that would offer refuge from Abraham's judgment or his meticulously crafted spectacle of authority. So she waited, spine straight, her face composed into a mask that revealed nothing of the storm raging within. The click of the door handle shattered the morning's stillness as Jacob's solid frame appeared in the doorway.

"It's time." He said, his voice a low rumble that filled the space between them. Beth's gaze lifted from the blank expanse of wall she'd been studying, her eyes steady on Jacob. Without a word, she stood and reached for her worn boots, their leather scuffed from use. She pulled them on mechanically, feeling the weight of each movement, then shrugged her coat over her shoulders. It was overly heavy on her thin frame, meant to ward off winter's chill yet it did nothing to ease the cold knot of dread lodged deep in her chest. Together they traversed the hallway, descending the grand staircase, its opulence a stark contrast to the sombre procession forming within its walls. Beth's fingers trailed along the ornate banister, the wood smooth under her touch. Below, the front door stood open, ushering guests into the unforgiving light of day. Outside, the air bit at her cheeks as she stepped onto the gravel, damp with winter dew which hung in the air from the frosty night before. Her eyes scanned the gathering crowd, searching without intent until they found the front row. There stood Ben, Austin, Reece, Val, Chase, and Tyler - an array of faces etched with varying shades of apprehension and resolve. Ben stood completely still, terrified that even the slightest motion might be interpreted as a rebellion. Austin's expression was particularly pained, his jaw set in grim determination. Reece appeared stoic, but a certain tightness around his eyes betrayed his unease. Val's posture was rigid, her gaze fixed forward as if willing herself to be anywhere but here, but determined to witness what was about to unfold. Chase's hands were balled into fists at his sides, while Tyler looked on with a furrowed brow, his thoughts unreadable. And there, before them all, loomed the platform - its wooden boards were freshly laid, the grain standing out in stark relief against the white snow. The noose dangled from the crossbeam, swaying ever so slightly in the breeze as if beckoned by an unseen hand. Dew clung to the hemp fibres like teardrops, reflecting the pallid sunlight. Each step Beth took towards the structure narrowed her world to the coarse rope and the void below. With every breath, her heart pounded a frenetic rhythm, echoing through her body like a drumbeat of impending finality. She swallowed hard against the lump in her throat, feeling the distance between herself and the platform shrink with agonising slowness. As she drew nearer, the murmurs of the crowd faded into silence, leaving only the whisper of wind through the trees and the creak of the rope as it swung, a harbinger of the judgement that awaited. Her heart thrummed in her chest as well as her fractured jaw, developing the slow onset of a headache. Her breath formed clouds in the frosty air as she aligned beside Val, whose eyes were stone-cold and unwavering. On her other flank stood Jacob, his presence like a silent sentinel. Across from Val, the others assumed their positions. Ben's gaze flickered with a blend of concern and something unspoken, while Austin's eyes held a quiet sadness. Beth ignored them both, her focus locked onto the noose that swayed with an eerie patience. The lines of residents became still, a collective breath held in anticipation. Abraham ascended the platform with deliberate steps, his figure casting a long shadow over the onlookers. He surveyed the crowd with a certain gravitas, his eyes passing over each person as if weighing their worth. The afternoon sun painted a golden halo around his silhouette, yet the chill remained, seeping into Beth's bones. Abraham's voice boomed across the open space, reaching every corner of the Biltmore Estate, and seemingly beyond.

"Let everyone be subject to the governing authorities, for there is no authority except that which God has established. The authorities that exist have been established by God. Consequently, whoever rebels against the authority is rebelling against what God has instituted, and those who do so will bring judgement on themselves." His words, authoritative and unyielding, hung heavy in the cold air. Beth felt the weight of his proclamation, the scripture resonating with an undercurrent of power and threat. A shiver ran down her spine, not from the cold but from the realisation of the finality that Abraham's sermon foretold. She could sense the unease that rippled through the crowd, the discomfort that came with the recognition of their own vulnerability under his rule. He continued to bellow as she watched him, seeking any hint of mercy in his stern features, but found none. Abraham's eyes seemed to pierce into each individual soul, demanding obedience.

"For rulers hold no terror for those who do right, but for those who do wrong. Do you want to be free from fear of the one in authority? Then do what is right and you will be commended. For the one in authority is God's servant for your good," Abraham's declaration was ironclad, leaving no room for dissent, "but if you do wrong, be afraid, for rulers do not bear the sword for no reason. They are God's servants, agents of wrath to bring punishment on the wrongdoer." As the last word echoed, a hush fell upon the assembly. Beth felt the gaze of the crowd shift towards the platform, towards the fate that awaited, and towards the man who wielded the power of life and death with the certainty of divine right. Beth's fingers curled into the fabric of her coat, the material offering scant comfort. She didn't dare look away from the noose that now seemed to beckon to her, its presence a grim reminder of the consequences laid bare before them. A subtle nod from Abraham, and the front door creaked open. The murmur of the crowd softened as Sabrina was led out, her hands bound behind her, her breaths coming in ragged gasps beneath the blindfold that concealed her eyes from the fate before her. As she stepped into the chilling air of judgment, most of the onlookers twisted around for a better view, their faces etched with a mix of fear and morbid curiosity. But Beth's gaze remained unyieldingly transfixed on the noose that danced gently with the winter breeze, its dark silhouette against the pale morning sky felt like an ominous portent. She watched, her heart pounding in her chest, as Sabrina was ushered towards the platform, each step faltering, a silent testament to her dread. Sabrina fumbled up the stairs as she was pulled forcefully, and when her blindfold was pulled away revealing the stark reality of the gallows, a sharp intake of breath escaped her lips. For a moment it seemed as if her knees would buckle, her body swaying precariously close to the edge before a steadying hand caught her.

"Please, Abraham," Sabrina's voice broke through the hush, her pleas raw and desperate, clawing at the hearts of those who dared to listen, "please don't do this." But the patriarch stood immobile, his face a mask of impassive resolve as the men flanked her, their grip firm and unrelenting. With deliberate movements, they positioned her atop the trapdoor, the rough hemp noose being secured around her neck, a grotesque necklace signifying the weight of her accused sins. Sabrina struggled, her cries growing more frantic, yet the crowd could only watch with a collective breath held in anticipation. Abraham approached, his shadow falling over her trembling form. His voice rose, clear and authoritative, casting the final verdict upon her like stones.

"But if out of hate someone lies in wait, assaults and kills a neighbour, and then flees to one of these cities," he intoned, his eyes locked onto Sabrina's, "the killer shall be sent for by the town elders, be brought back from the city, and be handed over to the avenger of blood to die. Show no pity. You must purge from Israel the guilt of shedding innocent blood, so that it may go well with you." There was a sacred gravity to his words, the ancient scripture resonating with a chilling finality.

"Please!" Sabrina's wails crescendoed, a haunting echo that carried across the open field. But Abraham, resolute as ever, turned his back on her. He had spoken, and there would be no reprieve.

His voice boomed across the assembly, each syllable falling like a hammer upon the anvil of silence that had befallen the crowd. "Sabrina has been found guilty," he proclaimed, his gaze unyielding as it swept over the sea of faces before him, "of murder most foul, and worse yet, the murder of an unborn child." The hushed murmurs of the onlookers were like the rustling of dry leaves in the wind, their collective unease palpable. Abraham's hand rose, gesturing for calm as he continued, drawing upon the ancient laws to justify the grim spectacle unfolding before them. Val's knees buckled slightly, only to be caught by Reece standing beside her. "It's almost over," he whispered gently into her ear, "stay with me." "Exodus 21, verses 22 to 25," he recited, his voice echoing off the grand walls of Biltmore, "if people are fighting and hit a pregnant woman and she gives birth prematurely but there is no serious injury, the offender must be fined whatever the woman's husband demands and the court allows. But if there is serious injury, you are to take life for life, eye for eye, tooth for tooth, hand for hand, foot for foot, burn for burn, wound for wound, bruise for bruise. Sabrina, do you have any last words?" Abraham's tone softened ever so slightly, an unsettling calm in the eye of the storm. Her response was a choked sob - words failed her, lost amidst the tide of despair that threatened to drown her very being. Her shoulders shook violently, the finality of her situation closing around her like a vice as her mind filled with thoughts of her newborn daughter, left alone in a world full of uncertainty. The crowd was stone-still, the gravity of the moment pressing down upon them all. Sabrina, her body wracked with tremors of fear, could scarcely stand as she faced the man who held her fate. Eyes wide, tears streaming down her cheeks, she was a picture of desperation incarnate. With a curt nod from Abraham, time seemed to slow. The soldier behind

Sabrina reached for the lever, his movements practiced and sure. There was a clank of metal, a rush of released breaths, and the trapdoor swung open beneath her feet. The sound was sickening, a sharp crack that cut through the air with fatal precision. Sabrina's body plummeted downwards, the rope snapping taut with a force that bordered on the obscene. For a moment she hung suspended, a tragic puppet in the hands of an unseen master, then stillness claimed her, leaving only the memory of her cries to echo in the hollow chests of all who bore witness. The crowd's collective gasp dissolved into an uneasy silence, punctuated only by the gentle creak of the rope as it swayed in the wind's embrace. Some turned away, shoulders hunched against the grim spectacle. Others squeezed their eyes shut, trying to un-see what had been seared into their memories, but not all averted their gaze. Val stood with an unsettling stillness, her expression one of eerie tranquility. In her eyes there was no horror or pity, only the cold satisfaction of retribution fulfilled. The serene set of her mouth spoke of closure - a belief that justice had been served for Chantelle, whose untimely death had left a chasm in her world. Beth remained motionless, her features a blank slate. The void in her stare mirrored the emptiness that had crept into her soul over countless days of sorrow and loss. She watched dispassionately, distantly, as Sabrina's body performed a macabre dance in the chilled air. A trickle of urine stained the condemned's legs, darkening the fabric before seeping into the snow below, an ignoble epilogue to the final act of despair. The two women, side by side, formed a stark contrast in the face of death's grim theatre - one finding peace in vengeance, the other lost to numb detachment, both united under the shadow of mortality.

CHAPTER 2

Beth sat stiffly on the edge of the infirmary cot, her posture a testament to weeks of forced immobility. Anne's fingers were gentle but probing as they examined Beth's jaw, which had seen better days before being fractured. The sterile scent of antiseptic lingered in the air, a sharp reminder of the clinical setting.

"How are you feeling? It's been almost seven weeks." Anne asked, her voice carrying the weight of professional concern. Beth offered a noncommittal shrug, her eyes betraying nothing. It was an answer without words, a habit she'd picked up since speaking became a luxury paid for with suffering.

"Still in pain?" Val pressed, her gaze searching Beth's face for clues as she assisted Anne's consultation. The raised eyebrow was Beth's only concession to expression, another shrug following suit as if her shoulders bore the world's indifference.

"Maybe some Tylenol for the discomfort?" Anne's tone was practical and formal. Beth's response was yet another shrug, that simple gesture becoming her voice, her shield. Anne gave a curt nod and turned to fetch the medication. Val scribbled something onto her clipboard, her pen scratching in the quiet room. When she looked up, her eyes caught Beth's, locking in a moment of silent understanding.

"I know what you're thinking," Val began, her voice low but clear, "and no, I don't feel bad for telling Abraham about Sabrina. I just didn't think, I didn't think it would lead to a hanging." Anne paused in her task, her back to them both but her attention unmistakably piqued.

"What did you expect Abraham to do? He has always been one to put the protection of children first, invoking the wrath of God if he deems it necessary." She turned slightly, her brow furrowed in confusion, or perhaps disapproval. Val's lips pressed into a thin line, her stance unyielding. She met Anne's gaze steadily, resolute in her convictions even in the face of doubt. Val's voice was firm, edged with a cold fury that had been simmering beneath her calm facade.

"Sabrina killed my daughter. My *pregnant* daughter. I will not apologise for demanding Chantelle justice." The finality in her tone suggested there was no room for debate.

"Whatever helps you sleep at night." Anne's footsteps echoed faintly as she moved across the infirmary, her presence diminishing with each step until she became just another fixture on the periphery of this charged moment. Beth, still seated on the examination table, turned her gaze to Val, whose eyes held a storm of grief and righteousness. Slowly, Beth lifted her hand, her movements deliberate, and grasped Val's arm with a grip that belied her weakened state. It was a grip laden with unspoken words, a silent affirmation of solidarity. Val looked down at Beth, searching her face for clues. There it was - a glint of something profound in Beth's eyes, an appreciation that needed no voice. Understanding passed between them, as tangible as the pressure of Beth's fingers on Val's arm.

"Thank you." Val uttered softly, the gratitude in her voice mingling with a hint of surprise before she withdrew, leaving Beth alone with Anne once again. Anne returned to Beth's side, a look of professional concern etched into her features. She sighed, a wistful note creeping into her voice.

"You should be able to talk now," she said, her hands deftly checking over the healing jaw, "your fracture has pretty much fully healed. In a perfect world we would've taken x-rays and maybe wired your jaw. But we make do, don't we? We have to hope everything's aligned properly." Beth nodded, the motion small but deliberate. Anne studied her patient, leaning in ever so slightly as her lips pursed tightly, a minute action that spoke volumes. Beth's eyes shifted away, fixating on the wall. In the silence, her reticence hung heavy, a testament to the trials etched deep into the grain of her being. She remained quiet, offering no words, only the weight of her gaze upon the indifferent surface. Anne retrieved a small bottle from the locked cabinet, shaking out two white pills.

"These should help with any lingering pain." She said, extending her hand towards Beth. Beth eyed the Vicodin with a mixture of reluctance and need before gently taking them from Anne's palm. She swallowed the medication without water, grimacing slightly as they went down. Jacob's lingering shadow appeared in the doorway, just in time to watch Beth as she swallowed the medication.

"Are we done here?" His tone was smooth and firm, laced with a hint of inconvenience at being handed the task of babysitter.

"She can go now," Anne said, her voice soft yet firm, "try to rest for the rest of the day." Beth nodded mutely, her movements sluggish and heavy with unspoken gratitude.

"How's she doing?" Jacob's gaze darted between them.

"I've given Beth some strong painkillers for her jaw. She needs to take it easy for the remainder of the day." Anne briefed him crisply.

"Understood." Jacob acknowledged with a curt nod. He stepped aside, gesturing for Beth to exit. With one foot in front of the other Beth shuffled past him, but not before casting a lingering glance back at Anne. Their eyes met, and Anne offered a subtle nod, an unspoken reassurance that lingered in the air as Beth departed.

The kitchen courtyard offered a striking difference to the estate's interior, with a thick layer of crisp white snow having blanketed the ground overnight. It was like a blank canvas, untouched and smooth except for the few boot prints that marred its pristine surface. Austin emerged from the archway, his boots making a crunching sound as he walked and his breath turned to a visible cloud in the chilly air. Ben sat on weathered crates, mechanically chewing on a lacklustre sandwich. The mundane activity was a small attempt at normalcy in a world where nothing was guaranteed. Austin glanced back and forth between Ben and a truck parked in the courtyard, its large door open to reveal a multitude of boxes filled with scavenged supplies. He opened his mouth to speak, but found no words suitable for the moment. Their lives had been monotonous, and filled with mundane tasks of unloading supplies and taking them to their necessary places around the estate. There had been no warrant for small talk, no light hearted conversations, no room for laughter or enjoyment or camaraderie. Austin faced Ben for a moment, eyeing the sandwich with a mix of envy and resignation as Ben took another bite, the action more out of necessity than enjoyment. With an acquiescent sigh, Austin continued his task, walking over to the truck to lift a heavy crate full of canned goods. He leaned against the truck as he pulled the box with a grunt, feeling the cold metal through his jacket, a reminder of the chill that permeated their existence as the muscles in his arms tensed under the strain. He then shuffled to the archway, dropping the crate in the opening and walked over to where Ben was perched, the wooden crates creaking under their combined weight as Austin took a seat beside him.

"Mind if I join you?" Austin asked casually, though the weight of recent events hung heavy between them.

"Suit yourself." Ben's voice was flat, colder than the air that surrounded them. He tore the remainder of his sandwich in two, offering half to Austin. He accepted the gesture, his fingers brushing against Ben's for a fleeting moment which caused Austin to flinch while Ben barely noticed. They ate in silence for a short spell, each lost in his own thoughts punctuated only by the rhythmic crunch of bread and the whisper of their breath misting in the frosty air.

"How're you holding up?" After a pause, Austin ventured the question.

"Good." Ben responded curtly, taking another bite of his sandwich without looking at Austin. His gaze was fixed on something distant, something beyond the confines of their makeshift refuge.

"Sorry about what happened with Julia." Austin said after a few moments, breaking the quiet that had settled around them. He wasn't sure what prompted him to bring it up - perhaps the need to fill the void or simply an attempt to reach out.

"Julia's made her feelings clear. She wants nothing to do with me." Ben shrugged nonchalantly, his shoulders rising and falling in a practiced motion that failed to mask the hurt lingering beneath.

"Think there's any chance you two could, I don't know, work things out?" Austin's inquiry held a hint of hope, though he knew reconciliation was a luxury rarely afforded in their world.

"Is this because you want Beth for yourself?" Ben turned to face Austin, his eyes sharp and searching.

"Nothing like that," Austin was quick to dismiss the implication, shaking his head slightly, "it's not—"

"Then why isn't Anne speaking to you?" Ben cut in before Austin could finish. His question wasn't accusatory, but there was a palpable tension underlying his words. Austin's eyes dropped to the half-eaten sandwich in his hand, suddenly finding the layers of ham and cheese far more interesting than they were a moment ago. "Things are complicated." Austin muttered, leaving an unsaid truth hanging between them. The silence stretched between them, as weighty and tangible as the frosty air that enveloped the courtyard. The quiet was finally broken by Ben's steady voice.

"I know what I'm about to hear," he said, "but I need it from you." The words seemed to unlock something within Austin.

"Beth and I, we slept together," the admission came out in a hushed tone, barely audible above the crisp rustling of dead leaves nearby, "it was a mistake."

"I'm tired, Austin. Tired of being angry at the whole fucking world. There's no room for happiness anymore." Ben drew in a slow breath, the steam of it mingling with the winter chill. He let it out slowly, his exhalation a physical release of pent-up frustrations. "Maybe not now," Austin conceded softly, "but we had our moments, didn't we? Before all this." There was a wistful note in his voice, a yearning for a semblance of normalcy they both knew was long gone. Ben nodded, acknowledging the truth in Austin's words as he finished his sandwich with a final, decisive bite. Meanwhile, Austin fiddled with the remaining half in his hands before offering it back to Ben.

"You don't want it?" Ben asked, raising an eyebrow.

"No, and I'm sorry. For everything. I've been a shit friend." Austin shook his head, unable to meet Ben's gaze.

"Should've listened to you." Ben replied, accepting the sandwich without judgment.

"About what?"

"About complicating things, but that's water under the bridge now." His teeth sank into the bread, the mundane act oddly grounding. Their shared understanding hung in the air, as did their regrets - words unspoken but felt deeply as they each contemplated the tenuous threads that held their world together. Ben stood, walking into the middle of the courtyard and stretching out his legs and arms as he paced back and forth slowly. He shifted his weight from one foot to the other, the frozen ground beneath him unyielding and cold. He glanced sidelong at Austin, who seemed lost in thought for a moment before breaking the silence.

"Think we could ever be happy under Abraham's rule?" Austin's voice was tentative and probing. A wry expression crossed Ben's face as he raised an eyebrow.

"Do we even have a choice?" The question hung between them like the icy breaths that clouded the air.

"I guess not—"

"Why'd you go after Luis like that?" Ben's gaze hardened slightly as he turned the conversation, pressing for answers. Austin's jaw clenched and he looked away, eyes distant with the memory.

"It was impulse," he admitted, his voice barely above a whisper, "I wish I had finished it though. Killed him when I had the chance."

"Then you'd be swinging from a noose right beside Sabrina." Ben pointed out bluntly, his eyes narrowing. There were lines in the sand now, drawn by grief and vengeance.

"Maybe so," Austin conceded, then his tone turned bitter, "Sabrina, she got what she deserved. Maybe now Val can find some peace with Chantelle's death."

"Agreed." Ben pushed off from where he had been leaning against the wall and began to stretch his arms, feeling the pull of muscles too long kept idle. As he paced, each step deliberate, he could feel the restless energy coursing through him.

"Have you talked to Beth lately?" Austin asked, watching Ben move across the courtyard. Ben let out a scoff, more out of frustration than humour.

"Has Beth spoken to anyone since Luis fractured her jaw?" It was a rhetorical question, they both knew the answer.

"No." Austin shook his head, confirming the silence that had fallen over their once vibrant friend. The conversation dwindled, leaving only the frigid air and their shared understanding of the harsh new world they inhabited. Ben stopped pacing and looked up to the grey expanse above, wondering if there was any warmth left to be found. The cold bit into Austin's skin as he shifted, his eyes never leaving Ben's haunted face.

"After the storeroom," he started, his voice tentative in the biting air, "the night Beth found you and then Luis attacked her. What happened?" Ben seemed to retreat into himself, his gaze fixed on some distant point only he could see. His jaw clenched tightly before he spoke.

"I heard everything," he said, a tremor of suppressed rage in his low tones, "Luis dragged her away and into the corridor. I heard punching and yelling, and then a loud crack. I think he dragged her into another storeroom. Just within earshot, as if he wanted me to hear her. The sounds, they were gut-wrenching. And then, just punches and thuds. I tried to get free, but I couldn't do anything."

The memory clawed at him, the sounds of struggle, the helpless fury. Austin watched his friend closely, the lines of strain etched deep into Ben's face. With reluctant words, he broached the question that had been burning in his thoughts.

"Do you think, did Luis, did he—" Austin couldn't bring himself to finish the sentence, but the horror in his eyes spoke volumes. Ben met Austin's gaze squarely, his expression darkening.

"I don't think so," he replied, his voice carrying an edge sharp enough to cut through the winter chill, "but once Beth can talk again and if I find out he did, Luis is a dead man."

"If I can't kill him, neither can you," Austin warned, a measure of resolve stiffening his posture, "or you'd be up there swinging too."

A cold laugh escaped Ben, devoid of any real mirth.

"We've both got our reasons for wanting him gone." He retorted, the undercurrent of animosity towards Luis clear in his tone. Austin let out a hollow chuckle, acknowledging the twisted camaraderie in their shared disdain. They stood there, two men bound by the grim realities of their existence, each grappling with their own ghosts and grievances. The silence between them stretched out, a tangible thing against the backdrop of their breaths hanging in the cold air.

"How'd you get out of that storeroom after?" Austin broke it with a question, his eyes searching Ben's face for clues.

"Wasn't much to it," Ben replied, brushing a hand through his hair, a gesture that spoke of weariness more than tidiness, "couple weeks later they just opened the door. Told me to prove I could fall in line, keep my head down. I looked for Beth, but she wouldn't come out of her room much after she was released from the infirmary. Eventually I just stopped trying. Worked, kept quiet, did what I had to." His gaze drifted, landing on nothing in particular as a shadow of frustration crossed his features. Austin watched him, the lines around his eyes softening.

"I'm sorry, Ben. I should've been there." He said, the regret clear in his voice.

"Hey, no," Ben lifted his eyes, meeting Austin's with a hardened resolve, "nothing to apologise for. You didn't do any of this, and I wanted to talk to you sooner. But with all the chaos, thought it best to lay low until things settled." He paused, a deep breath filling his chest before he exhaled slowly.

"Still." Austin began, but Ben shook his head.

"None of us knew how it would play out," he said firmly, "we were all just trying to survive." A moment passed, and then Austin was on his feet, closing the distance between them in a few strides. His arms wrapped around Ben in a brotherly embrace, a silent pact of forgiveness and solidarity. Ben returned the hug, the tension easing from his shoulders.

"Alright, break it up," the sharp command cut through their brief respite as another guard approached, his face set in a stern mask of duty, "get back to work." They parted, each giving a nod of understanding. They reached for the nearest boxes on the truck, the weight of them grounding as they carried them inside. The normalcy of the task was a stark contrast to the turmoil that lingered beneath the surface, but for now it was enough to keep them moving forward.

The flickering torchlight cast long shadows against the damp walls of the sub-basement storeroom as Tyler paced restlessly, his ears straining for the sound of approaching footsteps. He clutched the torch tighter, its warm glow a stark contrast to the cold apprehension that gnawed at him. Every creak and groan of the old building set his heart racing. At last the soft click of the door latch broke the silence and Chase slipped through the narrow opening, his eyes darting around the room before he closed the door behind him with practiced caution. The sight of Chase sent a rush of relief through Tyler, and without hesitation he closed the distance between them in a few eager strides.

"Chase." Tyler breathed out, his voice barely above a whisper as he held up the torch to illuminate the man he'd been longing to see. Chase's arrival ignited something within Tyler, a flame of defiance that burned away the chill of fear. He wrapped his arms around Chase, pulling him close, and kissed him with a passion that had been suppressed by their dangerous circumstances. For a moment they lost themselves in the intensity of their forbidden embrace, a fleeting escape from the world outside. Chase, caught off guard, yielded to the kiss but quickly regained his senses and stepped back with a wary glance towards the door.

"Tyler, why did you ask me to meet you here? You know we'd be punished if we're caught." The urgency in Chase's voice pulled Tyler back from the brink of reckless abandon, and he lowered the torch, casting his gaze downward.

"I needed to see you," Tyler admitted, the raw need in his words evident, "I missed you." A momentary struggle played across Chase's face, torn between the fear of discovery and the ache of separation. Then, tenderness overcame caution and he reached out, drawing Tyler into another hug. His voice was a hushed murmur against Tyler's ear, a frail thread of hope amidst the surrounding darkness.

"I've missed you too," Chase confessed, "but we have to be careful." The warmth of his breath against Tyler's skin sent shivers down his spine, a sharp contrast to the cold of the storeroom. Tyler nodded, his forehead resting against Chase's. In the dim light cast by the torch, their shadows danced on the walls, merging together as one. For a brief moment in that embrace, the world outside with its ever-looming threats and watchful eyes seemed to vanish, leaving only the two of them in a cocoon of muted hope.

"Every second is worth it," Tyler whispered back, his voice barely audible above the sound of their synchronised breathing, "but you're right. We can't let our guard down. Not here." They lingered there, savouring the closeness, each heartbeat a silent vow of solidarity. In the silence of the sub-basement, hidden from the prying eyes above, Tyler and Chase held onto each other - a small act of rebellion in a place where their love was subject to scrutiny and punishment. The storeroom was a tomb of shadows, the air thick with the stench of damp concrete and the faint, metallic tang of rust. Tyler's back pressed against the cold wall, his breath hitching as Chase's body loomed closer, their chests almost touching. The silence was deafening, broken only by the muffled thud of boots above and the low hum of workers in the kitchen. Chase's eyes gleamed in the dim light, dark and hungry. His lips slightly parted as he leaned in, the heat of his breath ghosting over Tyler's neck. Tyler's pulse quickened, his throat dry as he tilted his head back, exposing the vulnerable curve of his throat. Chase's calloused fingers trailed down Tyler's chest, rough and possessive, sliding beneath the hem of his threadbare shirt. The touch was electric, skimming over the ridges of his body, igniting a fire that burned low and dangerous in Tyler's gut. Chase's hand dipped lower, fingers brushing the waistband of Tyler's pants, teasing his sensitive skin as his hips buckled involuntarily, grinding against Chase's thigh. Tyler's breath came in ragged gasps, his hands clenching Chase's shirt, pulling him closer until their bodies were flush. He could feel Chase pressing against him, the heat radiating through their clothes. Chase's fingers finally slipped beneath Tyler's waistband and his hips jerked forward, a choked moan escaping his lips as Chase's hand began to move, slow and deliberate. Tyler let out a moan that was too loud for comfort, causing Chase to freeze. He pulled away quickly, his expression dark and conflicted as he took a step back, leaving Tyler panting and desperate against the wall. They listened for footsteps, for any signs that their dalliance had given them away.

"We can't," Chase muttered, his voice strained and his jaw clenched tight, "not here. Not now." Tyler stared at him, his chest heaving and his body aching with frustration. The rejection stung worse than any slap, leaving him raw and exposed. He opened his mouth to argue, to beg, but the look in Chase's eyes stopped him cold. There was a flicker of something there, the fear of being caught lingered in Chase's expression. It was enough to silence Tyler, leaving them both standing there in the suffocating silence, the heat between them still simmering beneath the surface.

"We can't hide like this forever." Tyler's fingers traced the cold, rough surface of the storeroom wall as he turned to face Chase, his eyes searching, the quiver in his voice betraying an urgency that had been building over the last few weeks. Chase's gaze dropped to the floor, a mixture of defeat and resignation lining his features. "I know," he admitted, kicking at a small pebble with the toe of his boot, "but we can't just leave, not with everything covered in snow. Remember last winter? We barely made it out alive, almost starved—" He looked up, his eyes meeting Tyler's. Tyler's jaw set firmly as memories of hunger pangs and chilling winds flashed through his mind.

"I remember," his voice was steady despite the recollections, his expression softening as he stepped forward to close the gap between them, "but I also remember what it's like to be free, to be who we are without hiding. We spent so long fighting for our friends and family to accept us. I won't accept that our relationship is now punishable by death." Tyler paused, his heartbreak evident in his tone. Understanding flickered in Chase's eyes - he reached out tentatively, his hand brushing against Tyler's cheek. It was a gesture filled with warmth that seemed to push back against the chill of their surroundings.

"Abraham doesn't look kindly on Reece and Val," Chase murmured, "her skin colour is enough for him to cast judgment, let alone us—" His thumb caressed Tyler's skin gently, grounding them in the reality of their situation.

"Chase—"

"Don't think I haven't noticed the kind of person he is," Chase continued, his voice low but clear, "the way he views the world, it's twisted and it's dangerous for us." Tyler leaned into the touch, feeling the weight of their shared truth. He knew the risks, they both did, but there was something in Chase's touch, in the resolve of his words, that fortified Tyler's determination. They might have been ensnared by the bitter cold outside and the oppressive regime within, but Tyler felt a spark of defiance ignite within him - a silent promise that they wouldn't let the winter, nor Abraham, dictate the bounds of their love. Tyler's hand trembled as he clasped it around the cold, rusted metal of the lantern hanging from the storeroom's low ceiling. The dim light cast long shadows across Chase's face, making his features appear sharper, more resolute.

"Promise me," Tyler said, his voice steady despite the anxiety that knotted his stomach, "as soon as the frost breaks, we make our move. But we have to bring the others with us." Chase shifted, his gaze drifting towards the door as if considering the weight of their escape.

"Wouldn't it be easier if it was just us?" His question hung in the air, laden with a practicality that stung Tyler.

"Easier," Tyler took a step back, releasing the lantern as it swayed slightly, creaking in protest, "how can you even suggest that?" Disbelief laced his words. They had survived because of the strength they found in each other, in unity. To abandon those who had become family seemed an unfathomable betrayal.

"It's always been us, Tyler," Chase's voice was soft but insistent, a stark contrast to the cold stone walls that enclosed them, "we don't need anyone else. We'll be okay."

"Okay," Tyler echoed, incredulous, "after everything we've faced together? After every sacrifice? No, we leave together or not at all." He shook his head, the flickering light casting erratic shadows across the storeroom. Chase's jaw tightened, the muscle there twitching with tension.

"You know we are the ones in the greatest danger," he pointed out, trying to appeal to Tyler's sense of self-preservation, "we need to think of ourselves first." Tyler felt a surge of frustration course through him, hot and unyielding.

"It's not just about us," he countered, his voice growing louder, "we're not the only ones at risk here. And what about loyalty, huh? What about honour? This isn't you, Chase. This is a version of you I don't lo—" Tyler stopped himself from finishing the word as he swallowed hard and clenched his fists at his side. They stood there, locked in a silent battle of wills, their breaths visible puffs in the chill of the storeroom. Tyler could see the conflict playing out in Chase's eyes - the urge to survive warring with the bonds they'd formed.

"You don't love me?" Chase's brows furrowed as he processed Tyler's words, the ones both said and unsaid.

"I didn't say that, Chase. I love you, but this version of you? It's not the man I fell in love with. Survival doesn't mean anything if we lose ourselves in the process," Tyler finally added, his tone softening, "I can't do that, Chase. I won't." Tyler's clenched fists released slowly as he stared at Chase, his heart pounding against his ribcage like a caged bird desperate for escape, but this was no simple flight to freedom. Chase's voice finally broke the tense silence.

"Tyler—"

"You do realise," Tyler interrupted angrily, "Val and Beth, they're not safe either." Chase's eyes flickered away momentarily, a furtive shift that didn't go unnoticed.

"They won't be persecuted for—"

"We left them," Tyler pressed on, the weight of their past decisions heavy on his shoulders, "we left, and look what happened. Beth broken, and Chantelle—"

"Dead." Chase finished, his voice barely above a whisper, but it was enough to send a chill through the air that wasn't from the creeping cold of the basement.

"Yes, dead," Tyler's exasperation burst forth like steam from a vent, "I love you Chase. God knows I do, but not this. Not this cowardly version that's willing to abandon our people." The words cut through the darkness, each one laden with betrayal and hurt.

"Cowardly," Chase's retort was quick and sharp, "no Tyler, you're being idealistic. We'll all go together if we can, but if it comes down to it, just us two." There was a finality in his voice, an unspoken ultimatum hanging between them.

"I don't think I've ever been this, this disappointed." Tyler breathed the word out, tasting the bitterness of it on his tongue. He had never felt such profound letdown, not by the man he considered his partner, his equal. Without another word he turned on his heel, his footsteps echoing off the walls as he stormed away, leaving Chase shrouded in both darkness and doubt. Chase remained motionless, the beam from the torch casting a lone circle of light that failed to reach the corners where shadows lurked. As Tyler's presence receded, so too did the light of their unity, leaving Chase to ponder the solitary path his choices might carve out.

Beth lay sprawled across the stiff mattress, a gentle buzz humming in her veins from the Vicodin Anne had reluctantly pressed into her palm. Her fingers, pale and weightless, rose languidly above her. She watched them, entranced as if they belonged to someone else, as they danced through the air to trace the water-stained patterns that marred the ceiling of her room. The drugs dulled the pain but also everything else, wrapping her thoughts in a thick fog. Visions flickered like old film reels - she saw herself darting through the snow-blanketed wilderness that bordered the imposing Biltmore Estate. With each bound, her boots launched clouds of powdery flakes skyward, dissipating into the grey expanse above. Her mind's eye painted a picture of liberation, a world away from the grim reality of her confinement. The biting chill of the wind whipped through her hair, unbound and wild as she raced between the skeletal trees. Twigs snapped underfoot, branches clawed at her dress, plucking threads and fabric as she plunged deeper into the forest leaving the oppressive stone walls farther behind with every desperate stride. It was a fleeting escape, one conjured by the haze of medication, yet it beckoned with the promise of freedom - a freedom that felt achingly out of reach within the confines of her drug-induced reverie. The tendrils of the numbness wove through Beth's body, thickening the fog that enveloped her mind. Yet amidst this haze, a persistent gnawing sensation clawed at the edges of her consciousness - the instinctual urge to return to gather Ben and Austin. To find Val and Reece and Chase and Tyler. They were her tether to a world that could be kinder than the one they knew, a world where a farm awaited them, promising sanctuary and peace. With each shallow breath, an invisible force seemed to pull her deeper into the lulling abyss of the Vicodin's embrace. Her limbs felt buoyant as if she might drift away from the confines of her bed and float into an expanse where worry could not follow. But this weightless freedom was marred by the burgeoning threat of nausea. It crept upon her stealthily, like a predator stalking its prey. Beth's head began to spin, a carousel set in motion by the swirling room around her. She clenched her eyes shut, tighter still, willing the vertigo to cease. The thought of vomiting sent a shudder throughout her body. Her jaw, which had known only the ache of healing bones for weeks, protested even the idea of opening wide enough to expel the sickness building within her. She inhaled deeply, focusing on the cool air traveling down her throat, trying to anchor herself to something stable in the midst of the relentless spinning. There was a place out there, a refuge where life could be more than just survival, where laughter might once again fill their days. She held onto that image as a lifeline, knowing she couldn't risk losing it to the churning darkness that threatened to consume her now. Beth's feet crunched against the frozen crust of snow, her breaths visible as puffs of vapour in the frigid air. Her legs pumped harder, propelling her through the barren trees that clawed at the sky with skeletal branches. The cold bit at her cheeks, but it was a welcome sensation against the flush of heat from her churning stomach. With each stride, she tried to outrun the drug-induced haze clouding her mind. A stark white expanse stretched ahead - the snow fields that bordered Biltmore's imposing silhouette. She skidded to a stop, snowflakes swirling around her. She had run in a straight line for what had felt like forever, yet had found herself approaching the oppressive walls of Biltmore despite running away from it. The looming estate stood silent, a giant spectre of what once was. As realisation dawned, a shadowy figure reached out for her from the periphery of her vision. Panic surged as she suddenly jolted upright, her pulse throbbing in her ears. A knock echoed through her room, insistent and real. Her heart hammered against her ribcage as the remnants of the dream clung to her like cobwebs. Jacob stepped into the room, his presence grounding. Beth blinked away the last vestiges of sleep and surveyed her surroundings - her room, not the endless snow fields. Sunlight filtered weakly through the curtains, signalling the start of another day under Abraham's rule.

"Are you okay," Jacob's concern cut through her disorientation as Beth nodded slowly, her hand instinctively rising to massage her temple, "Vicodin is nasty stuff. Had some after I broke my arm. It can mess with your head." The world felt slightly off its axis, the Vicodin tugging at the edges of her consciousness.

"Mmm." Beth offered a gentle murmur and a weak smile in acknowledgement, grateful for the small gesture of solidarity. Jacob, though often quiet and stoic, seemed to understand the battle she waged within herself - a war between enduring pain and seeking oblivion. Beth's cautious gaze lingered on him, the guard whose stoicism had always seemed impenetrable. His features softened just slightly, not quite a smile but an acknowledgment of shared human frailty. It was the first genuine exchange between them since her arrival at Biltmore, and it stood out in stark contrast to the usual orders and stern looks.

"Abraham wants to see you in the library." Jacob said, his voice steady but betraying a hint of urgency that Beth couldn't ignore. Her heart skipped a beat at the mention of Abraham's name. The library, a place of knowledge turned into a chamber for passing decrees and rendering judgments. She swallowed hard, the action sending a twinge along her jawline, a reminder of the injury that still haunted her. Her hands trembled as she pushed off the blankets, a sense of foreboding settling over her like a shroud. With every ounce of strength left in her body, she swung her legs over the edge of the bed, feeling the room sway around her. Jacob watched her with an inscrutable expression, offering no assistance, but his eyes held a glimmer of understanding. Beth steadied herself, took a deep breath, and rose to meet whatever fate awaited her in the library.

CHAPTER 3

The sharp scent of the infirmary intertwined with the lingering and pungent odour of antiseptic, creating an unmistakable atmosphere of cleanliness and care. Val stood amidst the sterile environment, her focus unwavering as she methodically checked off boxes on her clipboard. Each deliberate stroke of her pen against the paper created a rhythmic, steady scratching that echoed softly in the otherwise hushed room. This tranquil silence was only interrupted by the sound of heavy, familiar footsteps resonating through the stillness, a presence that filtered into the space with an unmistakable familiarity.

"*Hermanita*," Luis's voice sliced through the silence, his tone light and teasing, "it's so good to see you, finally." Val didn't bother looking up from her clipboard, her fingers tightening imperceptibly around it as she continued to work.

"I'm busy." Her response was sharp and disinterested in entertaining a conversation.

"You've been avoiding me around these halls for weeks." Luis continued, taking a few steps further into the room. Val continued with her tasks, deliberately avoiding eye contact and instinctively stepping slightly away from him. When she talked, her words were deliberate and measured, aiming to acknowledge him just enough to avoid provoking his anger without encouraging further discussion.

"I've had nothing to say to you."

"Is that so," a chuckle escaped him, resonating in the confined space, "not even a *hello* for your dear brother?" She felt him move closer, his presence like an unwanted shadow. "Brother, yes. Dear, not so much." Val continued to jot down notes, her jaw set in determination as she focused on anything but the man who now invaded her sanctuary of solitude.

"Really Val? Too busy even for a little banter," his voice inched closer, carrying an undercurrent of something darker beneath the surface cheerfulness, "or even a quick catch up? It's been so long since we talked." Val frowned, finally pausing to glance up at him.

"If it's company you're after, I'm not it," her eyes were wary, her posture rigid, "is there something else you need?" He leaned against a nearby bed, arms crossed. His refusal to leave drew a brief pause from her, a flicker of pain across her features before she quickly masked it with cold indifference.

"Are you relieved that we finally have justice for Chantelle?" Luis prodded, watching her carefully. Val placed the clipboard down with a soft click against the metal surface of the infirmary bed, meeting his gaze head-on, her brown eyes icy.

"We? Luis, you're the last person I'd discuss my grief with." Her words hung between them, a chasm that neither sibling seemed willing to bridge. The air shifted as Luis' laughter died, replaced by a weighty silence that bore down on Val's shoulders. His eyes, once alight with mockery now harboured storms of unspoken pain.

"Believe me Val," he said, his voice low and grave, "if anyone understands the grief over Chantelle, it's me." Val's hand tightened around the bed frame, her knuckles whitening. Anger, hot and fierce, bubbled up inside her.

"Understand? You? You did nothing," she spat the words out like poison, "I was there for her. Every step, every fall. I was her shield while you, you were nothing!" Luis' face contorted, his brows knitting together as if her accusation had struck a nerve. In one swift movement, his hand shot out, gripping her arm just above the wrist. His fingers pressed into her flesh, twisting only enough to send a jolt of discomfort through her, his tone a venomous hiss. "Nothing, huh?"

"Let go of me." Val said through gritted teeth as she tried to pull away, but his grip was ironclad.

"Let's be clear," Luis leaned in, his breath hot against her ear, "had you both left with me when Austin cast me aside, none of this would've happened. Not the situation at Alcatraz, not the murder on Catalina. All of it could've been avoided. But you chose to stay, so don't you dare pin her death on anyone but yourself." His words crashed into her like waves, relentless and suffocating.

"Luis, you're hurting me." Val's voice trembled, a mixture of pain and defiance as she glared at her brother. Val wrenched her arm free, stepping back as she processed his vicious blame. The sting of betrayal from her own brother burned deeper than any physical wound could ever inflict. His eyes widened in fleeting surprise as he released her arm with a jerk, stepping back as though her skin had scorched him.

"I'm sorry Val," he said, his voice soft but laced with the familiar undercurrent of fervour that always made her wary, "I love you. You're my sister." Val's laugh was bitter, an echo of incredulity and scorn

"Love? Just because you're my brother doesn't mean I have to love you. In fact, I hate you. More than you know. More than anyone else living." Her voice rose, breaking the silence of the infirmary like a curse. The words hung between them, a chasm too wide to bridge. Luis' face twisted into a mask of fury and hurt, and with a sudden, explosive movement, he struck her across the face. The force of the blow sent Val staggering backward. She fell onto the infirmary bed, the impact resonating through the room as her body slammed against the wall. The doorway framed Anne, her presence sudden and still, her eyes wide as scenes from some ancient tragedy played out before her. For a heartbeat she stood frozen, witnessing the aftermath of betrayal and violence. Luis loomed over Val, his shadow darkening her features and contorting with blame.

"Remember this Val," he hissed, each word punctuated by the venom of his conviction, "Chantelle's death is on your hands." He turned sharply on his heel, brushing past Anne with such force that she stumbled against the frame of the doorway, her shoulder slamming hard against it. She barely noticed the pain, her focus fixed on the fallen figure of her friend.

"Are you okay?" Anne rushed to her side, her voice thick with concern. But Val was already pushing herself upright, wiping away the tears that betrayed her vulnerability. With a shaky hand she grasped her clipboard, her fingers white-knuckled around the edges.

"I'm fine." She insisted, her voice steady despite the tears carving clean paths down her cheeks. Anne watched as Val straightened her spine, the lines of her body rigid with resolve. She returned to her work, the scratching of her pen against paper a testament to her determination not to let Luis, or anyone, break her spirit.

Sunlight streamed generously through the tall windows of the Oak Sitting Room, casting an inviting warmth over the plush carpet where Jennifer and baby Victoria were ensconced in their own little world. Jennifer sat cross-legged, her long hair cascading over her shoulders as she leaned forward, her eyes twinkling with affection. Her hands moved gently, guiding a colourful set of building blocks as she stacked them into a wobbly tower, much to Victoria's delight. She giggled with glee, her tiny fingers reaching out to explore and occasionally send the tower tumbling down, prompting peals of laughter from them both. The room was alive with the soft, cheerful babble of other children playing in the distance, their sounds mingling to form a gentle symphony that underscored the tender moment shared between the two. Victoria's eyes, wide with curiosity, followed Jennifer's every move, her smile as bright as the sunlight that bathed the room.

"Boo!" Jennifer teased, wiggling her fingers like ghosts hovering above Victoria's cherubic face. The baby's laughter bubbled up as she grasped at the tantalising digits, eyes alight with the simple joy of the game. Her tiny hands finally caught hold of Jennifer's index finger, triumphantly bringing it to her mouth for a slobbery victory chew. Jennifer's heart swelled with a maternal warmth that seemed to push away the darker thoughts that often lurked at the edges of her consciousness. They had fashioned this sanctuary for them, a safe haven from the chaos outside these walls, even if only temporarily. Even if under the oppressive regime of Abraham's control. The door creaked open, drawing Jennifer's attention. A young woman stepped inside balancing a tray laden with bowls of sliced fruit and small sandwiches - nourishment for the growing brood within the makeshift playroom. Jennifer offered a smile, an unspoken thank you for the care being brought to the children under their watchful eyes. As the woman made the rounds, distributing snacks with practiced efficiency, some of the children paused their play and flocked around her like ducklings to a mother. Their chatter rose in excitement, a chorus of thanks and hungry pleas. With the children momentarily preoccupied, Jennifer turned her gaze back to Victoria, resuming their play. Yet she couldn't help but steal glances at the woman now seated across the room. The newcomer sat with a quiet grace, observing the children with a tenderness that spoke volumes of her character, a silent guardian keeping watch over the innocent. Jennifer cooed to Victoria who simply gurgled in response as her eyes locked onto Jennifer's face with unwavering adoration. It was moments like these that fortified Jennifer's resolve - amidst the uncertainty of their fractured world, she found purpose and clarity in the laughter of a child. The silence, punctured only by the soft murmurs of children and the occasional giggle, stretched between them like a tangible thing. The woman's gaze lingered on Victoria for a few beats longer before she directed her attention to Jennifer, breaking the quiet with a tone that was gentle yet carried an undercurrent of curiosity, a hint of an Italian accent flavouring her voice.

"Did you know her mother?" Her eyes searched Jennifer's face for traces of emotion. Jennifer paused, her fingers stilling over Victoria's tiny hands.

"Unfortunately." She replied, the word laden with a history she wasn't prepared to unpack in this tranquil setting. With a sigh she pushed herself up to sit straighter, meeting the woman's inquiring eyes.

"Ah, I'm sorry," her expression softened as she realised the intrusion of the question, "we haven't been properly introduced. My name is Eve."

"Jennifer." She managed a tight smile, feeling the weight of Eve's empathy. Standing, she hoisted Victoria into her arms, the baby's warmth a comforting presence against her chest, and crossed to where Eve had placed the tray earlier. She picked up the bottle, checking the temperature against her wrist before placing it gently to the baby's mouth. Eve observed the care with which Jennifer fed Victoria, her own arms hugging her middle as if bracing against a chill.

"The hanging, it was quite the spectacle." Eve remarked, the words trailing off and leaving space for the unsaid to resonate. Jennifer looked up, her gaze steady.

"It was justified." She stated firmly, the conviction in her voice belying the gentle rocking motion she maintained with Victoria cradled in her arms.

"Was it? Even if Sabrina really killed a pregnant woman?"

"Chantelle," Jennifer interjected quickly, "her name was Chantelle. Sabrina murdered my friend." She continued to feed Victoria, the rhythm unbroken.

"I'm sorry." Eve said quietly before sinking back slowly into her seat.

"That hanging is the only just thing Abraham has done around here since he began his oppressive rule." Jennifer confided, her voice low but laced with a bitterness that hinted at a storm beneath the calm. Eve absorbed the words, her lips parting slightly as if to speak further but then closed them again, choosing instead to let the statement hang in the air - a testament to shared grievances and an acknowledgment of the harsh realities that bound them all.

"You know," Eve's eyebrows arched in surprise, her gaze flickering with a mixture of amusement and caution, "you shouldn't be so open with your thoughts to strangers." Jennifer's laugh was tinged with defiance, a spark of rebellion that refused to be quelled even in the face of danger.

"What are you going to do? Report me?" She challenged, meeting Eve's eyes with a steely gaze. A gentle shake of the head was Eve's response, her expression softening.

"No," she assured, "your thoughts are safe with me." Curiosity piqued, Jennifer leaned closer, her protective stance over Victoria momentarily forgotten.

"So where are you from then?" She probed, seeking common ground, or perhaps a kindred spirit.

"Prescott," Eve said, her voice carrying a wistful note as she glanced away, "I came with the group."

"And before that?"

"Las Vegas." Eve spoke softly, her voice fading and her gaze drifting as if she were recalling a distant memory. A silence settled between them, contrasting with the cheerful sounds of children playing and laughing, which formed an oddly joyful backdrop to their sombre moods.

"But originally, I am from Italy." Eve shattered the quiet with a statement delivered so monotonously that it sounded as if she were reciting from a book. Her voice was devoid of emotion, as though she was trying to avoid thinking about her home.

"Italy," Jennifer raised an eyebrow, "what're you doing here?"

"A fresh start, I suppose." Eve laughed, her tone laced with a hint of sarcasm.

"Well, it doesn't get as fresh as this. World wiped clean with a clean slate." Jennifer looked down mournfully at the baby in her arms, cooing away at nothing in particular as her eyes darted around the ceiling.

"You seem sad."

"I'm mourning the world," Jennifer spoke quietly, gently rocking Victoria back and forth, "worried about what these kids will have to grow up in." Eve walked around the room slowly, pacing on the soft carpet and dodging scattered toys left idly by disinterested children.

"Have you ever been?" Eve asked, turning back to Jennifer with a curious tilt of her head.

"To Italy? No, I've never been outside the States," Jennifer replied with a small shake of her head, "this is as far east as I've ever been." Her world had been small, confined by boundaries both seen and unseen.

"That's a shame," with a fluid motion, Eve began gathering the plates scattered across the floor and furniture, "as now you have probably missed the opportunity to do so." The clink of porcelain served as a subtle backdrop to their clumsy conversation.

"Tell me, what was Abraham like at Prescott?" Jennifer's voice held a trace of urgency now, her need for understanding evident. Eve paused, her movements stilling as she considered the question.

"He was always a devout man, but this," she gestured vaguely, encompassing the room and all it symbolised, "this dystopian evangelical community? I never would have imagined he'd be capable of creating something like this." Jennifer nodded, absorbing Eve's words, her mind racing with the implications. The portrait of Abraham painted by his past was at odds with the man who ruled their lives now, a man whose vision had darkened into something unrecognisable, something far more menacing. Victoria's suckling had slowed, her tiny fingers relaxing their grip on Jennifer's shirt. Jennifer gently nudged the bottle with her thumb, coaxing the infant to take in the last of the milk, but Victoria simply turned her head away, mouth closed, eyes fluttering towards sleep. With a tender sigh, Jennifer withdrew the bottle and nestled Victoria against her chest to burp her, the baby's warm weight a comforting presence in her arms.

"So he wasn't like this before?" Jennifer pressed as she rocked back and forth absentmindedly with the infant.

"No. He was kind, and absent a lot of the time. Abraham always struck me as peculiar," Eve mused, watching Jennifer with thoughtful eyes, "but I never picked him to be the kind of man to seek vengeance or resort to violence." Jennifer patted Victoria's back softly, eliciting a small burp from the child.

"Sabrina's hanging wasn't about revenge," she stated firmly, meeting Eve's gaze, "it was about justice. Plain and simple."

"And what about justice for her?" Eve's gaze drifted to the dozing infant. Looking down at the baby whose peaceful slumber contrasted starkly with the turmoil surrounding her birth, Jennifer felt a surge of protective instinct. She removed the empty bottle and set it aside, shifting Victoria to burp her properly and patting her back with a rhythmic thud.

"Victoria's got a chance now," Jennifer replied, her voice tinged with a resolve that brooked no argument, "a chance to grow up free from the shadow of her mother's influence." Eve pressed her lips together, her expression caught between concern and restraint, an unspoken retort lingering on the verge of being voiced. But before Eve could articulate her thoughts, the heavy tread of boots announced the arrival of a guard at the door.

"Eve," the guard intoned with practiced authority, "Abraham requests your presence." Jennifer glanced up, her maternal facade giving way to a flash of solidarity with Eve.

"Don't worry about this mess," she said, gesturing to the scattered plates, "I'll take care of it." There was more than just reassurance in her words, a silent acknowledgement of the unspoken bond that adversity had woven between them. With a hesitant nod and a lingering look at the children, Eve followed the guard out of the room. Her departure cast a palpable void in the once light-hearted space, leaving Jennifer alone with the slumbering child and the remnants of an unfinished conversation that hovered like ghosts in the air.

The heavy oak door creaked shut, the finality of its click resounding in the hushed space. Beth's footsteps were muted against the plush rug as she entered the dimly lit library where shadows clung to the walls like spectres. A crackling fire danced in the hearth, casting a warm glow that licked at her skin, the heat warring with the drowsy current of medication flowing through her veins. Abraham stood by the mahogany chess table, an inscrutable silhouette framed by the flickering light. With a courteous tilt of his head, he gestured towards the board adorned with its meticulously arranged pieces. A simple nod sufficed as she approached the table. Her movements carried the weight of caution, each step deliberate and measured. In a theatrical display, Abraham presented two clenched fists for her to choose from. Beth extended a trembling hand, guided by some unseen force, and pointed towards his right. Unfurling his fingers like the petals of a bloom, he revealed the white pawn nestled in his palm. As he spoke, his voice was a velvet baritone that seemed to wrap around the quiet room while he placed the piece before her on the board with an air of ceremony. They took their seats opposite one another, the game set between them as another kind of battleground.

"White makes the first move. The colour of purity and innocence, peace and calm, neutrality and balance, and new beginnings. How fitting," Abraham lifted his gaze, meeting hers across the battlefield of black and white squares, "and black, power and authority, elegance, mystery, formality. Perhaps we are both represented appropriately here." He leaned back, his chair creaking softly, the ghost of a smile playing upon his lips. Beth stared at him, wondering how pure and innocent she truly was, contemplating how powerful and authoritative Abraham had made himself out to be. He gestured across the board as Beth's fingers hovered, her eyes tracing the potential paths of the pieces. She could feel Abraham's scrutiny, the weight of his expectation settling upon her shoulders. With a steadiness borne from a resolve hardened by recent trials, she reached forward and moved her pawn. The game was alive, and though silent Beth's every move spoke volumes. The chess pieces clacked softly as Beth executed another swift advance, her bishop now menacing a vulnerable knight. She sat poised, with an air of quiet determination that belied the tumult within. The game had transformed into a silent dialogue, each move a word, each strategy a sentence in their muted conversation. Abraham's hand hovered over the board, his fingers dancing lightly above his remaining pieces as if he were coaxing them to reveal their secrets. He was a man unused to hesitation, yet here he paused and deliberated his next play with an uncharacteristic measure of contemplation. His eyes, sharp and calculating, flicked from the board to Beth, then back again. Finally, with the care of one stepping onto uncertain ground, he slid his queen forward, a daring gambit that broke the pattern of rapid exchanges. As their eyes locked, the flickering firelight played across his pale features, throwing half his face into shadow while the other half seemed to glow with an inner intensity.

"I wanted to thank you Beth," Abraham's voice pierced the stillness, his tone sincere yet tinged with the gravity of their situation, "your cooperation during the investigation into Sabrina was invaluable."

"Mmm." Beth met his gratitude with a measured nod and a quiet gesture. Her silence was not of choice, but it lent her an enigmatic quality that she wielded as deftly as the chess pieces before her. She leaned forward, her hand steady as she moved a rook along its straight path and claimed his knight with a soft tap against the wood. Leaning back, her gaze never wavered from Abraham's, her stoicism a shield against the undercurrents of power at play. The silence that enveloped the room was as thick as the tension between them, only disturbed by the occasional crackle from the fireplace. Abraham's eyes studied Beth with a mixture of curiosity and reprimand.

"It is considered quite rude to remain silent when spoken to," he chided gently while Beth remained unflinching under his gaze, her fingers brushing against her jaw with a deliberate motion in a subtle but clear reminder of her inability to respond, "ahh, my apologies. Does it hurt to speak?" Abraham's expression softened fractionally, a hint of concern creeping into his otherwise stern features.

"Yes." She whispered almost inaudibly with a slight nod, her eyes momentarily dropping to the chessboard as if seeking refuge among the battleground of black and white. Abraham seized the moment, advancing his bishop with a swift slide across the checkered landscape, claiming one of her pawns in an aggressive strike. He then reclined in his chair, crossing his legs, his posture reflective of the control he felt over the game, and perhaps over more than just that.

"I must say, what Luis did to you, it was abhorrent," Abraham continued, his voice dipping to a sombre tone as the air between them seemed to grow heavy, charged with the weight of unspoken history, "but we must remember, Austin's reaction was equally condemnable. We should not combat violence with violence."

"No." Beth's brow arched slightly at his words, a flicker of something unreadable passing through her eyes. With deliberate grace she leaned forward, her arm extending towards the board. Her fingers closed around the knight, sliding it smoothly to a new square with an almost imperceptible click. She then settled back into her chair, her posture mirroring Abraham's, a silent dance of wills that spoke louder than words ever could. Abraham surveyed the board with a contemplative gaze, his fingers drumming lightly on the armrest of his chair. The silence stretched between them, punctuated only by the soft crackling of the fire. He finally broke it, moving his queen forward with a decisive clack against the wooden surface. His hand waved vaguely in the air as if brushing away the memory of violence and retribution.

"Chantelle's justice has been meted out. It is time we moved past these recent unpleasantries. I intend to focus on rebuilding society, and I believe," he paused, turning his sharp gaze towards Beth, "you could be quite instrumental in this endeavour." Her eyes darted abruptly from the chessboard to Abraham's face, her whole body becoming tense and still as though immobilised, except for her intense green eyes that locked onto his with a mix of skepticism and fiery curiosity.

"How?" Beth's muted response reflected her intense scrutiny, her eyes narrowing as she leaned forward, her movements measured and silent. She stared at him, a question forming in the depth of her gaze, unspoken yet palpable. Abraham, perhaps sensing the pessimism behind her stare, swiftly changed course.

"Have you attempted to speak properly? Other than hushed monosyllabic responses?" His voice held a tinge of genuine concern, though it was difficult to discern whether it was for her well-being or for the functionality she offered him.

"No." She whispered as she shook her head, a gentle shake that sent a loose strand of hair across her face. Abraham nodded, his lips pressed into a thin line. She looked down once more, her fingers hovering over a rook before sliding it along its path. Beth remained there, leaning towards him, her silent gaze unwavering and reflecting a depth of thought he could not reach. Even without words Beth communicated volumes, her presence a counterbalance to Abraham's carefully curated control. The flicker of the flames from the fireplace cast dancing shadows across the chessboard, creating an almost ethereal atmosphere. Abraham's fingers brushed against a knight before he withdrew his hand and looked up at Beth with a contemplative gaze. He clasped his hands together, resting them on the table as if in prayer. Beth's eyes met his, her gaze devoid of any discernible emotion. Abraham pressed a finger to the bishop before sliding it decisively across the board and leaning back into his chair.

"Everything that has befallen us," he began, his voice measured and solemn, "it's all leading to something greater, a divine plan unfolding before us. I am destined to bring about the second coming of Christ, Beth. And for this sacred mission I require a partner. Pure, noble, untainted by the chaos of our time. A vital step in this plan is selecting a worthy wife. One who will stand by my side as we guide humanity out of its current state of damnation." Beth sat motionless as she absorbed his proclamation, her mind working to grasp the full inference of his words. As the implications of his statement began to sink in, Beth felt a tremor run through her fingers. Her hand had been reaching for a pawn which now hovered momentarily, trembling in the air like a leaf caught in an unseen breeze.

"A wife." Slowly she lowered her gaze to the board, the pieces now seemingly trivial in the shadow of Abraham's ambition.

"Amongst the few candidates," he said, his voice carrying the weight of his conviction, "you stand out. Your resilience, your fortitude in these trying times, it has not gone unnoticed. What you did for everyone at Fort Irwin, checking in on the civilians and keeping a thorough regimen through such a difficult situation, it was truly commendable." Beth's hand gripped the arm of her chair, and her eyes lifted to meet his. In the silence, her stillness spoke louder than any words could. The gravity of Abraham's intentions hung between them, as tangible as the wooden pieces they manoeuvred in their game of strategy and power. Abraham's smile unfurled gradually, like the slow opening of a deadly blossom.

"I once thought the second coming would be through an arbitrary birth," he mused softly, his eyes never leaving Beth's face, "but revelation has guided me to my true role as the father. I will steer the path for our saviour. Do you understand?" Beth's response was measured, a deliberate glide of her knight over the checkered battlefield. The piece clicked into place and she reclined, the leather of the chair groaning under her weight.

"Yes." Her fingers curled tightly around the armrests, knuckles whitening with the force of her grip that betrayed the storm brewing within her silence. Abraham continued to observe her intently, his gaze lingering on her features. He stared into her eyes, unblinking. She studied his face, trying to reconcile his stoic demeanour with the grand declarations he had just made. For a man so entrenched in the apocalypse, for a man so sure of rebellion and divine destiny, Abraham displayed no hint of dishevelment, no sign of the chaos he espoused. His beard was neatly trimmed, each hair in its place like the most diligent of soldiers. It sat meticulously combed and styled. His glasses perched precisely on the bridge of his nose, a perfect accent to his immaculate poise. From the suspenders resting symmetrically on his shoulders to the careful part in his hair, everything about him radiated control, as if even the smallest detail was part of a master plan. He looked down at Beth with an air of superiority, his personality exuding an almost supernatural aura of command. His persona seemed surreal, a living paradox of flesh and philosophy as if his very existence was an act of will perfected by a grand design. His appearance was so unbelievably flawless it was almost as if he were untouched by the disorder of the world, and for a brief moment, Beth found herself incredulous, wondering if his sense of order truly extended into the chaos inside. Even the flickering shadows from the fire had no power over him, casting no doubt on his control. It was as though he believed his mere presence could bend reality to his ambition. She felt a swell of incredulity, almost a disbelief that he could sit there, so perfectly composed.

"Check." Abraham announced triumphantly, advancing one of his pawns with a confident flick which broke her from her trance. His gaze sought hers, searching for cracks in her composed facade. In a fluid motion, Beth leaned in, her focus narrowing to the chessboard. Her hand danced swiftly, a rook cutting through the tension as it claimed a bishop. She retreated, then lunged again, her queen sweeping forward with quiet authority, each move an unspoken challenge. The room was a symphony of silence and strategy, the only sound the ticking of the clock and the whisper of wood on wood. Abraham studied the board, his brow furrowing momentarily before a smirk played at the edge of his lips.

"You've got me on the run, it seems." He conceded, yet there was no defeat in his voice, only admiration laced with the thrill of the chase.

"So it seems." Beth remained still, her gaze fixed on the game, where kings and pawns stood in silent judgment. The flicker of the fire illuminated Beth's face as a soft laugh escaped her as she barely opened her mouth, not one of amusement but an involuntary response to a farce too grand to be taken seriously. She rose slowly from her chair, the sound of her movements muffled by the crackle of the flames. The room seemed to hold its breath as she started pacing before the hearth, the shadows dancing across her features in a macabre waltz. Abraham's chair scraped against the floorboards as he stood, his eyes never leaving her form.

"Your potential role, it is no small matter," he said with solemnity, moving a bishop across the board with purposeful precision, "it would be a gift, indeed, to mother the saviour. I have every intention of setting things right with the world." He declared, as though his words could bend reality to his will. His voice was a blend of conviction and prophecy, intended to ensnare. He stepped closer, invading the space between them with a presence that seemed to command the very air. Beth continued her measured pacing, each step a silent assertion of her autonomy. She glanced over at him, feigning indifference, yet aware of his calculating gaze tracking her every move. Her eyes roamed across the shelves lined with books, their spines an array of muted colours and gold lettering, telling stories of knowledge and history that contrasted sharply with the narrative Abraham sought to weave. As she approached his desk, her attention was drawn to the neat stack of papers resting atop it. Pausing, she allowed herself a moment to study the files, recognising the methodical nature of their arrangement. Each folder was a dossier, a life condensed into pages and numbers, a piece in Abraham's grand design. Beth's silence was her fortress, her lack of speech a shield against the deluge of Abraham's aspirations. She lingered by the files, her eyes tracing the edges of the paper, her mind alight with unvoiced questions and contemplations. Beth's fingers hovered momentarily over the topmost file, a shiver of unease trickling down her spine as Abraham broke the silence with a casual remark.

"Health checks," he said, his eyes following her every move, "necessary assessments for each of my potential candidates." His voice was matter-of-fact, yet laced with a subtle sense of pride. He gestured then to the chessboard, drawing Beth's attention away from the calculated documentation of human worth. Reluctantly, she turned back towards the game, the gravity of her situation settling heavily upon her shoulders. With grace born of necessity, she lowered herself into the chair opposite him, her expression unreadable. The creak of the door announced the arrival of a guard, his posture stiff as he delivered his message.

"Eve is here to see you, sir." He said, his gaze darting briefly to Beth before returning to Abraham.

"Very well," Abraham responded, nodding dismissively at the guard, "give us a few moments."

"Yes, sir." Once the man had exited, Abraham turned his steely gaze back to Beth, weighing her with an intensity that felt like a physical touch.

"The decision will be made soon." He told her, the corners of his mouth twitching upwards in anticipation of his imminent choice. Beth met his stare, her own eyes cool and unyielding. The silence between them stretched taut, filled with the unsaid. She was a silent observer in this game of control, a player without a voice, yet her presence spoke volumes. The air was still, laced with the scent of old wood and the subtle hint of burning embers from the fireplace. The chessboard lay between them, their battlefield of black and white, reflecting the stark contrasts that governed their lives. Beth's hand hovered over the board, her fingers pale ghosts in the dim light, decisive despite her quietude. With a grace that belied the tension coiled within her, Beth moved her queen with surgical precision, sliding the piece into position. The soft clack of chess piece against polished wood was a thunderclap in the silence of the library. She lifted her eyes to Abraham, the man who fancied himself the architect of a new world. His features were etched with the confidence of one who believed destiny bowed to his command. But as Beth held his gaze, something shifted - the flicker of uncertainty in the depths of his eyes, a crack in the facade of control.

"Checkmate." She whispered, her voice a raspy thread weaving through the space that separated them. It was more than a declaration of victory on the chessboard, it was an assertion of her own agency - a reminder that even without words, she was far from powerless. Beth rose from her chair, her movements composed, the whisper of her clothing the only sound as she withdrew from the table. She did not wait for him to absorb the finality of the game, nor did she linger to savour the moment. There was nothing left to be said - she had spoken volumes with her strategy, her tenacity, her unspoken defiance. With her head held high, Beth crossed the threshold of the library, leaving behind the chessboard and the man who mistook her silence for submission.

CHAPTER 4

Reece's hand moved over Val's injured arm, trailing with exquisite care, as though each touch required the gentleness of handling fragile porcelain. It hovered above her tender skin, light as if he were brushing a thread of gossamer. The early morning light poured in through the gaudy curtains, and the room took on a honeyed hue, casting the warm glow of dawn upon their entwined figures beneath the sheets. His jaw clenched, tensing in a visceral response to the thought of anyone inflicting harm upon her. An ache settled deep within him - an anguish that matched his helpless rage at the violence she endured. The shadows of that day still haunted them, lurking in corners, darkening moments of would-be comfort. Despite the softness of their cocoon, the need to protect her surged as fiercely as ever. The feeling gnawed at his insides and fuelled a resolve he could not suppress. He would not lose her to pain, not when his devotion could serve as shield and sword alike.

"If Luis lays a finger on you again, I swear I'll kill him." Reece murmured, the low timbre of his voice vibrating with a protective ferocity that echoed in the quiet of their sanctuary. Val shifted in his embrace, the pain from her injury flaring up briefly as she nestled closer to him. She met his statement with a firmness that belied her gentle demeanour.

"And then you'd hang for it," she countered, her voice soft

but wrought with conviction, "I can't lose you too. Not after everything. It's selfish, but I refuse to lose someone else I love." A silence enveloped them, profound and resonant. Reece's heart hammered against his ribcage, not from the mention of danger or death, but from the weight of her words. He looked down at Val, her head cradled against his chest, her tousled hair splayed across his skin.

"That's the first time you've said you love me." He whispered, the sound barely more than the rustling of the sheets around them.

"I know." Val, feeling the echo of their earlier passion with each breath they shared, pressed her face deeper into the warmth of Reece's chest. The ache in her arm couldn't compare to the yearning that tightened her chest. They breathed together, the rhythm syncing as if their bodies remembered the dance of intimacy they had indulged in just moments before. Each inhale was a silent vow, each exhale a release of all the fears that lurked beyond the walls of their current reprieve. In that moment, they found solace in the simple truth of their connectedness, in the heat that radiated between them - a testament to life and defiant love amidst the chaos of their world. The rumbling of an engine clawed its way through the stillness, a jarring reminder of the world's persistent march forward. Reece tensed slightly beside Val, his protective instincts never fully at rest. The noise mingled with the murmurs and footsteps of people in the hallways, life continuing outside their sanctuary. He leaned in, his lips brushing the shell of Val's ear as he whispered a tender echo of her own confession.

"I love you too." His voice held a reverence, a sacred timbre reserved for moments like these. The words seemed to linger in the air, a fragile promise in the wake of vulnerability.

"I know," she whispered softly into his chest, nuzzling her face further against his skin, "you remind me every day." Carefully, Reece began to untangle himself from the warmth of their embrace. He slipped from beneath the sheets, the cool morning air kissing his skin as he moved across the room. With each article of clothing he donned, he felt the armour of reality settle back upon him, piece by piece. Yet, glancing back at Val, still nestled in the bed they'd shared, there was a sense of fortitude in his movements, a silent oath to protect the love that had blossomed amidst chaos.

Beth stood alone before her mirror, the reflection staring back at her from within the confines of an unfamiliar, archaic bathroom. It lacked the modern touch of her ensuite back at Fort Irwin, but it wasn't the design that held her gaze. Her fingers paused, a dollop of white toothpaste adorning her lower lip. With a practiced swipe, she cleared the residue away, setting the toothbrush down with deliberate care. Her eyes, darkened with unspoken thoughts, met their counterparts in the glass. Beth cleared her throat, an attempt to shake off the discomfort that clung to her like a second skin. She opened her mouth slowly, a grimace passing fleetingly as she worked her jaw side to side. Her thumbs pressed against her cheeks, fingers curling to cradle her jawline as she silently tested the healing that time had afforded her. In the reflection, there was a glimpse of the woman she had been, juxtaposed with the one she was becoming - a survivor marked by resilience and marred by the brutality of her past. Beth's gaze hardened, not at what she saw, but at what she knew lay ahead. Her eyes flickered with a hint of trepidation as she faced the mirror, her lips parting for words that refused to come. Instead, she exhaled a silent sigh and shook her head, dismissing an unspoken confession to her reflection. The knock at the door was expected, its rhythm familiar, yet it elicited no start from her, only an acknowledgment of punctuality as she murmured out loud to herself.

"Right on queue, as always." She turned away, the lingering stiffness in her jaw a reminder of past indignities, now easing into a dull ache that spoke of healing rather than hurt. Her steps were measured as she navigated the small hallway connecting the sanctuary of the bathroom to the vulnerability of the bedroom beyond. His presence filled the doorway, a subtle barrier between her and the world she had yet to fully rejoin. She nodded towards him softly. His smile held a semblance of warmth, though his eyes betrayed the burden of duty. When he spoke, his voice was tinged with the politeness that served as armour in their interactions. "Abraham has decided you've earned some trust. It's been almost three months since you arrived, and he feels you've more than proven your obedience. You won't be needing my *guidance* around the estate anymore. You're free to explore the building as you wish," he paused, ensuring the gravity of his words settled upon her while she eyed him cautiously, looking past him to the open hallway which now seemed so much bigger, "you are to stay inside, but otherwise, move freely around the building." Her mind was already racing through the myriad of possibilities this sliver of freedom presented. There was power in movement, however limited, and Beth intended to wield it with the same precision she had used to place her toothbrush on the sink. As Jacob left her to her thoughts, Beth lingered in the doorway, her fingers tracing the frame as if to assure herself it was real. The open door symbolised more than a mere absence of barriers, it whispered of autonomy, a luxury she hadn't savoured in far too long. She glanced back at the room that had become both her refuge and her cage. With a deep breath, she stepped out, leaving behind the confines of her assigned quarters. It had been almost a month since the meeting with Abraham in the library, and he had barely called her back since. She had wondered if their casual game of chess had rendered her a difficult candidate to control in his search for his wife, his mother to his child. She had wondered if her uttering a word to him had been the undoing, now that he knew she could speak, even if only a little. The hallway was quiet, the early morning light casting long shadows across the floor. Her steps were tentative at first, like those of a fawn testing its legs, but with each stride, her confidence grew. She descended the creaky wooden staircase, the sounds of life below drawing her onward. The dining hall unfolded before her, a tableau of morning routines and unspoken hierarchies. Austin and Ben sat opposite each other, their plates holding the remnants of a meal eaten more out of necessity than enjoyment. Their conversation was a low murmur lost amid the hum of others, their exchanged glances speaking volumes in the silence. Reece, a solitary figure with an unreadable expression, slid into the seat next to Austin. His arrival went largely unnoticed, his presence folding seamlessly into the tapestry of the room. A fork clinked against a plate, a subtle symphony to their muted assembly. Across the room, Chase and Tyler were islands amongst a sea of random guards. Their stoic silence spoke volumes of their animosity while others' laughter punctuated the air, occasional bursts of camaraderie in an otherwise subdued atmosphere. They ate with the ease of men accustomed to the unpredictable ripples of their environment. Beth's gaze swept over the scene, a silent observer cataloging details and dynamics. The scent of coffee and toasted bread mingled with the undercurrent of antiseptic cleanliness that never quite masked the building's aged musk. She felt the weight of eyes upon her, the whispers of curiosity and suspicion that trailed in her wake. Beth paused at the threshold of the dining hall, her presence casting a hush over the previously vibrant conversations. A quick scan over the room brought her eyes to Ben, his posture alert as he offered a subtle nod in her direction. Austin and Reece, immersed in their own silent communion, followed Ben's gaze and turned towards her, a silent acknowledgement passing between them. With measured steps, Beth navigated the maze of tables, her bearings set on a distant corner. She caught Jennifer's inviting glance, a beacon in the throng of unfamiliar faces, and with it a gentle wave that beckoned her over. The surrounding whispers seemed to dissipate into the background hum of the hall as she made her approach. Jennifer shuffled aside, creating space for Beth beside her.

"Morning, Beth," she said warmly, then gestured to the others, "this is Eve, Rebecca, Grace, and Hannah." Beth nodded softly as she sat down beside Jennifer, her hands placed gingerly on the table in front of her.

"Welcome to the lion's den." Hannah quipped, her tone laced with irony. Her eyes danced with mischief as she looked around their small congregation.

"Beth is another one of the contenders," Eve's eyes darted around the table, addressing the others in equal measure, "in the running to be Abraham's wife." Beth's brows knitted together as she peered at Eve, uncertain how to respond to the sarcasm dripping from her words.

"Let's keep it down," Grace interjected softly, her eyes flitting nervously across the room, "there are ears everywhere."

"It's not like it's a secret, though. Everyone knows about the," Hannah leaned in, her smile tinged with resignation, "the *selection*."

"Still," Rebecca chimed in, her voice holding an edge of caution, "there's no need for hostility in our tones, even if the whole place is buzzing with the rumours."

"Abraham will think you're ungrateful," Jennifer whispered softly, "he sees the opportunity as an honour. You'd be punished if he thought you weren't grateful." Their introductions woven with underlying currents of tension, the women exchanged looks that carried more weight than their words, each bearing her own silent battles while trapped in the grand scheme of Abraham's vision. The murmurs at the adjoining table slipped into an uneasy lull, as if the very air grew thick with the weight of whispered judgments. A voice, not quite hushed enough to escape notice, pierced the silence that had settled around Beth and her unexpected companions.

"Heard she's turned into quite the junkie now," the disembodied words floated over, tinged with a false pity that did little to mask their scorn, "always after something from the infirmary."

"I don't blame her," another replied, the clinking of cutlery punctuating their speech, "after that guy broke her jaw—" Beth's eyes remained fixed in front of her. She could feel the speculative gaze of the room prickling against her skin like a rash that refused to fade.

"Fractured, not broken," Jennifer's voice rang out, turning towards the source of the gossip with a protective sharpness, "and she's not a junkie, she's fine." Her eyes flashed back to Beth, searching for some sign of reassurance or distress. Beth met her look with a vacant one of her own, her gaze cutting through Eve, who sat across from her. The chatter was nothing but noise, a distant echo she couldn't, and wouldn't let touch her.

"Maybe she's silent because Abraham decided to take her tongue as punishment," came another barb, louder this time and tinged with mirth that curdled the air around them, "which wouldn't surprise anyone. She always had something to say back at Fort Irwin. She never knew when to shut up really—"

"Go fuck yourself Amanda." Jennifer snapped, her voice a whip-crack in the increasingly tense atmosphere. Beth's eyes grew wide in surprise at hearing the curse come from someone she considered more reserved. Jennifer turned again to face the accuser, her posture daring further comment, her loyalty to Beth a shield raised high. Eve's voice cut through the thickening air, her eyes darting between Beth and the provocateur.

"And then there's Amanda," she drawled, a smirk playing on her lips as if to mock the competition for Abraham's favour, "another contender." Jennifer's response came like the rumble before a storm.

"Might be looking at another Sabrina here. You remember what she was like at Alcatraz and Catalina," she murmured darkly as her eyes darted from Amanda to Beth, "Amanda is just like her. Could be worse, given enough time." The room's ambient noise dwindled to nothing, each ear seemingly tuned to the brewing conflict.

"Oh, Jenny, don't be so jealous. You know you're not his type," Amanda's smile twisted into a sneer, and her words slithered out venomously, "he likes us pure and clean. It's not your fault you were born with a little *darkness* in you. You can't blame him because you're filth." Beth felt a cold shiver run down her spine as Amanda's insidious words hung in the air, vile and unforgivable. Jennifer was on her feet in a heartbeat, her chair clattering to the floor behind her with a violence that matched the rage in her eyes. "What the fuck did you just say to me?" Jennifer's voice boomed, every syllable a thunderclap of fury. In the momentary lull that followed, Beth's instincts kicked in - she rose from her seat, the muscles in her legs tensing for flight. Eve, Hannah, Grace, and Rebecca mirrored her actions, their collective movements a ripple of unease. As Jennifer lunged across the table, hands outstretched and eyes ablaze, the guards sprang into action, converging on the scene like hounds to a hunt. Austin, Ben, and Reece were just a breath behind, their faces set in grim determination as they corralled the others towards the relative safety of the room's periphery. Chaos erupted, the sound of scuffling feet and shouted curses blending into a discordant symphony. Beth glanced back once to see Jennifer grappling with Amanda, both women caught in a maelstrom of flailing limbs and raw emotion, other women from Amanda's table joining the fray in a tangle of hostility.

"Come on, this way." Ben's voice was close, a steadying presence amidst the bedlam, guiding them away from the epicentre of violence. Beth allowed herself to be moved, her back to the commotion, but her mind still reeling from the ugliness of the words that had sparked it all. Ben's presence was a fortress, his arm a battlement encircling the small of Beth's back as he drew her into the shelter of his body. The grip on her hip was firm yet careful, mindful of the chaos that swirled around them. Amidst the cacophony of the brawl, his touch anchored her to a semblance of safety. Beth felt the rough pads of his fingers, the warmth seeping through the fabric of her clothing, spreading a reassurance that words could not convey. In a gesture that seemed both delicate and desperate, she reached down and entwined her fingers with his, the slight movement belying the strength with which she held on. It was a silent plea for something steadfast in the maelstrom.

"Are you okay?" With a lean that brought his lips close to the shell of her ear, Ben whispered, his breath a contrast to the din. Her eyes remained fixed on the undulating mass of bodies where loyalty and fury clashed. She could only manage a slow nod in response, her gaze locked onto the spectacle, her mind grappling with the brutality of it all. She squeezed his hand more firmly as he gently manoeuvred her to stand just behind him, always the vigilant protector shielding her from the world. She rested her forehead against his shoulder, savouring the closeness of his presence for the first time in months.

"What is going on here?" The sudden entrance of Abraham cut through the tumult like a blade. His voice thundered across the hall, a clarion call that demanded order. The command in his tone was absolute, brooking no dissent. As if a switch had been flicked, the brawl stuttered to a halt - the combatants froze mid-motion, and the dining hall descended into an eerie silence. Beth felt Ben's hand slip from hers as they instinctively distanced themselves from one another. Everyone seemed to hold their breath, waiting for the storm that was Abraham's wrath. He surveyed the room with a scowl etched deep into his features before raising his voice once more. This time, his words carried a different weight, one that sought to remind rather than chastise.

"Everyone should be quick to listen, slow to speak and slow to become angry because human anger does not produce the righteousness that God desires." The scripture hung heavy in the air, a rebuke that settled over the crowd like a shroud. In that moment, the fervour of the fight seemed distant and misplaced, leaving behind a collective sense of reflection and unease.

"I would have come for you sooner," Jacob spoke softly in

Abraham's ear, his authority over the dining hall crushed in his commander's presence, "but it all happened so suddenly—"

"Take my girls to the library," Abraham motioned towards him and Luis, eyeing each of his candidates one by one until his eyes settled on Jennifer, "this one too." In an instant Luis's grip was iron on Beth's arm, his fingers pressing into her flesh with unnecessary force. His eyes, dark and taunting, locked onto Ben's, challenging him silently. Beth felt the tension in Ben's posture, saw the white-knuckled fists at his side, and the vein throbbing in his neck as he fought to keep his composure.

"Easy now." Jacob muttered under his breath, a cautious glance thrown towards Ben, but it was Luis who seemed to drink in the silent fury, his smirk widening.

"Don't make it worse." Austin shifted beside Ben, a subtle movement that betrayed his protective instinct. His jaw set, his gaze never leaving the exchange, his body tensed as if coiled to spring. But restraint prevailed, his foot retreated back to its original position, a testament to his control in the volatile atmosphere. As she was led from the dining hall by Luis, Beth turned her head, her eyes meeting Ben's for a fleeting moment. In that glance, there was an entire conversation - her shake of the head quietly urging him to let her go without incident, to trust her. With a final, lingering look that conveyed more than words could express, she allowed herself to be led away. One by one the women filed through the door and settled in front of the fire. Beth's gaze traveled slowly across the expanse of the library, a space that felt more like an extravagant cage than a room for reading. Her eyes settled on each figure - Eve with her defiant posture, Grace and Hannah nestled together in mutual comfort, their familial bond evident in the curve of their arms around one another. Rebecca sat slightly apart, her expression unreadable, while Amanda lounged with a casual arrogance that belied the recent chaos she had incited. Other candidates sat quietly around the fire - Samantha, Rachel, and Sarah - the latter's youth stark against the gravity of their situation as each bore marks of shared history, traces of a world now fractured, all seven of them familiar faces from Fort Irwin. Then there was Jennifer, her presence a thread connecting Beth to the days when Alcatraz was their reality, a lifeline in an ocean of uncertainty, the only one she truly trusted in the room. The heavy door to the library creaked open, drawing Beth's attention away from the silent assembly. A voice spilled through the gap, too soft for her to discern the message, but it prompted Jacob to address the room.

"I'll be right back." He said, tone clipped and official. As he slipped out the door, a palpable tension filled the void he left behind. Now, with only Luis as their sentinel, a shiver of unease whispered through the air. The man leaned against the doorframe, his eyes roaming over the group with a predatory laziness. Beth's memories of his grasp on her arm were still fresh, the imprint of his fingers a ghostly pressure she could almost feel radiating through her skin. In the shared silence, Beth thought of Ben's clenched fists and Austin's halted step, their restraint a small victory against Luis's provocation. She held onto that thought, a silent mantra of strength, as she watched him, waiting for whatever came next. Luis's boots thudded softly against the worn carpet as he approached, each step deliberate, echoing in the stillness of the library. The flickering flames from the fireplace cast an ominous glow on his face, shadows dancing across his features as his eyes lingered on each of the women before him.

"Quite the predicament," he mused aloud, a smirk playing at the corner of his mouth as his gaze finally settled on Beth, "on one hand, I long for the day you're no longer protected, so I can have my fun without restraint. But then seeing Austin and Ben's faces should you become Abraham's wife, now that would be a sight." His voice trailed off into a chuckle, rich with malice. Beth felt the weight of his words, heavy and threatening, but she refused to shrink under his scrutiny. Instead, she rose slowly, her movements measured, her expression unreadable. A deafening silence blanketed the room, punctuated only by the crackling of the fire as all eyes turned to witness the confrontation. Meeting Luis's gaze head-on, Beth's lips curled into a defiant smirk, a silent challenge that hung between them like a taunt. And then, quick as lightning, her hand shot out, her palm connecting sharply with his cheek. The sound of the slap reverberated through the library, a sharp crack that seemed to halt time itself. "Beth!" Jennifer hissed while the room filled with a collective gasp as the others looked back and forth between Beth and Luis, holding their breath in anticipation of his response. For a breathless moment, Luis remained motionless, his head turned slightly from the force of the impact. When he finally looked back at her, his eyes were cold, his face betraying no sign of pain or anger.

"Remember this moment," he whispered, his voice low and menacing, "one day when you least expect it, whether you are Abraham's wife or not I'll get you back for that. One way or another." The heavy library door swung open with a resounding thud and Abraham's towering figure filled the doorway. His presence was like a sudden drop in temperature, sending an icy hush across the room.

"Luis, leave us." He commanded without preamble, his voice brooking no argument.

"Yes, sir." Luis cast a lingering glance at Beth, a silent promise etched into his steely gaze, before turning on his heel and walking out. Once the door clicked shut behind him, Abraham began to pace like a caged lion, his eyes scanning the group of young women with a barely contained fury.

"Sit down," he ordered, pointing at the scattered chairs around the grand fireplace, "not you two, you stand." All complied, except for Jennifer and Amanda, who remained standing at his command, their postures rigid with tension. Abraham stopped and faced them, his hands clasped behind his back. When he finally spoke, his tone was laced with a preacher's cadence.

"Scripture teaches us, get rid of all bitterness, rage and anger, brawling and slander, along with every form of malice. Be kind and compassionate to one another, forgiving each other, just as in Christ God forgave you," he turned slightly, addressing the room as a whole, "don't have anything to do with foolish and stupid arguments, because you know they produce quarrels. And the Lord's servant must not be quarrelsome but must be kind to everyone, able to teach, not resentful." With the verses hanging in the air, Abraham focused his attention on Jennifer.

"Sir, I—"

"Indignation has no place here, I won't tolerate it. But this is your first offence and you have become quite valuable to the children under this roof, or so I'm told," Abraham took a few measured steps towards Jennifer, placing his body square in front of her, "if this happens again there will be consequences, I hope I am clear on this. Do you understand?" He looked down his nose at her as she stared at the floor solemnly

"Of course," Jennifer's chin lifted a fraction, her eyes meeting Abraham's, "it won't happen again." He dismissed her with a wave of his hand, and she turned and walked out of the library with a quiet dignity that spoke volumes. Now alone under Abraham's scrutiny, Amanda shifted uncomfortably. Abraham's eyes bore into hers, as if willing her to understand the gravity of her actions. "I'm well aware it was you who provoked the incident," he said, his voice low and controlled, "your spirit is commendable, but my wife must embody more than just passion. She will be a leader, a beacon, guiding our child and our community on the path of righteousness." Amanda nodded, a flicker of something, perhaps fear or respect, crossing her features as she absorbed his words. The room held its breath, awaiting Abraham's next move. Amanda's voice trembled slightly as she offered her contrite words to Abraham.

"I apologise, I really do. I didn't mean to upset Jennifer. And perhaps," her eyes darted around the room, avoiding direct contact with Abraham's stern gaze, "perhaps she misheard me."

"That's bullshit," Sarah interjected sharply from the corner, her voice a stark contrast to Amanda's quivering tone, "I was sitting right behind her, and I heard every word Amanda said." She continued with a bravado that defied her youthful appearance.

"Enough!" The single word erupted from Abraham's lips like thunder, his step forward quick and heavy. The air thickened, a collective gasp was barely audible over the tension that now strangled the room.

"Sir, I," Sarah's defiance melted into retreat, her body sinking back against the chair as if wishing it could swallow her whole, "I'm sorry." Abraham paused, his chest heaving with the effort of regaining composure.

"Amanda," he straightened his collar as though realigning his very self before continuing in a calmer voice, "please take a seat." As

Amanda lowered herself onto one of the plush chairs, Beth's gaze swept across the room. Her eyes were sharp, missing nothing - the small flinches, the downcast looks, the way shoulders hunched inward as if to shield against an unseen blow. All except for herself, Amanda, and Eve. Eve remained still, her posture relaxed but alert, a mocking serenity about her. When their eyes met, no words passed between them, yet volumes seemed to be exchanged within that silent communion. Beth observed the willingness and unwillingness between the nine of them - Hannah, Grace, Sarah, Rebecca, Samantha and Rachel all avoiding his gaze, their body language subdued and unprotesting, hoping not to draw attention to themselves. While herself, Eve and Amanda all sat upright and alert, staring at Abraham as he spoke. Beth was unsure of their motives, knowing her own desire to play the game and destroy his world from within, but Eve and Amanda seemingly had their own stakes and she wasn't sure which rules they were willing to play by. The stillness stretched on, the quiet only disturbed by the crackling of fire until at last, Abraham's voice sliced through the silence once more. His presence filled the library, a towering figure of authority among the collected women. His gaze settled on each face, lingering just long enough to remind them of their place within his world. Beth watched him as he spoke, her silence a fortress of thought. The words washed over her like a ritual chant, predictable yet laden with unspoken implications.

"You are all here for a reason. Your health checks have been nothing short of exemplary, and I am genuinely excited at the prospect of what one of you, and myself, will accomplish together," his voice was a firm but measured timbre that commanded attention, "however, let it be known that insubordination is something I will not tolerate. Do you understand?" His eyes swept the room, pinning each woman momentarily under a steely scrutiny.

"Yes." A collective hush of whispered responses filled the void before Abraham continued.

"We stand on the brink of salvation, and in this new world, there is no room for rebellion," he paused, allowing the weight of his declaration to sink in, "consider Sabrina. A promising candidate - my favourite, in fact. Clearly fertile, very intelligent, she had so much potential. Yet, her actions betrayed her promise, and ultimately, they cost her everything." The fire crackled in the hearth, its warmth a stark contrast to the chill settling over the group. His hands clasped behind his back as he paced slowly. Eyes, now more watchful than ever, followed his every move. Abraham stopped pacing and locked his gaze onto Amanda.

"Sir—"

"I will not overlook flaws for my personal preference, even if you are the favourite as Sabrina was." Abraham's gaze bore down on her as if he were drilling into her very soul. Amanda held his stare, unflinching, but Beth saw the slightest tremor in her hand, a telltale sign of nerves belying her composed exterior. Beth remained motionless, absorbing the gravity of Abraham's words, her own thoughts obscured behind the veil of her imposed muteness. Her unwillingness to speak did not mean she couldn't listen, couldn't understand the game being played around her. And in that moment, the stakes had never seemed higher.

"I am sorry. It won't happen again." The tension in the library stretched taut as a bowstring, every eye fixed on Amanda under the weight of Abraham's stern visage. With a gesture that seemed to command the very air they breathed, he pointed at her, his voice a low rumble.

"Another outburst like today, and you are finished." His words didn't just echo, they reverberated through the silence, insistent and ominous. Amanda's response was subdued, an almost imperceptible dip of her chin affirming her understanding.

"Of course." Her eyes, once filled with a fiery defiance, now stared at the floor, the spark of rebellion extinguished, at least for the moment.

"Let me remind you of the virtues expected of a woman," Abraham's voice continued, his tone now edged with the authority of scripture as he recited the verses from Titus with deliberation, "then they can urge the younger women to love their husbands and children, to be self-controlled and pure, to be busy at home, to be kind, and to be subject to their husbands, so that no one will malign the word of God." Each word seemed to hang in the air, a palpable weight upon the room, and on Amanda most of all. Beth felt the eyes of Eve and the others on her, as if expecting her to react, but she remained a silent observer, her own feelings shrouded. Abraham then shifted his focus to the broader gathering, his gaze sweeping over the assembly of young women like a lighthouse beam cutting through fog. His proclamation and the certainty in his voice left no room for doubt or debate.

"I vow to be a good husband. Together we shall bring about the second coming of Christ and save the human race," he paused before quoting Ephesians, each sentence falling like the stroke of a bell, "husbands, love your wives, just as Christ loved the church and gave himself up for her to make her holy, cleansing her by the washing with water through the word, and to present her to himself as a radiant church, without stain or wrinkle or any other blemish, but holy and blameless. In this same way, husbands ought to love their wives as their own bodies. He who loves his wife loves himself." Even though silenced, Beth's presence was as strong as any spoken word. Her steady gaze held a flicker of something indiscernible - skepticism, resolve, perhaps a touch of quiet defiance. Her silence wasn't simply the absence of sound, it was a statement, a refusal to play the part Abraham had scripted for them. As Abraham's speech concluded, the room remained hushed, the echo of his promises lingering amongst the gathered, who were bound by more than just their shared circumstance. They were united too, in the unspoken understanding that this man wielded his words as weapons, shaping a destiny they were expected to embrace without question. Yet within that silence there was a subtle undercurrent, a collective breath held in anticipation of what was to come. The tension in the library seemed to coil tighter, like a spring compressing with every word that fell from Abraham's lips. His command was clear and immediate, reverberating through the silence that had taken hold of the room after his sermon on marriage and righteousness.

"Let us pray," he announced, his voice leaving no room for dissent, "let us pray together. Stand and join hands." Beth felt the movement around her as the women rose to their feet, hesitancy mingling with obedience. She stood, her own movements deliberate and measured, the air around her charged with the residue of earlier confrontations and unspoken alliances. With a subtle shift of her body, Beth extended her hand, feeling the warm clasp of Abraham's fingers envelope hers. To his right, Amanda's touch was tentative and almost cautious, as if the reprimand she'd received moments before lingered like a bad taste. On Beth's left, Eve's soft grasp laced between her fingers. She felt Eve's hands shaking slightly, her palm laced with a hint of nervous sweat. Amanda turned marginally, her eyes locking with Beth's in a silent exchange. The corners of Amanda's mouth twitched into a smirk, a fleeting expression that carried a mix of arrogance and challenge before her gaze dropped to the floor, as if the gravity of Abraham's words finally settled upon her shoulders. Beth's own eyes remained steady, impassive. Her silence wasn't a choice, but in that moment it became her armour, shielding her thoughts and preserving her dignity amidst the circling storm of Abraham's making. With the circle formed and each woman connected, they awaited Abraham's next move, an unbroken chain of reluctant hopefuls under the weight of an uncertain future.

CHAPTER 5

Austin's boots echoed softly against the cool concrete, his shadow elongating and receding with every step as he descended into the basement. The faint hum of the bustling in the kitchens mingled with the subtle scent of mildew that clung to the air, a constant reminder of the world below ground level. Tucked away past the hustle of the kitchens, this part of the building was familiar territory for Austin, though no less unsettling in its quietness. His eyes narrowed, adjusting to the dimming light that filtered through dusty windows, casting an eerie glow on the hallway's end. His hand instinctively grazed the wall, fingers tracing over the rough texture of the bricks as if they could guide him through the trepidation that knotted in his stomach. He knew every crevice here, each corner that led to his own secluded bedroom, but today, his focus was fixed on the unassuming closet door ahead. As Austin neared the closet, the sound of muffled voices seeped through the thin wood, causing him to slow his approach. With a cautious exhale, he pressed his ear against the door, trying to discern the conversation within, but finding only indistinct murmurs. A sense of foreboding gripped him as he reached for the handle, steeling himself for what might come next. The door creaked open, betraying his silent entry, and three pairs of eyes instantly snapped in his direction. Eve's gaze was the first to meet his, her posture stiffening as she turned to face him fully. Barnett and Stone, already alert to the intrusion, faced the doorway with an air of anticipation. For a moment, time seemed to hang suspended. Austin hesitated on the threshold, his heart pounding in his chest as he scrutinised their faces, searching for any sign of deception. The tension in the air was almost tangible, wrapping around him like a shroud. Eve's voice broke through the unease, calm and reassuring.

"This isn't an ambush, Austin," she said, a hint of earnestness threading through her words, "you're safe down here with us." The reassurance should have eased his mind, but it only served to pique his curiosity further.

"What's going on?" Austin asked, his voice carrying a measured edge as he stepped fully into the room. Every instinct screamed for him to be wary, to be ready. He watched as Eve exchanged a fleeting look with Barnett and Stone before returning her attention to him.

"Barnett and Stone have assured me that I can trust them." She explained, her eyes holding his in a silent plea for understanding. The statement hung heavy in the air, dense with implications Austin wasn't sure he wanted to unravel. Trust was a currency in short supply these days, and the value of it seemed only to rise with each passing hour. Eve's words carried weight, but Austin knew all too well the cost of misplaced faith. Austin's scoff echoed off the bare concrete walls, a sharp sound in the dimly lit corridor.

"Barnett betrayed us at Fort Irwin." He accused, his eyes narrowing as they fixated on Barnett's stoic face. The undercurrent of betrayal still stung, and trust was not something easily rebuilt.

"I took a bullet for Beth," Stone shifted slightly, the light catching the stark lines of his jaw, "and I trust him. That should give you some comfort." He interjected, his tone matter-of-fact as though the action spoke for itself. His gaze held steady, no flicker of regret or bravado, just the plain truth laid bare. Barnett met Austin's skeptical look with a level stare.

"The betrayal was a ruse," he said calmly, each word deliberate and measured, "a play to gain Abraham's confidence."

"Convenient." Austin muttered, his distrust a tangible thing that filled the space between them.

"Believe what you will," Barnett replied, shoulders squared, "but I—"

"Enough," Eve interrupted before Barnett could escalate the situation any further, "we don't have time for this."

"And how did you all manage to slink down here without raising alarms?" Austin's gaze lingered on Barnett a moment longer before turning towards Eve.

"Perks of the inner circle," Stone responded dryly, "we're allowed freedom others aren't privy to." There was a hint of disdain in his voice, a subtle jab at the hierarchy that granted them such liberties.

"Freedom, or a leash?" Austin mused aloud, his thoughts tracing the fine line between the two.

"Both." Barnett conceded with a shrug. Eve stepped forward then, her presence grounding.

"I bring food to the children," she said, gesturing vaguely towards the direction of the stairs, "no one questions my comings and goings here so close to the kitchen."

"Very convenient." Austin echoed his earlier sentiment, though this time it was tinged with a reluctant understanding. They each had their roles to play, their masks to wear. It was a game of shadows and deceit, and they were all unwilling players on Abraham's twisted stage.

"Convenience means survival." Eve replied, her eyes locking onto Austin's, a silent plea for him to see the bigger picture. In that moment, surrounded by the cold embrace of the basement, Austin felt the weight of their shared circumstance settle upon him like a mantle. Allies or enemies, they were bound by a common goal - a desperate need to navigate the treacherous waters they found themselves in. Whether he liked it or not, their fates were intertwined. Austin exhaled slowly, the air cool in his lungs, and nodded once.

"Alright," he said, the single word an unspoken agreement to move forward, "what's all this about?" Austin's eyes narrowed, the dim light casting shadows across his face as he scrutinised the trio before him. His voice echoed faintly against the concrete walls, skepticism lacing each word. Eve met his gaze steadily, a flicker of urgency in her eyes.

"I need to understand Beth better," she said, her tone earnest, "from what I've seen, she doesn't strike me as a true believer in Abraham's vision." A questioning look etched itself onto Austin's features, his brow furrowing in thought.

"Why?" He prodded, trying to piece together Eve's sudden interest.

"Because," Eve leaned in slightly, lowering her voice as if sharing a secret, "Beth has a strength that Abraham hasn't managed to quell. She could be powerful enough to topple his reign from the inside." There was a note of admiration, perhaps even hope, threading through her words.

"Powerful, sure," Austin allowed, his thoughts drifting momentarily to Beth's fierce independence, "but she isn't one for playing by someone else's rules." He knew Beth well enough, knew the restless spirit that drove her, the fire that Abraham's restrictions could never dampen. Barnett let out a short, barking laugh, a sound harsh and grating in the quiet of the basement. Austin's head whipped around, his eyes flashing a warning at Barnett, a silent command to tread carefully.

"Sorry," Barnett managed, though the smirk on his lips belied any real apology, "it's just amusing, imagining Beth bending to anyone's will."

"Exactly," Eve interjected before more tension could brew between the men, "that's why we need to make her believe leading this coup is her own idea. If it comes from us, she'll reject it outright." She gave Barnett a sharp glance before turning back to Austin, her expression serious. Austin crossed his arms, considering the implications. Beth, leading a rebellion wasn't far-fetched, not with the simmering defiance he'd seen in her eyes time and again.

"Manipulation's a dangerous game." He murmured, more to himself than to the plotters before him. Yet as the silence stretched between them, filled only by the distant drip of a leaking water somewhere unseen, Austin felt the weight of possibility settle upon him, the chance to change everything, if only they could steer Beth without breaking her.

"Isn't it always?" Eve responded softly, her eyes reflecting a resolve as unyielding as the walls that enclosed them. Austin's gaze shifted from Eve to the others, weighing their silent, expectant faces in the dim light of the basement.

"So the goal is to play Beth," his statement fell flat, his voice echoing softly off the concrete walls, "why aren't we planning an escape? Why can't we—"

"No," Barnett interrupted suddenly, raising his hand as he spoke, "this place is locked down so tightly we'd just end up getting too many people killed."

"We need to take Abraham down," Stone concluded for him, "leave the flock without their shepherd, so to speak." Austin shifted uncomfortably from one foot to another, looking between the three of them before settling his eyes on Eve.

"So your only solution is playing Beth?"

"Yes," Eve nodded once, resolute, "but we must be subtle, Austin."

"Subtlety isn't exactly a surplus around here," Austin mused, his thoughts drifting briefly to Beth's own cunning nature, "Beth's probably got her own agenda. Wouldn't surprise me if she's playing a long game herself."

"We can't assume anything at this point," Barnett chimed in, a flicker of respect in his eyes at the mention of her name, "she always seems like she's one step ahead."

"Which brings me to the next point," Austin's gaze landed on Stone, who seemed uncomfortable under the scrutiny, "why are you two involved in this?" Stone faltered, his throat convulsing as he swallowed. After a tense moment, he found his voice.

"I follow a different religion to Abraham," he admitted, his words nearly a whisper, "I have no interest in converting." The revelation hung heavy in the air, charged with the potential for dire consequences. The confession was met by a silence that felt like a held breath.

"And telling me this, do you think it's going to make me trust you?" Austin studied him closely, searching for any hint of deceit.

"No," Stone shook his head, a certain vulnerability breaking through his usual stoicism, "but sharing something that could see me punished seems like a step towards trust, doesn't it?" Austin thought for a moment before turning his attention to Eve who had been quietly observing the exchange. Her eyes met his squarely.

"And you," Austin prodded gently, "what secrets are you hiding from Abraham?" Eve let out a slow, steady breath, her hand subconsciously drifting up to touch the cross at her neck, an action that spoke volumes in the silence.

"Let's just say my *preferences* are distasteful to Abraham," she said, her voice steady despite the danger her admission carried, "if they were known, I'd likely find myself at the end of a noose."

"Preferences." Austin repeated, the word tasting of risk and rebellion. He took a moment to let the implications settle, feeling the weight of their shared peril. Each of them, marked by their truths, united in their deception. Austin's gaze lingered on Eve, a silent question hanging between them. She met his look unflinchingly, the dim basement light casting shadows that seemed to accentuate the gravity of her next words.

"Abraham doesn't approve of whom I prefer to share my life with." She said quietly, her voice carrying the weight of unspoken stories. Understanding dawned in Austin's eyes as he gave a slow nod, acknowledging the personal cost of her truth. He turned towards Barnett, who stood with his arms crossed, an unreadable expression on his face.

"Your turn." Austin remarked, his tone laced with curiosity and a hint of caution. Barnett shrugged, a casual gesture that belied the tension in the air.

"I'm not here for religious reasons or because of who I love," he began, his eyes scanning the faces of the conspirators, "it's simple. I just don't buy into Abraham's regime." The room was thick with their collective dissent, each one of them bound by a common thread of defiance.

"So why did you turn against us?" Austin pressed further, seeking the logic behind Barnett's betrayal as he raised his voice.

"Austin," Eve took a few steps towards the doorway, listening for any footsteps before turning back to him, "stay quiet, please. Or we'll all face the consequences."

"Someone had to be on the inside," Barnett whispered, the corner of his mouth quirking up in a wry half-smile, "you and Ben, you're smart, good leaders. But Ben's too wrapped up in Beth to see straight, and you. Well, Abraham has his reasons for not taking a shine to you." Austin's gaze dropped to the pigmentation that marked him differently in a world where differences were not just noted, they were often condemned. The weight of his heritage was a silent player in every room, an unspoken character in every interaction. He lifted his eyes from the contrast of his skin against the dimly lit corridor and met Barnett's gaze squarely. The message in that look was clear, a nonverbal pact sealed with hard-won trust.

"Besides," Barnett shrugged nonchalantly, "no one would believe that one of you had turned against the others."

"If you're playing us," Austin said, his voice low but carrying the sharp edge of a blade, "if you betray us again, I swear I will kill you myself." Barnett held his stare, neither flinching nor backing down. Instead he offered a nod, the gesture sombre and earnest.

"I wouldn't expect anything less from you, Austin." The air between them crackled with the gravity of their situation, the unspoken acknowledgement that life and death hung precariously in the balance of their choices. It was a dance on the razor's edge, and they all knew it.

"Alright," Austin exhaled slowly, as if dispelling the tension with his breath, "what do you want me to do?" His eyes shifted to Eve, who had been silently observing the exchange, her face a mask of determination. Eve stepped forward, her hands clasped together as though she was gathering her thoughts into a cohesive plan.

"We need you to talk to Beth," she began, her voice steady and sure, "you have her ear, her respect. We believe you can influence her, make her see reason—"

"Cut the bullshit," Austin interjected, his eyebrows knitting together, "you said yourself that we don't have time. What do you want me to do." He had a sense of where this was leading, but he needed to hear it spoken aloud, to understand the full scope of their intentions. Eve took a deep breath, and when she spoke the words seemed to hang heavy in the stale basement air.

"We need Beth to agree to become Abraham's wife, and she needs to pretend that she's committed to the role." The silence that followed was punctuated by the distant echo of footsteps above, a reminder of the world that continued oblivious to the conspiracy being hatched beneath its surface. Austin felt a chill run down his spine at the implications of Eve's words. This wasn't just a gamble, it was asking someone to walk willingly into the lion's den.

"His wife," Austin repeated, the concept bitter on his tongue, "you're asking her to step into a role that could very well be a death sentence." Eve met his gaze with an intensity that matched his own.

"Yes, because she's the one who can get close enough, earn his trust, and eventually—" She let the sentence hang unfinished, yet its meaning was unmistakable. Austin looked between the faces of those gathered, each set with resolute lines borne of desperation and hope. They were all playing their parts in a dangerous game, but it was Beth who would be asked to take centre stage, and if the curtain fell on their performance, it would mean the end for all of them. Austin's jaw clenched as he considered the gravity of what Eve was proposing. The low hum of a flickering lantern above did little to brighten the dim closet, nor did it ease the tension that hung like a shroud in the cramped space.

"Why Beth?" He finally asked, his voice a low growl of skepticism.

"Hannah, Grace, the others," Eve's expression was solemn, her eyes flickering to the small cross pendant that rested against her chest before her fingers curled around it, "they don't have the strength to survive Abraham, let alone overthrow him. And Amanda won't want to, but Beth—"

"Why not you?" Austin cut in, his gaze fixed on the symbol of faith at her neck. Eve's grip tightened on the cross, the edge biting into her palm.

"Because I couldn't kill him," she confessed, her voice barely a whisper, "even if I could get close enough, I don't think I could do it." Austin's brow furrowed, the lines deepening as he considered her admission. He understood faith, had seen how it could both anchor and bind. But this plan, it would test more than faith - it would test the very limits of their humanity.

"Are you saying the plan is for Beth to marry him, share his bed, pretend to like it? You realise what you're suggesting? That she endure him, that she willingly—" Austin couldn't keep the disgust from seeping into his questions.

"Yes. Play the doting wife until she gains his trust," Eve's nod was almost imperceptible, but it sent a ripple of disquiet through Austin, "and once she's alone with him, long enough to—"

"Kill him," Austin's words fell heavy between them, "even if she succeeds, they'll hang her for it. You're asking her to sacrifice everything."

"They won't hang her for it. The rest of them won't know what to do without their leader," Eve's face was stricken, yet resolved, "it's the only way. Beth's strong, she's cunning, and she doesn't bow to anyone's rule, not even Abraham's." Austin looked away, the weight of their scheme pressing down on him like the darkness of the room. This wasn't just about toppling a tyrant, it was about manipulating a friend into becoming an assassin, all under the guise of matrimony - a twisted play where the final act promised bloodshed.

"Let's say Beth agrees to go through with your plan," Austin said slowly, "will she know it's *your* plan?"

"No," Eve's eyes held sorrow now, the kind born of necessity, "but we're hoping you can convince her, to make her see it's *her* idea." Austin's hands balled into fists at his sides.

"Fuck Eve, you're playing with fire."

"Then let's hope we don't get burned." Barnett interjected, his words starkly pragmatic. Austin cast a final look at each of them, their faces set with grim determination. They were united by a common enemy, but divided by the horrors they were willing to embrace to see their mission through. As the reality settled in his gut like lead, Austin knew there was no turning back now. They were all committed to the path laid out before them, the path that led through darkness, deceit, and potential destruction. Austin stood still, his mind churning with the weight of Eve's revelation. The thick air of the basement felt stifling, and the dim light cast long shadows across the group's faces, mirroring the murky plan they were concocting. Eve had a resolute look in her eyes as she addressed the unspoken dread lingering between them.

"Look, it's a long game," Eve said, her voice steady despite the tremor that threatened to break through, "they won't let Beth out of their sight for a good while after she marries Abraham. She'll need to be the perfect wife, at least on the surface." Austin felt a knot tighten in his stomach. Beth playing housewife to a monster like Abraham, all the while plotting his demise - it was a dangerous performance, one that could cost her everything if even a single step faltered. He turned away from the conspirators, pacing the length of the cramped space, the cold concrete underfoot reminding him of the harsh reality they faced. Each step he took was a moment spent wrestling with the implications, considering angles and outcomes.

Finally, he stopped and faced Eve again, his expression grave.

"So what's the endgame? Beth kills Abraham, and then what? We just walk out the front gates?" Austin asked, his voice barely above a whisper as though speaking louder might make it all too real.

"We'd have to move fast," Eve met his gaze, unflinching, "she'd have to do it at night, when they're alone. Then we escape before dawn breaks and his body is found. It'll be chaos then. Our best chance to slip away unnoticed." Austin ran a hand through his hair, the enormity of the scheme pressing down on him.

"There are so many moving parts, Eve. This plan, it's patchy. Too many things can go wrong." He looked at each face in turn, searching for any sign of doubt that mirrored his own.

"Patchy or not, it's what we have," Eve replied, her fingers absently touching the cross at her neck, "we can refine it, but we need to start somewhere, and soon." As silence filled the room, Austin knew there was no simple way out. They were threading a needle in the dark, hoping against hope that when the time came, their shaky tapestry would hold together long enough to see them all through to the other side. Austin leaned back against the cool concrete wall, the weight of their precarious plan making his shoulders slump. The dim light from the overhead lantern cast long shadows across the room, mirroring the dark thoughts that flickered through his mind.

"Listen," Eve's voice cut through the tense air, "I know we've got a lot to figure out, but we can't afford to wait until we've mapped out every step. Abraham's going to pick a wife soon, and we need Beth to be ready, to start laying the groundwork now." He straightened up, his eyes narrowing.

"You're talking about pushing her into danger without a solid strategy. I can't, I *won't* do that without my friends knowing. They have to be in on it." Austin's voice was firm, his stance resolute.

"The fewer who know, the better," Eve shook her head slowly, the motion almost imperceptible, "secrecy is our ally here, Austin. Every additional person in the loop is another risk."

"Especially Ben," Barnett chimed in, his tone sombre, "his need to protect Beth is instinctual. It'll cloud his judgment, make him act rashly. We can't afford that kind of exposure." Austin felt the frustration boiling inside him. His loyalty to his friends warred with the necessity of stealth, and he found himself caught between the stark reality of their situation and the bonds that tethered him to those he trusted most.

"Ben's not just going to stand by," Austin countered, gritting his teeth, the muscle in his jaw tightening, "you expect me to keep him in the dark while his world is turned upside down?"

"Exactly that," Barnett said, his gaze steady, "he'll want to protect her regardless, but if he knows what's at stake his actions might betray us all. You get that, right?" A heavy silence settled over them as Austin wrestled with the implications. It felt like betrayal, yet the logic was cold and unforgiving. In this game of subterfuge and survival, the less they knew the safer they were.

"Ben's instincts to protect her are key," Eve continued, a grim certainty in his tone, "they'll provide the perfect cover. If he knew our intentions, it might influence his behaviour, make it seem contrived. We can't risk raising suspicions."

"Fine," Austin finally conceded, the word tasting like ash in his mouth, "but if anything happens to her—"

"Nothing will," Eve interjected, her voice soft but carrying an edge of steel, "Abraham is old school, I'm sure he won't object to Beth having a sort of lady in waiting once they're married. I'll watch over her." Austin pushed off the wall, his resolve hardening. He didn't have to like it, but he understood. For Beth, for all of them, he'd play his part.

"Okay, but I want Reece in on this. He needs to know." Austin's jaw clenched at the thought - involving Reece was one thing, but keeping Ben out of the loop felt like walking a knife's edge. Yet as he locked eyes with Barnett, he recognised the hard truth in the man's words. Reluctantly, he nodded, giving in to the necessary evil of secrecy. Eve exchanged a glance with Stone before returning her attention to Austin.

"Agreed," she said, "Reece, and no one else. It's imperative that Val doesn't find out—"

"Look," Austin interrupted, the frustration evident in his voice, "I can't promise what Reece will do with the information, but he knows how to handle classified intel. Secrecy is second nature to him, you have my word on that." Barnett leaned back against the cool concrete wall, arms folded, studying Austin with a calculating eye. Stone simply nodded, his expression unreadable behind the stoic mask he wore so well.

"Good. Then that's settled." Eve's voice cut through the tension, decisive and clear.

"How do you plan to communicate with Beth? You know every corner of this place is under surveillance, except some dark corners of the basements." Austin's gaze lingered on Eve, his brows furrowing in skepticism.

"True," Eve conceded, a wisp of a smile playing on her lips, "but it hasn't been too difficult to find ways around that. Barnett has been my escort on the grounds without raising suspicion, and Stone has acted as my chaperone for some time now. Our movements together have become expected."

"Right," Austin muttered, still unconvinced, "but Beth can't just waltz down here to the basement or sub-basement. She's not allowed unless someone's taking her to the infirmary."

"Leave that to me." Eve replied with a hint of confidence that seemed out of place in the dimly lit corridor. Austin nodded slowly, the gears turning in his head as he considered the implications of their plan. Yet, he couldn't shake the unease that clung to him like a second skin.

"I should get back," he said, glancing over his shoulder towards the stairs, "if I'm gone much longer, they'll start wondering why the trucks aren't being unloaded."

"Of course," Eve agreed, her nod resolute, "we can't afford any slip-ups, not now." Stepping away from the whisper of conspiratorial tension, Austin walked back towards his day-to-day responsibilities, the echo of his boots against the concrete floor punctuating each step. The weight of the impending deceit lay heavy in his chest as he ascended, leaving the hushed murmurs of revolution behind him. Eve's gaze lingered on the retreating echo of his steps before she pivoted to face Barnett and Stone, her expression etched with the gravity of their scheme.

"Think he can do it?" Stone's voice cut through the stillness, his eyes sharp on the others. Barnett leaned back against the wall, arms crossed, a contemplative look shadowing his features.

"At Fort Irwin, I kept my distance," he began, his tone measured, "but even from afar, it was clear. Austin's mind weaves through complexity like a blade. He sees beyond the immediate horizon."

"I hope you're right," Eve's lips pressed into a thin line, her hands clasped as if in silent prayer, "for all of our sakes." She murmured, and there was a tremor in her voice that spoke volumes of the perilous tightrope they walked.

In the sanctuary of the Oak Sitting Room, speckles of sunlight danced across the polished floors that cast warm hues on the walls. The children's laughter filled the air, a gentle balm against the undercurrent of tension among the women gathered there.

"Hannah, are you alright?" Eve's question was soft but laden with concern as she observed her distant gaze. Hannah exhaled slowly, her eyes never leaving the innocent playing among the children.

"I'm worried about Grace," she confessed, her voice barely above a whisper, "she's not handling this very well." Samantha offered a rueful smile that failed to reach her eyes.

"We're all in this together," she said, her hands wringing the fabric of her shirt, "none of us aren't scared, though some hide it better than others." The weight of unspoken truths settled heavily in the room, as the innocence of play contrasted starkly with the foreboding reality that encroached upon them all. Eve's gaze drifted towards the window, where shadows lengthened as the afternoon waned.

"There's a way to avoid being chosen." She said, her voice steady but low enough not to carry over the children's merriment. Samantha and Hannah turned, their movements synchronised in the tension of the moment.

"What do you mean?" Hannah whispered, leaning in closer as her eyes darted towards the doorway. Jennifer, her fingers gently guiding Victoria's small hands as her little fingers wrapped around Jennifer's own, remained focused on the child, the epitome of maternal distraction.

"Abraham has no patience for defiance," Eve continued, her eyes now fixed on the delicate mug cradled in her hands, "a public display of insubordination, an unwillingness to conform to the role of community matriarch. He would likely cast aside anyone who dared such rebellion."

"But that kind of resistance," Samantha's lips formed the words with caution, her eyes darting towards the children before settling back on Eve, "it could get you killed." Eve shook her head, a strand of hair falling loose from her bun.

"Not unless it's a matter of grave concern. Abraham is many things, but he prefers his punishments to serve as examples rather than to end lives prematurely," her eyes met theirs, a spark of something fierce within their depths, "an act serious enough to warrant a whipping, however, might just disqualify you from his selection." Samantha's hands clenched at her shirt again, her knuckles whitening, while Hannah's expression grew pensive, a silent communication passing between them.

"I don't think I could—"

"Sometimes," there was a hard edge of resolve in Eve's tone as she added, "scars can save us from a fate far worse than their sting."

"I heard about Austin," Hannah's voice trembled slightly, "whipped for laying into Luis." She brushed a stray lock of hair behind her ear, the memory of the incident darkening her normally bright eyes.

"Better a single whipping than what awaits the chosen wife." Eve murmured, her gaze distant, as if she could see past the walls of the Oak Sitting Room to a much grimmer place.

"What do you mean?" Samantha's expression clouded with confusion and fear. Her voice was barely a whisper, betraying the terror that gripped her heart at the unspoken implications. Eve met Samantha's eyes, her voice steady, yet heavy with unspoken sorrow.

"Becoming Abraham's wife, it would mean subjecting oneself to him completely. His need for an heir would justify his actions in his mind, daily rituals masked as marital duties." A palpable chill settled over the room as Samantha swallowed hard, her attention instinctively shifting back to the children. The innocence of their play stood in stark contrast to the darkness of their conversation.

"I don't want that life for Grace," Hannah whispered, her protective instincts for her sister shining through the worry etched on her face, "or for myself." Jennifer rose from where she had been sitting beside Victoria, her movement drawing the eyes of the others.

"None of us would wish that fate upon anyone," she said, her voice laced with conviction, "have any of you ever been raped?" In a moment of vulnerability, she posed a question that hung heavy in the air. The word itself seemed to echo ominously around them. Eve, Samantha, and Hannah shook their heads in unison, each grappling with the gravity of Jennifer's inquiry and the shared understanding of what it represented - a violation none of them had experienced but all feared. Jennifer's gaze held a depth of sorrow as she addressed the sombre group, her voice barely more than a whisper.

"It's like losing a piece of yourself," she began, her hands subconsciously twisting together as if to wring out the memories that clung to her words, "you do everything in your power to keep them off you, to keep them out of you. But when you're overpowered, when they have complete domination over you—" Her eyes darkened, reflecting a pain so visceral it seemed to momentarily paralyse the room. Hannah slowly sat up, her eyes welling with tears and softening.

"Jennifer—"

"If you thought you were scared in the beginning, if you thought you already felt violated when it started, it's nothing compared to," Jennifer paused, her voice strained with the effort of speaking the truth, her expression one of someone trapped within a memory rather than the safety of the sitting room, "to the second he's inside you. It's like being clamped in a bear trap. That weight on top of you, your arms pinned down and your legs crushed. Sometimes, you just surrender, just to get through it, waiting for it to end." The others watched her, feeling the weight of her experience without having lived it.

"I can't imagine—" Eve's knuckles whitened where they continued to grip at her shirt. Jennifer's eyes glossed over, staring at something only she could see. The air was heavy, each breath shared between them laden with the burden of understanding.

"But the anticipation," Jennifer whispered, and it was almost as if the shadows in the corners of the room leaned closer, drawn to the gravity and the confession of horror Jennifer painted with her words, "knowing it could happen again every night. That dread consumes you, infecting every moment of daylight with fear." Samantha hugged herself tighter, as though the action could shield her from the inevitability of such a fate. Hannah's face was a mask of stoic terror. They all understood now, the true nature of the threat that loomed over them, a spectre haunting their every step within Abraham's domain. The silence in the sitting room lingered, oppressive and thick, a tangible presence that seemed to swell with each passing second. Jennifer's harrowing tale had left an indelible mark, painting the walls with the shadow of fear that now hung over them. Hannah's hands were white from her vice-like grip, her knuckles bleaching from the force.

"Grace, she's," Hannah began, her voice barely more than a whisper yet slicing through the stillness like a knife, "she's never, she's a—" The words stumbled, tripped by emotion. She couldn't finish, but the unfinished sentence hung there, heavy with implication. Without another word, Hannah rose from her seat, her posture rigid with a resolve that belied the quiver in her lips. With a swift turn, she strode out of the room, her departure an echo of the defiance she'd voiced. Samantha glanced at the tray of empty plates, using it as an excuse to divert her gaze from the raw pain etched on Jennifer's face.

"I should get these back to the kitchen." She murmured, standing and scooping up the tray with practiced ease. It was a small act, but the normalcy of the gesture felt like a lifeline in the midst of the chaos threatening to engulf them. Eve nodded in response, her movements supportive but distant, her mind already racing ahead. As Samantha's footsteps receded down the hallway, Eve found herself moving towards Jennifer, who stood motionless, lost in the aftermath of her own brutal honesty. Standing beside her, Eve watched the corridor where Hannah and Samantha had vanished, feeling the weight of their collective fate pressing down upon them.

"That was very convincing." Eve's voice was soft, barely above a whisper, as she reached out tentatively, resting a hand on Jennifer's arm.

"Easy enough to draw from experience." Jennifer's gaze shifted from the emptiness of the hallway to meet Eve's questioning eyes. There was a vulnerability there, a shared understanding of the stakes at play. She drew in a deep breath, steadying herself with the intake of air.

"Do you think it worked?"

"We'll have to wait and see." Jennifer's voice was steady despite the uncertainty that clouded her expression. They both knew the gravity of what they were attempting, the seeds of doubt and rebellion they were sowing could mean salvation or destruction - only time would reveal which.

CHAPTER 6

As the iron grip of winter began to loosen, Beth found herself trapped in a different kind of cold. Her room had become her cell, and in it she languished as the walls echoed with the silent cacophony of her chaotic thoughts. Now that she had been allowed more leniency to her comings and goings of the building, she had never felt more compelled to stay in her room. It was as if she'd been given permission to slip up, the temptation of escape becoming too real once she no longer had a chaperone. She couldn't escape the feeling of being watched now more-so than ever. She lay on her bed, staring at the ceiling, her once vigilant spirit now dulled by a growing lethargy. Food had lost its appeal - the trays left by her door remained untouched, the contents congealing into an unappetising mass. Her body felt frail, each limb heavy as if weighed down by leaden shackles, yet her mind raced with fervent plans of rebellion and flight. The thought of bending to Abraham's will churned her stomach, and with every passing day the fuse of her resolve grew shorter. Defiance was the fire that kept her warm against the chill of defeat seeping through the walls. Outside her self-imposed solitude, the library had taken on the air of a sacred battleground. The prayer circles that once filled the room had dwindled as Abraham cast aside candidate after candidate, his divine selection process winnowing the group to just three - Beth, Eve, and Amanda. Where there had once been a chorus of voices lifted in supplication, now there was only a hushed murmur of the remaining faithful, or those good at feigning it. Beth stood up, her legs unsteady, and made her way to the edge of her room where her jeans and shirt lay strewn from the day before. She sniffed at her clothes, wondering whether a small change in outfit might lighten her mood. As she dressed, Beth was lost in thought, tracing the frayed stitching of the coat with her finger when a soft knock at her open door roused her. She lifted her head, eyes narrowing at the intrusion. Eve stood there, an uncertain smile playing upon her lips, with Barnett's imposing figure looming behind her.

"May we come in?" Barnett asked tentatively. Beth's nod was curt, more reflex than permission. She straightened as they entered, a ripple of tension passing through her as she assessed their unexpected presence. The air felt thick with unspoken words.
"We've been given permission to get some fresh air," Eve said, her voice a gentle prod, "would you like to join us for a walk?" Beth considered the offer - a walk meant facing the outside world, confronting the remnants of a life she was still tethered to. With a slow nod she acquiesced, reaching for her coat with hands that betrayed a faint tremor. It clung to her thinner frame, a reminder of the weeks spent in isolation. The three stepped into the biting cold, a welcome shock against Beth's pallid skin. She pulled the coat tighter around her as they began their silent procession. Eve matched her pace, offering quiet companionship while Barnett trailed behind, his watchful gaze a silent sentinel over them both. They passed beneath barren trees, their branches clawing at a heavy, grey sky. The sound of gravel crunching underfoot mingled with the distant caws of crows, creating a rhythmic cadence to their steps. There was a sombreness in the air, a weight that grew heavier

as they neared the platform where Sabrina had met her fate. Beth's throat tightened at the sight, memories pressing in like thorns. She could almost hear the echo of the gathered crowd, the finality of the rope snapping taut. She swallowed hard, her breath visible in the frigid air, as the stable structure cast a daunting realisation that it was to remain for future hangings, future punishments for Abraham's convictions. Eve cast a sidelong glance at Beth, her eyes filled with a quiet understanding. They shared this grim history, a bond forged in the shadow of tragedy. Yet, neither spoke of it, letting the silence between them carry the burden of remembrance as they continued on. The platform loomed beside them, stark against the winter landscape, a monument to the cost of defiance. Beth felt the ghost of anger stir within her, and she clenched her jaw against it, the cold air's numbing embrace dulling its edges. They moved past the platform, leaving it and its dark memories behind, as the path wound away towards parts of the compound less tainted with sorrow. For a moment, Beth allowed herself the simple pleasure of the chill on her cheeks, the freedom of movement, however fleeting it might be. The chill of the air seemed to relent as they approached the rose garden, its withered beauty a dramatic contrast to the bleakness of winter.

"I talked to Jennifer about the hanging," Eve's breath formed small clouds as she spoke, "she said it was justified." Her voice held a reverence that hinted at unspoken fears.

"Mmm." Beth's response was a mere sound in acknowledgement, her features set in stone masking the turmoil beneath. The path ahead forked, leading to the dormant rose bushes, their thorny branches like the barbs of the past that pricked at her heart. Eve's voice dropped to a conspiratorial whisper, pulling Beth from her reverie.

"Beth, we can't let Amanda win." She implored, urgency lacing her words. Beth halted, her gaze drifting to Barnett who lingered behind, feigning disinterest in their conversation. There was a practiced nonchalance in his stance, but the slight tension in his shoulders betrayed his awareness.

"Your secrets are safe with me." He said slowly before taking a few steps towards them.

"You can trust Barnett," Eve assured her softly, stepping closer, "he's been aiding me, helping to talk to the others one by one over the last few weeks." Beth looked at Barnett, skepticism clouding her eyes. Trust was a currency she couldn't afford, yet Eve's certainty gave her pause. With a subtle shake of her head, Beth remained wary. Understanding the silent exchange, Eve gestured subtly to Barnett.

"Not too far ahead." He nodded once, a sentinel accepting his dismissal, and turned away to leave the women alone amidst the naked roses. They moved off the gravel path, their steps careful among the sleeping blooms. The silence hung between them as they trudged through the converging blanket of snow and gravel, each step a crunchy echo in the still air. Beth's breath formed ghostly wisps before her, dissipating quickly as though trying to escape the weight of the situation. The conservatory loomed ahead, its glass panels frosted over, a cold sentry amidst the winter landscape. Eve slowed her pace, turning to Beth with an earnest look that seemed to chisel away at the fortress Beth had built around herself.

"You can trust me, you know," Eve said, her voice barely above the breeze, "I detest what Abraham stands for, his tyranny—" Beth's reaction was almost reflexive, an involuntary roll of her eyes as she came to a standstill, her arms crossed defensively. Trust - the word soured on her tongue even as it went unspoken. She eyed Eve warily, searching for any hint of duplicity behind those resolved eyes. But Eve stood firm, meeting Beth's scrutiny with a steady gaze.

"Barnett confided in me," she continued, her tone laced with a mix of frustration and hope, "Abraham can't make up his mind among us. Amanda with her relentless enthusiasm, you with that sharp wit of yours, and then there's my devotion." Beth's gaze flickered away briefly, considering the information. Abraham, a man whose decisions were as fickle as the shifting winds, now caught in a mire of indecision. It was almost laughable, if it weren't so deeply unsettling.

"Enthusiasm, wit and faith," Beth finally acknowledged in a low whisper, weighing Eve's words against her own desire for rebellion, "the bar is set extremely low if that's all Abraham sees in us." If Abraham's choice teetered on such traits that left them caught in a game of pretence, their true selves were obscured by the roles they were forced to play. Beth's gaze drifted from the frozen earth to Eve's face as she witnessed a smile pull at the corners of her mouth, a glint of triumph in her eyes.

"So you can talk." Eve remarked, her voice low and conspiratorial.

"Only when necessary." Beth responded curtly, her voice a hoarse whisper from disuse. She watched Eve closely, noting the subtle shift in her demeanour.

"Strange," Eve tilted her head slightly, curiosity lighting up her features, "I haven't heard anyone mention that you *could* talk."

"It hadn't been necessary until now. And even still I'm not convinced that it is," a silence fell between them filled only by the sound of their breaths misting in the frigid air, "besides, when you don't talk, you learn. I learned to shut up and listen for a change."

"Makes sense." Eve acknowledged with a nod. They continued on the path, their steps synchronised. As they walked, Beth's mind raced, measuring Eve's intentions, weighing her own options.

"So what is it about Amanda's enthusiasm, my wit and your *faith* that has Abraham so torn?" Beth asked curiously.

"Exactly that," Eve affirmed, a shadow of triumph in her voice as if revealing a secret stratagem, "he struggles to choose between us because we all possess something he wants but neither of us display all three. But we're more than just the parts he sees in us." Her eyes held a fervour that went beyond the religious zeal she wore like a cloak. Beth's gaze lingered on the silver cross that dangled from Eve's neck, a stark contrast to the stern lines of the woman's face. With a delicate touch, Eve cupped the heirloom in her palm, and a sliver of vulnerability flashed across her features.

"This was my grandmother's," she confided, her voice softening with reverence, "I wear my faith proudly. And I may seem clever, but I'll admit I don't think I'm as clever as you and it's difficult for me to muster the kind of fanaticism Amanda shows so effortlessly." Beth's eyebrows arched skeptically. It wasn't like Eve to concede to any shortcoming, especially not in their current game of survival and subterfuge.

"Amanda does make a show of her enthusiasm during prayer," she scoffed, "how she cried when he told the story of Abraham and Isaac—"

"Genesis," Eve said thoughtfully, her gaze fixed on the ground, "it tests the limits of trust in God and speaks to the pain of letting go. It is used to talk about surrender, faith, and parental love."

"How fitting to say to the women you're attempting to have surrender to you." Beth rolled her eyes, glancing back to where

Barnett had vanished, unable to detect any sign of him.

"Abraham doesn't see it as a surrender," Eve smirked, a sly edge returning to her voice, "I can show my religion and emulate intelligence convincingly enough. Maybe enough to outshine you."

"Intelligence and wit are two very different things." Beth let out a mocking breath as she turned away, her eyes scanning the path ahead. The brittle branches of winter-bare trees framed the walkway, reaching skyward like imploring hands. She could hear Eve's footsteps falling into step behind her as they neared the conservatory. Eve matched Beth's pace, the crunch of snow beneath their boots punctuating the silence.

"Beth, what do I need to do to prove to you that you're the one who should win this twisted contest? What will convince you?" The question hung heavy in the air, and Beth felt its weight settle coldly in her chest. She paused, her back to Eve, considering the implications of victory in this perverse selection process. A breeze whispered through the trees, carrying with it the stench of inevitability.

"To what end?" Beth's whisper barely carried, yet it bore the gravity of a thousand unspoken fears. Ahead, the conservatory loomed - a glass sanctuary filled with life that defied the surrounding chill. A symbol of resistance, perhaps, or merely another cage within which to be displayed.

"What other end could there be?" Eve's gentle voice bore the coldness of the inevitable conclusion to the story they were writing. A quiet fell between them as Beth imagined the story unfolding in countless ways, each ending in the same grand finale.

"Tell me something," Beth finally broke the silence, her words slicing through the air, "why do you think you can fake your intelligence but not the enthusiasm?" Eve's stride didn't falter, but her eyes held a faraway look for a moment before she turned to Beth.

"Because I have no interest in being Abraham's wife." She confessed, her voice carrying a certain bitterness. Beth stopped abruptly, causing Eve to halt and face her.

"And what makes you think that I'm any more interested than you are?" Beth challenged, her expression hardening. Eve's gaze traveled over Beth, appraising her, as if seeing her for the first time.

"I would never take a husband," she stated plainly, implying much more than the words alone conveyed, "I would never take *any* husband." Beth met her gaze steadily, considering the unspoken implications behind Eve's scrutiny. The air seemed to grow colder between them, the weight of their conversation heavier than the snow clinging to the barren branches overhead.

"Trust isn't given easily here," Beth ventured, her voice low and trailing grey plumes in the chilled air, "why do you trust me?" Eve glanced sidelong at Beth, her eyes reflecting a resolve that seemed etched into her very soul.

"In this place, we must decipher our allies from our enemies," she replied, "to survive Abraham's game, we need to have faith in each other and in the strengths we each bring."

"Faith is a luxury I don't have much of anymore," Beth admitted, her gaze flickering over the dormant garden beds they passed, "and my trust, it's been worn thin." A small, knowing smile touched Eve's lips, barely there, then disappeared as quickly as it had emerged.

"I thought that might be the case," she said, "but sometimes, necessity forges unexpected bonds." The conservatory loomed before them now, a cathedral of glass and wrought iron. Eve reached out, her gloved hand grasping the frigid handle and pulling the door open. A rush of humid air greeted them, carrying the scent of damp earth and greenery. Beth stepped through the doorway, her senses instantly assaulted by the lushness within. Towering palms stretched towards the high ceiling, their leaves whispering secrets. Exotic flowers flaunted vibrant hues, their colours impossibly bright amidst the monochrome world outside. It was an oasis of life defying the deathly grip of winter. As they moved down the path, the foliage parting before Eve's confident stride, Beth caught sight of Ben. He stood near a tangle of ferns, his posture rigid with anticipation. His eyes found hers, and something unspoken passed between them - a mix of relief and tension. Eve paused, turning back to Beth.

"Barnett and I will wait for you in the gardens," she said, her voice taking on a hushed quality amongst the rustling leaves, "don't take too long." With those words, Eve slipped away, melting into the verdant maze, and leaving Beth to navigate the final steps towards whatever awaited her. Beth's footsteps were muted against the path, her gaze fixed on Ben's steady presence. The air around them was thick with the scent of jasmine and orange blossoms, a natural perfume that seemed to underscore the gravity of the moment. As Eve's silhouette disappeared amongst the greenery, Beth exhaled softly, releasing the breath she hadn't realised she'd been holding. Her advance was tentative until a flicker of understanding crossed Ben's features, an unspoken invitation that spurred her into motion. In a few brisk strides, the space between them vanished, and she found herself enveloped in his embrace. The warmth of his body was a distinct variance to the chill that had settled deep in her bones. And she clung to him, seeking refuge from the shadows that haunted both their lives. Ben's arms wrapped securely around her, one hand resting gently at the small of her back while the other cradled her neck - a protective gesture that spoke volumes in the silence of their seclusion. There in the conservatory's lush cocoon, they held each other, two kindred spirits momentarily insulated from the treachery beyond the glass walls.

"Are you okay?" Ben murmured, the concern in his voice palpable as they reluctantly parted. Beth hesitated, her instinct to maintain her facade warring with the need for honesty in his earnest gaze. With a mental shrug, she cast aside the pretence.

"I'm fine." She assured him quietly. His eyes searched hers, seeking the truth behind her words.

"Beth—"

"Really, I'm fine," the question lingered on her lips before she gave it voice, a whisper of vulnerability amidst the strength she projected, "are you okay?" He nodded once, the simple gesture belying the complexities that lay beneath.

"I've wanted to talk to you since that night in the storeroom." Ben confessed, catching his breath as if the prospect of speaking freely were a forbidden indulgence. His voice came out low, an urgent whisper just barely audible above the conversations of rustling leaves. He drew closer to Beth, his need to express unspoken words almost palpable in the air between them.

"It's okay—"

"I'm so sorry, Beth. When I heard what Luis did, and then Austin beating the shit out of him. I've wanted to just be alone with you for five fucking minutes so I could—"

"It's okay." Beth interrupted tenderly, her voice a soothing balm to his mounting desperation. She leaned into him, her gesture an offering of solace, brushing his lips with a fleeting kiss that spoke of understanding and empathy. Her forehead rested against his in a quiet moment of connection, the simple intimacy providing a stark contrast to the chaos surrounding them. Ben's tension visibly eased, his chest rising and falling in a long, slow exhale that seemed to release the weight he carried. He drew her into an embrace, their cheeks touching softly as she melted against him. The firmness of his hug belied a vulnerability that he only revealed in these rare moments with her. It was a tenderness that promised protection yet acknowledged their shared uncertainty, a delicate dance between fragility and strength. The silence around them was thick, but it was the kind of silence that spoke volumes - a silence both comforting and fraught, each aware that time was slipping away, and with it, the privacy they so desperately craved. His glance shifted momentarily, as if expecting the foliage itself to be listening. The hushed rustle of leaves announced Austin's approach before he stepped into the clearing, his presence pulling Beth back from her cocoon of comfort with Ben.

"Didn't mean to intrude," with a knowing tilt of his head, he offered them a wry smile that didn't quite reach his eyes, "just thought you might want a moment." Beth felt the tension in her shoulders ease as she crossed the short distance to Austin. She wrapped her arms around him in an embrace as tight as the one she'd shared with Ben moments earlier.

"I'm glad you're both okay." She whispered against his ear, the weight of her relief heavy in her voice. Pulling back, she searched their faces, a frown creasing her brow as she stood between the two men, glancing back and forth between them.

"What're we doing here?" She asked, her gaze flitting between the two men who were more than allies, her pillars in this precarious existence. Austin glanced over his shoulder, as if to confirm they were truly alone, before locking eyes with her.

"It's the safest place to talk to you." He murmured, his voice barely audible above the whisper of wind through the glass structure. Beth's hand moved subconsciously to her jaw, pressing lightly against the spot where pain had once been a constant companion. The action caught Ben's attention.

"Are you still in pain?" He asked, his voice laden with concern.

"Surely it doesn't still hurt." Austin interjected, equally concerned yet a hint of skepticism laced his tone. She shook her head, the movement brisk.

"I'm fine." She met Ben's gaze squarely, reinforcing the truth of her words, then turned to Austin. His proximity brought a sense of urgency that made her heart beat faster. Austin leaned in closer, and his next words chilled her to the bone.

"You can't let Abraham choose you as his wife, Beth." It was a plea wrapped in a warning, spoken with the gravity of one who knew too well the stakes they were playing for. A shiver ran down Beth's spine, not from cold but from the raw fear that skulked in the shadows of her mind. She studied the earnest expressions on the faces of the two men before her, realising the depth of their concern and the complexity of the path she tread.

"Do either of you know what it's like," she flinched, her voice steady despite the turmoil within, "to be alone with him?" The question lingered in the air, stark and unanswerable, as they faced each other amidst the sanctuary of greenery that seemed so at odds with the darkness of their conversation.

"Yes," Austin's eyes narrowed on her, creasing his brow as his gaze bore into her, "but I suspect in a different way than you do."

"You don't think I—"

"No, nothing like that," Austin shook his head quickly, "I just mean, I assume he's more forward with you and his intentions." The silence stretched before Beth broke it with a declaration that seemed to come from the core of her being.

"We have to do something to stop him. I can't go through what I went through with Marcus again. I can't let someone else go through that either. I'm going to do everything I can to become his wife," she said, her voice low and resolute, "and for everyone's sake, when I'm close enough I'll kill him." Austin's face was a study in contradictions, as he raised an eyebrow, feigning displeasure at her words. Yet, there was a glint in his eye that betrayed his belief in her. "I knew you'd have a plan." He murmured, though his voice carried an undercurrent of worry. Ben, however, looked as if she had struck him physically. His features contorted with outrage.

"You can't do that Beth," he protested vehemently, "think of what he could do to you. He's strong, and he would overpower you. You can't let that happen." Beth turned to face Ben squarely, her gaze unflinching. She took a step closer, shortening the distance between them.

"Ben," she said firmly, "you will never get close enough to Abraham to take him out. The only person who could is with someone who shares his bed." In one fluid motion, she reached up and placed her hand gently against the rough stubble on the side of his face. It was a tender gesture, but within it lay all the strength of iron. Ben's eyes shut for a moment, seeking solace in the warmth of her touch. When they opened again, they were filled with an unspeakable mixture of fear and acceptance. He leaned into her palm, his action wordlessly conveying both his desire to protect her and his understanding of her resolve. Beth's eyes, steeled with the resolve of a survivor, held Ben's wavering gaze.

"Alcatraz, Catalina, Marcus and Victor," her voice was low but clear, each word laden with the weight of her past, of challenges faced and conquered alone, "I've weathered storms you couldn't even imagine, Ben. I had to learn to stand on my own." She paused, her hand still resting against his face, an anchor amidst the turmoil.

"Beth—"

"You need to trust me." She whispered, offering him a soft smile as her eyes pleaded. He swallowed hard, his eyes clouded with concern yet shimmering with respect. It was the silent battle between protection and faith, and she knew it tore at him.

"Okay." After a long moment he nodded, a promise etched in the firm set of his piercing eyes. Withdrawing her hand slowly, Beth turned towards Austin, her movements deliberate. She caught the guarded look on his face - it was apparent to her that he wasn't entirely sold on her plan either.

"You don't approve, do you?" She asked, though her tone suggested she already knew the answer.

"Not especially," Austin admitted, his brow creasing, "but it's not about what I think. You're just not exactly fighting fit, Beth." A wry smile tugged at the corners of her lips, her eyes glinting with a hint of mischief.

"You might be surprised," reaching into the pocket of her coat, she pulled out a small bottle filled with little white pills, rolling the bottle between her fingers, "I've been collecting Vicodin from the infirmary. Crushed up and mixed into his drink, they'll make sure he sleeps through anything." Austin's eyes narrowed slightly, assessing her with a new level of intrigue. The gears were turning behind his gaze, piecing together the layers of her strategy. She could almost see the reluctant admiration dawning on him as he realised the depths of her cunning.

"Sleeping pills and subterfuge," Austin mused, "I should say I'm surprised, but honestly I'm not."

"Survival demanded that I get creative," she replied, slipping the bottle back into her pocket, "and I intend to survive this too." Ben's brow furrowed, a mixture of confusion and relief etching across his rugged features.

"So you're not actually using those pills?" He asked, gesturing towards the pocket where she had just secreted the bottle. Beth shook her head, a strand of hair falling across her face, which she brushed aside with a slender hand.

"No," she said, her voice steady despite the freezing air that wafted through the conservatory, "I've been feeling fine for weeks now. The pain in my jaw is mostly gone, but I needed a believable excuse to keep going to the infirmary for more Vicodin." Austin shifted his weight from one foot to the other, uncertainty clouding his normally impassive gaze.

"But why not just tell Anne what you were planning? I'm sure she would've played along, given them to you if you'd asked."

"Anne has her reasons to hate me," Beth replied, the flicker of distrust in her eyes as sharp as the frost on the ground outside, "I could've asked but hate can make people unpredictable and I couldn't risk it."

"For obvious reasons." There was a beat of silence before Ben interjected, his tone carrying an undercurrent of accusation. Beth's head snapped towards him, emerald eyes narrowing. The quiet intensity of her gaze demanded an explanation, and Ben didn't shy away. He knew he had touched a nerve.

"Austin filled me in." He admitted, meeting her stare. Turning her head, Beth's gaze found Austin who stood with a certain stoicism, betraying nothing. It was clear then - there were layers upon layers between them, and trust was a currency in short supply. But there was also an unspoken understanding, a recognition of the roles each had to play in the dangerous game they were ensnared in.

"Alright," she finally said, breaking the momentary standoff, "let's focus on what we need to do now." Her voice, though soft, carried the weight of command and it was clear she intended to steer their course forward. The rustling of feet against the footpath broke the silence as Beth shifted her weight, her gaze lingering on Austin.

"No more lies, no more secrets." He murmured, a tinge of regret lining his words like a shadow. His eyes met hers, searching for absolution in the depths of her weary stare. Beth offered him a nod, an unspoken pardon that seemed to lift the invisible burden from his shoulders. She turned to Ben, whose expression was carved with concern, yet he echoed her silent forgiveness.

"No more." He said softly, the words barely audible above the whispering foliage.

"Good," she replied, her voice a mere whisper, "I should get back." The conservatory, with its lush greenery and floral perfume, felt like a world away from the stark reality waiting beyond its walls. With another nod, this time more resolute, Beth wrapped her resolve around her like the coat she had donned against the chill. She started towards the door, the loose gravel on the path crunching beneath her steps, a steady rhythm amidst the chaos of her thoughts.

"Will you keep up the act?" Austin called after her, his voice carrying a note of caution. Without turning, Beth paused and glanced over her shoulder, her profile etched against the dimming light filtering through the glass panes.

"Yes," she confirmed with a nod, her voice low but clear, "everyone thinks I'm a mute junkie. It keeps their guard down, so we should keep it that way." With those final words hanging in the cool air between them, she moved along the path, her silhouette receding into the fading daylight outside. Each step was measured, purposeful - each breath a quiet reaffirmation of the role she had chosen to play in this treacherous game. Ben's jaw was set hard, tension radiating from him like heat from a furnace as he turned to face Austin.

"I can't stomach the thought," he admitted, his voice low and tight with barely suppressed anger, "Beth, alone with that monster." Austin met Ben's gaze, a flicker of remorse shadowing his features before he masked it with a nod of feigned agreement.

"I know," he conceded, his tone carefully measured, "but she's stronger than we give her credit for. She's weathered storms we can't even imagine. If she says we need to trust her, then that's what we've gotta do." With a grunt of frustration, Ben spun on his heel, his boots crunching against the ground as he strode back down the path. His broad shoulders were hunched as if carrying the weight of their shared concern, the fading light casting long shadows that danced alongside him. As Ben's figure disappeared through the conservatory doors, the quiet rustle of movement announced Stone's presence. He emerged from where the dense foliage began to thin, his approach almost undetectable in the twilight.

"Better than expected, huh?" Stone's voice was low but carried an undertone of satisfaction as he came up beside Austin who watched Ben's retreating back before replying.

"I knew she'd want to kill him. She hasn't trusted Abraham since Fort Irwin, and since then he's done nothing but make it worse. She's determined to be the one to end his reign." His words were laced with a mixture of pride and concern, a testament to both

Beth's resolve and the perilous path she had chosen.

"She's got guts, I'll give her that." Stone's eyes followed Ben's exit before settling back on Austin.

"More than guts," Austin said, turning to survey the darkening sky, "she's got a plan, and if anyone can pull it off it's Beth." His statement was more than mere reassurance, it was a declaration of faith in a woman who had proven herself time and again.

"I thought she'd given up," Stone confessed, turning back towards the door, "I don't know her well enough but she seemed like she'd stopped caring. I'll admit I was fooled as well. I was convinced she was a mute junkie."

"I was too, for a short time," Austin admitted despondently, disappointed in himself for assuming the worst, "I thought it would take more convincing to get her back to her old self, but I should've given her more credit. She's more resilient than that." The conservatory's air was thick with the scent of damp earth and lush greenery. Austin watched the fog curl from his breath as they sauntered down the narrow path lined with exotic plants, their vibrant leaves whispering secrets.

"Resilient," Stone mused, breaking the silence as he ran a hand over a broad fern leaf, "I remember seeing Beth on Catalina. She took everything that place threw at her and came out standing." Austin halted beside a bed of orchids, their delicate petals defiant in the artificial warmth.

"How close did you get to her back then?" He turned to face Stone, his eyes searching. Stone shook his head slightly, a wry smile touching his lips.

"Not close enough to make much difference. But I've never liked dictators, people who put themselves above others without earning it." His gaze drifted to a patch of shadow where a spider plant hung like a silent observer.

"Is that why you helped us? Because of Victor?" Austin pressed, leaning against the wooden railing that separated them from the foliage.

"Every day, Victor played God with those women's lives," Stone said, anger simmering beneath his measured tone, "and every day, Beth stood up for them. Chantelle and Jennifer, they pushed her away, but she never backed down. She'd be shaking inside, you could tell, but she never let it stop her. Even when her own confidence wavered, she never backed down." Austin nodded, recognising the fierce tenacity that defined Beth. It wasn't just strength - it was the raw, unyielding spirit that had carried her through countless trials. He realised then that their faith in her wasn't misplaced, it was built on the foundation of her unwavering resolve. Stone glanced at Austin, an acknowledgment of the heavy truth between them. They both knew the cost of this fight, the toll it took to stand in defiance. But in that moment, amid the verdant life thriving under glass, the two men found a renewed certainty in their shared cause, bound by the resilience of one woman who refused to be broken. Stone shifted, his gaze lingering on the path they had taken. Scratching at the stubble on his chin, he finally spoke, his voice low and matter-of-fact.

"I'll be straight with you Austin. I don't know Beth like you do, but from the pieces I've seen she's our ace in the hole." Austin, hands tucked into his pockets, let out a slow breath, the condensation visible in the cooling air of the conservatory.

"I hope you're right." He murmured, his eyes tracing the intricate patterns of frost on the panes of glass above them.

"Hope's got nothing to do with it," Stone countered with a wry smile, "It's all about playing the hand we're dealt. Right now, she's holding all the right cards."

"And she doesn't even realise we gave her the winning hand." Austin glanced around at the lush greenery that enveloped them, an oasis of calm in a world that seemed increasingly chaotic.

"Speaking of playing," Stone added with a sudden briskness, "we should get back to pretending to work before someone notices we're missing." A low laugh escaped Austin as he nodded, the tension easing from his shoulders momentarily.

"The art of looking busy while plotting a revolution." He said, irony colouring his tone.

"Something like that." Stone agreed. With a last glance at the verdant foliage, Austin followed, the sound of their footsteps mingling with the distant murmur of water from a nearby fountain. Together, they slipped back into the roles assigned to them, their conversation folding away into the recesses of their minds, where plans and whispered confidences lay hidden beneath the guise of everyday labor.

CHAPTER 7

Beth's hand trembled slightly as it reached for the grand, wooden library door of the Biltmore Estate. She tapped twice, a soft echo whispering into the hushed corridor beyond. When no response came, she pushed the door open with a gentle creak that seemed much louder in the silence and stepped inside. The room was a sanctuary of knowledge left untouched by the chaos outside its walls, with shelves lined with books that held worlds within them. But it was the desk in the middle piled with files that drew Beth's attention. Her fingers grazed over the neat labels - her name first, then Eve's, and Amanda's. The faint scent of old paper filled her nostrils as she flipped through the contents, each page a testament to their lives under Abraham's rule. The sudden rustle of fabric from the doorway pulled her gaze up. Abraham stood there, his imposing figure framed against the dim light filtering in from the hallway. Startled, he eyed her with an intensity that sent a chill down her spine.

"What brings you here, Beth?" He asked, his baritone voice steady yet tinged with surprise. Without a word, she moved towards the desk and picked up his bible, its leather cover worn from use. Holding it like a shield, she approached him, her steps measured and deliberate. The familiar weight of the holy text provided an odd comfort as she closed the distance between them.

"I was wondering if I could ask you something." She whispered, her voice barely above the crackling of the fire that cast flickering shadows across the room. Abraham's expression softened fractionally, a hint of gratification in his eyes.

"I'm glad you are able to speak again." He stated flatly, his words laced with the authority of a man accustomed to obedience.

"Thank you," she murmured, her grip on the bible tightening ever so slightly as she anticipated his next move, "it still hurts, but I can manage a few words. Just trying to move my jaw as I've been clenching it so much in my silence." Beth's voice was a strained whisper when she lied. Abraham paced by her, his eyes scanning the dimly lit room with a hint of disapproval.

"You're alone in here? That's not wise," he chastised gently as his gaze lingered on the door, considering the negligence, "there should be someone with you."

"No one was at the door." Beth replied, a subtle edge of accusation in her tone. She watched him closely, seeking any sign of his intentions. He nodded gravely.

"I'll see to it that changes," he promised before turning back to her, his demeanour shifting to one of service, "now how may I assist you?" Beth moved towards him, the bible in her hands. Her fingers traced the embossed cross on its cover, feeling the grooves of the leather.

"Can you tell me," she asked, her voice low and filled with an earnest yearning, "what does this book say about starting over?" Abraham's blue eyes narrowed, studying her face as if searching for the truth hidden beneath the surface.

"Starting over?" He echoed, clearly intrigued by the question.

"From what I understand," she continued, carefully avoiding direct eye contact, "you've heard quite a bit about me from

Luis." Abraham's posture stiffened slightly, a flicker of something unreadable crossing his stern features.

"Yes, Luis has shared his thoughts and opinions with me," he confirmed, leaving the weight of his unspoken judgment hanging between them like a thick fog, "he has spoken unfavourably of all of his former companions, even his sister." Beth's gaze lingered on Abraham's imposing figure as he paced the length of the library, his broad shoulders casting a long shadow in the flickering firelight. The air was thick with the musk of old books and the crackling hearth added a soft undertone to the tense atmosphere.

"Luis," she began, her voice steady despite the fluttering in her chest, "he is not known for kindness. I'd like you to form your own thoughts and opinions of me." She watched Abraham closely, searching for any hint of reaction. Abraham stopped in his tracks, turning to face her. His blue eyes were sharp, penetrating.

"I'm not blind to Luis's nature," he stated flatly, "the man is flawed, but he has his role within our walls."

"True, every man has his place," Beth conceded, her fingers brushing against the spine of the bible as if drawing strength from its mere presence, "but I ask that you get to know me for who I am, beyond what Luis or anyone else might say." Abraham's lips tightened into a thin line, his expression unreadable. He let out a low sigh, then gestured towards an ornate chair by the fireplace.

"Sit." He commanded softly. She complied, moving gracefully across the room. The heat from the fire embraced her as she settled into the chair, her posture rigid, her eyes never leaving Abraham. He held his bible like a shield, his reverence for the text evident in the gentle way he cradled it in his hands. The pages whispered under his touch as he leafed through them, each turn methodical and deliberate. Dust motes danced in the slanting light as he searched for the passage that lay dormant among the scriptures, waiting to be brought forth. Beth stared at his face, the way his brows furrowed when he was deep in concentration. She studied him, every line and expression and the way that his eyes changed with his emotions. His eyes scanned the words, his lips moving slightly as he internalised their meaning. She couldn't help but admire the way his face softened as he read, a peacefulness settling over him. She swallowed hard, hating herself for thinking he could be attractive had he not been so sinister. Finally, Abraham found the page he sought. His finger rested upon it, as if marking the words that would shape the conversation to come. Silence stretched between them, punctuated only by the occasional pop and hiss of burning logs. Abraham's voice resonated through the library, his timbre imbued with a solemn gravity as he recited the ancient words.

"For I will take you out of the nations. I will gather you from all the countries and bring you back into your own land. I will sprinkle clean water on you, and you will be clean. I will cleanse you from all your impurities and from all your idols. I will give you a new heart and put a new spirit in you. I will remove from you your heart of stone and give you a heart of flesh," his eyes lifted momentarily to gauge Beth's reaction, then returned to the scripture, the steady cadence of his reading filled the room, each sentence punctuated by the crackling of the fire, "and I will put my Spirit in you and move you to follow my decrees and be careful to keep my laws. Then you will live in the land I gave your ancestors. You will be my people, and I will be your God. I will save you from all your uncleanness. I will call for the grain and make it plentiful and will not bring famine upon you. I will increase the fruit of the trees and the crops of the field, so that you will no longer suffer disgrace among the nations because of famine. Then you will remember your evil ways and wicked deeds, and you will loathe yourselves for your sins and detestable practices. I want you to know that I am not doing this for your sake, declares the Sovereign Lord. Be ashamed and disgraced for your conduct." Beth remained motionless, her gaze fixed on Abraham, absorbing the promise of redemption and renewal. The flickering flames cast a soft glow on her face, reflecting in her eyes the light that danced across the room. As Abraham spoke of cleansing and new hearts, the shadows seemed to retreat, banished by the hopeful undertones of the passage. The final words hung in the air as Abraham closed the bible, the sound soft yet final. He looked up at Beth, his blue eyes clear and unyielding.

"That was beautiful." She whispered, her tone deliberately soft in an attempt to suppress any unintentional sarcasm or disdain.

"This passage from Ezekiel highlights God's promise to cleanse, renew, and restore His people, giving them a new heart and spirit, and guiding them to follow His ways. It is a profound declaration of God's ability to bring about complete transformation and a fresh start," he studied her for a moment, his gaze intense yet not unkind, "would you like a new start, Beth?" His question was direct, an offering laid bare between them, waiting for her to reach out and claim it.

"Yes." Beth's throat tightened as she gave a small nod, her eyes drifting to the worn floorboards beneath her feet. With a measured motion, Abraham set the bible aside on the table and eased into the chair beside her. The leather of his gloves creaked faintly as he removed them and reached for her hands, enveloping them with a gentle firmness.

"Have you been cleansed in baptism?" He doubted, his voice low and steady.

"No." She shook her head, the movement almost imperceptible and the sound inaudible.

"Then let us wash away the past," Abraham said, his words carrying the weight of solemnity, "I can offer you baptism this very day, surrounded by those who have walked the path of faith alongside you." Beth's pulse quickened, her composure a mask that threatened to slip.

"On our wedding day," she hesitated slightly, the cracking in her voice threatening to betray her ruse, "I should be baptised just before we are married, so that everything can begin anew all at once."

"You are presumptuous—"

"And I would wish it to be a private affair," she murmured, the tightness in her chest betraying the calm she sought to project, "among believers only, so that nothing may taint this new beginning." His smile was a slow unfurling, like dawn breaking across his features. He reached out, his hand hovering momentarily before touching her cheek with a tenderness that contrasted sharply with the strength of his grip. Beth's muscles tensed, but she managed to curve her lips upward, allowing her eyelids to flutter closed, shutting out the sight of him. The warmth from his palm seeped through her skin, an unwelcome comfort that she endured in silence. She could feel the rough texture of his thumb as he stroked her cheek, a silent acknowledgment of her acquiescence. A solitary tear betrayed Beth's facade, trailing a glistening path down her cheek. Abraham caught it with his thumb, the gesture almost gentle in its execution.

"Tell me your troubles." He urged. Beth strained against the bile that rose in her throat as she spoke the lie.

"I have never been happier, the potential to be cleansed of my sins and begin again. Abraham, to be your wife would be my greatest honour." Poison seemed to coat her tongue, and she fought hard to keep her composure. Abraham stood, his height towering over her as he pulled her to her feet. Beth's gaze swept over his visage, noting the stark contrast of his dark hair against the fairness of his skin, and the penetrating blue of his eyes that held a fervour she found both repelling and somehow magnetic. It was such a waste, she had thought, as her gaze lingered on the rigid set of his jaw. Memories of Marcus' deranged behaviour flashed through her mind, followed by the recollection of Victor's unyielding cruelty. Yet Abraham stood apart from them all, an enigma wrapped in conviction. He wasn't cruel physically, just deranged. Abraham's approach was measured, his eyes holding her gaze with a passion that seemed to reach beyond the mortal coil. His lips met hers with calculated softness, an act that carried the weight of both temptation and promise. Beth's survival instincts warred with the revulsion coiling in her gut, but she managed to suppress it, responding to the kiss with feigned tenderness. The warmth of his mouth contrasted starkly with the chill of the vast library around them. She felt his fingers tighten at her waist, pulling her closer into the sphere of his influence. Her hands moved of their own volition, tracing the line of his neck, feeling the pulse that beat a steady rhythm beneath his skin. Every touch was a betrayal to her own senses, yet necessary in the intricate dance of deceit she had forced herself to perform. Abruptly, Abraham broke away, his forehead coming to rest against hers. His breath mingled with hers, creating a fleeting intimacy that belied the tumultuous storm raging in Beth's very soul.

"Forgive me." He whispered, a tremor in his voice that might have been mistaken for vulnerability if not for the steel in his gaze. Beth exhaled, the air leaving her lungs as though it carried the weight of her unspoken dread.

"For what?" She asked, her voice steady despite the chaos within. He drew back slightly, enough to look into her eyes, his own reflecting a battle between desire and doctrine.

"Lustful thoughts are considered sinful," he began, each word deliberate, "I equate them to the act of adultery itself." He paused, then recited from memory, his cadence reverent.

"You have heard that it was said, 'You shall not commit adultery.' But I tell you that anyone who looks at a woman lustfully has already committed adultery with her in his heart." His recitation hung between them, a reminder of the chasm that lay beneath the surface of their interaction. Abraham's beliefs, unyielding as the stone walls that encased them, loomed over Beth, a spectre of judgment and expectation. As Abraham retreated, the space between them seemed to swell with unspoken tension.

"Abraham—"

"My apologies," he said, his voice a low timbre that resonated through the quiet of the library, "it was not my intention to corrupt your efforts to begin anew." Beth's reply came softly, barely more than a breath.

"Abraham, there is nothing to apologise for," she looked up at him through lashes heavy with unshed tears, "if we are to be man and wife, forgiveness for each other's flaws should come easily." Abraham's reaction was swift, his head snapping towards her, eyes ablaze with an intensity that belied his earlier contrition.

"You presume too much," he spat out, the anger in his words cutting through the air like a sharp winter wind, "I have yet to make my decision." The rebuke stung, and Beth recoiled, her hands instinctively coming up as if to shield herself from the force of his words.

"I'm sorry." She murmured, the bite of regret bitter on her tongue. She averted his gaze, but not before noticing the telltale bulge straining against the fabric of his pants.

"You are forgiven." He uttered a soft growl.

"Is lust considered a sin between man and wife?" She asked coyly, swallowing hard as she fought to ask the question yet unable to stop herself. Abraham considered her probing for a moment, before turning away from her.

"Lust, as defined in the Bible, generally refers to an intense and uncontrolled desire, often of a sexual nature, that is self-centred and objectifies others," he bit his lip hard and adjusted his waistband before turning back to her, "in the context of marriage, sexual desire between a husband and wife is not considered sinful. Rather, it is seen as a natural and good part of the marital relationship. The Bible encourages marital love and sexual intimacy between spouses. Hebrews chapter thirteen, verse four tells us that 'Marriage should be honoured by all, and the marriage bed kept pure, for God will judge the adulterer and all the sexually immoral.' This verse implies that sexual relations within marriage are pure and honourable. The key distinction is that within marriage, sexual desire is part of the loving, committed relationship between husband and wife, rather than a selfish, objectifying lust." He placed a gentle hand against her cheek.

"So," she began softly, fighting her temptation to brush his hand away, "you're saying that while sexual desire within marriage is natural and good, it should be expressed in a way that honours and respects one's spouse, rather than reducing them to an object of lust."

"Indeed." Abraham whispered, bringing his face closer to hers.

"The focus is on mutual love, respect, and selflessness within the marital relationship." Beth concluded, raising her face to his, their lips a mere inch apart.

"You are learning quickly." He remarked, closing his eyes and taking in a deep breath as his lips neared hers. She was picking things up quickly, though not in the way he had intended with his compliment. Eve had a firm grasp of her beliefs and deep understanding of their religion. Amanda was eager to learn and aspired to become Abraham's wife. However, Beth was certain there was something Amanda hadn't attempted and Eve would never consider to do so. Beth lightly touched his lips with hers, closing her eyes and swallowing hard before gently placing her right hand on his cheek. She understood that a man like Abraham would respect someone so assured in their beliefs and self-confidence, and she intended to use it to her advantage. She inhaled softly, her chest rising and pressing against his. Her left hand slowly moved up his forearm, resting gently on his elbow as she caressed his arm with her thumb.

"I am," Beth chose her words carefully, pulling her head back slightly and opening her eyes, speaking softly with a hint of desire colouring her tone, "I am committed. I'm committed to learning. I'm committed to you, Abraham." Her breathing was shallow and her heart raced in her chest as she brought her right hand to rest gently on his neck. Abraham opened his eyes suddenly and stared at her, inches from her face.

"You need to leave," his tone had suddenly turned cold and distant, "I need you to leave." Stepping back, Abraham turned on his heel and approached the fireplace, placing a steady hand on the hearth as he stared into the flames.

"As you wish," Beth whispered, almost seductively, "I look forward to my next lesson." With a turn that sent her hair swirling around her shoulders, Beth moved towards the exit, her steps measured and deliberate. She left the library without looking back, the echo of her departure lingering in the silence that followed. As she walked, the events replayed in her mind, causing a wave of confusion. She had slipped so effortlessly into a seductive and convincing role that she had deluded herself into believing she wasn't just acting for a fleeting moment. She no longer felt the earlier revulsion when she touched him, nor did she experience the expected nausea when they had nearly kissed. Beth's footsteps were a soft cadence of urgency as she moved with haste through the dimly lit hallways of the estate. Her shadow, a fleeting companion against the opulent wallpapers, barely disturbed the haunting stillness that enveloped Biltmore. Up the grand staircase she ascended, her palms pressing into the polished wooden banisters for balance, her breaths shallow and quick. Reaching her bedroom door, she pushed it open, the familiar scent of stale air and dust greeting her in a bitter embrace. The adjoining washroom loomed ahead, its white porcelain fixtures a stark contrast to the encroaching gloom. Beth lurched forward, clutching the edges of the sink, and surrendered to the convulsions that wracked her body. The acrid bile splattered against the basin, droplets rebounding onto her trembling arms. Eve appeared in the doorway, hazel eyes wide with concern.

"What happened?" She asked, her voice a soft Italian lilt that cut through the silence. Beth could only respond with another wave of retching, her empty stomach clenching mercilessly. Her body desperately sought to purge the toxic memory of recent events, but her stomach was empty, leaving her with only a fitful heave of bile that splattered across the sink. Eve was at her side in an instant, her light brown hair brushing against Beth's shoulder as she placed a comforting hand on her back.

"Are you following me?" Beth managed between heaves, her voice hoarse and strained. A gentle laugh escaped Eve, tinged with relief at the absurdity of the question.

"No, I heard you almost running through the hall. My room is next door." She explained, her gaze never leaving Beth's ashen face.

"Of course." Beth whispered, leaning heavily against the cool tile wall, her body finally easing from its violent spasms. She grabbed her water bottle from the shelf and rinsed her mouth, washing the remnants of sickness from her skin, the water a soothing balm to her raw senses. Eve remained close, her presence a steady anchor in the storm that had become their lives. Together, they stood in the muted light, bound by secrets and the unspoken understanding that survival often meant wearing masks too painful to bear alone. Beth steadied herself against the cold porcelain, shakily pushing off from the sink. Water dripped from her fingertips, mingling with the last of her sickness swirling down the drain.

"Easy." Eve whispered as she poured some water onto a cloth and dabbed at Beth's forehead.

"Have you been there this whole time?" She asked, her voice echoing faintly in the tiled room.

"Right next door," Eve confirmed, a wry smile touching her lips, "you've barely left your room since the snow began to melt." The memory of Abraham's kiss surged back, bile rising in Beth's throat once more as she threw her face back towards the sink and began to vomit again.

"He was too close," she said between heaves, the words barely above a whisper, "I got too close. His touch, his lips. I almost couldn't hold this back." Eve's eyes softened, her hands reaching out to steady Beth's quivering form.

"But you did, and that's what matters," she reassured her, "that took strength."

"Strength," Beth scoffed, doubt bleeding into her tone, "I don't know if I can keep this up. I was repulsed at first, but then it started to feel natural. It's like I *convinced* myself that I wanted it, that I wanted him to—"

"Listen," Eve interrupted, her hand squeezing Beth's shoulder, "you know that you don't want that. If you convinced yourself, then you surely convinced him too. What you did today, it's a triumph over Amanda. You may have tipped the scales in your favour."

"Or perhaps I only angered him," Beth's gaze dropped to the damp tile floor, "he might see me as a lustful object now."

"How do you mean?" Eve scrutinised her, watching as Beth wiped her mouth with her hand and sank against the wall onto the floor.

"He said lust before marriage is a sin. But he kissed me," she whispered cautiously, making sure no more bile would return at the thought, "he ran his hands over me and he liked it."

"Isn't that a good thing?" Eve gingerly put some toothpaste onto Beth's toothbrush and handed it to her.

"It might've been, before he turned away and started cursing himself for sinful lust," Beth leaned forward and placed her head between her knees, "but I think I made the mistake of doing it again. It's like he couldn't help himself, so I tried to play into it. And then he got angry. Not furious angry, just like a low burning anger." She held the toothbrush to her mouth and slowly began brushing her teeth.

"Abraham is not immune to human desires," Eve pointed out, her voice even and matter-of-fact, "that could work to our advantage."

Beth remained silent as she brushed her teeth, her chest tight with conflicting emotions. Eve's presence was a comfort, yet the path ahead seemed fraught with shadows too dense to navigate. They were silent together, two souls adrift in the aftermath of an unwanted kiss, bound by circumstance and the unyielding will to endure. Eve's words hovered in the air, a thin veil of hope cast over the grim reality of their situation.

"Abraham is still a man." She murmured, her voice a quiet anchor in the storm of Beth's emotions. The brushing subsided, leaving Beth spent. She slowly pulled her face to the sink and spat out the toothpaste, leaving a trail of white foam to dance down the porcelain side. Eve handed her some water as Beth rinsed out her mouth and spat it down the sink as well, watching the water wash the toothpaste away.

"A man with conviction. I went one step too far," kneeling at the sink, she sagged against the cold wall, the weight of her body dragging her down until she sat huddled on the floor once more, "and even if I didn't, if he does choose me, I can't keep this up."

"Yes you can," Eve moved beside her, an arm slipping around Beth's shoulders with practiced care, drawing her head to rest upon the soft curve of her shoulder, "you have to. Just keep convincing yourself like before."

"I don't know if I can." A low sigh escaped Beth's lips as she surrendered to the momentary refuge offered by Eve's embrace.

"You're doing the right thing." Eve whispered into the silence, her fingers tenderly threading through Beth's hair. The rhythmic motion was soothing, a lullaby without words, and Beth's tension ebbed away with each gentle stroke.

"Hope so." Beth replied, the words barely audible. Her eyes fluttered shut as weariness seeped into her bones, the events of the day taking their toll. Time stretched out, marked only by the cadence of Eve's touch and the crackling whispers of the nearby fire in her room. Beth's breaths grew deeper, teetering on the edge of sleep, when the sudden creak of the door jolted her back to alertness. Stone stood in the threshold, his silhouette framed by the dim light of the hallway beyond. The interruption shattered the fragile calm, sending a sharp spike of adrenaline through Beth's veins.

"Eve," Stone's voice cut through the quietude of the room, "Abraham wants to see you." With a reluctant shift of her body, Eve disentangled herself from Beth and stood.

"Hopefully he wants to dismiss me." Her gaze lingered on Beth for a moment longer than necessary, a silent exchange of shared strength. Stone's eyes scanned the room, settling on the sink where small remnants of Beth's ordeal clung to the porcelain, the smell of bile and toothpaste lingering in the air.

"Is everything okay?" He asked, his tone laced with concern. Beth managed a nod, her throat too raw for words. Eve stepped forward, her voice steady despite the tension threading through it.

"She wasn't feeling well." Eve explained, sparing Beth any further scrutiny. In that brief interaction, Eve leaned close to Beth, her breath a whisper against Beth's ear.

"Stone is with us." She murmured, ensuring only Beth could hear. The knowledge brought a faint release to Beth's taut nerves, a small sigh escaping her lips as relief trickled in.

"Better not keep him waiting," Stone cautioned, glancing back towards the hallway with an urgency that conveyed more than his words, "Abraham's not in the best mood."

"I wonder why." Eve smiled coyly before turning back to Beth.

Beth caught Eve's eye, her mouth dry as she whispered an apology. Understanding flickered across Eve's face, a silent acceptance of the unspoken burden they both carried. With a curt nod, she followed Stone out of the room, leaving Beth to confront the aftermath alone. Once the door clicked shut behind them, Beth rose unsteadily to her feet. She approached the sink, grabbing her water bottle to take another drink. She splashed the clear liquid onto her arms, watching as it diluted the rest of the bile and rinsed away the evidence of her distress. The coolness against her skin was a stark contrast to the warmth of Eve's embrace, but it grounded her. As she scrubbed, each motion was methodical, a ritual of erasure, preparing her for whatever trials lay ahead.

Tyler paced the cold, concrete floor of the storeroom, each step echoing off the walls of the sub-basement. The air felt damp and carried the musty scent of neglect. Dust particles danced in the scarce light filtering through a grime-covered window high above. He stopped as the door creaked open, revealing Chase's rugged form silhouetted against the dim corridor.

"Tyler," Chase said, stepping inside, "we can't keep sneaking around like this." His voice held a tired edge, a sound that seemed to bounce off the shelves lined with cans and dry goods.

"Leaving things unresolved isn't any better." Tyler shot back, his face hardening. The storeroom, once a place of provisions, now served as their secret meeting point, but the weight of their previous argument lingered like the shadows around them.

"That wasn't a conversation, Tyler," Chase ran a hand through his swept-back hair, "it was a fight. A damn loud one at that."

"Because you're not hearing me," Tyler countered, stepping closer to him, "we stick together, all of us. That's how we make it out, not just you and me, but everyone." Chase shook his head, his grey-blue eyes reflecting frustration rather than their usual resolute calm.

"You're insane if you think we can orchestrate something like that. This place," his gaze flickered back towards the door, "it's a fortress."

"Then let it be without me," Tyler's words came out sharp, his stance unwavering as he met Chase's stare, "if you want to leave, you'll do it alone." A muscle twitched in Chase's jaw, and he threw his hands up, the gesture filled with exasperation. He closed the distance between them until they stood mere inches apart, his breath mixing with Tyler's in the cool air. The tension was palpable, a silent standoff in the heart of Biltmore's forgotten cache. Under the dim flicker of a solitary lantern, Chase's resolve faltered. The storeroom's musty air hung thick between them as he stepped forward, closing the space that anger and fear had wedged open. His lips met Tyler's in a soft entreaty for forgiveness, an olive branch tendered with the hope of reconciliation. Tyler responded, his kiss hesitant, a mirror of their fractured trust. The pressure of Chase's mouth was gentle, a stark contrast to the turbulent emotions that swirled around them. Chase drew back, his eyes searching Tyler's face.

"What's wrong?" He asked, voice low, the sound resonating off the concrete walls.

"Can't shake it," Tyler admitted, the taste of Chase's worry lingering on his lips, "you were ready to leave them behind." He wrapped his arms around Tyler, seeking the warmth that only shared human contact could afford in the cold underground room.

Chase's apology was sincere, a whisper lost in the vastness of their predicament.

"I'm sorry. When you went missing with Ben, I felt hollow. But finding out you were okay, it was like coming up for air." The embrace lasted, two men anchored together amidst the chaos of their world, finding solace where little remained. Tyler's eyes held a glint of determination as he faced Chase, the storeroom's dim light casting half his rugged face in shadow.

"It's okay," he said, his voice steady and sure despite the uncertainty that haunted their sanctuary, "we're as safe as we can be here. We just need to stay under the radar until we figure out how to get everyone out." Chase nodded, the steel in Tyler's tone bolstering his own resolve.

"We'll need a plan," he acknowledged, his eyes scanning the room as if the walls themselves might offer up a strategy, "and if we have to bring the others into this, then together we might stand a chance."

"Then it's decided." Tyler stepped closer, the gap between them charged with unspoken vows of solidarity. Their arms found each other once more, and they embraced fiercely, sealing their pact with the warmth of shared breath and the promise of a future fought for side by side. Their lips met in a long, deep kiss, a moment of peace snatched from the jaws of their grim reality. The tranquility shattered as the storeroom door burst open with the violence of a thunderclap. A guard barrelled into the room, his bulky frame a dark silhouette against the sudden intrusion of hallway light.

"Shit!" Tyler cursed, caught mid-embrace and utterly unprepared. Before Chase could react, blunt force crashed down upon him, and his world spun into darkness. A second guard rushed in, his grip iron as he seized Tyler's arm, dragging him away from Chase's crumpled form. Tyler's voice was a raw surge of panic and fury, but the guard's hold was unyielding, pulling him relentlessly towards an uncertain fate.

"Chase!" The name ripped from Tyler's throat, his voice a blend of desperation and rage as he struggled against the iron grip of the guard. His boots scraped against the storeroom's concrete floor, streaking dust and old grime in chaotic arcs as he was hauled backward.

"Quiet!" The guard's hold tightened around Tyler's arm, the man's breath hot and heavy against the nape of Tyler's neck. He twisted, trying to catch sight of Chase to ensure he was still breathing, but the room was a blur of shadows and turmoil.

"Let me go!" Tyler shouted, his words echoing off the high ceilings. The clamour of his own pulse thundered in his ears, drowning out the distant hum of the Biltmore estate's life going on unaware outside these walls. Chase remained motionless on the cold floor, a heap of untended strength and quiet loyalty. His dark hair splayed out like a shadow beneath him, and for a moment, Tyler saw him not as the unwavering defender he had always been, but as something fragile, something that could be broken.

"I said be quiet!" The fist of a guard landed squarely on Tyler's jaw, sending a jarring pain through his head and down his neck.

"Please—" Tyler pleaded, his voice cracking as a new wave of guards flooded into the room, their faces set with purpose and authority derived from Abraham's divine decree. They were indifferent to the bond they tore at with each step they forced Tyler to take away from Chase. Outside the storeroom, the corridor stretched endlessly, flanked by doors hiding secrets and stories much like their own. Tyler's eyes stung, not from tears but from the stark realisation that every inch he moved was an inch further from the man who had become his anchor in this fractured world. And then he was through the door, the echo of his plea swallowed by the stone walls of Biltmore, leaving behind only the silence and the fallen.

CHAPTER 8

Austin's gaze was irresistibly drawn to the lush tapestry of green hues flourishing behind the glass walls of the conservatory, each shade a reminder of nature's boundless creativity and resilience. It was a sanctuary, a vibrant refuge that recalled a time when the world thrived uninhibited by the shadows of apprehension. His eyes wandered over the verdant landscape, tracing the intricate patterns of life that unfolded in every corner. Delicate ferns, their fronds unfurling with languid grace, pressed against the glass, each leaf a masterpiece of intricate design. The veins of one particular fern leaf caught his attention - they were like a network of emerald rivers, guiding life-giving nutrients to every corner of its being. Dewdrops adorned the leaf's surface, clinging tenaciously as if they were nature's own precious gems, capturing the light and refracting it into a spectrum of colors. Beyond the ferns, the conservatory was alive with an orchestra of greenery. There were towering palms that swayed gently as if moved by an invisible breeze, their leaves rustling softly in a whispered symphony. The air was thick with the earthy scent of soil and the fresh aroma of chlorophyll, mingling to create a heady fragrance that spoke of life and growth. Vines cascaded down from above, their tendrils reaching out like curious fingers exploring the world around them. Small flowering plants dotted the landscape, their blossoms adding vibrant splashes of color amidst the sea of green. Austin marveled at this enclosed

Eden, a living, breathing testament to nature's enduring beauty and strength.

"Such a shame," Ben murmured from beside him, his breath misting in the cold air, "all this effort, just to be ripped out for some crops." Austin only half-heard him, his mind elsewhere, but he managed an absent grunt in response. The crunch of gravel announced Reece's approach before his shadow fell over them. Austin glanced up, catching the flicker of concern in Reece's normally composed demeanour.

"How are things at the motel?" Austin asked, steering his thoughts back to the present.

"Fine." Reece replied with a casual shrug, though his eyes also lingered on the botanical haven they were about to lose. Together, the three men stood as sentinels, bound by a shared mourning for the inevitable.

"You lot, why aren't you working?" Their reverie was broken by the stern voice of a guard, boots halting on the path. Reece turned, the picture of authority despite his relaxed posture.

"I've been instructed to keep an eye on these two." He said, nodding towards Austin and Ben. The guard faltered, his face softening into an apology.

"Right. Carry on, then." He resumed his patrol, leaving them to their solemn watch over the lush greenery that faced its final days. Ben wrapped his arms around himself, a shiver disrupting the stillness.

"I can't stand this cold anymore." Without waiting for a response, he made his way into the relative warmth of the conservatory to begin ripping out the flowers and ferns and trees. Left alone with Reece, Austin shifted his weight from one foot to the other, the gravel beneath his boots crunching softly. He glanced over his shoulder, ensuring they were out of earshot before leaning in closer to Reece.

"We've got a plan to get out," he said, his voice barely above a whisper, "it's not set in stone yet, but it's in motion." Reece's brow furrowed.

"What plan?" There was a notable edge of skepticism in his tone.

"It involves Beth," Austin watched Reece's face closely, "but Beth doesn't know she's the key. We're pulling the strings. Eve, Barnett, Stone, and myself." The information seemed to settle heavily on Reece, who ran a hand through his hair, pushing back the strands that had fallen into his eyes.

"Haven't seen much action around here myself," he admitted, his gaze drifting off towards the motel's direction, "mostly with the families and Phillip, it's pretty quiet over there. But Val fills me in on what happens here sometimes."

"What about?" Austin asked, his instincts prickling with the need for more information.

"Beth being hooked on painkillers, for starters." Reece murmured, his voice tinged with concern. It was clear that even though he was often detached from the day-to-day drama, the threads of tension wove their way to him eventually. Austin took in the news, filing away the detail as another piece of a complex puzzle they were all entangled in. The weight of responsibility pressed down on him, a reminder of the risks they each carried on their shoulders. The chilled air carried the scent of moist soil and greenery as Austin watched a leaf fall lazily to the ground, its life inside the conservatory now at an end. The quiet rustling of the plants in response to their movements seemed almost like whispers of secrets they were not privy to.

"An act," Austin finally said, breaking the silence with a dismissive wave of his hand, "she's smarter than we all give her credit for."

"Even so," Reece crossed his arms over his chest, his face betraying a hint of unease, "but she's impulsive and emotional. That's a hell of a weak link to hinge an escape on." Austin let out a short, humourless laugh.

"Look around. We're all running on instinct, man. Emotion's all we've got left." He met Reece's gaze, searching for signs of shared understanding. A low grunt emanated from Reece's throat, the sound carrying a mix of assent and lingering doubt. They stood side by side, their breaths visible in the cold air, forming transient clouds that drifted up towards the grey sky. For a moment, there was nothing but the shared solitude of two men contemplating the fragile nature of their current existence. Reece broke the quietude with a question that seemed to hang heavier than the mist around them.

"Do you miss it?"

"Miss what?" Austin turned his head slightly, catching Reece's profile.

"Being out there, with all the drama, fighting, surviving, starving—" Reece's voice trailed off, as if he was reliving memories that were better left undisturbed.

"Miss being constantly on edge, you mean," Austin's eyes narrowed thoughtfully, "do you want to stay here, is that it?" He pressed, his tone shifting from one of quiet strategizing to annoyed bemusement.

"We're safe at Biltmore. At least, safer than we've been in a long time." Reece shrugged, a half-hearted gesture that spoke volumes.

"Safe is relative when you're trapped behind walls." Austin mused, his gaze returning to the green sanctuary before them, soon to be dismantled - a metaphor, perhaps, for the illusion of security they had found within the confines of Biltmore.

"Not all of us are trapped—"

"With Abraham in charge, no one here is really safe," he said, voice barely above a whisper but carrying an edge sharp enough to slice through the cold silence, "especially the women." Austin let out a breath that turned to mist in the chill air, his eyes hardening as they shifted from the conservatory's lush interior to the imposing structure of Biltmore looming in the distance. Reece's response was clipped, almost dismissive.

"One woman." He said, and Austin felt the anger flare up within him, a fire stoked by fear and concern.

"Protecting one should be damn well enough, Reece," Austin's words were tinged with vehemence, his fists clenching at his sides involuntarily, "and if you think otherwise, you're already part of the problem." The loyalty in Reece's eyes flickered like a steadfast flame as he met Austin's gaze.

"Austin—"

"What if it were Val in this position?" Austin pressed. Reece shook his head, a pensive expression crossing his face as he furrowed his brow.

"If Beth weren't in this position, would you be trying this hard to take Abraham out?"

"He's a parasite," the taste of fresh, clean air lingered on Austin's tongue as he tried to control his angered breaths, "we wouldn't be safe anywhere as long as he's around to spread his influence."

"You saved my life, you know. Pulled me back from a ledge. And I know you've saved Val's life more than once. So yeah, we're with you Austin, all the way. We always have been," there was a pause, heavy with unspoken thoughts, before he continued, "but have you really thought this through? The second we move, we'll be in a war we can't walk back from." Austin's jaw tightened, the muscles working as he processed Reece's words. He knew the risks, weighed them against the lives at stake every day since they'd devised the plan.

"I know what I'm doing," he stated with a conviction that betrayed no room for doubt, "Abraham's reign ends with us." Without another word, Austin turned on his heel, his boots crunching on the frost-covered ground as he made his way back towards the fortress that held them all captive in one way or another. Behind him, Reece let out a sigh that seemed to carry the weight of their predicament, his breath visible against the backdrop of the conservatory's soon-to-be-lost paradise. Then, with a shake of his head that might have been resignation or resolve, Reece turned too, making his solitary path back to the motel where other fates were entwined with their own - a silent sentinel guarding the hopeful and the hopeless alike.

The sterile scent of antiseptics hung heavy in the infirmary, doing little to mask the undercurrent of despair that seemed to permeate the very walls. Anne stood beside a stainless steel tray, her hands methodically arranging medical instruments, each placed with precision - a small attempt to impose order in a world turned chaotic. Her gaze drifted to Mary, hunched on the cot, the trembling sobs shaking her frame punctuating the silence.

"Mary, listen to me," Anne's voice was a gentle but firm anchor in the tempest of grief, "everything will be okay. We'll get through this." Mary's head bobbed up, her eyes red-rimmed and hopeless. "But is there anything you can," her voice cracked with despondency and fear, "anything at all you can do for me?" Anne's heart ached. She knew far too well the pain etched on the younger woman's face. With a shake of her head, she uttered the truth that clawed at her own insides.

"You're too far along," she whispered softly, "and I don't have the right equipment to—" A knock on the door fractured the momentary stillness.

"Sorry to interrupt." Austin's voice, low and tinged with regret, seeped through the wood.

"Come back later, Austin." Anne responded without turning, her patience stretched thin by the day's burdens. Mary took the intrusion as her cue, rising abruptly.

"I should go." She mumbled, brushing past Anne with haste born of discomfort. Her hasty exit left Anne alone with the weight of responsibility pressing down on her. She exhaled slowly, forcing her shoulders to relax before facing Austin. His presence loomed in the doorway, his silhouette framed against the dim corridor light.

"What do you want?" Despite her attempts at neutrality, her words came out sharper than intended, a reflection of the strain that gripped them all. Austin closed the distance between them with a few measured steps, his boots whispering across the sterile floor of the infirmary. Anne's gaze, sharp and clear, met his - an unspoken challenge hanging between them. Her discomfort was evident in his presence, yet she remained firmly planted in place, matching his determined stance with equal measure.

"Anne," Austin began, the weight of his purpose anchoring him to the spot, "I know you have important things on your plate—"

"Then get on with it." She interjected, her voice a scalpel cutting through his hesitation. Her hands never ceased their work, arranging instruments with an efficiency born from necessity, not desire. He took a breath, steadying himself against the storm he was about to unleash.

"I need to apologise to you," he began firmly, his voice carrying a wave of determination and regret, "and I am also sorry for not having done this sooner." Anne's movements halted, her eyes flashing with an intensity that could have ignited the very air.

"I don't want to hear it, Austin." She snapped, her words biting into the space that separated them. Yet he pressed on, resolute.

"You need to hear this." It wasn't just for her, it was for him too - a chance to exorcise demons that had carved deep grooves into his soul. With a slow, deliberate motion, Anne set the clipboard down on the nearest counter.

"Fine." She turned to face him fully, arms folded across her chest, and one brow arched - an invitation for him to continue, though her stance screamed of skepticism. Austin knew that what came next required more courage than any battlefield he'd ever walked upon.

"Anne, I loved you. More than I knew how to say," Austin's voice was a low thrum of earnestness, his gaze never wavered from hers, seeking absolution in the oceans of her eyes, "what happened with Beth, it wasn't meant to hurt you. It wasn't meant to be betrayal. It was grief, dressed up as comfort. I was trying to fill a hole that I thought was gonna consume me for the rest of my life." He swallowed the lump forming in his throat. A sharp intake of breath escaped Anne, her eyes fluttering shut as if to ward off the sting of his confession. When her eyelids lifted, they revealed a storm brewing within. Her words were clipped, laced with a pain that resonated through the sterile air of the infirmary.

"So I was just filling a hole for you?"

"God no, Anne," Austin protested, shaking his head fiercely as he stepped closer, compelled by an invisible force, "you and Beth, you're like night and day. She's this darkness, and it's consuming—"

"I don't want your excuses, Austin—"

"I'm not trying to give you excuses. I'm just trying to give you the reasons why I did what I did. I'm trying to give you the truth. You were everything good I wanted to hold onto. You hadn't been scarred by harsh reality beyond Fort Irwin since the outbreak. But Beth, she's been through hell with me. She didn't just survive it, she owned it. She clawed her way through. And I," he paused, his heart hammering against his ribcage as he spoke, his voice cracking, "I think I loved you for what I hoped the world could still be. But I needed Beth just to survive what it really was." His eyes held a faraway look, one that spoke volumes of the battles fought and the resilience forged in the ashes of their shared past. The silence that filled the room afterward was heavy, charged with unspoken thoughts and turbulent emotions. Austin watched, his breath caught in his chest, as she processed the raw truths laid bare before her. Anne's eyes, once narrowed in hurt, now widened with a glimmer of curiosity that softened the hard line of her mouth.

"What happened, Austin? How did it all change?" The infirmary seemed to shrink around them, the walls closing in as Austin took a breath, his gaze flickering down to the cold linoleum floor before meeting Anne's expectant stare.

"At first, I resented Beth. Not for who she was, but for what she represented. Before the outbreak, when I was deployed, I used to be someone who'd never leave a soul behind. Then there she was, sick and weak, needing someone to take care of her all the time," he shifted uncomfortably on his feet, as if the weight of memories was pressing down on him, "and for a moment I faltered and I wanted to abandon her." Anne's arms were still folded across her chest, but her defensive posture had lessened slightly, her expression now painted with intrigue rather than disdain.

"So why didn't you?"

"Ben. He kept reminding me that it's not who I am. And she fought against every weakness," he admitted, the edge of admiration creeping into his voice despite the gravity of their conversation, "she fought against her flaws, eager to stand on her own, to pull her weight. Even when Luis told her she was worth nothing, it made her more determined to prove him wrong. Her determination, her stubborn refusal to be seen as a liability. It made me see shades of grey where I'd only seen black and white." He paused, locking eyes with Anne, ensuring she understood the depth of his confession.

"And I fell in love with her. On Alcatraz, we were played against each other like pawns in a fucked up chess match, and I watched her harden up in moments others would have been broken. But through it all, all the time even before we were taken there, she was slowly falling in love with Ben, not me. I hadn't seen her for what she was, or who she'd become, until it was too late." There was a vulnerability in Austin's admission, an earnestness that resonated in the silence that followed. It was a tale of reluctant admiration turned to unexpected affection, one he had not fully acknowledged until the night they had left her behind. Austin's fingers traced the coarse edge of the infirmary table, eyes downcast, a veil of guilt shadowing his features.

"Austin—"

"Leaving Beth there," his voice broke off, a mere whisper among the sterile white walls, "it crushed something in me. I thought I was doing what needed to be done, but seeing her arrive at Fort Irwin, so broken and defeated, so far from who she'd become, it clawed at my conscience. It felt like, like *I* broke her." Anne's posture softened, her analytical gaze searching his face as if trying to dissect the sincerity of his words.

"You didn't break her, Austin. That wasn't your fault."

"But it's how I feel," he lifted his eyes to meet hers, a flicker of old warmth briefly igniting in the dark brown of his eyes, "then there was you, Anne. Meeting you when I did, it was like stumbling on an oasis in a desert at just the right moment. You were untouched by the chaos, untainted by the savagery outside that haven. With you, I found comfort and peace. A fleeting glimpse of the life that should have been, the normalcy we all lost." He took a step closer, the intensity clear in his stance.

"Don't—"

"You became my refuge, a reminder of how things could've been. But it was more than that," he continued, his voice gaining strength, "you were real, not just a fantasy to cling to. You made me believe that even in this twisted world, what we want can still exist. That hope and reality don't have to be mutually exclusive. And then I saw her, after I'd let my guard down and finally came to terms with what I'd done, leaving Beth and Chantelle behind. Everything that you'd represented just, it faded away. It doesn't mean what we had wasn't real, it just meant that, at the time I felt like I'd let *her* down by forgetting what I'd done. I felt guilty for being so happy." Anne's brow furrowed, digesting his confession, her arms unfolding, a sign of barriers breaking. They stood locked in a moment of raw honesty, where the past and the present collided, revealing the intricate tapestry of their tangled emotions. Austin shifted his weight from one foot to the other, the air between them heavy with unspoken words and lingering heartache. His gaze fell to the sterile floor of the infirmary, tracing the lines between the tiles as if they might lead him to the right words.

"I wish you'd told me how you felt," Anne sighed softly, her voice a timid sound whispering into the void, "when we met, when she came back. I wish you had just told me."

"I didn't know how," he began, his voice a whisper of vulnerability that seemed foreign in the stoic frame he normally presented, "that night with Beth, it wasn't about us, or anyone else. She was consumed by rage for what she went through. And I, I was blinded by my guilt over what I'd left her to become. In my mind, I'd abandoned her to a fate worse than death. So when she came back, it was desperation. An attempt to end the anger boiling inside her, and the guilt inside me." He lifted his head, eyes meeting Anne's, brimming with a storm of emotions he could no longer contain. His confession hung in the silence, each word a raw wound reopened.

"So you replaced your guilt for what you did to her with guilt for what you did to me?" Anne rolled her eyes, though her body language had softened slightly.

"It was reckless, a moment fuelled by the worst kind of emotion," he shrugged lightly, his eyes growing tired and weary from hindsight, "I never said it was a smart decision. We weren't thinking of you, or Ben, or the consequences. Only the pain we needed to escape." Anne absorbed his admission, the flicker of hurt in her eyes betraying the composed facade she maintained. As she exhaled slowly, her breath seemed to carry the weight of all they had lost, all that had been broken. She reached up, brushing away the tear that had escaped despite her resolve. Her gaze softened as she regarded him - a man weathered by loss and the gruelling fight for survival.

"I understand, Austin," she said quietly, her voice trembling with empathy, "you were both caught in a whirlpool of grief and regret. And perhaps I was fortunate, shielded from the harshest blows of this new world. I can see that you've been carrying this burden for far too long. And you're right, I'd been sheltered at Fort Irwin, while you and Beth, and all the others, you faced the storm head-on." Her words offered a solace he hadn't known he craved, a gentle acknowledgment of the harrowing journey that had led them to this point.

"Thank you—"

"I forgive you, Austin," she interrupted, her voice raw with the effort of speaking the words, "but I'll never forget what happened. I understand why you did it but it hurt me so deeply that I can't ever forget it." Austin's throat tightened, his eyes meeting hers in a solemn understanding.

"I know," he said softly, "and I have to live with that." And in that moment of shared understanding, the walls between them eased ever so slightly, allowing a glimmer of forgiveness to shine through the cracks of their fractured past. Anne's gaze lingered on Austin, the conflict of her emotions etched into the lines of her face. A brief silence fell between them before Anne shifted the topic away from their personal wounds.

"How's Beth doing? Is she okay?" She asked, her tone laced with genuine concern.

"Okay," Austin echoed, his brow furrowing slightly, "in what way?"

"The painkillers," Anne clarified, "she's been taking a lot for her jaw. By now, I would've expected her to need less. The pain should be gone by now." Austin's jaw tensed at the mention, and he gave a noncommittal shrug.

"Are they locked up? Just in case?" He pressed, looking around the room in an attempt to feign concern.

"Of course," Anne replied, her professional demeanour resurfacing as she turned around, "they're kept secure in a cupboard." Her eyes flicked towards a corner of the infirmary where a sturdy cabinet stood, its surface unmarked by the chaos of the outside world.

"That's good." Austin's attention had followed her gaze, noting the precise location of the cupboard.

"Only Val and I have a key," she continued, her hand absentmindedly brushing against her pocket, a subtle but deliberate gesture, "Abraham has one too, somewhere." The weight of their conversation still hung heavily in the air, but his mind was already turning over the implications of what she had said, pieces of a larger puzzle clicking into place. He nodded, a silent acknowledgment of the information she'd unwittingly provided.

"Thank you, Anne." He said quietly, the words carrying more than just gratitude for the forgiveness she'd extended. His eyes stayed fixed on the cupboard for a heartbeat longer before he turned. He was almost to the doorway when Anne's voice reached him, soft but clear.

"I don't blame her, you know." She offered, her voice cracking as she spoke. He paused, turning back to face her, confusion shadowing his features as he met her gaze.

"What do you mean?"

"Beth," Anne said simply, a depth of empathy in her eyes, "for all she's done, for her actions, and for you. I'm tired of feeling mad about it. I can't find it in me to hold it against her. Not anymore." Understanding dawned on Austin's face, softened by relief. He nodded slowly, recognising the strength it took for Anne to release that burden.

"That means a lot." He admitted.

"And I forgive her," Anne added, her voice steady and sure, "more for my sake than for hers. But I do forgive her too. It's over, I don't want to talk about it anymore. I just want to move on." It was a declaration of peace, an offering to close old wounds. A smile, genuine and grateful, broke across Austin's face. His words were a quiet echo in the stillness of the infirmary.

"Thank you."

"You're welcome." She called after him as he stepped out into the corridor, the weight of their past lingering just a moment before dissipating into the air.

Beth stepped into the library with a cautious grace, her senses attuned to the space she knew so well. As she crossed the threshold, the muted light filtered through high windows, casting an ethereal glow over the rows of books that loomed on either side. These tomes, once a source of comfort and knowledge, now seemed to stand in silent judgment, their spines lined like sentinels watching her every move. The air was thick, saturated with the heady scent of leather bindings and the musty aroma of aged paper. At the heart of this sanctuary sat Abraham, a figure as enigmatic as he was imposing. His presence was palpable, a dark sun whose gravitational pull seemed to warp the atmosphere around him. Every object, every thought, seemed to orbit him, drawn inexorably into his sphere. Beth's footsteps were deliberate and slow, each one placed with care so as not to betray the tremor of anxiety that rippled beneath her composed exterior. Internally, she quaked with an anticipation that was both thrilling and terrifying, yet outwardly she maintained a calm facade, determined not to let her inner turmoil show in the face of his inscrutable gaze.

"Ah, Beth," Abraham greeted her, his lips curving into a semblance of warmth, "thank you for coming." She managed a tight smile, her guard never dropping. Her voice was a whisper of sound in the cavernous room, and she held her breath, waiting.

"You wanted to see me?"

"Indeed," he replied, gesturing for her to come further inside, "I have a surprise for you." The door chose that moment to click shut behind her, the sound jolting through her like a bolt. Beth's heart skipped a beat, but she masked her startle with a practiced ease that came from too many unexpected turns. Steeling herself, she took those few steps forward, each one resonating with the silent question of what lay hidden in Abraham's intentions. He held out a bible towards Beth, its leather cover pristine and uncreased. She swallowed hard, mustering all her strength to feign pleasure.

"A bible?"

"For you," he said, a note of pride in his voice, "I asked my men to find one for you on their last run. I thought it fitting that you have your own copy." Beth's fingers brushed against the cool leather as she took the item from him, feigning a warmth in her gaze that failed to reach the depths of her eyes.

"Thank you, Abraham." She murmured, the words like stones on her tongue. She forced the corners of her mouth upwards into a semblance of gratitude, hoping her disquiet was well concealed. Her hand hesitated before she compelled it forward, gently pressing her lips to his cheek in an act so mechanically performed it might as well have been rehearsed. The contact was fleeting, impersonal, yet it was all she could muster.

"Ah, but there's more." Abraham's voice halted her retreat, drawing her attention back to his towering figure as he moved deeper into the library.

"More?" Beth turned, her heart pacing a little quicker, her nerves tensed for whatever revelation lay ahead. He reached towards a shelf where a plain white cotton dress hung solitary amidst the books, its simplicity a stark contrast to the ornate surroundings. With deliberate care, he lifted it from the hanger, holding it up for her to see.

"Beautiful, isn't it?" He stated, though it sounded more like a decree than a question. His eyes sought hers, searching for a reaction, while Beth worked to maintain the delicate balance between showing enough pleasure to appease him and not betraying her true feelings. Beth's pulse hammered in her ears, drowning out the library's silence as Abraham approached with the dress. Its fabric whispered promises of a future she never asked for, each step he took towards her amplifying the urge to flee. Yet her feet remained rooted, and she managed a stiff nod in response to his expectant look.

"Yes," she managed, "beautiful—"

"Found just the thing for your christening." He said, the pride in his voice unmistakable. The dress swung slightly as he held it before him, a ghostly spectre of purity.

"My christening," she exhaled a breath she hadn't realised she was holding, her shoulders dropping the slightest bit at the word *christening* and not *wedding*, "yes, it's perfect." A formality, nothing more - she could endure that. But the momentary relief shattered like fragile glass as Abraham continued, calmly spelling out the path he had set for her.

"You will be christened first, naturally," a smile of genuine warmth crept across his face, "as you should be before we are married." The room spun dizzyingly around Beth, her body numbed by the shock of his words.

"What do you mean?" She whispered, her voice a strained thread of sound barely carrying across the distance between them.

"Exactly what I said, Beth," he replied, mistaking her muted horror for jovial surprise, "I have made my decision. You will stand beside me, as my wife, the matriarch to our new beginning." His eyes glinted with a sense of ownership, a future laid out without her consent. Her mind reeled, trapped between the impending walls of Abraham's vision and the primal scream of instinct inside her, begging her to resist the destiny he had so casually dictated. This was the plan she had set out to do. This was the idea she had contrived to see through so she could get close enough to him. Yet, her mind and body reeled in disgust now that it was coming to fruition. Beth's muscles tensed, urging her to create distance as she measured a cautious step backwards. The corners of her mouth lifted in a mechanical mimicry of joy, an expression far from reaching the apprehensive eyes that met Abraham's. His brow furrowed slightly, a subtle shift that betrayed his perception of her unease. His concern, however, was edged with anticipation, awaiting the gratitude and adoration he felt due.

"Forgive me," she paused, her voice softening into a plea for understanding, "my exhaustion shows too readily these days. My recovery has been slow, and it takes all my strength to simply keep on sometimes. But I'm working on regaining what I've lost. I am really so very, truly happy." She offered a small laugh, as hollow as the chamber of her chest where her heart raced a frantic rhythm.

"I'm glad to hear it." His eyes scrutinised her, and she knew she had faltered. With the bible's weight still palpable in her hands, Beth approached the table and carefully set the sacred tome down. The leather cover whispered against the wood, a quiet testament to the gravity of the object now lying inert between them. She turned then, her movements deliberate yet fluid, as if drawn by the gravity of the white dress Abraham held. Her fingers brushed the fabric, tracing the fine lines and simple elegance of its design.

"It's beautiful," she breathed, allowing herself a moment to appreciate the craftsmanship before lifting her gaze to meet his, "thank you, Abraham. For this, for all of it. Most of all, for your vision of our life together." The words, although expertly crafted, tasted like ash on her tongue. There was no denying the mild allure of the life he promised - stability and security - but at the cost of her freedom, her will, and her very self. Still, she adorned her face with the mask of gratitude, hoping to conceal the dread that curled tight in her belly.

"To become your wife," she concluded, her voice steadier than she felt, "is the greatest surprise of all." Beth felt a wave of nausea surge through her, an unwelcome tide rising from the pit of her stomach. She fought to maintain the facade of joy, steadying her voice as it threatened to quiver under the weight of her discomfort.

"It's not just a surprise," he took a small step towards her, his hand reaching out slightly as if he were about to take her hands in his own, "it's an honour that you are truly worthy of." Beth had to summon all her inner strength to avoid flinching at the gesture.

"I've never been happier." She lied, the words feeling like shards of glass in her throat. Abraham's eyes narrowed slightly, a hint of concern shadowing his features.

"Are you sure you're okay?" He asked, stepping closer. His presence was oppressive, suffocating, and Beth could feel the walls of the library closing in around her.

"Absolutely," she managed with a brightness that didn't quite reach her eyes, "I'm just overwhelmed. With happiness, I promise." Her heart hammered against her ribs, a frantic drumbeat echoing her mounting panic. The room spun, a carousel of books and shadows blurring before her eyes, and the floor seemed to lurch beneath her feet. Beth's last conscious thought was a desperate hope that her collapse might be seen as nothing more than a fainting spell, rather than the physical rejection of the future being forced upon her. Darkness engulfed her as she slipped into oblivion, the world fading away to nothing but the sound of Abraham calling her name from far, far away.

CHAPTER 9

Beth's eyelids fluttered open, the world gradually taking shape as her vision cleared. The room was dimly lit, and for a moment she couldn't place herself. She blinked at the ceiling, and for a moment she saw the off-white paint from her house in Fort Irwin. Blinking again to clear her vision, she saw the concrete ceiling of her cell at Alcatraz, causing a shiver to run down her spine. The white and the gray twisted and merged until she couldn't distinguish one from the other. Her mind was a delicate balance between innocence and strength, constantly shifting and struggling to find its footing in a world that had taken so much from her. There was a metallic taste in her mouth, almost like the taste of fear. It was a taste that she had become all too familiar with. Her memories swirled and overlapped like watercolors, blending her past and present in a disorienting yet strangely comforting way. The whispering of familiar voices, kind voices, told her that she wasn't there, that her mind was playing tricks on her. Her fragile mind, one that had developed from a naive girl to a strong survivor, one that occasionally flipped between the two, was trying desperately to ground her now. Then the familiar scent of the old blankets wrapped around her filled her senses, anchoring her back to reality. She felt the warmth of another body on either side of her bed - Val and Eve, their faces carved in quiet distress.

"Hey," Val said softly, her voice steady but with an undercurrent of worry, "you gave us a bit of a scare, but your blood pressure just took a nosedive. That's all." Beth tried to speak, but her throat felt like it was lined with cotton.

"I've been trying to eat." She managed a raspy whisper.

"I know you have," Eve's hand found Beth's, giving it a gentle squeeze, "but you need more strength in you." Val's gaze shifted between the two of them, a silent command passing through her eyes before she stood with purpose.

"I'm going to let Abraham know you're awake." Her tone was matter-of-fact, yet carried the weight of unspoken authority. Once Val had left, the air in the room seemed to change, becoming both heavier and lighter at the same time. Eve moved closer, her presence comforting as she perched on the edge of the mattress.

"I was so worried about you." She murmured, her eyes searching Beth's face for signs of recovery.

"Help me up?" Beth asked, her voice a mere wisp. Eve's hands slipped behind Beth's shoulders, gentleness personified as she assisted Beth into a sitting position. Pillows were adjusted behind her back, propping her up against the headboard. With a tenderness that belied her usual stoicism, Eve reached for the tray on the side table, laden with an assortment of food that Beth hadn't smelled in what felt like ages. She set the tray in front of Beth on the bed.

"Try to eat something." Eve encouraged, her tone a mix of maternal care and the subtle firmness of someone who knew too well the importance of sustenance in times of weakness. Beth's gaze lingered on the tray, a colourful mosaic of nourishment that seemed foreign in its abundance. Her fingers trembled slightly as they hovered over the bowl of canned beef and vegetable soup. Beside it lay a bread roll, golden and warm, freshly baked. Scrambled eggs sat fluffy and inviting next to a dollop of creamed spinach, its deep green colour stark against the white plate. A glass of orange juice gleamed like captured sunshine, while an apple, its skin polished to a glossy sheen, promised a crisp bite.

"Why so much?" She whispered, her voice barely carrying across the short distance to Eve's attentive ears.

"Abraham," Eve replied, her tone a mix of respect and a hint of something more complicated, "he insisted that some of the better food they'd been saving be prepared for you. He wants you to regain your strength." The thought of Abraham investing such care was discomforting, yet Beth couldn't deny the gnawing hunger clawing at her insides. With a tentative hand, she reached for the spoon resting against the bowl and scooped up a small amount of soup. The aroma, rich and savoury, teased her senses, a reminder of a time when meals were not just scraps to survive on. Closing her eyes, she brought the spoon to her lips, steeling herself for the first taste. The liquid warmth spread across her tongue, but it was the act of swallowing that brought pain. Each gulp felt like it scraped down her throat, sharp and unyielding. She could almost imagine the food turning into tiny daggers, reminding her body of its prolonged deprivation. The sensation left her fighting a wave of nausea, the mere thought of eating sending her stomach into a silent protest.

"I can't—"

"Slowly," Eve instructed softly, "it will get easier." Beth nodded, taking another painstaking mouthful, showing no sign of the turmoil roiling within. The silence stretched between them, a tangible entity as Eve's watchful eyes followed each tentative bite Beth took. Halfway through the roll, nibbling at the edges of scrambled eggs, and with just a sip of orange juice left, Beth pushed the tray away, her hand trembling slightly.

"I can't eat any more," she murmured, "I'm full."

"You did good," Eve said, a note of pride edging her concern as she leaned forward, her elbows resting on her knees, "how do you feel?" Beth's gaze flitted to the window where the light was a soft grey, then back to Eve, her expression raw.

"Horrified. He told me—" she whispered, pausing suddenly for a while before taking a deep breath, "he told me I would be his wife. He gave me these gifts. A dress and a bible." Eve's eyes moved slowly from Beth's pale face to the chest where the leather-bound bible lay, its pages crisp and untouched.

"Abraham insisted on it being in here when you wake up," Eve's gaze traveled further to the dress draped elegantly on a hanger over the front of the ornate armoire, the fabric unnervingly pure and untarnished, "he wanted them both here to offer you some comfort." Beth followed the trajectory of Eve's stare, her own eyes landing on the symbols of her impending fate. She closed them quickly, a shudder passing through her body. When she spoke again, her voice was barely audible.

"How long was I out for?"

"Only for the night," Eve reassured her, reaching out to pat her hand, "your body clearly needed the rest, especially after—" She trailed off, biting her lip.

"After what?"

"Amanda's obviously been dismissed. It happened yesterday morning and Abraham wanted to tell you himself about being chosen. But Amanda, well, she's been ranting about it since."

"*Dismissed.*" Beth repeated, the word tasting like ash in her mouth. She turned her head away from the oppressive sight of the dress and the bible, seeking refuge in the blank wall.

"Abraham made her promise to keep her mouth shut until he could tell you himself but she wouldn't shut up about it, ranting and raving," Eve continued, her tone low and dismissive, "but at least she didn't get to you first. Who knows how cruel she might have been."

"I'd rather she had," Beth sighed, "then at least I would have been more prepared. I can handle Amanda, she's nothing. Abraham is the one that's difficult to deal with."

"There's something else," Eve's voice was soft, but it carried the weight of an unspoken command as she leaned closer to Beth, "Abraham has asked me to take care of you, to be a guide in your faith." She said, and a ripple of apprehension coursed through Beth's already fragile composure. Beth's eyes, rimmed with shadows of her recent ordeal, met Eve's earnest gaze. A guide, she thought, or a warden.

"You're going to teach me how to be more *faithful*?"

"Abraham understands that I might feel passed over," Eve continued, pressing her lips together in a thin line before offering a slight, almost imperceptible shrug, "but he trusts my devotion. He believes I can support you through this, help you understand God's path for you." For a moment, Beth's response was merely a nod, her acknowledgment slow as if each motion required immense effort. She glanced down at her hands, trembling betrayals of her inner turmoil. They were pale against the dark woollen blanket, stark reminders of her vulnerability.

"God has no path for any of us," Beth whispered, clutching at the blanket, "at the very least, if I believed in any of it, I think he abandoned all of us long ago."

"I know you don't believe in it," sensing the need for comfort, Eve reached out, enveloping Beth's cold fingers with a warmth that felt foreign yet desperately needed, "but you need to pretend, or none of this is going to work."

"I know."

"I'm here," she promised, her voice firmer now, "whenever you need me, I'm right here." The reassuring squeeze was abruptly cut short by the sound of the door swinging open with such force that it struck the wall. Startled, Eve jerked upright, her hands withdrawing from Beth's as if scorched by the sudden intrusion. Beth barely had time to process the disruption before Abraham's imposing figure filled the doorway. His presence seemed to suck the air from the room, leaving behind a heavy silence that settled over them like a shroud. The quilt whispered across the cotton sheets as Beth gathered it, inch by cautious inch, closer to her chest. The fabric formed a slight bulge - an inconspicuous rampart in the space between her and the man whose shadow now loomed over the bed.

"I didn't mean to startle you, my dear." Abraham's voice was a deep timbre that filled the room as he approached, his steps assured and unhurried. He perched on the edge of the mattress, the weight of his presence causing the springs to protest softly. With a paternal gentleness belying his stature, he took Beth's hands, cupping them in his large, calloused ones. His thumb brushed over her knuckles in what might have been an attempt at soothing, or perhaps claiming.

"Let me look at you." He said, lifting his hands away from hers to feel her forehead, his touch carrying the warmth of a fever she did not possess. Her pulse fluttered like a captured bird under his fingers. Beth managed a small smile, the corners of her lips twitching upwards in a facsimile of reassurance. She sought out Eve in her peripheral vision, looking for an anchor in the storm that was Abraham. Eve stood by, her eyes a well of encouragement, nodding faintly as if to will strength into Beth's faltering facade.

"She's eaten quite a bit," Eve took a small step forward, "so she has some strength back."

"How are you feeling?" Abraham's inquiry demanded honesty, ignoring Eve's statement, but Beth could only muster the courage for another half-truth.

"Better," she whispered, "now that you're here." Her voice, a fragile thread, seemed to please him. His response came as a kiss pressed to her forehead, a benediction that lingered longer than necessary before he allowed his lips to descend upon hers. The touch was brief, a soft claim that still spelled ownership. Beth tilted her chin up to meet him, submitting to the contact while her mind raced with silent dissent. As he drew back, a flicker of pride brightened Abraham's eyes.

"I didn't have the chance to tell you last night," he began, the baritone of his voice threading through the quiet of the room, "the christening was set for this morning, but we've pushed it back so it will be held the morning of the wedding. You need time to recover." Beth nodded, absorbing his words. In the respite they offered, her heart found a momentary calm. The christening, the wedding - each word was a stone added to the weight she carried, yet for now, she had been granted a reprieve.

"Isn't it bad luck for you to see me on the morning of—" she paused, swallowing hard, unsure of what her protest might accomplish, "the morning of our wedding day?" Abraham let out a light laugh, placing his hand on her cheek.

"The idea that the groom shouldn't see the bride before the wedding is a tradition, not a biblical rule. It's not mentioned in the Bible and has no religious basis. You have nothing to worry about."

"Oh," she managed a small smile, "I'm glad." In that pause, she clung to the hope that somehow, she might still find a way through the labyrinth that Abraham's devotion had constructed around her. Abraham's gaze drifted towards the tray, where half-eaten morsels lay abandoned amidst the china.

"You're doing well," he said, a note of approval lacing his words, "it's important that you regain your strength." Beth's eyes flicked to Eve, who stood quietly behind Abraham, the very image of dutiful care.

"Eve has been looking after me," she offered softly, her voice still weak but steady, "she's making sure I eat."

"Thank you, Eve," Abraham said, turning his attention to her now with a nod of recognition, "I know this can't be easy for you, helping Beth after, well, after everything. But I trust there are no hard feelings." His inquiry lingered in the air, heavy with unspoken expectations. Beth watched as Eve's resolve hardened - the subtle tension in her shoulders spoke volumes to those who knew her well. Yet, her voice was calm and reassuring when she finally spoke. "Of course not, Abraham. You made the right choice. Beth will be our salvation." Their exchange hung like a delicate truce, fragile and fraught with complexity. Abraham seemed satisfied as he turned back to Beth, his hand reaching out to caress her cheek once more with an almost reverent touch. The gesture was meant to comfort, but it left a trail of unease on her skin.

"I have faith in you," he said quietly, "I know you'll fulfil your role." Beth felt the pressure of his fingers, cool and commanding.

"I just hope that I'm worthy." She said softly as she held his gaze, searching for some sign of suitability of the man in front of her. But all she found was the unwavering certainty of a leader, a prophet to his people, who saw in her a means to an end that she could neither embrace nor escape. Abraham's departing words fell heavily in the cramped bedroom, his presence lingering like a shadow even as he exited.

"As soon as you're well, we'll have the christening at Bass Pond. The wedding will follow immediately." His voice held a note of command that brooked no argument. Beth managed only a silent nod, her throat tight with unspoken fears. As the door swung heavily behind Abraham's departure, she allowed herself the smallest of reprieves - a slow inhalation that seemed to fill the room with its quiet defiance. Eve's hands were deft as she closed the door, her fingers lingering on the knob as if to ensure the finality of their privacy. She turned back to Beth, her brow knit with concern.

"Do you need anything?" Eve asked, voice soft but insistent. Beth's request was hesitant, eyes darting to the leather-bound book resting atop the chest of drawers

"Can you please pass me the bible?"

"Of course." Eve fetched it with an ease that suggested familiarity, returning to sit close beside Beth on the bed. The book was placed gently in Beth's lap, its pages soft and new and full of secrets. Beth flipped through the thin leaves before pausing, her voice barely above a whisper.

"Is there anything in here about ending a life for something greater?" The question hung between them, delicate and dangerous. Eve reached out to still Beth's trembling hands, her touch grounding.

"The Bible consistently upholds the sanctity of human life and explicitly condemns murder, regardless of the perceived greater good," her voice was firm, echoing the conviction of her beliefs, "biblical teachings emphasise that the ends do not justify the means when it comes to taking a life." In the dim light of the room, Beth's face was a map of conflict, her eyes tracing the passages as if seeking a hidden message among the unfamiliar verses. The weight of the book in her hands felt like the gravity of all that was yet to come, a future bound by words she was only beginning to learn. Beth's fingers paused on a verse, the ink barely visible in the dimming light. She raised her gaze to Eve, her expression clouded by worry.

"Why are you so intent on having Abraham killed?" She asked, her voice a thin thread of sound in the heavy air. Eve's expression remained unreadable, her hands folding around the edges of the tray with calculated calm.

"I don't see the Bible in black and white, Beth," she murmured, her eyes not quite meeting Beth's, "I could never take a life myself, but I'm not opposed to the idea of someone else stepping in."

"Sounds hypocritical." Beth countered softly, the words spilling out with a bitterness she hadn't intended to reveal.

"Perhaps," Eve conceded, standing up, the tray now a shield between them, "but I won't lose sleep over it." Her voice carried a firmness that belied any doubt she might have felt.

"You say that," Beth whispered, tracing the wood grain of the nightstand with a trembling finger, "but there are many who wouldn't bat an eye if I were the one to die." Eve's face softened for a moment, the mask slipping.

"Don't be stupid, Beth. You know that's not true."

"Isn't it?" Beth mused aloud, her thoughts wandering like leaves in a slow-moving stream; "Abraham wasn't hesitant to rid himself of sinners before—"

"True," Eve interjected, her tone tinged with disdain, "he had no qualms about casting judgment as if he held divine authority."

"Then where does that leave those among us who carry their sins like stones in their pockets?" Beth's eyes lingered on the fading daylight creeping through the window, her voice a mere wisp of sound.

"Beth—"

"Wouldn't it be merciful, perhaps, to let a stone fall into the ocean and sink beneath the surface?"

"You're starting to sound like him," Eve studied Beth for a long moment, her eyes searching, "speaking in riddles and proclamations—"

"Isn't that the point," Beth snapped her head towards Eve, anger and frustration etched into the hollows of her eyes, "for me to drink the Kool Aid?"

"If you're talking about what I *think* you're talking about, it's a sin."

"So your line is drawn at suicide but not murder," Beth scoffed, "got it."

"Your thoughts are veering into dark waters, Beth. Best steer clear of them." There was a warning in her tone, a subtle plea for Beth to tread lightly.

"Of course," Beth replied, a ghost of a smile touching her lips, "just idle thoughts." Eve nodded, though the lines of worry didn't disappear from her forehead.

"Rest your mind as well as your body," she advised, "you'll need your strength for what's to come." Eve cast a backward glance at the pale figure nestled among the linens, her expression a mask sculpted in unease that she carefully concealed beneath a practiced calm. Beth's eyes fluttered, heavy with the remnants of weariness and the burden of unspoken thoughts. A faint nod was her only reply, and with it Eve turned to leave, her steps measured as she balanced the tray in her hands, the clink of the empty glassware a soft discordant symphony in the hush of Beth's room as she closed the door behind her with a gentle click, leaving Beth alone with her thoughts and the heavy silence of the encroaching night.

The sub-basement corridor was cooler than the rest of the facility, its dim light casting long shadows that seemed to dance upon the walls as Eve moved through them. She navigated the familiar path with ease, her mind replaying the veiled words, the subtle hints of despair that had slipped from Beth's lips. She shook her head, trying to dislodge the unease that clung to her like an unwanted shroud. Leaving the tray of half-eaten food in the kitchen, Eve stepped into the corridor once more, her footsteps hurried with a sense of purpose.

"*Eve*!" The hushed call came just as she reached the intersection leading to the kitchen. Austin's lean frame emerged from the shadows, Ben a silent figure beside him. Their faces were drawn tight with worry, the lines around their eyes deepened by the weight of the situation. The air was stale, carrying a weight that seemed to press against her chest with every breath she took.

"I'm sure you heard what happened," Eve whispered, stepping further into the darkness, "Beth's fine."

"We heard she'd fainted," Austin's voice was low, "that's all we know." Eve paused, her fingers lightly brushing against the fabric of her skirt.

"That's all there is to know. She's fine," she assured, though the heaviness in her heart belied her calm exterior, "just exhausted. She fainted after Abraham, well, he gave her a bible and a white dress for the christening. She collapsed when he told her she'd been chosen to be his wife." Eve's gaze drifted away momentarily before locking back onto theirs. A silence fell between them, fraught with unspoken fears and simmering anger. Ben's face hardened, the lines around his mouth growing more pronounced.

"So it's done then." He said, his words like ice. Eve nodded solemnly, an unspoken understanding flashing between her and Austin.

"Beth has taken on the burden she set out for herself." She replied, her voice steady despite the storm raging inside her. Ben's eyes narrowed, darting between Eve and Austin.

"And why do you know all this?" He probed, suspicion lacing his tone.

"Abraham has tasked me with taking care of her," Eve responded, her resolve unwavering, "he believes I can guide her, seeing as how we once walked the same path, and she trusts me. She confessed her plan to me." She held Ben's gaze as she lied, her own eyes reflecting a depth of conviction and strength borne from trials by fire.

"Sounds convenient." Ben muttered, but there was no further challenge in his voice. He understood the gravity of their situation, the roles they each had to play in the theatre of survival they found themselves entangled within.

"Convenient or not, I'll be watching over her," Eve declared, a fierce protectress ready to shield Beth from the tempest that awaited, "you don't have to like me, and you don't have to trust me, and I know you want to be the one to watch over her but you can't. So right now, I'm all you've got—" A sudden clamour from the kitchen echoed through the dimly lit corridor, shattering the hushed conversation between the three. Startled, they glanced towards the source of the noise, an instinctive unease tightening their features. Without a word, Austin reached out, his hand finding Eve's elbow, guiding her swiftly to an adjacent storeroom nestled in shadows. The door clicked shut behind them, muting the outside world.

"Anne keeps the Vicodin in a locked cupboard in the corner of the infirmary," Austin whispered, urgency lacing his voice as he leaned closer to Eve, "if Beth needs more, Anne and Val have keys, and apparently Abraham too. We'll have to find a way to steal one." Eve nodded, her eyes reflecting an unyielding resolve. Ben, arms folded across his chest, shifted his weight.

"She already has enough to lay a man out," he remarked, skepticism furrowing his brow, "but Abraham's strong. He's young, fit and healthy. He might pull through even with what Beth's got."

"Definitely enough to put him to sleep," Eve murmured, pondering the gravity of their plan as her gaze flickered to Austin, seeking silent agreement, "but if it's death, she may need more." She let the thought hang, heavy in the air. Austin's response cut through the tension, decisive and clear.

"It'll knock him out cold," he said, confidence underscored by necessity, "that gives Beth the chance to finish him off another way if she has to." They stood in silence for a moment, each lost in their own calculations of risk and resolve. The stakes were high, and the next moves they made would set the course for all that followed.

"Or for one of us to sneak in and do it." Ben shrugged, staring at the wall as if he saw the events playing out in his mind. Eve faced him squarely now, her eyes searching his blank stare.

"I don't see how that would be possible if their room would be guarded—"

"If someone was standing outside their door, then they'd hear a struggle anyway and Beth would be fucked before she even got the chance—"

"Stop it," Austin hissed as he glared between the two, "fighting isn't going to help. You're both right and there are a lot of ways this could go wrong, but getting into it with each other is not gonna help anyone." The silence that fell between them stretched on for what seemed like an eternity. Eve's gaze lingered in the empty space beyond the room for a moment, her mind racing with the weight of Ben's objections, Austin's reprimands, and then suddenly, Beth's cryptic words. She turned back to face Austin and Ben, noticing the confusion etched on their faces as they awaited an explanation. "What's wrong?" Ben asked, trouble chiseled into his expression.

"You look like you've seen a ghost." Austin added.

"Abraham is young, fit and healthy. It might not kill him." She repeated Ben's words, trailing off as she continued to look towards the door. Ben raised an eyebrow at her.

"That's what I said."

"Something's not right," Eve's voice was low and hollow, "Beth, she was talking about dying for the greater good." Her throat tightened at the memory, a cold unease settling over her.

"So she needs more? To make sure he's dead?" Austin asked, his eyes narrowing as he tried to grasp the full meaning of Eve's words. Ben and Austin exchanged looks of confusion, their faces lit softly by the dull lamplight.

"No," Eve shook her head slowly, her eyes haunted, "she specifically mentioned someone dying, not killing someone. There's a difference in her tone. It's like she's resigned to something." Austin and Ben exchanged a tense glance, the unspoken fear between them palpable.

"What did she say, Eve? Tell us exactly what she said." Ben pressed, taking a small step towards her. His figure was imposing in the dim light, the shadows casting a darkness around his eyes that made him look possessed. Eve swallowed hard, her stomach churning.

"She mentioned suicide, but I thought she was just thinking out loud." Eve felt the urgency building inside her, knowing she had to act fast.

"Beth mentions *suicide* and you left her alone?" Ben's voice was raised every so slightly, the anger building like thunder before lightning strikes.

"We all have dark thoughts, Ben. Don't tell me you haven't wanted to check out of this hell we live in. I thought she was just—"

"Just *what*?" His voice grew even louder before Austin managed to grab his arm to soothe him.

"I need to go check on her." Eve insisted, already stepping towards the door. Her pace quickened as she made her way down the dimly lit corridor, the echo of her footsteps a stark reminder of the looming threat.

"Eve!" Austin called out, his voice carrying a note of concern that spurred him into action. He caught up to her, his hand reaching out to grasp her arm. She spun around, her eyes fierce and determined. "I have to make sure Beth is alright," she told him firmly, yanking her arm away from his grasp, "stay here. If you're seen wandering around upstairs without purpose, it'll raise questions we can't afford, especially in the upstairs bedrooms." Without waiting for a response, Eve turned on her heel and dashed up the staircase as quickly as she could without raising suspicion, her heart pounding in sync with the rising stakes. As she disappeared from view, the heavy silence of the sub-basement closed in around Austin and Ben, leaving them with the echoes of a plan teetering on the brink of something unfathomable.

The library was steeped in the scent of aged books and rich tobacco, a haven amidst the chaos that encroached from the world outside. Abraham lounged in a leather armchair, a glass of whiskey swirling between his fingers as the gentle crackle of burning wood accompanied his thoughts. Across from him, Aaron and Adam settled into their own seats, forming a triangle of leadership in the dimly lit room.

"Your last supply run was quite the success, Aaron," Abraham remarked, the smoke from his cigar drawing lazy circles towards the coffered ceiling, "these cigars are a rarity." Aaron leaned back, a smirk playing on his lips.

"There's a little place in Biltmore Village," he disclosed with a sly tilt of his head, "I might have appropriated their entire collection for our enjoyment." Adam, silent until now, gave an approving nod, his gaze fixed on the dancing flames that reflected in his deep-set eyes. He seemed lost in thought, the orange glow painting shadows across his solemn face.

"You've been quiet, Adam," Abraham watched him for a moment before probing, "what's on your mind?"

"Communications," Adam replied, his voice low but clear, "picked up chatter from a group to the north, close to a town called Kingsport in Tennessee." His eyes didn't leave the fire, as if the answer lay within its embers.

"Kingsport," Aaron interjected, leaning forward with interest, "how far is that?"

"Close enough," Adam said with a half-hearted laugh, glancing at Aaron, "ninety minutes drive, give or take, assuming you could find a traffic jam these days." They shared a brief, strained laugh, the kind that recognised the absurdity of their reality, a world where roads lay empty and the relics of a bygone era like cigars and whiskey were luxuries hoarded by those who held power. Abraham took a deep draw from his cigar, letting the smoke fill him before exhaling slowly, his mind churning over the implications of Adam's words. The amber liquid in Abraham's glass caught the light as he swirled it thoughtfully, his gaze sharp upon Adam.

"Are they a threat?" His voice carried the weight of responsibility and an undercurrent of readiness for whatever answer might come. Adam's fingers traced the rim of his own glass before looking back at Abraham, his expression unreadable yet tinged with caution.

"Hard to say," he admitted, his eyes narrowing slightly, "we've only got fragments over the long wave radio, bits and pieces. But I'm keeping my ear to the ground."

"How do you know they're in Kingsport?" Aaron raised a questioning eyebrow at him, his tone laced with skepticism.

"Because they said so." Adam replied casually, sipping from his glass, not breaking his gaze in return. Aaron pondered for a moment before taking an idle sip of his drink.

"Seems careless for them to mention their location on an open line. Anyone could barge in."

"Then perhaps they're guarded enough that an ambush wouldn't hurt them," Abraham chimed in, his posture relaxed but his eyes keenly observant, "anything else going on out there?"

"Mostly quiet," Adam responded, shifting in his seat to face both men, "but there's been significant talk about the Kingsport group. And you're right. They're organised, that much is clear."

"Any military activity? Uniforms? Weapons?" Aaron queried, the interest in his tone edged with the precision of a man accustomed to strategic considerations.

"The chatter is mostly about supplies. They're not broadcasting manoeuvres, if that's what they're planning," Adam took a slow sip of his whiskey, "but they did mention a sighting, a group of well-prepared military men."

"Ours?" Abraham leaned forward, locking eyes with Adam. Adam set down his glass with a soft clink.

"I don't know, that's Aaron's department." He nodded towards their cousin, his statement hanging between them like a challenge. Aaron sat up straighter, his eyes flicking between Adam and Abraham. The tension in the room had thickened, an unspoken acknowledgement that the stakes were as high as ever in this fractured world they navigated. Aaron's jaw tightened, the muscle ticking in silent fury as he shot a glare at Adam. His fingers curled into fists briefly before he forced them to relax and turned his gaze to Abraham.

"Some of our patrols might have pushed beyond the usual boundaries," he said, voice steady despite the edge of irritation, "supplies don't just fall from the sky, we need to venture further out." Abraham's brows rose slightly, a clear signal of disapproval. He leaned back in his chair, a hand casually swirling the whiskey in his glass.

"This is why we set up what we could to be sustainable here. Vegetables and meat, animals and fruit. We planned for this. I didn't authorise any expedition north," he stated, his tone carrying the weight of command, "we agreed to a fifty-mile radius until we've thoroughly scouted. You know this, Aaron." The air hung heavy with tension, the smoke from their cigars twisting like serpents in the dimly lit library. Aaron met Abraham's gaze squarely, refusing to cower under the scrutiny.

"We spent a year scouting every inch of land before relocating to Biltmore," he reminded his cousin, a hint of steel underlying his words, "and we never encountered a soul past Louisville."

"Then it was a gross oversight." Abraham's reply was cold, dismissive. The scornful look he sent Aaron's way held a warning, a reminder of the power dynamics at play within the walls of their stronghold. Abraham's gaze shifted from Aaron to the third man in the room, his eyes narrowing thoughtfully.

"Cousin, I—"

"Perhaps I should have put you in charge of our military operations," he mused, directing his attention to Adam, ignoring Aaron's attempt at a plea, "someone with a keen sense for detail."

Adam stiffened, the muscles along his jaw clenching slightly.

"I handle communications," he said quickly, his voice steady despite the sudden spotlight, "field experience isn't my forte."

"Then maybe it's time to reconsider who sits at my table." Abraham intoned, the hint of a threat woven through his words. He leaned back against the plush leather of the chair and brought the cigar to his lips, drawing in deeply, the ember at its tip glowing fiercely for a moment in the dimly lit library. Across from him, Adam's eyes flickered over to Aaron, a silent exchange passing between them. It was a look that carried the weight of unspoken challenges and years of rivalry. Both men took a synchronised drag on their cigars, the smoke swirling above them like an omen. Aaron's voice broke the silence, laced with a sarcasm that barely masked his defiance.

"I'll make sure to be more thorough in the future." He declared, his tone dripping with insincerity.

"See that you are." Abraham responded coolly, unaffected by the barb in Aaron's voice, his eyes locked onto the dancing flames in the fireplace as if the entire conversation were no more than a minor distraction. The authority in his posture left no room for further debate, sealing the command with the quiet certainty of his rule.

CHAPTER 10

The echo of Eve's boots against the walls were like gunshots, bouncing off the empty hallway, the vibrations reverberating through her very soul. It was a frantic symphony, each step a staccato beat that reverberated through the opulent halls. She was a creature possessed, driven by a force that threatened to consume her. Her gasping breaths were loud and desperate while the urgency that clawed at her insides was almost tangible, propelling her forward until she collided with Stone's broad chest. Without preamble, her fingers latched onto his arm, her grip ironclad.

"Stone," her voice was a hushed blade, cutting through any pleasantries or hesitation, "I need you, *now*. Come with me." She didn't wait for an answer, already tugging him along, her strides eating up the distance to Beth's room. Jennifer sat perched on a chair in the third-floor living hall, her eyes widening in surprise as she watched Eve and Stone rush up the winding staircase. Their hurried ascent and their sense of urgency created a prickling sensation that crept up the back of her neck, causing her to clench her hands tightly into the fabric of her shirt. She couldn't shake off the sense of dread that enveloped her, like cold fingers grasping at her heart. She closed her book gingerly and listened to the sounds from above, hoping their haste would give Jennifer a sense of direction. Silence enveloped the space as muffled voices from the floors below began to filter through the air, until a loud thud from above startled her. Beth's door gave way under Eve's forceful push, the creak of its hinges underscoring the gravity of the situation. The sight that met them halted Eve for half a heartbeat. Beth lay on the bed, her breathing so faint it barely stirred the air, her body white and her lips almost blue. Stone remained motionless by the door, his complexion pale and filled with terror.

"Holy shit—"

"*Cazzo*," Eve whispered the Italian obscenity to herself, and she was moving again, her hands finding Beth's wrist, searching for the thready pulse of life beneath the skin, "it's weak but she's alive." She announced, more to convince herself than to inform Stone who stood rooted in place, his face a mask sculpted in horror. Frantic, Eve reached for the water glass perched precariously on the bedside table and flung its contents across Beth's pale face, hoping for some sign of revival. As the water trickled down her cheeks, it made a soft pattering sound, almost like gentle rain on a windowpane, hitting the dense ground after a thunderstorm. Droplets cascaded down Beth's skin like crystal tears, but they elicited no response. The droplets seemed to shimmer in the dim light, reflecting the faint outline of her face as it cascaded over her features. Eve's mouth was dry and parched from the panic and adrenaline coursing through her, and she couldn't help but take a drink from the half-empty bottle on the side table. Her hand closed around the little container of Vicodin that lay there, accusingly silent. A moment hung between them, laden with unspoken fears, before she let the plastic vial drop back onto the table, its rattle an incongruent sound amidst the tension. Beth's body tensed, a feeble moan escaping her lips as if she were fighting through the fog of unconsciousness. Eve's response was immediate, her hands gripping Beth's shoulders with urgent care. Stone moved closer to the bed, his expression still showing traces of terror, but his determination to assist in any way possible had strengthened.

"What do we do?"

"Quickly, help me turn her." Eve's voice was sharp, a command that brooked no hesitation. Stone, though clearly shaken, moved into action, his strong hands aiding Eve in rolling Beth onto her side. As he did so, Eve's fingers plunged decisively into Beth's mouth, pressing down to the back of her throat. Beth's gag reflex kicked in, her body convulsing with a violent cough.

"What the fuck was she thinking?"

"Come on, Beth," Eve urged, her voice tinged with desperation, ignoring Stone, "throw it up, *please.*" She doubled her efforts, her fingers a relentless force against Beth's throat. The sickening sound of retching filled the room, and then, amidst the spasms and convulsions and relentless heaving, small white fragments dotted the bedspread like grim confetti in a puddle of bile and saliva.

"Jesus—"

"Count them." Eve snapped without looking up, her attention riveted on Beth's ashen face.

"What?" Stone's voice came out strangled, disbelieving.

"The pills," Eve's whisper was fierce, a serrated edge to her words, "count them!" His face twisted with revulsion, Stone began the macabre task, his hands sifting through the mess for the broken remnants of the swallowed pills. His fingers moved with reluctant precision, trying to reconstruct the jigsaw of half-dissolved tablets.

"I don't know if I can piece these back together."

"How many?" Eve's voice was taut with urgency, every second stretching out interminably as she awaited the answer.

"It's hard to tell," Stone shook his head, "they're all in pieces, and half dissolved. I don't know if I've got two halves here or if it's a third of another pill." Frustration etched into his features as he continued to shift the pill fragments around frantically.

"*Cazzo.*" Eve's jaw clenched as she cursed again. Time was slipping away, and with it Beth's fragile grasp on life.

"Do you even know how many she had?" Stone continued sifting through the mess on the bed, his fingers sticky with bile.

"I could guess," Eve moved his fingers lightly across Beth's forehead, wiping away strands of hair that had stuck to her skin from the sweat and water, "I think it was about half full."

"There's nowhere near half a bottle here." Stone wiped his hand on the sheets, leaning back and surveying Beth with a concerned expression that bordered frustration. Jennifer's footsteps pounded against the floor, her heart racing as she entered the chaos of Beth's room. Barnett was just a shadow at her heels, their breaths mingling in short, sharp gasps. Eve, her hands smeared with the evidence of her frantic attempts to save Beth, rose like a barrier before them. She stood between them, a sentinel to protect Jennifer from the gruelling sight in front of her.

"Stay back." She commanded, but Barnett wasn't deterred. He manoeuvred around Eve and dropped to his knees beside the bed, his face a mask of trepidation and resolve.

"What the fuck was she thinking?" He placed a gentle hand on Beth's forehead, looking at the pill fragments scattered on the bed. Stone shifted his gaze between Eve and Jennifer, before settling his eyes on Barnett.

"That's exactly what I said—"

"She wasn't. Force your fingers down her throat and make her throw them up," Eve instructed, her voice steady despite the tremor that ran through her body, "she has more in her stomach that we need to get out." Barnett's nose wrinkled, the disgust evident even through his determination, but his fingers complied, prying open Beth's jaw with a gentleness that belied his reluctance. Beth's body shuddered, another wave of sickness rolling through her. Eve spun on her heel, her eyes locking with Jennifer's. She reached out, gripping Jennifer's hands with an intensity that left no room for doubt.

"Beth," Jennifer's wide eyes darted between Eve and the scene behind her, "what happened?"

"It's okay," Eve said, the lie clear in her eyes but necessary in her voice, "Beth is sick, but we can help her." Jennifer nodded, her own hands trembling within Eve's grasp, the reality of the situation imprinted into every line of her face. Reality set in, and Jennifer shook her head lightly, swallowing the lump that had formed in her throat.

"It's okay, Eve. I'm not stupid, and you don't need to protect me. I know what she's done. Just tell me what to do."

"Go to the infirmary and find Val," Eve said slowly, her words measured as if to calm the storm raging inside them both, "we need something for an overdose." Jennifer's forehead creased, her expression silently begging for understanding.

"What should I ask for?"

"Listen carefully," Eve said, her voice a low whisper as she glanced back at Beth's limp form, "you must be discreet. Find Val and only Val. Ask if they have something, *anything* to treat an overdose. But make sure neither she nor Anne follows you back here. We can't risk raising alarm. Do you understand?" Understanding slowly dawned in Jennifer's eyes - a flicker of apprehension shadowed by the weight of necessity. She hesitated only a moment, her gaze flitting to Beth's convulsing form before steeling with purpose.

"Yes," she released Eve's hands and nodded once, sharply, "I'll ask Val for something for an overdose and make sure no one follows me back here." She turned on her heel, her steps measured and deliberate as she hurried down the hallway, cloaking the urgency that screamed within her to run. Eve's attention snapped back to Beth, whose laboured breaths filled the room with a haunting rhythm.

"Stone, Barnett," she called over her shoulder, urgency bleeding through her composed facade, "we need someone at the door." Stone rose unsteadily, his face pale, a haunted look in his eyes as he confronted the scene before him.

"I can't—" his voice was barely audible, a choked murmur as he stumbled towards the door, "I can't watch this."

"Then stand guard," Eve commanded, the authority in her tone leaving no room for argument, "close it behind you. If anyone asks, say that Beth needs rest and is not to be disturbed under any circumstances." With a curt nod, Stone grasped the doorknob, his hand trembling as he pulled the door shut, the click of the latch resounding like a verdict. Alone now with Beth and Barnett, Eve's facade cracked ever so slightly, allowing a glimpse of the fear beneath, but her resolve remained unshaken.

Jennifer's footsteps echoed against the sterile walls of the sub-basement, her body a vessel for urgency as she forced herself to maintain an even pace. Her instincts screamed at her to sprint, yet the cool logic of Eve's instructions bound her movements to calculated normalcy. Each step was a battle between the adrenaline surging through her veins and the dire need for discretion.

"Jennifer." Austin's voice pierced her focus, causing her to startle slightly. He stood leaning against the wall, his eyes narrow with concern.

"Austin," she breathed slowly, attempting to control the shaking in her voice, "you startled me."

"Have you seen Eve?" His gaze followed her like a hawk tracking its prey, sensing the distress she worked so hard to mask, waiting for a hint in her expression. She met his eyes for a fleeting moment, the raw panic in hers speaking volumes more than words could convey. "I can't talk," she managed to say, the words rushed but quiet, betraying the semblance of calm she projected, "one of the kids is sick and I need something for them." Without waiting for his response, she continued onward, leaving him in the wake of her silent plea for understanding.

"Tell Eve I need to speak to her." Austin called out as he watched her retreat, his gut twisting with the knowledge that Jennifer's presence in the infirmary could only herald trouble. He took a deep breath, trying to quell the unease that settled over him as he considered following her. Instead, he remained stationary, a sentinel wrestling with the choice between intervention and trust. The cool air of the infirmary greeted Jennifer as she stepped inside, the antiseptic scent a stark contrast to the chaos of emotions within her.

"Val?" She called out, her voice steadier than she felt. Anne looked up from her paperwork, a smile fading into a concerned frown as she took in Jennifer's appearance.

"Val's not here," Anne said, tilting her head slightly, curiosity piqued, "she's off this afternoon. Spending some time with Reece in the gardens. What do you need?" Jennifer's heart sank - Val's absence was a complication she hadn't anticipated. She cursed inwardly, realising that improvisation was now essential. The weight of the situation bore down on her, the gravity of Beth's condition a shadow that loomed ever closer, and they couldn't wait for Val to return. Jennifer's fingers trembled as she covertly scanned the infirmary, shelves lined with meticulously labeled bottles and medical apparatus that gleamed under the stark lighting. She took a shallow breath, buying herself precious seconds before her words would betray the urgency that gnawed at her.

"Anne," she began, moistening her chapped lips, "I need, *we* need something, for an overdose." The request hung in the air like a discordant note, heavy with implications. Anne's eyes sharpened, her movements stilling as she processed the plea. Her voice was controlled but carried an undercurrent of authority.

"Jennifer, what's going on?" Anne's steps towards her were measured, each one echoing solemnly in the quiet room.

"I can't say," Jennifer whispered, shaking her head in a silent plea for discretion, "please, I need you to trust me." Before Anne could press further, Austin's silhouette appeared from the corridor and filled the doorway. His presence was unexpected, yet it offered a flicker of hope that he might understand the gravity of their plight.

"An overdose?"

"Austin," Jennifer breathed out, relief and fear mingling in her voice, "please, just help us." Jennifer implored, her eyes brimming with unshed tears as she turned back towards Anne. Austin stepped into the room, closing the gap with a few long strides. He addressed Anne with a graveness that demanded action.

"Give her what she needs." The weight of his words seemed to shift the balance, and Anne hesitated, caught between protocol and the urgency reflected in their eyes. Anne's hands hovered over the array of medications, her resolve unyielding.

"Not until someone tells me what's going on." She insisted, her eyes scanning their faces for the truth. Austin exchanged a weighted glance with Jennifer before stepping forward, his voice sombre.

"I can't be sure, but I'm wagering a guess that Beth—" he paused, swallowing hard, "she might be in trouble." The colour drained from Anne's face as horror carved its way into her features.

"Oh God," she whispered, her professional detachment crumbling, "I'll come with you right now—"

"No," Jennifer's protest cut through the tension like a knife, "you can't. It will cause a scene, and if Abraham finds out—" Her voice faltered, the unspoken consequences hanging in the air.

"Anne, please," Austin's plea was earnest, his hands clasped together as if in prayer, "she'll need something to counter it. Without that, we might lose her."

"Suicide is a sin here," Jennifer added, her voice trembling, "Beth could be punished. We just need to save her life. Quietly." Anne's knuckles blanched as she clenched her fists at her sides, a momentary reflection of the turmoil churning within her. But as quickly as the tension arose, her hands relaxed, opening like flowers to the sun. She whirled around and made for a cabinet, her movements swift and purposeful.

"Take this," Anne said, her voice was firm but laced with urgency as she thrust a small box into Jennifer's shaking hand, "spray it once into one nostril, covering the other nostril so she inhales it." Jennifer, her fingers cold around the box, peered at the label, a question in her eyes.

"What is it?" She asked, the words barely above a whisper.

"Narcan." Anne replied, her gaze never leaving Jennifer's face, ensuring the gravity of the situation was understood.

"Okay." Jennifer nodded, trying to mask her confusion with determination. Anne continued, her instructions falling over each other in haste.

"If she doesn't respond within a few minutes after the first dose, give her a second dose into her other nostril," her hands mimed the action, pressing an invisible vial to an unseen nose, "you can give additional doses every few minutes if necessary until she begins to breathe normally. It's important to continue monitoring her breathing and responsiveness. Do you understand?" The weight of responsibility settled on Jennifer's shoulders, heavy and daunting. She met Anne's gaze, finding a well of resolve deep within herself.

"I understand." She affirmed, gripping the Narcan like a lifeline. Jennifer's fingers tightened around the box as Anne's words echoed in her ears, a solemn testament to the gravity of their situation.

"This is all I have," Anne said, locking eyes with Jennifer, "if this runs out before she starts breathing normally, she needs to be closely monitored for any signs of relapse into respiratory depression, as the effects of the Narcan may wear off before the opioids do." The room seemed to contract around them, the air thickening with tension. Every second counted, and the burden on Jennifer grew heavier with each beat of her racing heart.

"What happens then?" Austin's voice cut through the stillness, his tone edged with apprehension. Anne's expression darkened, a shadow passing over her features as she turned away. She strode across the room to another cupboard, her movements deliberate and laden with purpose. The clatter of bottles and jars punctuated the silence as she searched, finally emerging with a small sachet which she handed to Jennifer.

"Activated charcoal," she explained, "it needs to be mixed with water, and Beth needs to drink it." Jennifer took the sachet, its weight insignificant yet somehow monumental. Anne's instructions were clear, but the challenge they posed was daunting. Getting Beth to drink would be no easy task, but it was one that could not be shirked.

"Understood." Jennifer murmured, clutching the sachet like a talisman against the chaos threatening to engulf them. There was no time for doubt or fear - Beth's life hung in the balance, and Jennifer was determined to tip the scales back in her favour.

"Get her breathing properly first, with this," Anne commanded, her grip on Jennifer's hand firm and unyielding as she raised the Narcan into view, "then sit her up and make her drink the charcoal, and she needs to keep it down. She will want to throw it up, but you need to make her swallow it." Her eyes blazed with a mix of urgency and trust, pressing the sachet of activated charcoal into Jennifer's palm.

"Thank you." Jennifer managed to stammer, her voice barely above a whisper. As she strode towards the doorway, trying to mask the tremble in her steps with forced calmness, Austin reached out to her.

"Wait." He said, his voice low but insistent. He quickly grabbed a towel from a nearby stack, spreading it open with a deft flick of his wrists.

"Thank you." With quick hands, Jennifer wrapped the Narcan and the sachet of charcoal within its folds, disguising them.

"You can't be seen with these." He stated firmly, his eyes locking onto hers for a brief moment, conveying a silent message of solidarity. Jennifer nodded, her lips pressed into a thin line. She understood the stakes all too well. Clutching the makeshift bundle close to her side, she stepped out into the corridor as her heart thudded against her ribs, yet she moved with deliberate ease, her gaze fixed ahead as she vanished into the network of hallways that would lead her back to Beth. Anne's fingers hovered in the air for a mere second before they found their place on Austin's back, light as a butterfly's touch.

His body trembled beneath her hand, the weight of uncertainty pressing down on him like the heavy air before a storm.

"What happened?" She asked, her voice a ghostly whisper in the sterile silence of the infirmary. Austin merely shook his head, the gesture sending his face deeper into his hands.

"I don't know." He murmured, the words muffled by his palms. He seemed to fold inward, an origami man collapsing under the burden of the unknown.

"What did she—"

"The Vicodin," Austin interrupted, removing his face from his hands and looking up at Anne, "she wasn't taking it, she was saving it. She must have—" His voice trailed off, looking past Anne at the wall, then directing his gaze above them, as if trying to see through the floors into the chaos that was unfolding in Beth's bedroom.

"If you knew she was saving the Vicodin, why didn't you take it from her? Or tell someone?" Anne pressed, her face laced with confusion as she wrinkled her forehead.

"It wasn't for this," Austin cried softly, "she wasn't saving it for this."

"Then what was she saving it for?" Anne demanded, her voice changing from the prior curious tone to frustration. Austin looked back at her, considering his options to bring her into the fold. With a deep sigh, he turned to face her properly, weighing the options in front of him while someone he once loved, someone he cared for deeply, was dying upstairs.

In the sanctuary of Beth's room, Jennifer's entrance was marked by the soft thud of fabric on linen as the towel hit the bed. With deft fingers, she unwrapped her bundle and extracted the Narcan with the urgency of a soldier pulling a pin from a grenade. Eve's gaze bore into her, demanding answers that Jennifer didn't have the luxury of providing.

"Did anyone see you?"

"No," Jennifer shook her head softly, her face a mask of stoicism, "I didn't run into anyone on the way back."

"What did Val say?" Eve looked up at her hopefully, her eyes glazed with a sense of purpose and urgency.

"Val wasn't there," Jennifer said, her voice steady despite the chaos churning inside her, "Anne gave this to me."

"I told you to find Val." Eve's frown deepened, her words clipped with frustration.

"She wouldn't have been back until later, possibly tomorrow, and I didn't think we had time to wait." Jennifer countered, moving with purpose. Her hands were firm but gentle as she held one of Beth's nostrils shut, positioning the Narcan with the precision of someone who knew that every second counted. She pressed the plunger, releasing a spray of hope into Beth's unresponsive body. Jennifer's eyes never strayed from Beth's face, watching, willing her shallow breaths to find depth and rhythm once again.

"Well what did Anne say?" Eve pressed, her question directed at Jennifer but her eyes fixed on Beth.

"One spray in her nostril, close the other nostril. Wait. Do it again after a few minutes if nothing changes. Wait." Jennifer repeated Anne's instructions mechanically as if she were reading from a list in her mind.

"What are we waiting for?" Barnett looked between Eve, Beth and Jennifer, but Jennifer remained silent. They waited moments, every second stretching into eternity. Jennifer's hand trembled slightly as she administered the second dose of Narcan into Beth's other nostril. The room was thick with tension, and a heavy silence fell over them, punctuated only by the laboured breaths of the girl on the bed. Eve's eyes were laser-focused, a mix of fear and determination embedded into her features, while Barnett stood somewhat aloof but rooted to the spot, unable to look away. Time stretched agonisingly, until Jennifer leaned in to provide a third dose of the Narcan. Without warning, Beth's chest heaved in a deep inhale that broke the stillness like a thunderclap which startled Jennifer, who jumped back slightly in fright. Beth gasped and coughed, her body convulsing with the effort to expel the toxins that had threatened to claim her life. Eve let out a sigh that seemed to carry the weight of the world, while Jennifer felt a surge of relief so powerful it nearly unmoored her, causing her momentary fright to dissipate. Barnett, still crouched at the other side of the bed, took Beth's hand in his and let out a slow, deep breath. They watched as Beth's erratic breathing smoothed out into a more regular rhythm, each breath a small victory against the shadow of death that had loomed so close.

"Quick, the charcoal." Jennifer urged, her voice cutting through the newfound hope with practical urgency. With hands that betrayed no hint of the anxiety churning within her, Eve snatched up the sachet of activated charcoal and tore it open. She handed it to Jennifer who emptied the dark powder into an awaiting water bottle, her movements brusque as she shook it, creating a murky solution meant to bind any remnants of poison still lurking within Beth's system.

"Help me get her up." Eve commanded, and together with Jennifer and Barnett, they coaxed Beth into a sitting position. Beth groaned, the sound raw and pained, but it was music to their ears. It signalled life where there had been perilous closeness to its absence.

"Here," Jennifer extended her hand, holding out the bottle for Eve to take, "I don't think I can do this part. Anne said she's going to fight against it." Eve took the bottle quickly and swirled it in the air, the black sludge dancing like a tornado within the confines of its plastic casing.

"Easy, Beth, easy." She murmured, her tone a sharp contrast to her earlier command as she sat beside Beth on the bed. With a gentle firmness, Eve brought the lip of the bottle to Beth's mouth and tilted it, allowing the gritty liquid to flow. Beth's reaction was immediate - she gagged at the unfamiliar and unpleasant sensation, her body recoiling instinctively. A spray of black-tinged sludge erupted from her lips, speckling Eve, Jennifer, and Barnett with the grim evidence of the life-saving procedure.

"She needs to keep it down." Jennifer whispered, brushing a damp strand of hair from her forehead, her own skin mottled with droplets of charcoal. There was no room for disgust or discomfort, only the singular focus on Beth's survival, on pulling her back from the precipice upon which she had teetered.

"Keep it down, Beth." Barnett pleaded, his voice taut with urgency as he helped steady Beth's convulsing body. The room was tense, the air thick with desperation and the acrid scent of charcoal. Eve's hands were steady, but her voice betrayed the panic that clawed at her insides.

"*Fucking drink it.*" She barked, her resolve hardening into steel as she tipped the bottle once more, pouring the life-saving sludge between Beth's chapped lips. With a firm press of her hand over Beth's mouth, she compelled her to swallow, her eyes locked onto Beth's, willing her to fight through the discomfort. Beth's throat worked against the viscous fluid, swallowing with difficulty as her consciousness clawed its way back from the clutches of darkness. Her body revolted against the invasion, heaving in protest. She tried to lurch forward, an instinctive escape from the bitter cure.

"She needs to keep it down." Jennifer repeated with more conviction, stepping closer to the bed and holding Beth's legs down.

"Don't you dare." Eve growled, a fierce protectiveness enveloping her. In one swift move, she pushed Beth firmly back against the headboard, her thighs straddling Beth's hips to keep her anchored. Eve's fingers slipped beneath Beth's chin, tilting her head back just enough to open her airway. Without hesitation, she continued to pour the charcoal mixture, a steady stream that carried both redemption and revulsion. Beth instinctively clawed at Eve's hands and the bottle at her mouth, pulling and pushing it away. Barnett reached over Eve, holding Beth's arms down on either side, caught in the crossfire between them. Droplets of charcoal dripped onto his head as he shook his hair, cursing as he struggled to hold down her arms.

"Come on, Beth." Jennifer whispered from the end of the bed, her hands holding Beth's body down helplessly as she watched the battle unfold. Barnett looked on with a grimace, staring at the wall beside them as he craned his neck up to see. The charcoal ebbed and flowed with each of Beth's forced gulps, a dark tide that held the promise of life or the peril of death. It was a dance as old as time, the struggle for survival, played out in the microcosm of this dimly lit room. Beth's body convulsed as she coughed and struggled against the three imposing figures - in her weakened state, Beth could do little to resist them. Despite her best efforts, their determined grip remained unshaken. As Eve held her head back, thick droplets of black sludge shot past her hands, splattering onto both of their faces and staining the pristine white sheets below. The putrid smell of the substance filled the air, making Eve gag as she fought to maintain her hold on Beth. Slowly, the black ooze dripped down Beth's chin, leaving a trail of dark stains in its wake. Eve's fingers, firm and unyielding, clamped Beth's mouth shut, the lines of her face taut with determination. Her other hand steadied the empty bottle that had once been full of life-saving charcoal slurry. She maintained her position astride Beth, a guardian against the abyss, as she watched for signs of life to steady in those feverish eyes.

"Swallow." Eve commanded steadily, her voice softened now to a coaxing murmur, though her grip did not wane. Beth's throat constricted and relaxed in response, betraying a cough that rattled through her frame, spattering more drops of black into the air. The room was silent save for the sound of struggle and survival, as Beth fought against the invasive cure with every laboured breath. Gradually, the spasms subsided, the gagging ceased, and Beth's breathing found a rhythm more akin to normalcy. It was only then that Eve lessened her hold, allowing Beth's head to rest back against the pillows. Beth's eyelids fluttered open, revealing the cloudy depths of confusion before focusing on Eve's shadowed face looming above her.

"Ow." She managed, her voice a hoarse whisper laden with pain and betrayal. Eve's gaze never faltered, her hands still framing Beth's face, the residual powder leaving a ghostly imprint on her skin.

"What the fuck are you doing?" Eve's words were a hiss, laced with a cocktail of anger and fear. There was no hiding the tremor that betrayed the steel in her voice, a tremor born from the desperate terror of nearly losing someone under her watch. To the side, Jennifer stood frozen, her own visage a mask of shock and distress.

The chaos had splashed her with the dark remnants of their frantic ministrations, tears carving clean paths down her cheeks through the grime. Each sob that escaped her was a testament to the room's collective relief and horror. Barnett, positioned opposite to Jennifer, was equally marked by the ordeal, his expression hollow as he tried to process the scene unfolding before him. His gaze lingered on Eve, a silent question in his stare, as if seeking some form of understanding in the madness they had just endured. In that tense tableau, each of them was bound by a singular, unspoken vow - to keep Beth tethered to this world, whatever the cost.

"Water." Beth coughed as more black dots flew through the air and landed on Eve's face. She didn't falter, didn't flinch, but instead stared at Beth with a gaze that could have turned her to stone.

"Get more water from my room." Eve commanded, her tone brooking no argument as she met Jennifer's watery eyes. Jennifer nodded, hastily wiping her cheeks with the back of her hand before scurrying out the door. Eve slowly removed herself from straddling Beth, sliding off the edge of the bed and straightening her posture. Barnett stood, staring at the scene before them with an expression of disbelief at what they had just witnessed.

"Will she be okay?"

"I hope so. Help me with these." She gestured towards the soiled linens and Beth's stained clothing, her words clipped and urgent. Barnett's voice was hesitant, his posture stiff with uncertainty.

"Shouldn't we wait for Jennifer?"

"No time. We clean this up now," Eve insisted, her eyes darting to the door, the weight of potential discovery pressing down on her, "someone could come any minute." Together, they moved Beth, a delicate shell of herself, to the tiled floor in the adjacent bathroom. Her body slouched against the cool wall, her body limp but alive, shivering from the cold tiles.

'"She looks uncomfortable."

"She can deal with it," Eve's hands were steady as she peeled the damp shirt away from Beth's fragile frame, her movements efficient despite the tremor that threatened to uncoil within her, "start stripping the bed." She instructed Barnett, who complied, peeling back the tainted sheets with a grimace. The room was filled with the rustle of fabric and the faint scent of charcoal and sickness. As if on cue, Jennifer burst back into the room, arms laden with bottles of water. Her face a portrait of silent concern as she caught sight of Eve.

"What will you do about your water allotment? How can you explain needing more?"

"Later," Eve said sharply, snatching a bottle and pouring its contents onto a cloth, "right now, we keep Beth safe. Everything else is just noise." Her gaze never left Beth, her protective instincts a fierce guardian against the chaos threatening to break through their makeshift sanctuary. Jennifer's hands were gentle yet hurried as she dabbed at the dark smudges on Beth's skin. The charcoal had spread like a shadow across her pale face, clinging to the fine lines of worry that had settled there long before the day's crisis. Beside her, Barnett worked with a more mechanical efficiency, scooping up the soiled sheets and tossing them into a heap on the floor.

"There should be more sheets in her cupboard." Jennifer said without looking up from her task. His eyes skirted over the white dress that had been hanging on the armoire door, thankfully covered in a clear plastic clothing protector. With a deft flick, he sent it sailing clear across the room.

"Careful," Eve's voice cut through the tense silence, her sharp gaze following the trajectory of the dress, "don't get charcoal on that."

"Sorry." He shrugged, an easy, dismissive gesture that belied the gravity of their situation.

"We can't find a replacement if it gets ruined." She watched him for a moment longer, ensuring her command had registered despite his nonchalance.

"What excuse would we give Abraham if she turned up in a dress speckled with black dots? It's not like we can run to the store for another one," Jennifer's tone changed, almost in anger, as she continued to wash Beth's skin, "might as well just confess now and save ourselves the trouble of cleaning up."

"Jennifer's right. Go to my room next door and wash off in the bathroom before you change the sheets," Eve said, her tone brooking no argument, "we can't afford to leave any trace behind." With a nod that was almost imperceptible, Barnett picked up a water bottle and disappeared into the hallway. The sound of trickling water was a quiet reminder of the precious resource they were now depleting with abandon. In the wake of his departure, Jennifer and Eve exchanged a glance, a silent conversation passing between them. Their expressions mingled fear with resolve, each knowing the stakes if they failed to erase every sign of the near catastrophe that had unfolded within these walls. Hands still trembling slightly from adrenaline, they returned to their task, peeling off their own clothes stained with the remnants of their frantic life-saving efforts. They moved in sync, stripping away the evidence, their movements as synchronised as their shared determination to protect Beth, and themselves, from any further harm.

CHAPTER 11

Shadows danced across the walls of the den - a perfect space to monitor communication and movement, an almost unnoticed space only accessible by a small door within the library - as Abraham leaned back in his chair, fingers interwoven behind his head. The glow from numerous screens cast an artificial blue tint on Adam's focused expression. A bank of radios and communication equipment hummed softly in the background, a symphony of static and the occasional crackle of voices that broke through the silence.

"Kingsport's been pretty chatty today," Adam remarked, his eyes scanning over a log of recent transmissions, "it's just about supply runs though. Nothing substantial." He turned to look at Abraham, his hand resting idly on a radio dial. Abraham's gaze lingered on Adam for a moment, reading the unspoken concern in his creased forehead. He rose from his seat, pacing with deliberate steps around the cramped space filled with maps and scattered papers. The question hung in the air, palpable and heavy.

"Have they mentioned any sort of hierarchy? Who their leader may be?" Abraham's voice had a way of filling a room, even one as modest as this den.

"No word on who calls the shots or how they manage things," Adam shook his head, a small gesture that conveyed both frustration and curiosity, "silence on that front." He adjusted the volume on the radio as if expecting it to suddenly reveal Kingsport's secrets. Abraham stopped pacing and stood by the window, staring out into the twilight that wrapped around their stronghold. His mind worked like a skilled weaver, threads of possibility intertwining into a tapestry of strategy and foresight.

"Maybe we need to reach out first." He finally said, turning from the window to face Adam. There was a resolve in his posture, a readiness to bridge gaps and forge bonds that might ensure their mutual survival. Adam looked up, caught off guard.

"What do you mean?"

"Neighbours," Abraham mused, tracing a line on a map that depicted the distance between them and Kingsport, "if we're to share this new world, it's only right we try to be friends. Or at the very least, understand each other." His voice held a note of diplomacy, a belief that connections could be just as vital as fortifications in the times ahead.

"Friends." Adam echoed, a hint of skepticism in his voice tempered by the respect he held for Abraham's judgment. He knew well that alliances were delicate, but also that Abraham had a knack for seeing potential where others saw only peril.

"Indeed," Abraham affirmed, his decision etched into the set of his jaw, "we'll start with an open hand, not a clenched fist." He turned away from the map, ready to plan their next move in a world where every gesture mattered. Abraham leaned against the window sill, stroking his beard thoughtfully as he considered their next steps. The den's walls, lined with static-filled monitors and maps marked with territories and notes, felt suffocatingly close after hours of strategizing. Adam's laugh was dry, a sound that bounced off the dense bookshelves and sombre paraphernalia of their makeshift command centre.

"Are you talking about making friends, or are we going to end up *persuading* them to join us?"

"Persuasion implies I've given them no choice," Abraham replied, his gaze steady, "I haven't done that, not once."

"Ben and Tyler might disagree," Adam countered, leaning against a sturdy oak desk cluttered with radio equipment, "their abduction wasn't exactly voluntary. Austin, Chase, and the others, they followed because they had to, not out of some newfound loyalty to you." Abraham's expression didn't waver, but there was a flicker, a momentary dimming behind his eyes.

"Fort Irwin was an option for them. They chose to come here, to see their friends." He said firmly, the words more of a mantra than a statement. Adam shook his head, strands of hair falling into his eyes before he pushed them back impatiently.

"Sure, they came," he conceded with a reluctant shrug, "but let's not kid ourselves about why, brother." Silence settled between them for a moment, a quiet acknowledgment of the complexity of their situation.

"Like I said," Abraham finally spoke, "they had a choice."

"Not a fair one," Adam smiled, "and Kingsport doesn't seem interested in power plays. So far, they're just surviving like the rest of us."

"Which is precisely why we should learn if they have a place in this new world alongside us." Abraham stood straight, his shadow stretching across the room as the sun dipped behind the horizon outside.

"Alongside us, or with us?"

"We'll figure out where they stand," Abraham interjected, "before someone else decides for them." He looked at Adam, his face set in determination, hinting at the gravity of their responsibility. It wasn't just about survival - it was about shaping the future, one alliance at a time. Adam's hand hovered over the radio, the static hiss a low whisper in the den.

"You want to try reaching out to them?" He glanced at Abraham, a question unspoken yet evident in his features. Abraham's gaze lingered on the radio as if weighing its potential against unseen risks. Finally, he shook his head, the movement decisive. He turned to Adam, his eyes reflecting a strategic calculation.

"No," he said slowly, "it might be time for something more *personal*. Aaron has been desperate for new ground. We'll send him, let them see we're about more than just words crackling through the air."

"An envoy," Adam nodded, setting the radio down with care, "face to face has weight in times like these."

"Exactly." Abraham agreed, his voice steady and assured.

In the Oak Sitting Room, the children's makeshift play area, Jennifer sat detached from the cheerful chaos around her. Her eyes were distant, lost in thought while the children's laughter echoed off the walls, their small hands busy with toys and games. The door swung open abruptly, disrupting the cadence of play. Austin stepped through the threshold, balancing a tray laden with bowls and cups, the aroma of stewed vegetables preceding him. The children paid him no mind, engrossed in their imaginary worlds. Jennifer's focus snapped back to the present, and she gestured towards an empty table on the far side of the room.

"How did you manage to get up here with that?" Her voice was soft, almost disinterested, yet tinged with a hint of curiosity.

"Everyone else was busy," Austin replied, his tone casual but his eyes scanning the room as he navigated through the sea of scattered toys to set the tray down where Jennifer had indicated, "so I offered to bring lunch up for the kids." Austin set the tray on the table with a clatter that went unnoticed by the children, absorbed in their play.

"How convenient." Jennifer's gaze followed him, her expression unreadable as she ignored the vibrant energy of the room.

"Got past the guards by saying Hannah sent me," Austin confessed with a half-shrug, as if it were nothing more than daily mischief, "told them the others were tied up and couldn't make it."

"And they believed you?" Jennifer raised an eyebrow, mildly impressed despite herself.

"Why wouldn't they?" Austin's lips quirked into a fleeting smirk, quickly replaced by a solemnity that matched the weight of the air between them. As he spoke, Jennifer began distributing the food, her movements mechanical but efficient. She handed out bowls of stew to each child, pausing only briefly to ensure they had utensils.

"You want to know what happened?"

"I don't want to know what happened. I just want to know how she is." Austin ventured, leaning against the wall, his arms crossed, eyes fixating on Jennifer for any hint of the situation's gravity.

"Alive." She responded curtly, hands steady as she poured water into cups with practiced precision. The word hung heavily between them, a stark contrast to the innocence and blissful ignorance enveloping the children. The little ones continued their games, laughter punctuating the sombre conversation. They remained oblivious to the undercurrents of concern and intrigue that ebbed and flowed around them, their joy unfettered by the complexities looming over their guardians' heads. Austin's gaze lingered on

Jennifer, noting the tension that seemed to radiate from her. Curiosity took over, his face dropping as he tensed his body.

"What happened?" He inquired, his voice low, almost cautious. Jennifer met his eyes and for a moment, it was as if the din of the children's play faded into the background.

"I thought you didn't want to know—"

"I lied," he lifted his gaze, his eyes meeting hers with resolve, "if I can pretend that I don't care then maybe I'll trick myself into believing it."

"It was horrific." She said blankly, the words seeming to leave a bitter taste in her mouth.

"Horrific *how*?" Austin pressed, edging closer, his concern drawing his brows together.

"She rejected the charcoal, as Anne said she would, and it was pretty violent," Jennifer's voice was steady, but her hands trembled as she set down an empty water pitcher, "Eve had to hold her down, force her to drink. You didn't see her, Austin. The desperation, the—"

"I should let Ben know that she's been sick," he interrupted her, his gaze distant, "but that she's okay, or he'll start asking questions why she isn't walking around the grounds."

"Is that wise?"

"He was there when Eve took off to check on Beth. He's already worried. I don't want his emotions to get the better of him and cause a scene. He just needs to know that she's okay." He cut across her narrative with a nod, his expression grim. Jennifer paused, a frown creasing her forehead as she regarded him.

"But should we worry? Is this the right thing? Beth's mind is getting weaker, slipping away—"

"How many pills are left?" Austin's response came not in words of comfort but in practicality, his focus narrowing. The question hung in the air, jarring against the gravity of their conversation. Jennifer gave him a questioning look, her mind grappling with the shift from life and death to counting capsules.

"I don't know—"

"The pills, Jennifer," Austin urged, his tone firm, "how many?" She hesitated, then sighed, the weight of their secret mission pressing down upon her.

"Enough," she whispered, turning away to hide the conflict etched into her features, "she didn't take them all, and we salvaged some fragments from her vomit." Jennifer's fingers clenched into fists at her sides, the fabric of her shirt bunching under the force of her grip.

"Good—"

"Is that all you care about?" She spat suddenly, incredulity painting her voice as she faced Austin. Her chest heaved with more than just the exertion of her earlier task - it was laden with the weight of unspoken fears and moral quandaries. Austin seemed confused by the question, focusing on Jennifer's pained expression as if he'd find the answers within.

"Is what all I care about?"

"Enough Vicodin to kill Abraham?" She continued, her voice rising despite the children playing obliviously in the corner. The words echoed like a sinister whisper through the room, carrying the weight of their grim implications.

"Jennifer, keep your voice down—"

"Austin, is that *all* you care about?" Jennifer's eyes blazed with a furious fire as she repeated herself, her resolve hardening. She took a step towards the door, her movements rigid with anger.

"Jennifer—"

"Beth tried to kill herself, and you're worried that she didn't leave enough pills behind to kill Abraham?"

"Not to kill," Austin corrected quickly, his eyes darting towards the door as if to ensure their conspiracy remained within these walls, "just enough to knock him out." His hands were steady, betraying none of the tension that gripped his voice.

"I think so." She snapped back, her tone biting. The air between them crackled with the dangerous dance of their intentions, a delicate balance between desperation and duty.

"I care about her, you know," he shifted on his feet uncomfortably, "I left her on that island and took my chance to escape, and she's made me feel guilty about that ever since. Now, I need to protect her, I *want* to protect her. But this isn't about her, or me, or you. It's about *everyone* else here. So don't come at me thinking that I don't care. I care *too* much, so much it hurts, so sometimes I need to pretend that I don't, sometimes I need to care about something else, or I'm gonna fucking break." The silence that filled the air was thin, and even the sound of the children playing had quietened down. They sensed the tension and the anger that had filled the space. Jennifer looked around the room, forcing a smile at the children before closing the space between herself and Austin.

"What you're doing to her, this game we're playing, caused her to try and kill herself. Think about that the next time you're contemplating your own existential crisis. Now *leave*." She commanded, her voice barely above a whisper now but no less formidable. It was an order, delivered with an authority that brooked no argument. Austin's nod came slowly, an acknowledgment of the rift that had formed between them. His footsteps were soft against the wooden floor as he edged back, his hand reaching for the doorknob.

"I'm thinking of everyone." He said, the apology in his voice sincere but failing to bridge the chasm of their divided loyalties. Jennifer remained silent, her gaze fixed on a point beyond him, beyond the room and its heavy atmosphere. With a gesture towards the open door, she dismissed him without words, her stance unyielding. He sighed, a sound that carried the weight of their shared burdens, before slipping out into the dim corridor. The door closed with a soft click, leaving Jennifer alone with the ghosts of their conversation and the uneasy quiet that followed.

Beth's feet tread the soft earth on the path to Bass Pond, her steps tentative yet drawn forward by an invisible thread of destiny. She was cocooned in a world awash with purity - the throng of friends flanking her passage were adorned in garments as white as the first snowfall of winter. Their faces, serene canvases of acceptance and communal spirit, watched her approach the water's edge. Mary emerged from the congregation, extending a white rose towards Beth with a smile that radiated warmth, a silent symbol of peace and new beginnings. The bloom felt delicate and alive in Beth's grasp, its petals softly brushing against her palm. Eve emerged from the crowd on the other side of the path, her touch was gentle as she took Beth's hand, leading her with unspoken encouragement through the gathering towards the pond where Abraham awaited. His form was a steadfast presence in the liquid expanse, arms outstretched in welcome, his stance both an invitation and a promise. The water glimmered beneath the sun's golden rays, like a field of diamonds dancing across the surface. Its crystal clear depths revealed a world of swirling colours and shimmering plants. The air was filled with the fresh, crisp aroma of water, carrying hints of earth throughout. It rippled with each gentle breeze, creating a symphony of soft splashes and tinkling melodies. The sound of nature's orchestra echoed in her ears, a soothing lullaby that beckoned her to continue on her path. It was a mirror, reflecting the soft hues of the setting sun and the silhouettes of the trees that lined its edge. It felt cool and inviting, a place of solace and release, and it beckoned to Beth with an irresistible pull. An ever-moving canvas of life, an aqueous universe that held within its depths an infinite expanse of secrets and mysteries, an ever-changing landscape that reflected the skies above in its shimmering surface. As Beth approached its edge, she felt as though she was stepping into a new world, one where anything was possible, where the weight of the past was gently washed away by each gentle ripple. The cool embrace of the water lapped at Beth's ankles, sending ripples through the tranquility of Bass Pond as she stepped forward. In that moment, surrounded by the stillness of nature, she turned her gaze to the shore. There stood Ben and Austin, their smiles beacons of solidarity amidst the sea of white. Each held a white rose, twin sentinels of the profound journey they all shared. Anne and Julia stood on either side of them, their hands clasping the forearms of each man, their faces passive and their eyes empty. Beth faced Abraham again, reading in his gaze the depth of their shared future together. He reached for her with hands that spoke of leadership and care, steadying her as she navigated the unfamiliar terrain beneath the surface. When his fingers brushed her shoulders, it was with the reverence one might show a rare treasure. As Abraham drew her closer, Beth embraced the vulnerability of the moment, allowing the distance between them to dissolve into the kiss that followed. It was a connection forged not only in the flesh but in the meeting of souls, an acknowledgment of their intertwined fates. Her lips parted seamlessly, welcoming the intimacy of the gesture, a silent dance that needed no music but the rhythm of their beating hearts. Abraham's gaze then traversed the crowd, sharing an unspoken triumph with those who had gathered, a leader basking in the unity of his flock. Beth also looked upon the faces of her companions, her eyes catching Val and Reece's joined hands, each holding the purity of a white rose. They stood together, a testament to the strength found in partnership, each couple within the multitude reflecting pieces of the same whole. In this tableau of silence, every glance was a conversation, every touch a declaration, and every rose a vow to the future they would cultivate together. Beth's gaze lingered on the gathered crowd, their white attire stark against the verdant backdrop of Bass Pond. Each face was a familiar story, a tapestry of survival and hope. Abraham's hand, warm against her cool flesh, pressed gently yet firmly onto her chest. A silent cue beckoning her to trust in the ritual. She acquiesced, bending her knees and letting the water rise to cradle her chin. The world above the surface, with its chorus of birdsong and rustling leaves, began to fade as she granted herself to the embrace of the water. Her eyes clung to her friends for a moment longer, etching their images into memory. Then, she closed her eyes and surrendered to the depths. The transition was serene, a descent into tranquility, until the water's caress turned insistent. Unseen hands gripped her, not with the tenderness she had known from Abraham, but with an urgency that spoke of darker intentions. Panic fluttered in her chest as she fought against the force, yearning for air and light. Her eyes snapped open, vision blurred by the ripples on the water's surface above. Through the veil, a figure materialised above her - Marcus, his presence an aberration in this sanctified scene. His hands, once laid upon her in forced intimacy, now sought to push her deeper into the aqueous abyss. No sound escaped her, just bubbles reaching skyward, bearing mute witness to the struggle below. She grappled against Marcus' spectral form, a phantom adversary in a world where silence reigned supreme. Beth's heart thundered in the silent watery chamber as her lids snapped shut, a scream rising within her - a soundless, desperate plea. The pressure around her intensified, and when she dared to look again, Victor's face hovered before her, contorted by the liquid curtain between them. His hands, once used for harm to threaten but never kill, now seemed like iron vices fastened onto her with homicidal intent. A shiver of disbelief coursed through her as she clamped her eyes closed once more, shaking her head in a futile attempt to dismiss the nightmare. When her gaze reopened to the murky world, the visage that confronted her had shifted. It was Luis, his expression unreadable, pressing down on her with a force that betrayed their shared past. Her limbs flailed, but each movement was a languid battle against the water's resistance. As she struggled against Luis' grip, her vision wavered, and his features morphed once more. Austin's face loomed over her, eyes devoid of the camaraderie they once held. Confusion entwined with dread as she questioned why Austin would be the means to her end. She ceased her thrashing, stilled by the haunting question. Her body surrendered to the stillness of the deep, her breath suspended in time. In this eerie calm, the water distorted reality again, presenting Ben's face staring down at her with an emotion that chilled her to the core. His eyes bore into hers with hate, disgust - an accusation and a sentence in one. Beth paused, her body still, in a small attempt to bring her hand to Ben's face with acceptance at his attempt to end her life. If Ben wanted her dead, then she must have done something to deserve it. Despite her brief moment of clarity, the betrayal seared her soul, and in that moment of despair the water's surface rippled anew. For a brief moment, she saw her own reflection staring back at her, mirroring her expression. The figure above her mirrored every movement, every tilt of the head, even her scrutinizing gaze. The metaphor was not lost on her - there was no one on earth who wanted her dead more than herself. She lifted her hand to touch the reflection, and the reflection did the same, slowly moving until their fingers touched. The figure turned dark, her clothes morphing from the white christening dress into the dark grey uniform of oppression that she was forced to wear on Alcatraz Island. The reflection smirked, no longer mirroring her own serene expression, but now masked with darkness and malice. Beth took in a deep breath, but only water filled her lungs as she struggled to breathe. Eve's face appeared, serene amidst the chaos, her hands reaching with purpose. A lifeline in the tumult, Eve's grasp was firm, pulling Beth free from the aquatic depths and the phantoms that dwelled beneath. Gasping for the breath that had so cruelly been denied to her in the drowning depths of her dreams, Beth's body jerked upright. Her lungs ached as they expanded, greedily pulling in the air that filled the dimly lit room. She clutched at Eve, who was perched beside her on the bed, her hands steady on Beth's shaking shoulders. Her coughing subsided, leaving behind an uncomfortable rawness in her throat. Her fingers trembled as they moved to touch the tender skin, the phantom sensation of water still lingering, inducing a fresh wave of panic-stricken breaths. Eve's voice pierced the silence, a mantra repeating Beth's name with urgent softness.

"Beth, it's okay, you're safe." Eve murmured, her tone firm yet soothing. Beth's eyes, wide with the horror of her recent ordeal, searched Eve's face for the truth of those words. But the spectre of death that had pursued her beneath the waves clung stubbornly to her senses.

"They want me dead," she sobbed, the words spilling out amidst her tears, "they all want me dead." The fear that enveloped her was a thick cloak, heavy and suffocating. Eve's response was immediate and protective - she gently pushed Beth aside to make room for herself, then climbed into the bed. With movements both tender and decisive, she gathered Beth into her arms, wrapping her in an embrace that served as a barricade against the horrors of the night. The warmth from Eve's body seeped into Beth's chilled limbs, her presence a solid reassurance against the chimeras of Beth's subconscious. In Eve's hold, there was no murky water or distorted faces, only the grounding reality of another person's heartbeat echoing against her own. Beth's frame heaved with each sob that tore through her, the fabric of Eve's shirt growing damp as her tears soaked into it. Eve's arms formed a cocoon around her, strong and unyielding, a sanctuary in the tumultuous remnants of Beth's nightmare.

"Shh, it's okay," Eve whispered again, stroking Beth's hair with a rhythmic gentleness that seemed to brush away the terror moment by moment, "it was just a dream. You're here with me." The door creaked softly, and Barnett's concerned face appeared in the dim light, his voice barely above a whisper.

"Is everything okay?"

"Bad dream," Eve assured him without looking up, her attention fixed on the trembling woman in her embrace, "she's fine." Barnett held their gaze for a heartbeat longer before nodding.

"Shout out if you need anything." His silhouette retreated as the door closed with a quiet click, leaving them once more in the privacy of their shared sorrow. As time threaded on, Beth's sobs began to subside into shuddering breaths, her body exhausted from the onslaught of fear and grief. She clung to Eve, the solidity of the other woman's presence anchoring her to the present. She felt the nightmares recede like the tide, leaving behind the safety of the shore. Eve's hand never ceased its comforting motion, tracing circles upon Beth's back. Finally, when Beth's cries had ebbed into silence, Eve dared to whisper the question that had been weighing on her heart.

"Beth, what were you thinking taking all those pills?" The query hung between them, delicate as gossamer yet heavy with unspoken concern. Beth's grip on Eve tightened, a silent plea for understanding, for absolution from the choices that had led her to this fragile state. Her eyes remained closed, unable to meet the gaze of her caretaker, her confidante, too ashamed to confront the vulnerability laid bare between them. Beth's fingers still clung to the fabric of Eve's shirt, her tears finally subsiding into damp tracks on her cheeks. The terror that had gripped her heart was now just a pulsing echo, held at bay by the warmth enveloping her.

"I wanted it to stop," Beth murmured, her voice a hoarse whisper against the quietude of the room, "the pain, the memories, Abraham's expectations, everyone else's expectations. I wanted to silence it all." Eve's arms remained steadfast around her, a lifeline in the storm that had raged within Beth.

"You're going to be okay." Eve assured her with gentle conviction. Her hand continued its soothing path along Beth's back, a balm to the raw edges of her spirit.

"How can you be so sure?" Beth asked, lifting her gaze to meet Eve's. There was a search for something unspoken in the depths of Eve's eyes, a hope for the kind of certainty that seemed to elude

Beth. Eve's lips curved into a light, knowing laugh, a soft sound that seemed out of place in the gravity of their situation yet perfectly fitting as a counterpoint to despair.

"Because I have faith." She said simply.

"Faith," Beth echoed, the word feeling foreign on her tongue, "I wish I could believe like you do."

"It didn't come naturally to me," Eve confessed, her own gaze becoming distant, as if traveling back through time, "I grew up in Italy, under the roof of very strict, religious parents." A shadow passed over her face, a remnant of old scars borne from a past that had demanded conformity.

"Religious?" Beth prompted, curiosity piqued despite the heaviness that lingered within her.

"*Si*," Eve's accent thickened with the memory, "my parents, they were *uncompromising*. But my *nonna*, she was different. She understood me better than they ever did." A fondness flickered across Eve's features, a testament to bonds that transcended judgment. Beth leaned in closer, drawn to the story unfolding before her.

"Understood how?"

"When they found me, in the arms of another woman, they couldn't accept it. My parents cast me out, like I was nothing more than a sinner undeserving of their love." The pain was there, in the slight tremble of Eve's voice, but it was tempered by the resilience that had carried her forward.

"And your *nonna*?" Beth pressed gently, sensing there was more to Eve's tale of faith regained. Eve's smile returned, softer this time.

"She took me in without a second thought. Her love never wavered, even when the rest of the world seemed ready to turn its back on me." In those words, Beth heard the strength that had shaped the woman beside her, a strength she found herself yearning to share.

"Love like that," Beth whispered, "it must have been a blessing."

"It was," Eve agreed, her eyes meeting Beth's once more, "and still is." She pulled Beth closer, a silent promise that no matter what darkness might try to claim her, she would not face it alone. Eve brushed a loose strand of hair from Beth's forehead, her touch gentle as the quiet night.

"So what happened?"

"*Nonna*," she said, the Italian endearment warming her voice, "she gave me sanctuary when my own parents wouldn't. She loved me, sins and all. Even when I was angry at God, convinced He'd turned His back on me for being gay, she stood by me." Her eyes held a distant glimmer, reflecting a love that had defied the harsh judgments of others. A tear traced Eve's cheek, but her voice remained steady, a testament to an inner peace hard-won over years of turmoil. Beth's eyes searched Eve's, seeking the source of her strength.

"She helped you find your faith again?" She asked, her own voice tinged with a longing for such unwavering support. Eve nodded, her gaze lifting as if seeing past the room's confining walls.

"I found God on my own terms, and realised that He loves all His children, without exception." Her conviction rang clear, leaving an echo of hope in the stillness between them.

"Even those who've sinned?" Beth's voice was small, vulnerable, as if fearing the answer. For a long moment, Eve said nothing. Instead, she wrapped her arms around Beth, pulling her into an embrace that spoke volumes more than words ever could. In the safety of Eve's hold, Beth felt a whisper of the faith that seemed to imbue every fibre of Eve's being - a faith that perhaps one day, she too might come to know.

"Yes, Beth. Even those who have sinned."

"Thank you," Beth's breath was a warm whisper against the curve of Eve's neck, her words muffled but sincere, "for everything." The air between them seemed to shimmer with an intensity that went beyond gratitude. Eve's response was not in words but in a tender gesture as she tilted her head, brushing her nose gently against Beth's. The space between them charged with a palpable energy, and Beth felt pulled by an unseen force, lifting her face to meet Eve's lips with a soft peck, which quickly deepened into a fervent kiss. As their lips moved together, Eve's hands found their way to the hem of Beth's shirt, carefully lifting it, skimming lightly over the sensitive skin of Beth's torso. Her touch was a balm, soothing the raw edges of Beth's frayed emotions, drawing her even closer. Beth responded instinctively, shifting her body towards Eve, feeling the rush of connection as they repositioned themselves. Now side by side, the two lay mirrored, gazes locked in silent conversation. Eve's eyes held a depth of understanding, a promise of solace that Beth found herself desperately wanting to believe in. Beth's fingertips traced the line of Eve's jaw, a path charged with electricity, as she pulled Eve closer by the nape of her neck. She wanted this. She didn't know if it would fix anything, but it was her decision to make. She was about to give away her entire self to a marriage she had no desire to be a part of. This act of desperation could very well be the last time she had any autonomy over her own decisions.

"Are you sure?" Eve pressed, her voice a light whisper in the dark atmosphere.

"Yes—"

"You're very vulnerable right now, Beth. I don't want to take advantage—"

"Eve," Beth interrupted, taking in a slow breath as the adrenaline coursed through her, "I'm about to hand myself over to a monster, and everything I do will be watched and scrutinised by everyone around me. Let me make one more decision for myself." Eve nodded slowly, bringing her lips to Beth's, closing the gap between them. Their kiss deepened, a dance of desperation and desire, each movement more insistent than the last. Eve's breath hitched, a shallow catch of air that vibrated between them as Beth's hand continued its descent, mapping the contours of Eve's body over the fabric of her clothing, venturing to the edge of her underwear. The world beyond their cocoon of intimacy fell away as Beth's fingers slipped beneath the elastic, touching Eve with a boldness fuelled by raw emotion. Eve's soft moan broke through the silence, a sound both vulnerable and wanting. Her own hands weren't idle - they glided down Beth's sides, taking with them any barriers as she eased Beth's underwear down her hips. In that moment, they were each other's anchor in the storm that raged within. As they pushed into one another, there was a sense of homecoming, a fierce affirmation of life amidst the chaos that surrounded them. Each touch, each breath shared, was an act of defiance, a silent vow that even in the darkest times, they would find light in each other. Beth's soft moan was muffled as Eve's hand gently covered her mouth, the world narrowing to the singular sensation of their urgent connection. The intensity in Beth's eyes flared as she gripped Eve's arm, pulling her into a fervent kiss that spoke volumes beyond words. Heat radiated from where they touched, a silent symphony of need and affection. Eve's forehead came to rest against Beth's, their breaths mingling, ragged and quick. There was an unspoken understanding between them, a shared rhythm that guided their movements as they continued to explore each other with a passionate urgency. They moved together, a perfect synchrony born of raw emotion and instinct. The crescendo of their shared pleasure approached, inevitable and exquisite. They clung to each other as if nothing else existed, no past regrets or future fears, just the present moment encapsulating everything they were and all they needed. A silent gasp escaped them as they reached the peak of their passion almost simultaneously, waves of release crashing over them, leaving them breathless and entwined. In the aftermath, they lay still, foreheads pressed together, the exchange of soft kisses punctuating the silence. It was a tender contrast to the storm of sensation that had just passed, a quiet affirmation of the bond they shared. In this space, in this time, they found solace in each other's arms, a refuge from the turmoil that awaited beyond the sanctuary of their embrace.

CHAPTER 12

Ben's boots echoed in the narrow sub-basement corridor, the rhythm of his steps syncing with the distant clatter of pots and the muted hum of conversation trickling down from the rooms above. His brows were drawn, as if bracing for bad news, his eyes darting around like they expected something to go wrong. Each turn in his relentless pacing marked a silent testament to the turmoil within. A week had crawled by since Beth's desperate act, and while whispers assured her safety, they offered no solace to Ben, who felt marooned on an island of uncertainty. The walls, lined with pipes and fading posters of a world long gone, seemed to close in around him with each pass, amplifying the sense of isolation that gnawed at his insides. He stopped momentarily, pressing a hand against the cold concrete, absorbing the vibrations of life above - life that continued unabated, ignorant of the shadow that lingered in his heart. With a deep breath that did little to steady his nerves, Ben pushed away from the wall and made his way up the musty stairwell. The transition from the gloom of the sub-basement to the sunlit upper floors was jarring, but he welcomed the change as a necessary step towards confronting his own helplessness. Reaching the top, he paused before the heavy oak door of the library. His fingers curled into a fist, hesitating as he caught the eye of the guard stationed there, a severe-looking man whose presence was as unfamiliar to Ben as his stoic expression.

"Can I speak with Abraham?" Ben asked, his voice steadier than he felt. The guard sized him up with a scrutinising gaze before slipping through the door without a word. Ben's heart hammered against his ribcage as he waited, the silence punctuated only by the steady ticking of a clock somewhere down the hall. Seconds stretched into minutes, and just as doubt began to creep into his mind, the door creaked open once more.

"Abraham will see you now." The guard announced, stepping aside to allow Ben passage. With a nod of acknowledgment, Ben crossed the threshold, the weight of his request heavy on his shoulders as he plunged into the lion's den. Ben cleared his throat, standing before Abraham with a mix of resolve and trepidation.

"Could we speak alone?" He ventured, glancing back towards the guard who remained in the library. Abraham, seated behind a mahogany desk piled with papers and open ledgers, peered up from his work and gave a slight nod. Ben took a step forward, only to be halted by the guard's firm hand on his chest. Misinterpreting Abraham's gesture, Ben was caught off guard as the guard's hands moved methodically over him, patting down his limbs with practiced efficiency. The brusque invasion of space left Ben's skin crawling. Still, he remained motionless, his eyes locked on Abraham, who watched the procedure with dispassionate interest. Once satisfied, the guard stepped back, giving Ben a cursory nod before exiting the room, leaving a palpable silence in his wake.

"What is it you need, Benjamin?" Abraham finally said, leaning back in his chair, his fingers tented before him.

"Ben, please. My father called me Benjamin when I was in trouble and it makes me think I'm in for it." Ben offered a light laugh, attempting to ease the tension in the room.

"I'm a busy man, *Ben*," Abraham cleared his throat and angled his body forward, staring at him, his face unchanged, "what can I help you with?" Ben gathered his thoughts, a rehearsed speech poised on his lips.

"I believe my abilities are being underutilized. I am tasked with moving supplies but," he paused, choosing his words carefully, "the frequency of the trucks has decreased. The others below can manage that without issue."

"And your point?" Abraham asked, his tone even but edged with impatience.

"Before this," Ben continued, gesturing vaguely to encompass the world outside their walls, "I served in the army, as you well know. My skills could be put to better use here, contributing to something more substantial than logistics."

"Every role is critical here, Ben," Abraham's voice held a note of reprimand, "the community functions because each person fulfils their duties."

"Of course," Ben conceded, feeling the weight of the unspoken hierarchy pressing down upon him, "but surely there's more I could do to ensure the safety and efficiency of your, I mean, *our* operations?" Abraham regarded him for a moment, his expression unreadable.

"Everyone wants to feel important, Ben. But aspirations must align with the needs of the community. We'll see if your proposal holds merit. For now, continue with your duties." Abraham rose with a measured grace that filled the room with his unspoken authority. His footsteps were silent against the plush carpet as he closed in on Ben, his presence towering despite the meagre height difference between them.

"Of course, sir." Ben straightened his spine, his military training kicking in, refusing to betray even a hint of the trepidation that gnawed at his insides. With hands clasped behind his back, Abraham began a slow orbit around Ben, scrutinising him like a specimen under a microscope. His analysing eyes, magnified slightly by the lenses of his glasses, pierced into Ben, searching, always searching for something unspoken. Despite standing only two inches taller, Abraham's stature seemed to swell, dwarfing Ben in both size and command.

"What exactly are your intentions, Ben?" Abraham's voice broke the silence, each word deliberate and heavy with implication. Ben faltered for a fraction of a second, the question catching him off-guard.

"My intentions?"

"You've been part of this community for some time now," Abraham prodded further, his circling coming to a pause as he faced Ben directly, "why is it that you've waited until now to seek elevation?" Ben wrestled with the words, the truth clawing at his throat while he searched for an acceptable lie.

"It's not about seeking a higher position," he said, struggling to maintain eye contact, "it's about wanting to contribute more meaningfully to what you're, *we're*, building here." The sentence was bitter, the taste of disloyalty masked beneath feigned devotion to Abraham's envisioned utopia. Abraham's gaze held Ben captive, a silent judge presiding over an unspoken trial. The air in the library seemed to thicken with the weight of expectation as Abraham's lips parted, his voice resonating in the hallowed space between towering shelves of books.

"Humble yourselves before the Lord, and he will lift you up." Abraham intoned, the scripture echoing off the walls.

"Which verse is that?" Ben asked, his voice steady despite the churning in his stomach.

"James, chapter 4 verse 10." Abraham replied without missing a beat. Ben's eyes drifted from the stern face before him to the rows of leather-bound spines, each one a sentinel of knowledge and doctrine. The room, once a sanctuary of thought and learning, now felt like a chessboard, and he was a pawn manoeuvring for position. His childhood lessons, hours spent pouring over verses and parables, became his unexpected arsenal.

"I might be a bit rusty," Ben ventured with a careful calm, "but didn't the Bible also tell us that 'you should use what gifts you have to help others, as faithful servants of God'? I think I remember learning that at Sunday school. Something like that." The corner of Abraham's mouth curled into a knowing smile, the slightest nod of appreciation for the counter-move.

"Peter, chapter 4 verse 10," he corrected gently, yet with authority, "each of you should use whatever gift you have received to serve others, as faithful stewards of God's grace in its various forms." Ben stood a little taller, bolstered by the words he'd dredged from memory, feeling them settle around him like armour. He met Abraham's eyes, finding in them a flicker of respect that hadn't been there before, a mutual recognition of the dance they were engaged in, a duel cloaked in scripture and subtlety.

"I'm impressed that you seem to know the bible cover to cover," Ben acknowledged, a slight nod accompanying his words as he fought to maintain an even keel, "it's truly admirable that you're so devoted to your beliefs." The silence that stretched between them was thick, charged with the weight of unspoken thoughts and careful calculations.

"Is there something more you wish to express, Ben?" Abraham's eyes narrowed slightly, not in suspicion but with the shrewdness of a leader measuring the worth of those who served him. Ben hesitated, choosing his words with precision.

"It would be a disservice to keep me at my current post, sir," he began, his voice steady despite the tension coiling within him, "my training and experience as a member of the United States Army has honed skills that I believe can be of greater use here. It is my desire to help ensure the safety and well-being of this community." The room seemed to grow stiller, if possible, as Abraham considered Ben's proposition further. His fingers interlaced in front of him, a steeple of contemplation. Outside the library's confines, life moved on, but within these walls, time hung suspended on Abraham's decision.

"You're persistent," Abraham finally said, "there is to be a heavy focus on scouting and recruitment after my official union with Miss Taylor." His words deliberate, each one a test of Ben's composure while he watched closely as Ben's hands formed fists at his sides, the only visible sign of the storm raging within.

"I am." Ben said calmly, his face neutral despite his unrest.

"Only after the celebrations have settled, Aaron has been instructed to embark on a mission to another community we have heard over the radios," Abraham continued, "you may accompany them, and this will be the perfect opportunity for you to demonstrate your discipline and the utility of your skills."

"Thank you. I won't disappoint you." Ben replied, his voice betraying none of the tumult caused by the mention of Beth. He gave a short, respectful nod, though his jaw remained set, muscles taut with restrained emotion.

"You're dismissed." Abraham concluded, turning his attention back to the papers before him, signalling the end of their discussion. As Ben turned to leave, the door closed behind him with a soft click, leaving Abraham enveloped in his thoughts and the quiet dominion of his library.

Mary's hand reached out and lightly rapped on the door, her knuckles barely grazing the polished wood. The sound was almost lost amidst the hush of the carpeted hallway, the softness of it sinking beneath her feet as she waited for a response. It was a gentle murmur, a secret whispered through the plush silence of the corridor.

"Come in." Aaron beckoned without looking up from the book laid open on his bed. The door swung open, revealing him standing tall and composed, his posture commanding and his features chiseled like polished stone.

"Brother." She whispered softly as she stepped into the room, her hand lingering on the doorknob before she clicked it shut with tentative finality. The air carried the scent of sandalwood, suffusing an ambiance that was as meticulously arranged as the rows of maps lining his armchairs and chest of drawers. Aaron finally glanced up, an eyebrow arching in mock surprise.

"I don't remember summoning you, Mary." His tone held a note of playful reprimand, yet underneath there was a current of something sharper, something colder. Swallowing the tightness in her throat, Mary edged closer.

"I need your help." She said, the words barely above a whisper but laden with a weight that seemed to fill the room, vying for space amongst the shadows cast by the morning light. In one fluid motion, Aaron rose from his bed and closed the distance between them, the casual grace of his movements belying the steel in his eyes.

"What can I do for my little sister?" He purred, reaching out to stroke her arm with exuberant affection. The touch sent a shiver through her, an involuntary recoil from a familiarity that had long since curdled into something grotesque.

"Not that." She whispered, pulling away from his touch as if it burned. His hand dropped to his side, and his face tightened, the veneer of charm peeling back to reveal a flash of anger.

"Then why are you here?" His voice took on a sharp edge as he stepped back, creating space that felt both like a chasm, and yet not nearly enough. Tears pooled in Mary's eyes as she faced her brother, the words catching in her throat like thorns.

"Aaron—" She managed softly, her voice a fragile whisper betraying the turmoil within. Words escaped her mind as she struggled to find the way to express their predicament, as she involuntarily raised her hand to her stomach, pressing an open palm across her abdomen as she looked down. The fleeting shock on Aaron's face transformed into a fury that contorted his features. His hand struck out, connecting with Mary's cheek with a sound that echoed violently off the walls. She stumbled, careening to the floor, her palms slapping the cold surface in a futile attempt to break her fall. The mood had shifted so suddenly that she barely had time to catch her breath. From the cold moment she stepped in, to his expectant advances, which had shifted so quickly to rage. Aaron's face twisted in rage, his features contorted and his eyes narrowed into slits. His body tensed and his fists clenched, veins protruding from his neck and arms in a display of pent-up anger. The taste of iron filled Mary's mouth as she tasted her own blood, a metallic tang that lingered on her tongue. The air was thick with it, a raging storm of emotion that left her trembling in its wake.

"How did you let this happen?"

"Stop, please," she begged, her plea muffled by the carpet as she tried to shield herself from him, "help me, Aaron. Abraham will kill me when he finds out."

"How could you be so stupid?" Aaron loomed over her, his words like lashes across her already bruised soul. She cringed, pressing herself further into the ground as if willing it to swallow her whole. "I'm sorry," she whimpered, her apology nothing more than a breath, an echo of despair, "I need your help Aaron, please—" Aaron's shadow fell upon her as he towered above, the rage in his eyes not yet abated.

"And what do you expect me to do about it?" He demanded, his voice cold and hard. Mary gathered the shreds of her courage, rising slightly to meet his gaze.

"The Bible," she said, her voice gaining strength from the conviction of her words, "clearly teaches us that incest is a sin. It's forbidden, a violation of God's law and natural order. You know this, Aaron. You knew this from the first night you—, the first night we—, we've sinned together. This is your baby too." Her eyes searched his, imploring. In the tense silence that followed, their shared transgression hung in the air between them, a spectre of guilt and fear that no scripture could exorcise. He leaned down to her, close enough that she could feel his breath on her cheeks.

"You want me to claim the wages of our sin? To bless what should never have been conceived?"

"You instigated this," she whispered louder, attempting to regain a semblance of control and strength within the conversation, "I'll tell him. I'll tell him *everything* and we'll both be punished for it."

"You would sacrifice your own life just to spite me?" Aaron's voice sliced through the tension like a knife, cold and unyielding; "Don't confuse your desperation with courage, Mary. You know what he'll do to you."

"You put me in this position," she stared up at him, her face a mix of fear and anger, "you put *us* in this position, and if you don't help me—"

"I'll deny it," he stated flatly, his eyes devoid of any brotherly warmth, "and who do you think Abraham will believe? His trusted cousin who commands his armed forces or a fallen woman, corrupted by lust, bearing the fruit of her shame?" He sneered down at her, still crumpled on the floor, her tear-stained face a mask of desperation. Mary's sobs hitched in her throat as she absorbed the weight of his words. She knew the truth of the matter - Aaron's position made him untouchable, while she was vulnerable and exposed.

"Please, Aaron," she begged between ragged breaths, her hands clenching into fists against the cold floor, "if you have any affection for me, for your own family, you have to help me."

"And what would you have me do, Mary?" Aaron's voice was laced with scorn as he folded his arms across his chest. The very image of military discipline, he stood impassive before her turmoil.

"Ask Abraham to marry me off," she said quickly, grasping at straws, "then I can say the baby belongs to my husband. He might be the leader of all of us but in his eyes, you own me. He'll approve a marriage if you ask—" The laughter that escaped Aaron was sharp and without humour.

"Our father would be the one to ask him, not me."

"He thinks George is old and weak. Abraham trusts you, not him—"

"Stupid girl," he chided her, shaking his head, "Abraham won't buy such a convenient story. Marriages take time, and he won't organise that before his own wedding to Beth. Even if he believed you, the baby would be born way too soon. You couldn't claim it was born prematurely at a full-term weight. Abraham is no fool."

Tears streamed down Mary's cheeks as the last vestiges of hope began to fade, her brother's rejection a stark confirmation of her deepest fears. In that moment, the realisation dawned on her - she was truly alone.

"Then what am I to do? You know I have no other choice." Her gaze was desperate, her voice barely above a whisper. Aaron's eyes, cold and calculating, met hers with a steely resolve.

"You tell Abraham you were raped," he said evenly, his tone suggesting a simple solution to an unsolvable problem, "he will take you in, Mary. To him, children are gifts from God, no matter the circumstances of their conception." *Raped*, she thought, was such a harsh conviction for someone who would be innocent, though it was not far from the truth, only with the conviction falling upon the wrong man.

"But who—" she implored, her eyes widening with horror at the suggestion, "Abraham will demand a name. I can't, I *won't* condemn an innocent man to be punished for this."

"Then you're out of options," Aaron replied curtly, offering a hand to lift her from the ground, "better for one man to suffer the consequences of your actions than for you and your child to be punished." She took it gingerly, the strength of his grip a stark contrast to the tremble in her own limbs. On her feet now, she struggled to steady herself, her body swaying like a reed in the wind. "Aaron, please—"

"How far along are you?" Aaron's question sliced through the tension, interrupting her further plea for salvation.

"Three months," Mary confessed, her voice so soft it was almost lost in the space between them, "at least three months." Three months of secret terror, three months of silent prayers for a way out that never came. His jaw tightened, anger flashing across his features.

"You should have told me sooner." He growled.

"I hoped, I *prayed*—" her voice broke as she admitted the truth, the words spilling out like the tears that had come before, "I prayed to God that I would lose it." The sinfulness of hope was a new concept to Mary, but in Aaron's presence, it took on a cruel clarity. Her brother's words fell upon her like judgement itself.

"To wish for death over life is a sin, Mary." His thumb came up to her cheek, brushing away a solitary tear with an intimacy that belittled the gravity of their conversation.

"I—, I know." She murmured, each word punctuated by a shudder that ran through her frame. Even as she acquiesced, there was a hollow resignation in her eyes, a knowing that beyond this room, more than just her own soul was at stake.

"Then you know what you must do," Aaron said, his voice laced with a feigned compassion that did not reach his cold gaze, "tell Abraham a tale of violence. He will forgive you, and he will shelter you and *your* child." Mary nodded, though her heart sank with the weight of the lie she would have to live.

"But who should I say did it?" The question hung between them, heavy with implications neither wished to address directly. Aaron's response was a dismissive shrug, as if he proposed she pick a name from a hat.

"You're smart, when you want to be. You'll think of someone." His detachment stung, a sharp contrast to the enormity of the decision before her. Her silence lingered, a testament to her internal struggle, before Aaron shifted in his stance.

"Brother—"

"You're dismissed. Unless, of course, you'd rather stay." He offered, the coy undertone of his suggestion impossible to miss. It was an offer she knew all too well, one that had led her to this precipice of despair in the first place. With a shake of her head, disgust etched deeply into the lines of her face, Mary wiped her remaining tears defiantly. She could not bear the thought of conceding any further to the man before her, who wore the mask of a brother but bore the heart of a stranger. Without a word, Mary turned and left the room, the door closing softly behind her, sealing away the sordid proposition and the choked air of betrayal.

Anne shuffled through the rows of neatly organised medication, her fingers tracing the faded labels as she conducted a meticulous inventory. The infirmary was dimly lit, its corners softened by the warm glow of a kerosene lantern perched on a nearby bench. A scavenged floor lamp hummed quietly in the corner, its light flickering sporadically from the small generator humming just outside in the corridor. Shadows danced across the shelves, lending the space a strange kind of intimacy, as if the room itself were holding its breath. Each bottle she inspected was a precious resource - antibiotics nearly out, gauze running low, morphine locked away like gold. Anne's gaze was sharp, but the crease between her brows deepened with every missing item she mentally tallied. Across the room, the soft rustling of Val's movements broke the silence, accompanied by the occasional clink of glass against metal.

"Anything else you reckon we need?" Anne asked without looking up, her voice echoing slightly in the sterile space. Val paused, a thoughtful expression crossing her face as she leaned against a metal shelf.

"An ultrasound wouldn't hurt," she mused sarcastically, "especially with Beth and Abraham's wedding on the horizon. You know he's eager to get her pregnant the second they're married." Anne chuckled dryly, finally glancing over at her colleague.

"And what good is an ultrasound without power? Might as well add a *reliable* generator to the wish list." They shared a brief, knowing laugh as they glanced at the flickering lamp, a momentary reprieve from the gravity of their duties.

"Weren't they getting solar panels?" Val inquired, flipping through a clipboard laden with notes and figures; "I thought Abraham was trying to get some power here."

"They were," Anne sighed, "but all the panels they found went into the cars so they didn't need to scavenge for fuel."

"Right, prioritising Aaron's department over ours. How typical," Val shook her head, "why does Abraham want these checks done so frequently?"

"Once a week," Anne replied, tucking a strand of hair behind her ear as she marked off another item, "have to make sure nothing goes missing, as if we have the luxury to pilfer." Val scoffed, placing her hands on her hips.

"Right, because there's just so much temptation here," she said, gesturing to the modest supply of bandages and over-the-counter painkillers, "what's he think anyone's gonna do? Run a black market for Tylenol?" Their laughter mingled again, softer this time, each keenly aware of the absurdity and yet the necessity of their simple task surrounded by a world that demanded constant vigilance, even among such meagre resources. Amidst the steady clattering of the kitchens down the corridor, Anne leaned back against the cold edge of the examination table, her gaze fixed on a particularly bland spot on the wall.

"At least this inventory gives us something to do." She said, her voice betraying a hint of weariness. Val's hand hovered over an open cupboard door, her brow furrowing as she scanned its contents.

"I could have sworn we had a full box of Narcan last week," she said, tone laced with confusion, "it's missing." Anne felt a knot tighten in her stomach but kept her eyes anchored away from Val's searching look.

"I thought you were counting bandages and stuff," she deflected, her fingers absentmindedly fiddling with a loose thread on her white coat, "I was about to check that cupboard for the pharmaceuticals." Val's suspicious gaze bore a hole into the back of Anne's head.

"I moved on—"

"I said I was going to do it." Anne interjected sharply, still facing the wall to which her eyes remained focused.

"Anne," Val pressed, her voice firm as she shut the cupboard with a soft click and turned to face her colleague, "why are you dodging the question? We're supposed to catalogue everything that comes in and out of this room. Where did the Narcan go?" The silence stretched between them, thick and heavy. Anne's hands stilled, and she finally allowed her eyes to meet Val's. She could see concern etched into the lines around Val's eyes, a look that demanded honesty.

"Val—"

"Was there an overdose I didn't hear about?" Val's words were more of a statement than a question. Anne let out a non-committal hum, shrugging her shoulders as if the loss of such crucial medication was a minor inconvenience.

"It must be around the infirmary somewhere." She replied, hoping her casual demeanour would dispel Val's suspicions. But Val's penetrating gaze told Anne that her attempt to deflect had fallen short. There was no paperwork for an overdose, and they both knew it. The unsaid hung between them like a dark cloud waiting to burst open at any moment. Val's hand hovered over the empty space where the charcoal should have been before glancing back at the bench where the clipboard lay abandoned, its pages fluttering slightly in the sterile breeze from the hallway.

"Anne," she began, the hint of a knowing smirk playing on her lips, "some charcoal is missing too." Anne exhaled slowly, her chest deflating as she faced Val.

"I must have misplaced it." She said, the words tasting like ash on her tongue.

"Come on," Val laughed dryly, shaking her head with disbelief, "this is you we're talking about. You don't misplace things." There was affection in her voice, but a sharp edge of curiosity cut through it. Anne remained silent, unsure of what to say. Her mouth was dry, a sudden bitter taste enveloping her tongue as she swallowed.

"Please, leave it alone."

"I can't leave it alone. We're supposed to report this kind of thing to Abraham. If he finds out—"

"He won't find out," Anne took two small steps towards Val, her hands held up in front of her body like a shield, "he doesn't know what comes in here half the time, so he'll never know if one or two things are missing."

"What if someone needs it? What if one of *his men* need it, and the scouts remember finding Narcan and charcoal and we don't have it in here?"

"I—," Anne hesitated, her mind overwhelmed with words and justifications, leaving her unable to articulate any excuse, "I don't know."

"Tell me what's going on." Val demanded, louder this time, her cadency filled with impatience.

"Val," Anne hissed, her tone suddenly urgent as she closed the distance between them, "please lower your voice." She reached out, gripping Val's arm with a gentle firmness. The aggravation died on Val's face as she registered the seriousness in Anne's eyes.

"What happened to the Narcan and the charcoal powder?" She demanded, though this time her voice was hushed, laced with unease. Anne glanced back towards the doorway, listening for anyone lurking in the corridor, ensuring the privacy of their conversation.

"There was a suicide attempt," she whispered, the gravity of her confession making her voice tremble ever so slightly, "I didn't log it because, well, because Abraham would see it as a sin." Val's face drained of colour, her eyes widening in shock. The clipboard and its inventory, the missing supplies, all of it fell away into insignificance against the weight of what Anne had just revealed. Val's knuckles whitened as she gripped the edge of the bench, her frustration simmering beneath a facade of professionalism.

"You need to tell me what happened," she pressed, her voice tight with contained anger, "if we don't account for the missing Narcan and charcoal, it'll be *our* necks on the line, not the person who tried to take their own life." Anne's eyes darted to the door before returning to Val's piercing gaze, her lips pressed into a thin line.

"And they won't know, Val," she said firmly, a hint of steel threading through her words, "it won't come up for a long time. No one's going to need it—"

"Until they do," Val cut in sharply, her fear for their precarious situation bleeding through, "what then, Anne? What if there's another overdose? We've got Narcan listed in the inventory." Anne leaned against the cool metal of the supply cabinet, her posture betraying a weariness that seemed bone-deep. She ran a hand through her hair, the gesture more of a surrender than a solution.

"I know, I know," she murmured, almost to herself, "even if it's listed on the inventory, not everyone's gonna know what it's used for. It's not like we'd be dealing with an overdose and someone's gonna ask for the Narcan. If—, if something happens again, we'll have to make do with the charcoal we have left. That's all we have."

"Shit." Val exhaled a ragged breath, her shoulders slumping slightly as the weight of the secret they now shared settled upon her. The infirmary walls felt too close, the silence too heavy with unspoken fears.

"Val, please try to calm down." Anne's voice was a whisper now, tinged with desperation as she motioned with her hands for her friend to calm down.

"Anne," Val's face was flushed with frustration, her stance rigid against the sterility of the infirmary, "you're not hearing me. If—"

The crisp sounds of footsteps on the concrete floor cut through Val's heated words like a scalpel, and both women turned to see Austin leaning against the frame, his presence an unexpected intrusion. His eyes flicked between the two, reading the tension in the room like one would scan a patient's chart.

"Everything okay here?" Austin's voice filled the space, a note of concern undercutting his casual demeanour.

"What are you doing here?" Val's tone didn't mask her irritation, but her body language shifted subtly, ready for another confrontation.

"Could hear you two halfway down the corridor," he replied, stepping inside, "you might want to keep it down." Anne's eyes met Val's in a silent plea, but Val was wound too tight, her sense of justice propelling her forward.

"We were—"

"It was Beth." Before she could launch into another argument,

Austin interjected with a gravity that immediately dampened the fire in her gaze. The words hung heavy in the air, carrying a weight that seemed to press on their chests. Anne's expression tightened, her scolding look aimed at Austin, silently chastising him for his bluntness. But there was no taking back the truth now that it had spilled out like medication from an overturned bottle.

"Beth? What happened?" Val's question trembled on the edge of panic, her previous anger deflated by concern. Austin's eyes softened, and he crossed the room to stand closer.

"Beth tried to take her own life," he said with a gentle firmness, "she couldn't deal with it all anymore." A cold shiver ran down Val's spine. The revelation struck a chord deep within her - Beth, always so determined, pushed beyond her breaking point. It was a sobering thought, one that echoed the unspoken fears lurking in the corners of their minds. She had survived Marcus on Alcatraz, and Victor at Catalina, but Biltmore had nearly killed her. The colour drained from Val's face as she processed Austin's words.

"She couldn't take any of it anymore," she repeated Austin's words, her voice was a mere whisper, the strength sapped from it by the gravity of Austin's revelation, "what do you mean?" Austin glanced at Anne briefly before returning his gaze to Val.

"The pressure," he said quietly, "our lives here. *Her* life here. She wanted to end it." Val's legs trembled, no longer able to support her. She sank into the nearest chair, pressing her hand against her forehead as if to physically hold back the pain throbbing behind her temples.

"When did this happen?" She asked, her eyes not meeting anyone's, fixated on some unseen point in the distance.

"About a week ago." Anne answered, her voice laced with a sadness that had settled like dust in the corners of the infirmary. Val felt a hollowness expanding within her chest. The walls, lined with shelves of medication and sterile equipment, seemed to close in around her, a stark reminder of their reality.

"Hey," Austin said gently, a note of reassurance threading through his tone, "Beth's okay now. She's getting the care she needs." At his words, something inside Val snapped. She surged to her feet, anger flashing in her eyes as she strode back to the clipboard. The names and numbers blurred together, but she didn't need to see them clearly - they were etched in her memory from countless checks before.

"Are any of us really okay though?" She spat out, her voice rising with each syllable. It wasn't just a question, it was an accusation, a challenge to the world they were all trapped in.

CHAPTER 13

Beth's heart jolted at the sharp rapping on her door, its suddenness sending a flutter of nervous birds into her stomach. She sat upright in the narrow bed that had become her sanctuary, her gaze involuntarily drawn to the white dress that loomed like a spectre from the wardrobe's exterior, a ghostly harbinger of the day ahead. The door creaked open and Hannah entered first, her arms laden with a tray filled with the morning's offerings, followed closely by Jennifer and Eve whose presence filled the small room with an air of expectant tension. The soft clink of porcelain against wood punctuated their arrival as they brought the ritual of breakfast, a semblance of normalcy on a day anything but ordinary.

"Are you ready?" Hannah's voice was gentle, a soothing balm to the chaos threatening to spill from within. Beth's eyes lingered on the dress once more, its fabric whispering promises and demands. With a breath that felt as heavy as lead, she managed a nod, a solemn dip of her head that conveyed her acquiescence to the inexorable march of time towards the ceremony awaiting her. Hannah approached, the tray balanced with practiced ease in her hands. The smell of toasted bread mingled with the citrus tang of orange juice, but the aroma did little to tempt Beth's appetite which seemed to have retreated deep within her. Still, she reached out, her fingers brushing against the warm crust of the toast before bringing it to her lips, taking a token bite to appease her attentive audience. Eve, in stark contrast to the others, perched herself on a chair across the room. Her posture was impeccable, legs crossed, hands resting demurely on her knees, a silent sentinel observing the scene before her. Even without words, her presence spoke volumes, a testament to the complicated threads that wove between them, threads now taut with unspoken questions and confessions. Beth's gaze flitted to Eve, a silent conversation hanging in the air, but the gravity of the moment pulled her attention away. Instead, her focus shifted to a small basket that Jennifer had placed at the foot of the bed, a nest of greenery and pastel colours amidst the rich reds and browns of her surroundings. Her hand abandoned the half-eaten toast, reaching instead for the basket's contents. The flowers within were fresh, their petals vibrant against the verdant leaves that cradled them - a splash of life on this day where so much seemed shrouded in shades of uncertainty. They were a gift, one last token of beauty before the inevitable tide of the day swept her along to an unknown fate. Jennifer's fingers danced among the delicate petals, a soft smile gracing her lips.

"Abraham insisted I pick these for you," she said, holding Beth's gaze with an earnestness that belied the morning's heavy air, "he wanted something fresh and alive from the conservatory before the last flower beds were ripped out." Jennifer made little attempt to hide the sadness on her face for the destroyed biome within the glass palace which was once the Biltmore Conservatory. Beth's response was empty, a perfect contrast to the words she spoke.

"They're beautiful—"

"I've forgotten the ribbon though," Jennifer added with a sudden start, "it's in my room, I'll be right back." And with that, she slipped away, her departure as swift as her entry, leaving behind the scent of the conservatory blooms. In the silence that followed, Hannah leaned in slightly, her voice a gentle intrusion.

"Beth, would you like some coffee instead?" Her eyes searched Beth's face for signs of sustenance beyond the meagre toast nibble. Beth, feeling the weight of the dress on her psyche as much as the fabric itself might weigh upon her shoulders, managed a small nod. Coffee seemed like an anchor, something to hold onto amidst the storm of emotions brewing within. Without another word, Hannah exited, the soft click of the door marking her departure. Eve rose from her distant chair like a spectre summoned forth by the solitude, closing the space between them with quiet steps. She settled onto the bed, her presence a palpable thing, yet her gaze wandered to the wall, avoiding the directness of an encounter. Beth's mouth parted, the beginning of a sentence forming, perhaps of gratitude or an explanation, but before the words could navigate the tightrope of their shared tension, Eve cut through them.

"You've barely spoken to me this last week, not since—" She trailed off, her tone was not accusatory but instead laced with a vulnerability that they both knew she rarely showed. It demanded honesty, even if cloaked in concern. Beth drew in a breath, her eyes tracing the lines of worry that creased Eve's forehead.

"There's been—," she hesitated, searching for words that wouldn't betray too much, "a lot on my mind. I needed time to process." Her voice barely rose above a whisper, a testament to the internal cacophony she battled with. The room held its breath as Eve watched her, a silent guardian of the moments they'd collected now scattered like the petals in Jennifer's basket. Beth, with her solemn nods and whispered admissions, clung to the fragments of peace before the day claimed her once more. Eve's fingers picked at the edge of the comforter, a gesture so small and fidgety it belied the calm she tried to exude.

"I'm sorry," she said suddenly, her voice a soft murmur in the quiet room, "for taking advantage of your vulnerability." Beth watched Eve's hands, the way they twisted the fabric, and felt a well of emotions threaten to overflow. She reached out, stilling Eve's restless fingers with her own.

"There's nothing to apologise for," Beth assured her, her tone gentle yet firm, "I don't regret a single thing. You were there when I needed someone." Eve's gaze finally met hers, searching Beth's eyes for any sign of insincerity. Finding none, something within her seemed to soften.

"If you're sure—"

"Your care meant everything to me," Beth continued, the weight of gratitude anchoring each word, "but it was a dark day. What I did, I wasn't in the right headspace to see things clearly." Her voice faltered as she acknowledged the chasm she'd almost surrendered to. Eve's scoff was quiet but sharp, carving through the tender atmosphere.

"You latch onto anyone who shows you kindness, Beth. It's like you fall for people just because they care." Stung by the remark, Beth withdrew her hand, wrapping her arms around herself protectively.

"Is that what you think this is?" She asked, hurt flickering across her features.

"Isn't it?" Eve challenged, her expression hardening as if preparing for an uncomfortable truth. She let the implication hang between them, unsaid but clear as the morning light filtering through the window. Beth's heart clenched, not just at the accusation, but at the worry that it might bear some truth.

"Maybe you're right," she admitted, though the words tasted like ash on her tongue, "maybe I do gravitate towards those who show me care, but is that so wrong?"

"Only if it blinds you to their real intentions," Eve replied, her voice losing its edge, replaced by a note of concern, "just be careful. Don't mistake gratitude for love." The warning echoed in Beth's mind, a cautionary whisper amidst the storm of her emotions. Acknowledging the truth in Eve's words, she nodded slowly - a silent promise to tread more carefully on the path her heart urged her to follow. Eve's words settled into the air like dust after a storm, coating the silence with their heavy implications. Beth's brow furrowed, the corners of her lips pulling down in a frown as she processed the insinuation that her affections were merely reflections of gratitude. Beth's voice cracked, a mix of offence and disbelief lacing her tone.

"So my feelings are just transactions?"

"Transactions? No, that's not what I meant." Eve said quickly, softer now, a tinge of regret seeping through.

"What did you mean then?"

"I'm saying be cautious with your heart. Austin, Ben, they cared for you, and you just," she hesitated, searching Beth's face for understanding, "you developed feelings for them, and me. Be vigilant, Beth. Otherwise, given time, you might even convince yourself you're in love with Abraham." The very thought sent a visceral shiver of revulsion through Beth's frame. Her stomach twisted at the mention of his name, and she recoiled from the bed as if it were on fire.

"Never." She spat out, the word tasting bitter. The image of Abraham, with his steely eyes and imposing presence and prejudice disguised as salvation, seemed to loom over her. She shook her head, dispelling the unwelcome spectre from her thoughts. At that moment the door creaked open and Hannah re-entered, carrying the promised coffee with an air of practiced calm. The rich aroma filled the room, acting as a temporary balm to the turmoil within. "Here you go," she offered a smile that didn't quite reach her eyes, a silent acknowledgment of the tension she had walked into, "something a bit more energising than orange juice." Beth reached for the cup gratefully, wrapping her fingers around its warmth, drawing comfort from its steadiness. As she took a tentative sip, the bitterness on her tongue was replaced by the smooth, robust flavour of it. Jennifer followed close behind, her arrival marked by a brighter energy. She cast a glance at the dress and then at Beth, her smile genuine and full of expectation.

"Are you ready?" She asked, clasping her hands together in anticipation. Beth paused for a moment, looking around the room at the three women who had attempted to make the morning as normal as possible, on an otherwise abnormal day.

"I can't procrastinate forever." Beth replied, her voice firm despite the quiver of nerves beneath. She swung her legs off the bed, her bare feet touching the cold floor, grounding her. She stood, feeling the weight of the day ahead. Her gaze lingered on the white dress once more before she turned to face the future, whatever it might hold.

Beth's feet carried her down the path that ribboned towards Bass Pond, each step a silent echo of her dream from the week before. The images clung to her memory like cobwebs, gossamer and persistent. As she hesitated, caught in the tangle of her reverie, Mary materialised beside her, a spectre of duty and expectation.

"Beth, I'm to walk with you," Mary said, her voice soft but laced with an authority that belied her young age, "you're becoming part of my family today." The words slipped into Beth's consciousness, urging her back to the present. She gave a solemn nod and accepted the solace of Mary's extended arm. Their steps synchronised, Beth cast a backward glance as Eve, Hannah, and Jennifer receded into the shadowy embrace of the trees, their figures blurring with distance until they were nothing more than part of the forest's whispers. The path unfurled before her, bordered by the last vestiges of winter's touch. Her white dress, innocent and expectant, fluttered around her legs, the fabric whispering secrets to the wind. Despite the early spring chill that nipped greedily at her exposed skin, Beth felt cocooned in a void of sensation, her body moved through the motions, yet her spirit remained detached, observant. As they descended the gravel footpath, the murmur of voices heralded the small gathering at the Bass Pond Lookout. The clearing unfolded slowly, an arena set before the murky expanse of water that did not mirror the crystalline clarity of her nocturnal visions. Relief washed over her, a gentle wave of gratitude that reality had granted her this divergence from her subconscious fears. There, standing sentinel by the pond's edge, was Abraham. His profile was etched against the backdrop of brooding water, his gaze transfixed upon its surface as if searching for omens, or perhaps absolution. Beth's heart skipped a beat - not in adoration, but in a rhythm of resolve. She reminded herself of Eve's cautionary words, how easily care could be mistaken for affection. No, she would not fall for Abraham, no matter how her mind sought connections in solitude. Mary's grip on her arm tightened, a wordless reminder that they were almost upon the gathered witnesses. Beth squared her shoulders, bracing against the cold and the unknown, ready to confront the ceremony that awaited her. The clearing by Bass Pond was a tableau of solemnity, the small group of onlookers casting long shadows in the early light. Beth's gaze swept over them, a silent inventory of presence and absence. Austin and Ben were conspicuously missing from the assembly, their absence a hollow note in the chord of attendees. Yet there was something comforting in them not being there, a subtle affirmation that Abraham had honoured her request for a select gathering. Still, an undercurrent of curiosity tugged at her. She wondered if he would have honoured the same request for the wedding itself, or if the whole community had been invited to watch him take possession of her. Beside Abraham stood George, his posture rigid with an air of ceremonial importance. Adam stood next to him, clutching Abraham's bible to his chest with a reverence that bordered on zealotry, while Aaron lingered a step behind, his expression unreadable. Beth's eyes then drifted across the faces dotting the clearing. Eve, wrapped in a shawl, watched with an intensity that seemed to reach out to Beth, laden with unspoken words. Hannah hovered near, her features twisted in a knot of concern and duty. Grace stood slightly apart, her hands clenched together as if in prayer, or perhaps in a bid for strength. Jennifer's eyes were bright, reflecting a cocktail of emotions, a mirror to the complexity of the day. Val's presence was like a pillar of quiet support, her sturdy frame exuding a sense of unwavering loyalty. Reece's jaw was set, his gaze fixed on the ground before him, his mind seemingly distant. Barnett's upper lip twitched ever so slightly, betraying his attempt at stoic indifference. Stone's face was a mask of neutrality, giving nothing away, while Sarah's eyes darted around the group, restless and seeking. Samantha's arms were folded, her stance suggesting a barricade of personal boundaries. Rebecca's chin lifted in a semblance of defiance, a subtle challenge to the proceedings. Mary's presence was a gentle one, her demeanour soft but tinged with the weight of expectation. Rachel stood serene, her eyes half-closed as if lost in contemplation, while Jacob's youthful face was set in a serious mould, far beyond his years. Amid all these familiar faces was the conspicuous absence of Amanda, a vacancy that filled Beth with a quiet relief. The assembled crowd formed a mosaic of loyalties and secrets, each person a thread in the tapestry of the moment. As Beth looked upon them, she felt the weight of their gazes, some heavy with judgment, others light with sympathy. But it was the unseen eyes, those of Austin and Ben, that haunted the fringes of her consciousness, a ghostly audience to her procession towards an uncertain future. The water lapped gently at Beth's ankles as she stepped into the cold embrace of Bass Pond, her white dress billowing softly around her legs. Abraham stood already ankle-deep, his presence a towering silhouette against the pale morning light filtering through the trees.

"You look beautiful." He said, his voice warm but carrying an undercurrent of command that resonated across the still water.

"Thank you." Beth mustered a smile, a fragile thing like frost on spring buds, and looked down at her dress, a cascade of white that now seemed more shroud than garment.

"Brothers and sisters," Abraham's voice boomed, turning to address the intimate congregation gathered at the water's edge, "we come together in this sacred place to witness a rebirth, a cleansing of spirit and body through the holy waters of baptism." His hands, firm and sure, guided Beth deeper into the pond until the water swirled around her waist. He raised his arms slightly, and the crowd fell silent, their attention fixed solely upon them.

"Before us stands Bethany, ready to renounce the old and embrace a new path in Christ," Abraham continued, locking eyes with Beth while speaking to all, "and so I ask you, before God and these witnesses. Do you believe in God, the Father Almighty, Creator of heaven and earth? Do you believe in Jesus Christ, His only Son, our Lord, who was conceived by the Holy Spirit, born of the Virgin Mary, suffered under Pontius Pilate, was crucified, died, and was buried, and on the third day rose again from the dead? Do you believe in the Holy Spirit, the holy catholic Church, the communion of saints, the forgiveness of sins, the resurrection of the body, and life everlasting?" Abraham's gaze was piercing, his questions laden with the weight of centuries-old tradition and expectation. Beth felt the words wrap around her like the chill of the water, seeping into her bones. She knew the affirmation expected of her, the declaration that would seal her in the covenant she was about to enter. Her lips parted, whispering acquiescence to the beliefs laid out before her, her voice barely audible over the rustle of leaves and the murmur of the pond.

"Yes." With a solemn nod, Beth surrendered to the ritual. Abraham's strong hands cradled the back of her head and shoulders as he gently lowered her backwards into the water. The cool liquid enveloped her, the surface breaking against her forehead in a sacred caress. His words resonated above her, seeming to ripple through the water itself. The sensation was unnerving, yet she fought against the panic that threatened to surge within her. Focusing on the firm grasp that held her safe, Beth allowed the symbolic act to unfold, trusting Abraham's control over her immersion. She felt the water trickle like a benediction over her skin, the droplets mingling with the deeper currents of her tangled thoughts. As she was slowly brought back to a standing position, Abraham's voice rose clear and commanding, projecting to all who witnessed this moment.

"I baptise you in the name of the Father, and of the Son, and of the Holy Spirit. Almighty God, the Father of our Lord Jesus Christ, who has given you new birth by water and the Holy Spirit and bestowed on you the forgiveness of sins, keep you in eternal life by His grace. May He anoint you with the Holy Spirit and mark you as Christ's own forever." The power behind his words seemed to vibrate in the cold air, wrapping around Beth like a shroud. Water dripped from her hair and lashes, yet there was a warmth in the promise of protection and belonging that left her momentarily comforted. It was a fleeting solace, for in the depths of her heart, where doubt lurked and truth whispered, Beth understood the unspoken covenant that was being forged - not just with the divine but with the man who now claimed her future.

"Amen." Whispers filled the crowd as they watched her tremble, the fabric sticking to her and outlining her silhouette. The chill from the baptismal waters clung to Beth as she ascended the field, her soaked dress weighing heavy against her skin. Abraham's voice resonated behind her, its timbre mingling with the rustle of wet fabric.

"We receive you into the household of God. Confess the faith of Christ crucified, proclaim His resurrection, and share with us in His eternal priesthood." Beth's gaze lingered on his retreating back, feeling a tangible shift in the air as the mantle of his words settled upon her. Mary's gentle grip on her hand tugged her forward, breaking the invisible thread that tethered her to Abraham. They walked together, but Beth felt alone in her thoughts, her mind adrift in a sea of unspoken fears and doubts. In the distance, the Walled Garden's grey wooden gates stood like solemn sentinels guarding the threshold of her new life. The murmuring of the crowd beyond crept into her ears, a distant cacophony that grew louder with each step. Mary halted at the garden's entrance, her eyes holding a hint of empathy that offered little comfort.

"Will I have a chance to change?" Beth's question was more a plea than an inquiry, a grasp for some semblance of normalcy in the ritualistic tide that swept her along. Mary shook her head, her voice soft but unwavering.

"Abraham wishes for you to be presented as you are, pure and reborn from the waters," she extended the bouquet, a vibrant contrast to the pallor of Beth's hands, "Jennifer made this for you." The flowers were fresh, their petals still dew-kissed from the conservatory. As Beth accepted the arrangement, the scent of lilies and roses wafted up to her, a fleeting reminder of a world where beauty was not bound by expectation or ceremony. Clutching the bouquet like a lifeline, she cast one last glance back at the pond that had borne witness to her transformation.

"Let's go." She whispered, more to herself than to Mary. With a deep breath, she stepped through the gates, her resolve fortified against the waves of uncertainty that threatened to erode her composure. Beth's gaze lingered on the open expanse beyond the gardens, the vastness of the estate beckoning to her with whispers of freedom. Her heart raced with the thought of escape - she wondered if she could vanish into the trees before anyone noticed. The sound of muffled conversations and shuffling feet from within the garden walls served as a stark reminder of the expectant eyes awaiting her entrance. The sound of her name, sharp and commanding, suddenly sliced through her contemplation. Beth turned, her pulse quickening, to find Adam standing just inside the threshold, his presence like a dark omen. His arm was outstretched towards her, a crooked smile playing across his features, a cruel mimicry of warmth that failed to reach his cold eyes.

"Time to go, Beth." He said, his voice carrying an edge that cut through the fragrant air. Hesitation clawed at her, but with the bouquet clutched in her damp hands, Beth placed her other hand atop Adam's arm. The rough fabric of his sleeve scraped against her skin as she allowed him to guide her forward. With each step, the possibility of flight diminished, replaced by an acute awareness of her surroundings. The assembled crowd came into view, a sea of faces that held traces of curiosity, anticipation, and in one case, venom. Amanda stood among them, her glare fixed on Beth with undisguised loathing. It was a look that could curdle the festive atmosphere, but Beth forced herself to meet it only briefly before shifting her attention away. At the rear of the crowd, two figures stood apart from the rest. Ben and Austin, their postures tense, offered silent witness to her procession. The white fabric of her dress, now a second skin clinging to her form, made Beth acutely aware of herself under their gazes. She felt the weight of the wet cotton and the chill of the air, yet the sensation seemed distant, numbed by the surreal procession in which she found herself ensnared. Adam's grip on her arm was firm, unyielding, as they moved past the silent observers. Beth focused on the path ahead, on the reality of her situation, and the strength she would need to face what was yet to come. Tremors rippled through her body, a silent testimony to the cold and her mounting dread. She kept her gaze lowered, focusing on the wet hem of her dress as it brushed against the gravel path. The faces of Austin and Ben hovered at the edge of her vision, two anchors in a stormy sea, but she dared not look at them directly. Their presence was both a balm and a curse, stirring up what ifs that had no place in the inevitability of her march. The clamour of the wind fell away, muffled by the bodies that lined her path, creating a corridor of solemn silence. The air grew still, yet the chill lingered, seeping into her bones. Unseen, Ben's eyes tracked her every step, his expression a mask of controlled anguish. His hands, fisted at his sides, spoke volumes of the struggle within, to act or to abide, knowing all too well the futility of resistance in this moment. As she approached the front, George stood with an air of sombre authority, cloaked in the vestments of his role. Abraham's figure loomed beside him, a pillar of expectation, while Aaron lingered just off to the side, his posture suggesting readiness to fulfil his part in the ceremony. Mary, resplendent in her chosen role as bridesmaid, mirrored Aaron on the opposite flank, her eyes soft with empathy that couldn't reach beyond the distance between them. In a ritual as old as time yet alien in its context, Aaron stepped forward and took Beth's arm from Adam. His touch was light, almost respectful, but it was Abraham's hand that reached for hers next, his fingers closing around her wrist with proprietary firmness. With a nod, Aaron retreated, leaving Beth before Abraham, their positions now mirroring those of countless couples before them, though none under quite such a pall of foreboding. Beth felt Abraham's eyes upon her, his grip insistent as he guided her to stand beside him. Her heart beat a staccato rhythm against her ribs, each throb a reminder of the life that surged within her despite the encroaching walls of a future she never chose. The chill from her dampened dress reached deep into Beth's bones, a shiver coursing through her as she stood beside Abraham. The crowd hushed, the only sound the rustling of leaves whispering secrets to the wind. George raised his hands for silence, and despite the tremors that shook her frame, Beth anchored herself in the present, her gaze fixed on a point just over George's shoulder.

"Dearly beloved," George intoned, his voice resonant with the gravity of ceremony, "we are gathered here today in the presence of God and these witnesses to join Abraham and Bethany in holy matrimony. Marriage is an honourable estate, instituted by God, signifying the mystical union between Christ and His Church. Therefore, it should not be entered into lightly but reverently, deliberately, and in accordance with the purposes for which it was instituted by God." His eyes swept over the assembly, lingering on each face as if to imprint upon them the weight of their observance. Beth's eyes darted around, seeking an anchor, but there was none to be found in the sea of faces that surrounded her. She felt the lightest of touches, a soft breeze perhaps, or the ghost of freedom, stirring the wet tendrils of hair at her neck. George's words were like stones cast into the still waters of her resolve, rippling outwards, distorting her reflection into something unrecognisable. Beside her, Abraham stood resolute, a proud smile playing upon his lips as he turned towards Beth. His eyes gleamed with satisfaction, the corners crinkling in anticipation as if he had already savoured this moment in countless dreams of conquest. George continued, his gaze now fixed on Abraham, who seemed to swell with self-importance.

"Will you, Abraham Joseph Bishop, have this woman to be your wedded wife, to live together in the covenant of marriage?" The question, though rhetorical, hung heavy in the air, a noose awaiting a neck; "Will you love her, comfort her, honour and keep her, in sickness and in health, and forsaking all others, be faithful to her as long as you both shall live?" George's voice boomed, reaching even the farthest corners of the gathered throng. The mask Beth wore was porcelain-thin, her features etched with a stoicism borne of necessity. Yet beneath the carefully sculpted exterior, a tempest churned. Every fibre of her being screamed in silent protest, the urge to flee, to scream, to reject the charade before her clawing its way up her throat. But the words would not come - they were prisoners too, shackled by circumstance and the piercing gaze of the man who claimed her future. Abraham's voice, fervent and clear, cut through the cool air, filling the space with a resonance that seemed to vibrate in Beth's chest.

"I do." He declared, his gaze locking onto hers with an intensity that belied the simplicity of the vow. A smile stretched across his face, a triumphant display of certainty, as he eagerly consumed the moment. Beth forced the corners of her mouth upwards, the motion mechanical and devoid of warmth. She swallowed the lump forming in her throat, the hard swallow audible only to herself amidst the murmur of the onlookers. Her skin prickled with anxiety as George turned his attention to her, his voice steady and expectant.

"Will you, Bethany Rose Taylor, have this man to be your wedded husband, to live together in the covenant of marriage?" George intoned, and Beth felt the weight of every syllable settle upon her shoulders like leaden shawls; "Will you love him, comfort him, honour and keep him, in sickness and in health, and forsaking all others, be faithful to him as long as you both shall live?" The mention of her middle name sent a jolt through Beth. A reminder of a past self, a fragment of identity not yet consumed by Abraham's shadow. The furrow lining her brow deepened as she wondered who unearthed that secret piece of her, and for a fleeting second, her composure faltered, revealing the barest glimpse of vulnerability. She had mentioned the name to no one, a conversation topic that had never really been brought to light - her real given name had barely crept into any conversation the last few years, never mind a seldom used middle name. Abraham's eyes narrowed almost imperceptibly, mistaking her pause for reluctance. Muscles tensed, he leaned just a fraction closer, ready to intervene, to steer her back to the path he had meticulously laid out for them. Beth recovered swiftly, pushing aside the swell of memories and doubts.

"I do." She affirmed, her voice carrying more strength than she felt. It was a performance worthy of the stage, a line delivered with practiced ease to appease the script of their unconventional ceremony.

"Bless, oh Lord, these rings, that they who give them and they who wear them may abide in thy peace, and continue in thy favour, unto their life's end, through Jesus Christ our Lord. Amen." George concluded, the solemn words lingered in the air as Beth watched Adam reach into the folds of his garment. He withdrew two simple bands, their gold glinting dully in the wan sunlight. With deliberate movement, he extended them towards Abraham, whose eyes never left Beth's face.

"Amen." Abraham's tone was firm, and accepted the rings with a nod that held no warmth, his fingers encircling the smaller one meant for Beth. His touch was clinical as he took her hand, sliding the ring onto her finger. The metal felt alien against her skin, a shackle disguised as a symbol of unity. Beth's breath caught in her throat as she lifted the remaining ring. It felt heavier than it looked, laden with the gravity of permanence.

"Amen." She whispered. Her fingertips grazed Abraham's hand, the contact sending an involuntary shiver up her spine. She mirrored his precise movements, placing the band upon his finger, the gesture hollow but necessary.

"By the authority vested in me by God, I now pronounce you

husband and wife. What therefore God hath joined together, let no man put asunder. You may now kiss the bride." George concluded, the words a decree, a final seal on the strange covenant between them. Abraham leant forward, the rough stubble of his chin grazing her cheek as he pressed a restrained kiss to her lips. It spoke volumes of his understanding of their public spectacle, a kiss for show, devoid of tenderness or passion. Beth's heart pounded with a rhythm of disquiet, aware of every eye upon them, each witness to this union that felt more like a binding contract than a marriage. Yet she mustered a smile, a facade as carefully crafted as Abraham's, for the assembled crowd who watched on, oblivious to the turmoil behind the veil of propriety.

"It is my great joy and privilege to present to you," George's voice rang out with a finality that turned the air leaden, "Mr. and Mrs. Abraham Joseph Bishop. Go in peace to love and serve the Lord." The words cascaded over Beth, each syllable erasing her identity like waves smoothing away footprints on a sandy shore. Her name, her essence it seemed, had dissolved into the title of wife, an appendage to the man beside her. The crowd's applause was meek and polite, a mere rustling of leaves in a vast forest of expectation. Abraham's grip on her hand was ironclad as he led her through the throng of well-wishers, their faces blurring into a sea of sameness. Her soaked gown clung to her legs, the fabric growing heavy with the weight of her new reality.
"Abraham," Beth ventured, her quiet and unassuming, "what's wrong?" His stride did not falter, nor did he glance at her behind him. The silence between them stretched taut as they made their way towards the gate, the palatial estate looming ahead like a silent judge. Beth's questions went unanswered as they passed, leaving

the murmur of the gathering behind. The firmness of his pace suggested urgency, a need to be removed from the public eye as dread pooled in her stomach. Abraham's silence was a cloak, obscuring his thoughts, his intentions, all while they crossed the threshold into the dim, hushed interior of the estate, the heavy doors closing with a resounding thud behind them. Austin's hand clamped down on Ben's forearm with a firmness that brooked no argument. From the edge of the gathered crowd, they watched as Abraham led Beth away, her figure growing smaller with each step towards the imposing house. The silent exchange between the newlyweds spoke volumes, and Ben's muscles tensed, a primal urge to protect rising within him.

"Leave it," Austin muttered, his gaze fixed on the retreating couple, "Beth knows how to take care of herself." Ben's jaw tightened, the protest dying in his throat. He had scanned Beth's posture throughout the ceremony, her subtle hesitation before saying 'I do'.

"She paused," he said, more to himself than to Austin, "Abraham saw it, you could tell by the way he grabbed her. He's not gonna like that."

"Trust her." Austin replied, though his eyes betrayed a flicker of doubt. He glanced back at the crowd, seeking a distraction from the uneasy feeling settling in his gut.

"Everyone's here." Ben noted, trying to shift his focus from Beth's plight.

"Yes," Austin observed, "I suppose he wanted everyone to witness it." His attention now sweeping over the assembled faces. A sudden realisation dawned on them both, a void where two familiar presences should be.

"Chase and Tyler," Ben murmured, "I haven't seen them for a

while." Austin followed Ben's searching gaze, his own concern mirrored in his friend's expression.

"Same." Austin confirmed, a crease forming on his forehead.

"So, if Abraham wanted everyone to see him take possession of Beth, where are they?" Ben's voice carried an edge, his casual demeanour slipping. They locked eyes, a silent communication passing between them. A gust of wind rustled through the leaves above, carrying with it an undercurrent of tension. As the crowd began to disperse, their shared unease hung in the air, an invisible thread pulling taut, the question of Chase and Tyler's whereabouts a new knot in the tangled web surrounding them.

CHAPTER 14

The heavy oak door slammed shut behind them as Abraham shoved Beth into the dimly lit library. Leather-bound tomes lined the walls, their musty scent mingling with the sharp tang of wood polish. Abraham planted himself between Beth and the exit, his imposing frame blocking any chance of escape. The silence stretched taut between them until she broke it with a question, her voice eerily calm.

"How did you know my middle name?" Beth's heart raced, but she kept her face impassive as she met Abraham's piercing blue gaze. Surprise flickered across his stern features before he let out a light, unsettling laugh.

"Is that why you hesitated?" He asked, a hint of amusement in his tone. Beth's expression remained stoic as she continued to stare him down. Beth's mind raced as she struggled with her conflicting emotions, her wet dress still clinging to her legs. She had been fighting an internal battle for so long, trying to navigate the precarious situation she found herself in. Despite her anger bubbling just beneath the surface, she knew that lashing out would only sabotage her carefully laid plans. Taking a deep breath, she cautiously considered her words before continuing their delicate conversation.

"Is that why you were so angry after the ceremony? You thought I was hesitant to marry you?" Her face remained passive, a move she had thought clever but only seemed to anger Abraham. The grin slid from his face as he realised her lack of amusement. Without a word, he strode to his ornate mahogany desk and yanked open a drawer. Rifling through papers, he extracted a manila folder and thrust it at Beth.

"Read it."

"What is it?" She asked, not reaching for it.

"The forms you filled out when you arrived at Fort Irwin," Abraham's jaw clenched, "*read it.*" Beth's fingers trembled slightly as she took the folder, the weight of its contents suddenly feeling far heavier than mere paper. She fought to keep her breathing steady, acutely aware of Abraham's intense scrutiny as she held the key to a past she couldn't fully remember. Beth slowly opened the folder, her eyes scanning the papers within. There, in her own familiar handwriting, was her full name - middle name included. She blinked, a frown creasing her brow.

"I—, I don't even remember writing this down." She murmured, her voice quiet.

"You must have done it out of habit." Abraham's tone softened slightly, though his posture remained rigid. Beth nodded numbly, handing the file back to him. She watched as he carefully returned it to the desk drawer, the soft scrape of wood against wood echoing in the oppressive silence of the library.

"I'm not trying to play a trick on you, Beth," Abraham turned back to her, his piercing blue eyes seeming to pierce into her very soul, "this isn't a game, you can trust me." Beth swallowed hard, suddenly aware of how dry her throat had become.

"I'm sorry—"

"What did you think was happening?" Abraham mused, walking

back around the desk to stand in front of her.

"I was just shocked. It wasn't something I had shared with anyone, or so I thought," she managed, her voice hoarse, "I don't know what I thought, to be honest. Forgive me."

"Forgiveness within a marriage is required," Abraham intoned, his words carrying the weight of a sermon, "but so is trust." Beth nodded again, her mind racing. Abraham walked back to the desk and his hand disappeared into another drawer, emerging with a small, velvet-covered box. He extended it towards her, his expression unreadable.

"What's this?" Beth asked, her heart hammering against her ribs as she stared at the unexpected offering. Beth's fingers trembled as she accepted the box, her eyes darting between Abraham's impassive face and the gift in her hands. She struggled to conceal her distaste, her mind reeling at the absurdity of a wedding present in their bleak post-apocalyptic world, but she knew Abraham had a different view of how things were.

"I got you a wedding gift." Abraham stated, his voice carrying a hint of pride.

"Thank you." Beth forced a smile as she carefully opened the box, revealing a delicate silver cross nestled inside. The polished metal caught the dim light, seeming to mock the harsh reality beyond the estate's walls.

"Do you like it?" He asked rhetorically - any answer other than something positive would have triggered another uncomfortable discussion, more uncomfortable than the present. She knew he expected her to say nothing other than 'yes'.

"It's beautiful." She whispered softly, blinking down at the ornate cross.

"May I?" Abraham gestured towards the necklace. Beth nodded, turning slightly as Abraham lifted the cross from its velvet bed. His fingers brushed against her neck as he fastened the clasp, sending an involuntary shiver down her spine. She touched the cross gently, feeling its cool weight against her skin.

"It's beautiful." She repeated, the words tasting like ash in her mouth. Abraham circled back to face her, his imposing figure blocking out the fading sunlight from the window.

"The only thanks I need," he said, his voice low and intense, "is for you to be a beautiful, obedient wife." Before Beth could respond, Abraham leaned in and pressed his lips against hers. The kiss was soft but insistent, a clear statement of ownership that made her stomach churn. A sharp knock at the door startled them both.

"Abraham, Mrs. Bishop," Jacob's voice called out, "everyone has returned to the hall."

"Mrs. Bishop," Abraham purred, "I like the sound of that."

"It will take some getting used to—"

"Shall we join our reception, wife?" Abraham's lips curled into a smile as he turned to Beth. The word made her feel like a possession, like she was an object outside of her own control. Beth nodded mechanically, her mind already searching for ways to survive this new, terrifying chapter of her life, wondering if she'd be able to muster up the courage to mask her inner turmoil every hour of every day. Beth followed Abraham through the gallery outside the library before crossing the entrance hall to the dining hall, her steps hesitant and unsure. A dull weight settled in her gut, a dread she couldn't shake. She wasn't legally bound to him, not by any court or any law, but in his eyes she belonged to him just the same. To him, she was a vessel, a means to carry his legacy. God had signed the contract, and that was enough for him to view her as his possession. As they approached, Abraham's hand tightened around hers, his grip almost painful. Beth bit back a gasp and forced herself to remain composed, plastering a fake smile on her face as they entered the room. The hall was filled with almost everyone from both the estate and the inn on the other side of the grounds. Beth recognised most of them, including some Prescott arrivals she had barely had a chance to speak to at Fort Irwin before the outbreak and consequent departure. The usual contented faces that she passed every day in the halls were now laced with delight as they ate and drank heartily - a rarity in their post-apocalyptic world. Abraham led her to the head of the room where a long table was set with an array of delicacies. Beth's stomach growled at the sight and smell of food - it had been days since she had eaten anything substantial, but she couldn't bring herself to indulge in this luxury when she knew what it had cost her. Abraham guided her to the head table. It sat alone, facing the rest of the room like a stage. Beth's skin prickled with unease. She took her seat next to Abraham and tried not to flinch as he wrapped his arm around her waist possessively. He leaned in close to whisper in her ear.

"You look stunning, my dear wife," he said with a smug smile, "but please try not to disgrace me today." Beth clenched her jaw but didn't respond. She knew that any sign of rebellion on her part would only lead to further punishment later on. She'd learned to read the air around Abraham, how it could thicken without warning, the way his jaw would set just before a storm rolled in. His mood could switch in an instant, without warning, and she knew he only needed a little ammunition to do so.

"This is different." She murmured, noting the unusual arrangement. "A special exemption for our wedding feast," Abraham's lips twitched in a smile, "but from tomorrow, we'll dine privately in my quarters for every meal." Beth's breath caught in her throat. "Every meal?"

"Our quarters now," he corrected himself as he ignored her dismayed tone, his grip on her arm tightening imperceptibly, "it's time we truly began our life together, away from distractions."

"Yes," she forced a smile, "distractions." The implication hung heavy in the air as Beth scanned the room. Dozens of eyes flickered between her and Abraham, a mix of envy, pity, and barely concealed fear. She felt exposed, vulnerable - a prized possession on display. As she listened to conversations close by, Beth kept up appearances, smiling and nodding politely as some came up to their table to congratulate them. The room was alight with casual conversation, comments on the food spread before them, and further hopes of future weddings so their community could grow and more food would be offered. Inside, Beth couldn't shake off the sense of being trapped and suffocated by this world that Abraham was forcing her into. Her eyes darted to a shadowy corner where Austin and Ben huddled. A pang of longing struck her heart, remembering easier days with them before Biltmore, before Fort Irwin and Catalina, before Alcatraz. She tried to catch their eyes, but they barely noticed her gaze.

"Is there something wrong?" Abraham's voice broke through her thoughts.

"No," she turned to face him, trying to school her features into a neutral expression, "just feeling a bit overwhelmed by everything." Abraham's grip on her waist tightened again.

"You'll get used to it," he said with a hint of impatience in his voice, "and remember, you're not just representing yourself now but also our family and our community." Beth nodded, her heart heavy with the weight of his expectations. She knew that from now on, every move she made would be scrutinised. Dinner continued in this way - Beth feeling suffocated and trapped while Abraham revelled in the attention and admiration from his followers. But as the night wore on and more wine was passed around, the room grew louder and more boisterous. Beth noticed that even Abraham seemed to relax slightly, his hand lingering on hers under the table as he laughed at someone's joke. Her mind wandered back to Austin and Ben, wondering what they were discussing so intently. The thought of escaping this life with them filled Beth with hope and longing. She continued to stare, picturing their escape, running through the town and beyond Asheville until Biltmore was just a dot on the horizon. As she daydreamed, something within her snapped. Escape was imminent, but not without Abraham's death and the subsequent downfall of his regime. She took in a deep breath, and stood, tapping her glass with a spoon and raising her drink towards the room. The hall fell silent as everyone turned to face her, frozen in their place to listen. Beth's eyes slowly moved around the room, catching glances from familiar faces. Eve smiled at her, nodding as an expression of admiration adorned her face. Beth's smile widened at Amanda's snarl from two seats over, smirking as she continued to look around the room. Austin's jaw was set in stone, clenched as he sat back in his chair cradling a glass of wine, while Ben sat next to him, looking away - the only face in the room refusing to meet her gaze, the only person she wanted more than anyone to see her strength.

"Friends, before we continue our celebrations, I would like to take a moment to express gratitude to the most invaluable person in this room," she said, turning towards Abraham and offering her hand for him to hold, a sweet smile graced her lips as she continued, "without my phenomenal husband, our dinner tonight, and every night, would not have been possible. He has kept us safe, warm, and well-fed." Applause and a few cheers erupted as she smiled out to the crowd, catching Abraham's gaze towards her through her peripheral vision, his expression a mix of surprise and adoration.

"My only wish in this new life he has been so gracious to provide is that I can live up to his expectations," she continued with feigned elation, casting a warm smile and light laugh towards the crowd, "and while I'm not as well-read in this sacred tome as my husband, I spent a few days recovering in bed and came across some words I think are perfectly fitting for today." At her subtle nod, Eve stepped forward from the side and walked up to the table, placing the white Bible gently into Beth's hands. She noticed the way Beth's fingers trembled, how tightly she gripped the edges in an attempt to steady herself.

"You've got this." Eve whispered, just loud enough for Beth to hear. Beth drew in a steadying breath, then set her glass down. She opened the book to the ribbon-marked page, her fingertips brushing across the passage like a prayer in motion.

"Then the King will say to those on his right, 'Come, you who are blessed by my Father; take your inheritance, the kingdom prepared for you since the creation of the world. For I was hungry and you gave me something to eat, I was thirsty and you gave me something to drink, I was a stranger and you invited me in, I needed clothes and you clothed me, I was sick and you looked after me, I was in prison and you came to visit me'," Beth glanced down at Abraham who had been gazing at her for some time, idolising her as she spoke, "then the righteous will answer him, 'Lord, when did we see you hungry and feed you, or thirsty and give you something to drink? When did we see you a stranger and invite you in, or needing clothes and clothe you? When did we see you sick or in prison and go to visit you?' The King will reply, 'Truly I tell you, whatever you did for one of the least of these brothers and sisters of mine, you did for me'." Beth closed the Bible and set it back down onto the table, taking Abraham's hand and holding it tightly. Abraham's face brimmed with pride, seemingly lost for words.

"Wife, I—" He stammered.

"You have taken care of all of us in only a way that a true man of God could ever do. We are his children, and you are our saviour, and one day our son will continue to do your work," she concluded, raising her glass once more to the room, "to Abraham!" She yelled triumphantly, as the room erupted once more as applause flooded the hall. Abraham stood suddenly, placing a gentle kiss on Beth's face. She smiled sweetly as he turned to face his followers.

"To new beginnings!" Abraham declared, raising his own glass. The room echoed his toast, a chorus of hollow voices. Beth lifted her own glass once more, mechanically, as the weight of her new reality crashed down upon her. She was no longer just Beth - she was Abraham's wife, his vessel for repopulating this broken world. As the lukewarm wine touched her lips, she steeled herself for the long night ahead, and the even longer future that stretched before her.

"I hope you're proud of me." She looked towards the back corner once more, as Ben looked down at his glass, swirling the wine before him. Austin nodded, raising his glass slightly at her and raising an eyebrow, before taking a sip of his own wine. She continued to stare, knowing she couldn't linger too long or Abraham would notice.

"Of course I am." Abraham beamed, assuming the statement was directed towards him, but she did not notice. Every second that passed without Ben looking at her felt like an eternity of pain stabbing at her heart. She wanted his approval, she *needed* it. She needed him to acknowledge that what she had done and everything she had said was a step in the right direction for all of them. Just one more second, any second, and he might look over, but she couldn't risk lingering any longer, and turned to face Abraham.

"Did I do well?"

"Wife," he said adoringly, placing a gentle hand on her cheek, "you have proved yourself an incredible advocate for the both of us."

"Thank you, husband." She tilted her head into his hand, resigning herself into his charge.

The stone walls of the South Tower loomed before Beth as Abraham and Jacob escorted her up the winding staircase. Her dress clung to her skin, each step a reminder of the christening ceremony and subsequent marriage that had sealed her fate. The flickering torchlight cast eerie shadows, distorting their silhouettes against the ancient masonry.

"Here we are." Abraham announced, his voice echoing in the narrow corridor. He halted abruptly before an ornate wooden door, causing Beth to stumble slightly. Beth's eyes widened as realisation dawned.

"This is your room? But it's so close—"

"To where you've been sleeping? Yes," Abraham interrupted, a hint of amusement in his tone, "proximity has its advantages." Before Beth could process this information, before she could think about what would have happened if Abraham had caught them the night she had tried to kill herself, Abraham nodded to Jacob. Without warning, Jacob's hands were on her, patting down her sides and legs. Beth gasped, instinctively recoiling.

"What are you doing?"

"Trust is a two-way street," Abraham's blue eyes bore into her, "we must earn it from each other."

"This is ridiculous. I'm wearing next to nothing, and it's been soaked through. You saw every curve as it clung to me. Where exactly do you think I'm hiding something?" Jacob's hands paused at her hips, hovering with uncertainty as he glanced at Abraham. Abraham considered her words, his gaze traveling from her hair to her bare feet.

"Very well," he waved his hand dismissively, "Jacob, you may go." As he retreated down the hallway, Jacob cast one last look at Beth. There was something in his eyes - perhaps pity, or even concern, and it made her stomach churn. Then he was gone, leaving her alone with her new husband and the imposing door that led to their shared future. Abraham's hand grasped the ornate brass doorknob, turning it with a soft click. The heavy door swung open, revealing a cavernous room bathed in flickering firelight. Beth stepped inside, her breath catching as her eyes swept across the opulent furnishings before settling on the enormous four-poster bed dominating the far wall. The door closed behind her with a thud that made Beth flinch. Abraham strode past, his imposing figure casting long shadows as he paced the room. He paused by an antique dresser, lifting a crystal decanter and pouring amber liquid into a glass. Beth hugged herself, suddenly aware of how the fabric clung to her skin.

"Can I—, may I have one too?" Her voice sounded small in the vast space. Abraham's piercing blue eyes studied her for a long moment. Without a word, he poured a second glass and extended it towards her. Beth took it with trembling fingers, careful not to brush his hand.

"You understand," Abraham began, his deep voice resonating in the quiet room, "that under ideal circumstances, I would have chosen a virgin bride. But these are far from ideal times. Your previous marriage, sanctified before God, makes you acceptable."

Beth's grip tightened on her glass. She raised it to her lips, letting the burn of alcohol steel her nerves.

"I'm honoured." She managed, the lie tasting bitter on her tongue. Beth shuddered as the whiskey seared down her throat. Abraham's gaze sharpened, misinterpreting her reaction.

"You must be cold," he gestured towards the crackling fireplace, "warm yourself. That dress was wet for far too long." Beth moved hesitantly towards the flames, grateful for the momentary reprieve. The heat seeped into her chilled bones, but did little to quell the dread coiling in her stomach. Abraham's footsteps approached, slow and deliberate.

"Thank you—"

"Your previous husband," he interrupted, his tone carefully neutral, "was he the only one you've been with?" Beth froze, her back to him. She knew honesty was vital, but the truth felt like ash in her mouth. Slowly, she shook her head.

"I see." Abraham said, his voice hardening. Before he could continue, Beth turned to face him.

"You know my past," she said quietly, "but I've renounced those sins. When I came here, I asked for a second chance, a new beginning."

"Yes. That you did." Abraham nodded, his expression inscrutable. He drained his glass and poured another. The silence stretched between them, heavy with unspoken judgment.

"I'm sorry," Beth whispered, "this must be difficult for you. If you've never been with someone—"

"That's not your concern." Abraham cut her off, his tone brooking no argument. He stared into the depths of his glass, lost in thought. Abraham's soft laugh broke the tense silence.

"While I am not without sin," he said, his voice low and contemplative, "I am repentant." He moved slowly towards the bed, his fingers absentmindedly touching the wedding ring on his left hand. The firelight caught his face, casting a warm glow across his skin.

"What's wrong?" Beth watched him, confusion creasing her brow. Abraham's gaze snapped to hers, a flicker of surprise crossing his face.

"I've been married before." He said quickly, as if the words had escaped unbidden. Beth's eyes widened, her lips parting in shock. This revelation shattered her perception of the stoic leader she thought she knew. A gentle laugh escaped Abraham as he turned to stare at the far wall. His eyes took on a distant quality, as if peering into a long-forgotten memory. The corners of his mouth twitched upwards, hinting at a happiness Beth had never seen him express.

"Was she—" Beth hesitated, her voice catching, "where is she?" Abraham shook his head slowly, his expression darkening. The room fell silent save for the crackling fire and their measured breaths. Beth waited, hardly daring to move. Finally, Abraham spoke, his voice heavy with an old pain.

"My wife and newborn son," he said, each word seeming to cost him dearly, "were killed in a car accident by a drunk driver." The weight of his confession hung in the air between them, altering the very atmosphere of the room. Beth's heart clenched at Abraham's revelation. She moved to the edge of the bed, her gaze drawn to the window where the last remnants of daylight painted the sky in muted oranges and purples.

"I'm so sorry." She whispered, her voice thick with genuine sympathy. Silence enveloped them, broken only by the occasional pop and hiss from the dying fire. Beth's mind raced, trying to reconcile this new information with the man she thought she knew. The flames in the fireplace dwindled, casting long shadows across the room. Suddenly, Abraham stood, the abrupt movement startling Beth. He strode to the dresser, placing his empty glass down with a soft clink. As he approached her, Beth's body tensed involuntarily. Abraham reached for the glass in her hand, his fingers brushing against hers as he took it and set it on the nearby table. A violent shudder ran through Beth as realisation dawned. This was their wedding night, and Abraham would expect to consummate their union. Fear and revulsion twisted in her gut, but she forced her face to remain impassive. Abraham's eyes locked onto hers, his gaze intense and filled with purpose. He placed his large hands on her stomach, the heat of his touch seeping through the thin fabric of her dress.

"Before I formed you in the womb I knew you," Abraham intoned, his voice taking on the cadence of a sermon, "before you were born I set you apart; I appointed you as a prophet to the nations." Beth's breath caught in her throat, her heart pounding so loudly she was sure Abraham could hear it. She struggled to find her voice, to say something, anything, that might delay the inevitable. Abraham took Beth's hands in his, lifting them to his chest. His touch was firm yet gentle, a stark contrast to the turmoil raging within her. Her lips parted, but each attempt at speech withered in her throat, leaving only the ghost of what might have been an objection.

"Abraham—" She swallowed hard.

"Let us pray together," Abraham said, his blue eyes piercing into hers, "heavenly Father, we come before You with hearts full of hope and desire, seeking Your blessing as we prepare to bring new life into the world." Beth's fingers trembled against Abraham's chest as he continued, his voice resonating with fervent conviction. The room seemed to close in around her, the air growing thick and oppressive. She fought to keep her breathing steady, to maintain the facade of the dutiful wife. Abraham's grip tightened slightly as he pressed on.

"You are the Creator of all things, the giver of every good and perfect gift, and we trust in Your perfect plan for our family. We ask that You guide us in this journey of parenthood, and if it is Your will, grant us the gift of a son. Prepare our hearts, minds, and bodies for this precious responsibility. May our love for one another grow stronger as we wait on Your timing," Abraham intoned, his words carrying the weight of a solemn vow, "and may we always seek to glorify You in our lives. We pray for health, peace, and patience during this process, and that any fears or anxieties we may have would be replaced with trust in Your provision and care." Beth's stomach churned at the mention of fears and anxieties. If only he knew the true depths of her dread. She forced herself to nod slightly, playing her part in this macabre performance. Her gaze darted to the window, searching for an escape that didn't exist. The distant mountains loomed dark against the night sky, a reminder of the isolation of her new reality.

"Abraham—" Beth's mouth opened, her lips forming words that never came. He knelt before her, eyelids pressed shut, lost in a devotion that rendered her silence invisible.

"You know the desires of our hearts, Lord," Abraham said, his voice dropping to a near-whisper, "and we place our hopes in Your hands. In Your mercy, bless our efforts to conceive, and if it be Your will, may we joyfully welcome a new life into our family, a son whom we will raise in faith, love, and devotion to You." Beth's breath caught in her throat. The reality of what was to come crashed over her like a tidal wave. The crackling fire cast dancing shadows across the room, its warmth doing nothing to thaw the chill that had settled in her bones. She longed to pull away, to run, but remained frozen in place by duty and fear. Abraham's grip on her hands tightened as he reached the crescendo of his supplication. She closed her eyes to suppress the tears that threatened to escape.

"We thank You for Your unfailing love and for the opportunity to seek Your blessing in this sacred moment," Abraham concluded, "we place our trust in Your goodness and Your wisdom. In Jesus' name, we pray, Amen."

"Amen." Beth whispered, opening her eyes to find Abraham's piercing blue gaze fixed upon her. The air between them crackled with an awful anticipation. She lowered her hands gingerly to her sides, her fingers trembling slightly. Abraham reached out, his touch feather-light as he gently pulled the side of her dress over her shoulder and down her arm. The fabric whispered against her skin, raising goosebumps in its wake.

"Turn around." Abraham instructed softly. Beth complied, facing away from him. She felt the cool metal of the zipper against her back as Abraham slowly lowered it. His fingers trailed down her spine, following the parting fabric until they reached her lower back and hips. Her heart thundered in her chest, a frantic rhythm born not of desire, but of dread. Beth's mind raced, searching for a way to steel herself for what was to come. Behind her, she heard the rustle of fabric and the soft pop of buttons. Beth turned slightly, catching a glimpse of Abraham's bare torso. Her eyes widened involuntarily. Despite his austere demeanour, Abraham's body was surprisingly fit and muscular - a fact she'd never had cause to consider before this moment.

"Abraham—"

"You're trembling," he observed, his voice low, "are you still cold?" Beth swallowed hard, forcing a small smile onto her face.

"A little," she lied, "it's just nerves, I suppose." Abraham's hand came to rest on her shoulder, warm and heavy.

"There's no need for nervousness between a husband and wife," he said, "this is a sacred act. A divine calling." Beth nodded, not trusting herself to speak. She closed her eyes, silently praying for strength to endure what lay ahead. Abraham's calloused fingers slid her underwear down her legs as she let out a gentle breath to steady her heart rate. She felt the coarse fabric brush over her ankles and drop to the floor. She willed herself not to think, not to feel anything. She sensed him studying her naked form, his gaze like icy pinpricks on her skin. Revulsion rose in her throat. She swallowed hard, choking it down. He leaned forward and lifted the blanket for her, pushing her slightly to climb inside the covers. Sliding in cautiously, she pulled the blankets over her breasts and lay on her side, facing the window. Abraham slowly walked around the bed and stood at the end, staring at her. Noting his fully naked form in front of her, she continued to look out the window, watching the fading light. Beth kept her eyes on the silhouettes of the trees as he watched her like a predator eyeing its prey. His gaze raked over her body, visible through the thin blanket. She resisted the urge to pull the covers higher, to hide from his lecherous stare. Instead she remained motionless, passive, the obedient wife he wanted her to be, even if it made her skin crawl. Finally, Abraham looked away, continuing his prowl around the bed to the fireplace. Beth released a quiet breath, her fingers curling into the bedsheets. Abraham stared at the flames. Abraham gazed into the fire, reciting Scripture in a low, reverent tone.

"Sovereign Lord, what can you give me since I remain childless and the one who will inherit my estate is Eliezer of Damascus? You have given me no children; so a servant in my household will be my heir," he paused, as if listening for God's reply, "then the word of the Lord came to him: 'This man will not be your heir, but a son who is your own flesh and blood will be your heir.' He took him outside and said, 'Look up at the sky and count the stars - if indeed you can count them.' Then he said to him, 'So shall your offspring be.' Abram believed the Lord, and he credited it to him as righteousness." Another pause, Abraham's eyes gleamed with zeal in the firelight, his lips curled into a faint, triumphant smile. The words of Scripture were a promise to him, a prophecy.

"You can do this." Beth suppressed a shudder, dread pooling in her stomach. Abraham turned from the fireplace and slipped under the covers beside Beth. The bed creaked as he climbed in beside her, his hand closed around her arm, tugging her onto her back. She kept her eyes closed, not wanting to see his smug smile or the hunger in his pale eyes. His skin was warm against hers as he pulled her close, kissing her deeply. Beth kept her eyes closed, trying to retreat into herself.

"Be fruitful and multiply," Abraham whispered against her lips, his hands roaming over her body as he positioned himself next to her, "through you, God will make me into a great nation. Look at me."

"Yes." She obeyed, blinking up at him. He loomed over her, all sharp angles and flushed skin.

"You're mine now," he said, his breath sour with wine and whiskey, "my wife."

"Yes." Beth gritted her teeth. He smiled at her, gingerly brushing hair off her face as he looked at her.

"Yes what?"

"Yes, husband." Beth released the tension in her jaw, swallowing her words as she let out another breath to steady herself. He grunted in approval and pressed his lips to hers. She endured his kiss, trying not to recoil from his touch. This was her duty now, her cross to bear. When he finally broke away, he stroked her cheek almost gently.

"You please me well, wife. Now, let's see if you can give me a son." He rolled on top of her further, pinning her in place with his weight. She squeezed her eyes shut as he thrust inside her, biting back a whimper of pain and revulsion. It will be over soon, she told herself, just get through this, and survive. She let out a hollow moan for his benefit and began the pretence of pleasure she knew he expected, hating herself for it. But she would do whatever it took to appease him, even this. She retreated into her mind, enduring each rhythmic thrust of his hips, letting out the occasional moan, running her hands through his hair and along his back. She parted her legs wider, bringing her knee up as he grabbed at her hip with one hand and her opposite shoulder with the other. She gritted her teeth and forced herself to stay still as Abraham continued to move, his hips grinding against hers in a painful rhythm she couldn't halt. She shut her eyes tightly and tried to focus on something, anything else besides the feeling of his sweaty skin against hers and the dull ache in her breasts from where he gripped them too tightly. The only sound in the room was their ragged breathing and the springs of the bed creaking under their weight. She could taste the wine and whiskey on his lips as he kissed down her neck, his hot breath sending shivers down her spine. His fingers dug into her hips with each thrust, leaving bruises that would only add to her misery. She bit her lip hard, trying not to cry out, but it was no use. Each time he pushed deeper inside her, she winced and let out a small whimper that echoed in the silent room, a noise he mistook as pleasure. As they moved together, Beth couldn't help but think about what it must be like for him - this man who had lost so much yet believed so fervently in God's plan for them, for everyone. If he was really able to find any pleasure in this act, or if it was just another duty expected of him by his faith. Despite her despair, Beth continued with their dark dance beneath the covers until finally, after what felt like an eternity but had realistically lasted only minutes, Abraham let out a hoarse cry and collapsed on top of her chest. It was a marathon, not a sprint. Her performance had only just begun.

CHAPTER 15

The rose garden's imposing walls loomed over Ben and Austin as they huddled in a secluded corner, the sweet scent of blooms mingling with the acrid smoke from Ben's cigarette. His fingers trembled slightly as he held out the pack to Austin, who shook his head.

"You sure? Might help you take the edge off." Ben commented, his voice low and gravelly.

"I'm good," Austin's jaw tightened, "need to keep a clear head." Ben nodded, taking another long drag. His mind raced with worry for Beth, trapped in Abraham's bedroom for days with no sign of her around the estate. The thought made his stomach churn.

"She'll be okay." Austin said suddenly, raising an eyebrow at his friend as if he could read his thoughts. Ben looked up at Austin, shielding the sunlight with his free hand, squinting into the sky.

"How do you know that?"

"Because she's always okay."

"Until she tries to kill herself again." Ben snorted, taking another drag of his cigarette, finishing it and lighting another one.

"You should really slow down on those," Austin nodded towards the half empty packet, "when did you get them?"

"Yesterday." Ben said flatly, staring at the ground. Before Austin could reply, Eve appeared suddenly, her eyes darting nervously as she approached.

"I can't stay long." She whispered urgently.

"Beth," Ben's heart leapt, "how is she?"

"She's okay, I think," Eve's face fell slightly, "I've brought her food, but she's mostly been in bed."

"Is she hurt?" Ben's fists clenched.

"Some bruising on her arms and shoulders," Eve hesitated, "but otherwise, she seems alright. I think she's just adjusting mentally more than anything." Ben's mind reeled with rage and helplessness. He wanted nothing more than to storm into that bedroom and rescue Beth, consequences be damned.

"What excuse is she giving this time?"

"She claims she's still unwell," Eve gave a non-commital shrug, "she told Abraham that she was still recovering from being sick and the wedding day exhausted her. She made him feel so bad for keeping her in a wet dress that he's actually doting on her like a dutiful husband."

"Don't try to humanise him," Ben spat, standing suddenly, "he doesn't deserve that—"

"The Vicodin," Austin spoke up, changing the subject, his voice tight with concern, "where is it?"

"Safe," Eve assured them, "I have it hidden away for when we need it." Ben nodded gratefully, though his chest ached. He should be the one caring for Beth, protecting her. Instead, he was relegated to secret meetings in gardens, relying on others for scraps of information about her wellbeing.

"Thank you, Eve," Austin managed, his voice thick with emotion, "for everything you're doing for her." Ben stubbed out his cigarette, his resolve hardening. Somehow, some way, he would find a way to save Beth from this nightmare, no matter the cost.

"Are you sure she's okay?"

"I said she was," Eve responded curtly, "she's playing her part well, and she's alive. What more do you want?"

"Did you find anything about Chase and Tyler?" Austin leaned in, his voice low and urgent as he tried once more to redirect the conversation.

"I've searched most of the basement and sub-basement, but nothing," Eve shook her head, frustration evident in her expression, "the only place I haven't been able to check is the attic."

"The attic," Austin's eyes lit up with determination, "that's where I'll start looking." Ben felt a surge of protectiveness for his impulsive friend.

"Austin, we can't just go poking around up there," he hissed, "it's too risky."

"I'll find a way," Austin insisted, his jaw set stubbornly, "maybe I can sneak up with some supplies for storage or something." Ben ran a hand through his hair, anxiety gnawing at his gut. He knew Austin's heart was in the right place.

"Your recklessness could get us all in trouble."

"*My* recklessness?" Austin faced Ben squarely, narrowing his eyes; "You're the one hellbent on going after Beth, guns blazing. We know she's safe, safe enough. We have no idea what's happened to Chase and Tyler." Ben offered a resigned sigh before sitting back down and lighting up another cigarette.

"You're right, I'm sorry," Ben shook his head regretfully, "I've got my new posting tomorrow, and I'm meeting with Aaron soon. Then we're heading out on some mission. I won't be back for a while. I won't be able to have your back if things go south. Just promise me you'll be careful, alright?" As Austin nodded reluctantly, Ben's mind raced. He hated leaving with so much unresolved, but maybe this mission would give him a chance to gather intel, find some leverage to help Beth, to help all of them. He had to believe there was still hope, even as the walls of Biltmore seemed to close in around them.

"Do you think they might be missing because Abraham found out they were in a relationship?" Eve asked suddenly as Ben took a long drag of his cigarette. Austin nodded grimly, his shoulders set with resolve as he turned towards the looming estate.

"I have to go." Austin said abruptly, taking a few steps towards the gate, "and lay off those smokes." He called back before disappearing. Ben watched his friend's retreating form vanish through the rose garden gate, a knot of worry tightening in his chest.

"Ben," Eve's soft voice broke through his thoughts, "why do you love her so much? Beth, I mean." The question caught Ben off guard, his breath catching in his throat. He turned to Eve, seeing genuine curiosity in her eyes. For a moment, he considered deflecting, but something in her gaze compelled honesty.

"It's not just—" Ben paused, struggling to articulate the depth of his feelings, "it's not just how I feel when I'm around her. It's like, everything else fades into the background. The world was too loud, too chaotic. Even after the pandemic, there was still chaos, and there was also nothing. But when I look at her, it's like everything falls into place. She was this calm in the middle of the storm, even when she was the storm. I don't just love her because of how she makes me feel, but her strength, her stubbornness, her fire. Even when she's at her lowest, she's still the bravest person I know."

"That's sweet," Eve's eyes widened, touched by the raw emotion in Ben's words, "you really do care for her."

"I do. When we found her, we thought she was dead, and then she moved and gasped and we raced into action to save her, all while

Luis complained about another mouth to feed," Ben clenched his fists, looking back towards the estate, "but once she was better, she was funny, and caring, and kind, and despite not being able to take care of herself she was always there to take care of others."

"Seems like she's pretty capable of taking care of herself now." Eve interrupted, shrugging as she shifted awkwardly on her feet.

"Is she though? You all keep saying she's capable of taking care of herself, but she tried to take her own life," Ben paced angrily, "she tried to kill herself because of the situation we're all in."

"It was a momentary lapse in judgement," Eve thought uncomfortably about their night together, their moment of grief-fuelled passion which could have resulted in their deaths if they'd been caught, "and we all make mistakes. Can you tell me you haven't made mistakes in judgement calls since the pandemic started?"

"Only when it comes to protecting her," Ben shook his head, "she clouds my judgement, but I can't help but want to protect her."

Eve smiled gingerly.

"Because you love her."

"Because I love her." Ben repeated, staggering his words, cementing them into the universe as if the cosmos would hear his heartache and bring them out of the nightmare.

"You need to tell her that," Eve insisted, "when you get the chance. No matter when that is, Ben, you need to tell Beth exactly what you just told me."

"That she clouds my judgement?" Ben shook his head, a bitter laugh escaping him as he took a final drag of his cigarette. He ground it out beneath his boot, watching the embers die.

"No," Eve laughed softly, "that you love her, the way that you love her. She needs to hear it, it will give her strength."

"I'll probably never get to tell her that." He muttered begrudgingly.

"There will come a time when this is over," Eve said reassuringly, "and you'll be able to talk to Beth freely again. We find a way to talk freely, don't we?" Ben felt a surge of gratitude for Eve's unwavering optimism, even as his own hope flickered.

"Thanks for believing that," he said, his voice rough, "but this world we're living in, it's not some fairytale where the guy gets the girl he wants. We're not watched as heavily as she is. We're not monitored every second." As he spoke the words aloud, the full weight of his situation crashed down on him. Beth was married to Abraham now, locked away in that room, in that monstrous estate, and tomorrow he'd be leaving on a mission, moving further away from any chance of reaching her.

"Can I—" Eve hesitated, her brow creasing, "is there anything you want me to pass along to her?" She asked gently. Ben's throat tightened. A thousand unspoken words crowded his mind, but he forced them back.

"Just, please tell her that I hope she's okay," he managed, his voice barely above a whisper, "and that there isn't one second that I'm not thinking about her safety."

"I promise." Eve nodded, her eyes filled with understanding. Without another word, she turned and hurried towards the gate, her slight form soon disappearing from view. Left alone, Ben sank onto a nearby stone bench. The fragrance of roses hung heavy in the air, a stark contrast to the turmoil in his heart. He tilted his head back, gazing up at the towering estate looming in the distance. His eyes traced the ornate windows of the upper floors, wondering which one concealed Beth.

"What are you doing right now?" He murmured aloud, the words carried away by a gentle breeze. His mind drifted to Chase and

Tyler, a flicker of hope kindling at the thought that they might be hidden away in the attic, and if they were there, maybe there was still a chance. Ben shook his head, forcing himself back to reality. He couldn't afford to indulge in wishful thinking. With a heavy sigh, he pushed himself to his feet. Every step towards the gate felt like a betrayal, but he had no choice. He had a role to play, and for now, that meant walking away from the woman he loved.

Abraham, Adam, and Aaron all huddled around the ornate coffee table in the library, the firelight casting amber flickers across their solemn faces. The scent of old paper and burning cedar hung thick in the air. Maps and documents lay scattered before them, corners weighed down with polished stones and half-drunk glasses. Abraham leaned forward, his fingers steepled, gaze locked on a route carved through hostile terrain. Adam sat stiff-backed, arms crossed tightly over his chest, a pulse ticking in his jaw as he read the fine print of tomorrow's strategy. Aaron shifted in his seat, one hand absentmindedly tapping a pencil against his knee, his foot keeping a restless rhythm on the rug beneath them. None of them spoke, but the silence was dense - packed with questions, calculations, and the kind of uncertainty that only bred among men who couldn't afford to admit doubt.

"Any more noise from Kingsport? Anything new on the radios?" Aaron's voice cut through the tense silence. Adam shook his head, frustration evident in his tight jaw.
"Not much to go on, I'm afraid. We know they're there, and there's some kind of military presence, but beyond that—" He trailed off

with a shrug. Abraham's eyes narrowed, his fingers drumming an impatient rhythm on the polished wood.

"Remember, Aaron," he said, his tone laced with warning, "I want no funny business. You go as a democratic convoy. We can't appear to be a threat." Aaron bristled slightly at the implication.

"Of course," he replied, his voice carefully neutral, "but we can't go in blind either. If they have significant military power—"

"We adapt," Abraham cut him off, "we observe, but we do *not* provoke. Is that understood?" His gaze swept over both men, brooking no argument. Aaron nodded, his tactical mind already whirring.

"What if we brought a civilian or two as representatives?" He suggested, leaning forward; "It might soften our appearance, make us seem less militaristic." Abraham's eyes lit up, a rare smile tugging at his lips.

"Now that's an idea, Aaron," he turned to Adam, brow furrowed in thought, "did we have anyone at Prescott or Fort Irwin with a political background? Someone who could speak diplomatically if needed?" Adam rubbed his chin, considering.

"You know," he said slowly, "your wife would be the best person to ask about that. She ran the census for Henry, after all. She'd know everyone's background." At the mention of her, Abraham's expression darkened slightly.

"My wife," he said, his tone clipped, "has other matters to attend to at present." Adam raised an eyebrow, sensing the tension. He chose his next words carefully.

"With all due respect, brother, asking her a simple question about the census wouldn't distract her from her duty to you," he held Abraham's gaze, a silent challenge in his eyes, "her main objective is to bear you a son and sitting around in your bedroom isn't going to will her body into becoming pregnant. It will happen when it happens, as God's will." For a moment, the air in the library grew thick with unspoken tension. Abraham's jaw clenched, and Adam wondered if he'd pushed too far. Finally, Abraham's shoulders relaxed slightly.

"Very well," he conceded, "fetch Jacob for me."

"Yes, of course." Adam nodded, relieved he would not receive a reprimand, and strode to the library door. He called out into the hallway, and moments later, Jacob appeared, looking slightly bewildered at the summons.

"Jacob, I need you to fetch my wife for me. Tell her it's urgent." Abraham fixed Jacob with an imperious stare.

"At once." He said quickly. As Jacob hurried off, Adam couldn't help but wonder what Beth's reaction would be. He'd seen the bruises, heard the whispers. He believed in his brother and he believed in the cause, but he knew what Abraham could be like behind closed doors. He only hoped that involving her in this mission might offer her some respite, however brief, from whatever was happening away from prying eyes. The heavy oak door creaked as Ben's knuckles rapped against it. His heart pounded, unsure of the reception he'd receive. Abraham stood to greet Beth, taking a few small strides towards the door.

"That was quick—" His voice cut off abruptly as Abraham caught sight of Ben. Surprise flashed across his face, quickly replaced by a carefully neutral expression.

"I apologise for the interruption," Ben swallowed hard, "I was told to meet Aaron here to discuss tomorrow's mission."

"Let him in, Abraham." Aaron's voice rang out from within the library. As Abraham stepped aside, Ben felt a wave of trepidation wash over him. He'd faced down insurgents without flinching, and carried injured brothers across a warzone during a firefight, but something about this trio of power made his palms sweat.

"Gentlemen." Ben greeted, his voice steadier than he felt. The weight of their combined gazes bore down on him. Aaron leaned back in his chair, eyeing Ben critically.

"I'll be frank, I'm not thrilled about adding new blood to our ranks this late in the game. Everyone here earned their place early on." Ben's stomach twisted, wondering if he had miscalculated Abraham's invitation to Aaron's ranks.

"I'm thankful—"

"But," Aaron continued, "Abraham here insisted we give you a shot." He gestured towards the settlement's leader.

"What can I say? I admired the boldness of his request," Abraham nodded, a faint smile playing at the corners of his mouth, "the audacity to enter my library, my *sanctuary*, and ask for a change in one's rank was inspiring." Ben relaxed slightly, but remained on edge. He'd gotten his foot in the door, but he knew he'd have to prove himself ten times over to truly earn their trust, and to have any hope of protecting Beth.

"Thank you for the opportunity," Ben said carefully, "I won't let you down." Ben straightened his posture, drawing on years of military discipline. Abraham settled back into his chair, a smile creeping across his face as he stared at Aaron.

"I am sure you will find a way to ensure he earns his place." He mused.

"I may be a bit rusty, but I assure you, I'm an excellent scout. My family has served this country for generations," Ben paused, letting the weight of his words sink in, "I was top of my class in reconnaissance and survival training." Aaron's eyebrows raised slightly, a smirk playing at the corner of his mouth.

"A true countryman, through and through." He remarked, his tone a mix of amusement and grudging respect. Ben inclined his head in acknowledgment, a surge of pride mingling with his apprehension. "Thank you, sir," he hesitated, then pressed on, "if I may ask, what exactly will we be doing tomorrow?" Before Aaron could respond, the soft click of hurried footsteps on the hardwood floors drew everyone's attention to the doorway. Ben's heart leapt into his throat as Beth entered the room, her presence both electrifying and terrifying. She froze mid-step, her eyes locking with Ben's. The air between them crackled with unspoken emotion. Ben's fingers twitched at his sides, every fibre of his being screaming to rush to her, to hold her, to whisk her away from this place. But he couldn't move. He could only stare, taking in the sight of her. His gaze traveled over her form, noting with a mixture of relief and fury the delicate features of her face – untouched, thank God – before cataloging the angry bruises marring her arms. Ben clenched his jaw as he fought to maintain his composure. He longed to gather her in his arms, to tell her everything would be alright. But he knew any such action would doom them both. Instead, he stood frozen, caught between duty and desire, as Beth's presence filled the room like a storm about to break. Abraham strode towards Beth, his face a mask of false tenderness. He planted a kiss on her cheek, his hand possessively gripping her arm.

"You look radiant, my dear," he purred, "and looking so much better. Your colour is returning to your cheeks." Beth's smile was brittle as glass.

"Thank you," she murmured, taking another step into the room as her eyes darted between the men, confusion and wariness evident in her expression, "what am I doing here?"

"Perfect timing," Abraham replied, his voice syrupy sweet, "we were just about to go over tomorrow's mission with Ben. He'll be joining Aaron's ranks in our military." Ben watched Beth carefully, noting the flicker of surprise that crossed her face. Her eyes met his again, and this time there was steel in her gaze. He felt a chill run down his spine, unsure of what her next move would be. Beth turned to face Aaron and Adam, her posture straightening as if bracing for impact.

"Adding Ben to your military ranks is an excellent decision," she stated, her voice steady despite the slight tremor in her hands, "he's a skilled soldier and will undoubtedly uphold the values of this community."

"What a testimonial." Aaron smirked. Ben's heart raced as Beth continued, her words measured.

"When I was in need, Ben did everything he could to help me. Just as Abraham has done for everyone here." The room fell silent. Ben held his breath, acutely aware of Abraham's piercing stare boring into him. He fought to keep his face neutral, even as his mind raced. Abraham's eyebrows shot up, a mixture of surprise and amusement playing across his features.

"My, my, such high praise for Ben," he remarked, his tone light but his eyes sharp, "I'm pleased to hear it." Beth felt her pulse quicken, realising she may have overplayed her hand. She took a steadying breath before attempting to recondition the situation.

"He is an asset to any community, but I'm sure that's not why I was summoned here. Surely not for a character reference, if you've already assigned him to your ranks." Looking around the room, she watched as the faces on all four men relaxed slightly at the change of topic. Abraham's lips quirked into a small smile as he moved past her, returning to his seat beside his brother and cousin. Beth fought the urge to shiver as he brushed by, the faint scent of his cologne lingering in the air.

"You're quite right, my dear," Abraham said, settling into his chair, "we actually wanted to inquire about your time at Fort Irwin. During your work there, did you come across anyone with a strong political background?" Beth's mind raced, trying to discern the motivation behind this question.

"None were as wise as your father, of course," she shrugged, aiming for nonchalance, "he was a strong political presence and led with integrity."

"While he would have been a tremendous asset, it's unfortunate the outbreak claimed him so soon." A flicker of something - perhaps pride, or even grief - passed over Abraham's face as he spoke. Beth noted his lack of genuine emotion, her stomach churning, and concluded that his expression was simply relief that Henry had died, and wasn't around to challenge Abraham's power.

"There was a state senator among the survivors," she pressed on, "he might be able to offer some assistance. May I ask why you're interested? Perhaps if I knew more I could think who might suit what you need—"

"We're considering taking some civilians with us to another community," Abraham leaned forward, his elbows resting on his knees as he studied the maps before them, "it would help us appear less threatening." Beth's heart rate spiked as she considered the implication of another community close by. She struggled to keep her face neutral as her mind whirled with potential dangers, or monumental possibilities.

"Was the senator Republican?" Adam leaned forward, his brow furrowed. His tone held a hint of eagerness, as if the answer might sway some unspoken calculation. Beth felt a twinge of frustration. American politics had always been a labyrinth to her, even before the world fell apart. She shook her head slightly, her voice calm despite her inner turmoil.

"There was a senator and a local councilman I think, but I'm afraid I'm not well-versed enough in American politics to comment on their affiliations." She desperately wished she'd paid more attention during those census interviews. Any scrap of information could be valuable now, a potential bargaining chip in this dangerous game she found herself playing. Before anyone could press further, Jacob cleared his throat.

"Abraham, if I may offer some advice?" All eyes in the room swivelled to the unassuming man, forgotten in his silence as he guarded the door. Beth felt a spark of curiosity. Jacob was there to be seen and not heard, so she wondered what was so important for him to interject his opinion. Jacob took a tentative step forward, his posture deferential but his eyes determined. Abraham leaned forward, intrigued by the interruption.

"Go on."

"It might be wise for you to go yourself, sir, and—" he hesitated for a moment before continuing, "to take Beth with you." A shocked silence fell over the room. Beth's heart hammered in her chest - the idea both terrified and intrigued her. It could be an opportunity, but it could also be walking into even greater danger. Jacob, seeming to sense the tension, hurried to explain.

"The community we're contacting might be more civilian than military, based on the radio communications you've come across. An alliance could benefit from showing that we, too, have women and children to protect," his gaze flickered briefly to Beth, "if you present Beth as your wife, along with a few other representatives, it might demonstrate that we're not a threat." Beth's mind raced.

The suggestion was bold, and potentially risky, but it also held possibilities. A chance to gather information, to see the world beyond Biltmore's suffocating walls. Maybe even emancipation, but she quickly banished the dangerous thought of escape before it could fully form. She kept her face carefully neutral, waiting to see how Abraham would react to this unexpected proposal.

"It could show great strength," Adam conceded, glancing between Jacob and Abraham, "showing that we are confident enough to bring along our civilians to meet with others. That you're willing to put your beloved wife at risk."

"It could also show weakness," Aaron's brow furrowed, his voice laced with skepticism, "bringing civilians, especially women, into unknown territory." Beth's eyes instinctively sought Ben's across the room. Their gazes locked, a silent understanding passing between them. Her heart ached at the concern etched on his face. Abraham abruptly stood, his imposing figure casting a shadow as he began to pace. The floorboards creaked under his measured steps, each one punctuating the strained silence. Beth's muscles tensed, awaiting his decision. Finally, Abraham turned to Aaron.

"Take Ben to the Music Room, brief him on our military plans." His voice was firm, brooking no argument.

"My *strategy room* has been designated for my most trusted men." Aaron interjected angrily, glancing towards Ben and then back at Abraham.

"Gather the rest of tomorrow's convoy," Abraham ignored Aaron's objection, "explain the new arrangements. Beth and I will be joining you tomorrow." Aaron's jaw clenched, but he nodded curtly.

"Yes, sir. We'll need to arrange extra transportation."

"See to it." Abraham commanded. Aaron rose reluctantly, gesturing for Ben to follow. As they moved towards the door, Ben brushed past Beth. His hand, rough and warm, grazed hers for the briefest moment. The touch sent electricity coursing through Beth's body. Memories flooded her mind – stolen moments, passionate embraces, the safety she'd felt in his arms. She bit her lip hard, willing herself not to cry. She internally begged her mind to pull herself together, blinking rapidly as she felt her heart surge in her chest. She glanced around, paranoid that someone had noticed the exchange. Her eyes swept the room, not catching Adam's keen gaze observing her from the corner of his eye. Abraham's voice cut through Beth's thoughts as she mentally rejoined the conversation.

"Mary will accompany us as well. A united family front will serve us well," Abraham turned to her, his eyes cold and calculating, "Beth, you'll go with Adam to speak with Mary. Then find that senator and councilman you mentioned. Convince them to join our convoy to Kingsport." She nodded mutely, her mind racing, desperately wondering how she was supposed to convince anyone of anything in her state. Adam's eyes flicked from Beth to Abraham. "Am I to come too, to represent this united family front?"

"We shouldn't be gone more than a few days," Abraham's gaze shifted to Adam, "while we're away, you're in charge. I expect Biltmore to be run with the same care that I have maintained."

"Of course, brother," Adam inclined his head, "you can count on me."

"Abraham," Jacob interjected, "shouldn't Adam be included in the welcome party? If it's to be a family affair, he should go as well." Beth looked between Jacob and Abraham, an inkling in her gut telling her that Jacob was trying to get them all away from Biltmore. "Husband," she stepped towards him and placed a gentle hand on his shoulder, "it would be ideal for our brother to attend as well."

Abraham paused for a moment, before shrugging her hand from his shoulder.

"Adam will remain here as instructed," he said dryly, "as much as this idea inspires me, I won't trust this community left in anyone else's hands other than my family, and I need Aaron with me on this. Adam is my best solution to being away for a long period of time. Now, go to Mary." As Adam led Beth from the room, she felt a mixture of relief and dread. Relief to be away from Abraham's suffocating presence, but dread at what lay ahead. The hallways seemed to stretch endlessly as they made their way to the second-floor sitting room. They found Mary reading by the fire, the warm glow softening her features. Beth approached cautiously, hyper-aware of Adam's presence behind her. She sank into a nearby chair, feeling the weight of her exhaustion. Mary looked up, a practiced smile gracing her lips.

"Ah, my dear cousins," she said, closing her book, "to what do I owe this pleasure?"

"Abraham has decided to join tomorrow's convoy to Kingsport," Adam stepped forward before Beth could speak, "and Beth will be accompanying him, and he'd like you to join them as well." Beth watched Mary's face carefully, searching for any hint of her true feelings. But Mary's expression remained pleasantly neutral, giving nothing away.

"Kingsport? How intriguing," Mary raised an eyebrow, "and what, pray tell, is the purpose of this little excursion?" Mary's eyes glinted with amusement as she tilted her head, a coy smile playing on her lips.

"There's a community there," Beth offered slowly, glancing to Adam and then back to Mary, "and Abraham wants us to present a familial approach, as opposed to a military appearance."

"Do I have a choice in the matter?" She leaned forward, placing her elbow on her knee and resting her chin on her hand.

"I'm afraid not, cousin," Adam's smirk was cold, devoid of any real humour, "Abraham's word is law, as you well know." Beth felt a chill run down her spine at the casual way Adam reinforced Abraham's authority. She fought to keep her face neutral, acutely aware of how every reaction could be scrutinised.

"As I well know," Mary mused, leaning back in her chair, "what time are we leaving?"

"Early," Adam responded, his tone brusque, "pack for a few days away. If you'll excuse me, I have other matters to attend to." As Adam's footsteps faded down the hallway, Beth found herself alone with Mary. The crackling fire seemed too loud in the sudden silence.

"So, cousin, how are you enjoying married life?" Mary leaned in, her voice dropping to a conspiratorial whisper.

"Mary—" Beth's stomach twisted. She opened her mouth, but no words came, even though she so desperately wanted to describe the nightmare of the past few days to someone who seemed so innocent in her family's scheming. Mary's smile never wavered, but something in her eyes softened.

"Don't piss him off," she glanced back at her book, suddenly murmuring, "not in public, and certainly not in private." Beth's heart raced. She wanted to press for more information, but fear kept her silent. Instead, she nodded slightly, acknowledging Mary's warning while her mind reeled with the implications.

"Whatever you do and whatever he says," Mary whispered, "just smile and nod."

"What do you mean?" Beth's eyes widened, her voice barely above a whisper. Mary's hand shot out, gripping Beth's wrist with surprising strength.

"Hush." She hissed, eyes darting to the doorway.

"Please, Mary. I need to understand." Beth's heart pounded as she leaned in closer. Mary sighed, her features softening.

"I noticed Abraham drinking at your wedding dinner," she murmured, her words barely audible, "he's supposed to be sober, or so I thought." Confusion clouded Beth's face as she searched Mary's expression for something, anything to give away what she was trying to say.

"He's been drinking for a while," Beth's face was lined with unease, "I've seen him drinking in the library when I've been in there, well before the wedding—"

"I must've missed it. When the pandemic hit, he found God and had stopped drinking," Mary offered, leaning forward and lowering her voice to mere decibels, "but it wasn't God he found, it was power."

"He told me about his wife and son," Beth's mind raced, piecing together fragments of information, "is that when he started drinking?"

"No," Mary's gaze hardened, her voice laced with long-buried pain, "that's when he started drinking more." Beth slouched back in her chair, her brow furrowed as she wrestled with the scattered pieces of the puzzle before her. Her mind was a foggy mess as she tried to make sense of it all. Mary sat across from her, her expression twisted into an eager leer as she waited for Beth to piece together the truth. The silence between them was thick and tense, broken only by the occasional crack of the fire. Outside, the sun continued to rise over the late morning, casting an orange glow through the windows that seemed to match the intensity of their conversation.

"I don't understand—"

"What did he tell you?" Mary asked, slightly louder than before as she leaned back into her chair, mirroring Beth's posture and expression.

"He told me they were killed in an accident," she offered slowly, "run off the road by a drunk driver."

"An accident? Is that what he's calling it now?" She inhaled sharply. Beth searched her wistful face for a hint or a clue as to what she was attempting to convey. Mary leaned in again, shuffling forward on the chair so that her knees touched Beth's. She waited patiently as Beth slowly sat up, leaning in, her ear merely an inch from Mary's mouth.

"Beth," Mary whispered softly, the sadness and honesty evident in her tone, "Abraham's wife was one of the sweetest women I had ever met, and she obeyed his every command. When he hit her, she took it in her stride and never faltered. When she told him she was pregnant, he was elated, and he never touched her again."

"What happened?" Beth pressed, unsure if she wanted the answer she knew was coming.

"She couldn't stop the baby from crying, she didn't want him to anger Abraham. But Abraham, he ran into the nursery and shook him so violently that he died." Mary took in a low, deep breath as Beth swallowed hard, shaking her head and closing her eyes to stop the tears from falling down her cheeks.

"He killed his son?"

"She grabbed the baby and ran to the car, determined to get to the hospital. Abraham followed close behind and ran them off the road when he tried to stop her." Mary concluded deplorably, her voice soft and laced with torment. Beth swallowed hard.

"How do you know this?"

"We all knew about it. Our own little *family secret*. Abraham confessed to his father, begging for redemption. Henry told my father, seeking his advice. Aaron and I overheard him telling our mother, and we told Adam," Mary's voice was surprisingly calm, but not without sorrow, "we have no secrets in this family, Beth, and now you're one of us. You should know the truth. Abraham was the drunk driver, he killed his wife and son." The words hit Beth like a physical blow. She struggled to breathe, her world tilting on its axis. Everything she thought she knew about her new husband crumbled, revealing a further darkness she'd only glimpsed. She thought she knew all she had needed to in order to play him, in order to manipulate him into trusting her. But in that moment, Beth realised just how precarious her position truly was.

CHAPTER 16

Dawn's light spilled through the cracks in the heavy drapes, casting a soft glow on the bedspread where Beth methodically packed her bag. Her fingers brushed over the rugged canvas, checking for the essentials she'd need for the trip to Kingsport. The route was etched into her mind – a path of survival rather than convenience, winding around the possible remnants of a world left to wither. A sudden knock at the door jolted her from her focus. Before she could call out, Ben pushed the door open and stepped inside, his presence an unspoken command.

"What are you doing here?" She asked softly, masking her surprise with a tone that bordered on indifference.

"Got orders to bring you down to the car." Ben replied as his gaze lingered on her, taking in the scene as Beth resumed folding a pair of jeans with precise corners.

"I thought Jacob was my *personal guard*." She picked up a battered paperback from the bed and slid it alongside her clothes. Ben's curiosity broke through his disciplined exterior.

"What's that you're reading?"

"Is this a social visit, or are you just here to make sure I don't dawdle?" Beth shot him a look, one eyebrow arching as if questioning his intent. He shook his head, a hint of embarrassment coloured his face. He advanced a few more steps, closing the distance between them, yet respectful of the space she guarded so fiercely. Satisfied, Beth zipped her bag shut, the sound echoing in the silence that followed. Her hand hesitated over the zipper of her bag, her attention fixed on the floorboards. Ben watched her every move, aware that their journey together was about to begin anew under the watchful eyes of Abraham in unfamiliar territory. Sensing his scrutiny, she finally relented to Ben's persistent gaze, turning her head in slow concession. She hoisted the bag onto her shoulder, ready to face whatever lay beyond the walls of Biltmore. With the morning light slicing through the gaps in the curtains, it revealed the stark discolouration against her pale skin - a canvas of bruising that encircled her neck like a morbid necklace. Ben's voice was quiet, almost a whisper, as if fearful to cast the words into existence. "What happened?"

"Take a guess." Beth said, her voice devoid of inflection. She didn't flinch when he reached out, his fingers tentatively tracing the outline of the bruises. The imprints mirrored the shape of fingers, an intimate signature of violence.

"What can I do to help?" Ben's touch retracted as quickly as a spark snuffed out, and a shadow crossed his face.

"Nothing," she replied with a wry twist of her lips, "unless you think you can undo the past."

"Beth—"

"Just trust me, and stay out of my way. When I'm close enough, Abraham will pay for it," her eyes locked onto his, fierce despite the vulnerability written on her flesh, "I'll make sure he pays for everything." There was a finality in her tone, a certainty that brooked no argument.

"I know your anger isn't directed at me," he whispered, "but I'll take it if you need someone to lash out on." He brought his hands to her face, stroking her cheek softly with his thumb.

"I know," she nodded, "I'm sorry." They paused briefly, her eyes shut as his fingers lightly grazed her skin. Her heart fluttered, aware of his proximity yet the distance between them. She longed to kiss him, to experience the warmth of his lips on hers. She yearned for a moment with him that would erase all the hurt and sorrow. His presence soothed and centered her, but being trapped here with him in a place where they couldn't be together felt suffocating. Beth shook her head, taking a small step back as she opened her eyes. Ben's jaw set in silent understanding, his soldier's discipline masking the turmoil beneath. He nodded once, his affirmation sharp and precise. Reaching for her bag without another word, he shouldered the weight of its contents and their shared resolve. He turned towards the door, his footsteps steady and resolute. Beth let out a slow breath before following him out of the room. The morning chill hung heavy in the air as Beth descended the grand staircase of the Biltmore Estate, her footsteps echoing through the opulent yet decaying halls. Abraham awaited at the foot of the stairs, his tall frame wrapped in a simple, well-kept coat that belied the authority he wielded within these walls. His blue eyes, piercing as ever, softened momentarily as he leaned in to plant a light kiss upon her cheek, a gesture as possessive as it was perfunctory.

"Good morning, wife." He greeted, his voice devoid of warmth despite the cordial words. Outside, the overgrown grounds of the estate sprawled out like a kingdom in ruins, the early light casting long shadows across the gravel driveway. Beth's gaze fell upon the Humvee idling nearby, its solar panels gleaming dully beneath the hazy sky. Luis sat behind the wheel, his wiry frame almost too lean for the robust vehicle he commanded.

"Time to go." Luis stated flatly, his brown eyes flickering to Ben as the latter climbed into the front passenger seat. Ben's expression remained unreadable, his focus fixed on some distant point ahead, deliberately ignoring Luis's smirk. The tension between the two men crackled in the air, an invisible but palpable force.

"Knock it off, Luis." Beth said sharply, breaking the silence. Her voice carried a steely edge, one honed by the trials she had faced and the resolve that steeled her will. Luis turned, his features twisting into a mocking sneer.

"What are you gonna do about it?" He challenged, his tone laced with derision.

"It's fine, Beth." Ben said sharply, maintaining his gaze forward.

"Yes," Luis smiled maliciously, enjoying every second of the discomfort that both Beth and Ben clearly expressed, "it's perfectly fine, we have ninety minutes together in this car, we might as well catch up." Beth leaned towards him, her whisper venomous, a dangerous promise delivered with chilling calm.

"The moment that I am certain I'm carrying Abraham's son, I'll get someone to hit me so hard it makes the time you broke my jaw seem like a love tap," she paused, letting the threat sink in, "and then I'll tell Abraham that *you* did it." Luis's smirk faltered, uncertainty flashing in his eyes, his voice edged with bravado.

"You think he'd believe that?"

"Everyone knows you've hit me before, Luis," Beth continued, her voice low and unyielding, "who wouldn't believe you'd do it again?"

"You wouldn't dare." Luis clenched his jaw, his eyes darting to Ben. The haunted look in Luis's eyes betrayed his attempt at nonchalance. Ben sat motionless, his gaze fixed on a point beyond the windshield, but in the reflection of the rearview mirror, his face was etched with a mix of fear and pride.

"Luis," Beth whispered menacingly, her eyes unblinking as she bore into Luis' soul, "what do you think Abraham would do to the man who would dare harm the woman carrying the saviour of the earth?" Her words were cold and staggered as she emphasised every syllable. The silence in the car was thick and suffocating. Ben's jaw was tight, his knuckles white as he gripped the door handle with one hand and dug his fingers into his knee with the other. Luis sat next to him, maintaining a facade of calmness, but fear and disdain flickered in his eyes, his body betraying the tension as he clutched the steering wheel with a death grip. Beth couldn't help but notice the way his fingers dug into the fabric of Ben's headrest, his casual demeanour a thin veil disguising the turmoil within him. Every muscle in his body seemed coiled, ready to react at any moment. She could feel the unspoken tension between them, like a storm brewing just beneath the surface. Then, suddenly, Luis' hollow laugh shattered the tension.

"Well, Ben," Luis' smirked, "what have you and Austin been teaching her? What happened to that fragile girl I last saw at that campsite?" Beth turned her head slightly, meeting Luis's taunt with a cold smile.

"The fragile girl who stabbed you in the shoulder, you mean? I didn't learn how to take care of myself from Ben and Austin," her words were like ice, veiled by a sickly sweet tone of sarcasm, "I learned it from men like you." In the confined space of the Humvee, a shiver of fear ran down Luis's spine at the implications. He knew all too well the wrath of Abraham and the fate that would await him should he be accused of such a crime. Beth's words painted a picture more terrifying than any physical blow could inflict. Outside, Abraham's voice cut through the air, authoritative as he directed the convoy. Aaron slipped into the driver's seat of the lead Humvee, nodding solemnly at Abraham's instructions. In the backseat, Zachary Brooks adjusted his spectacles, leaning forward to exchange a few hushed words with Patricia Cox, both dressed in attire that spoke of their political stature even amidst the decline of civilization. Beth thought about the conversation from the evening prior, when she had approached Zach and Pat separately. She had spoken to them once or twice at Fort Irwin, checking in on them during the outbreak, planning to include them in a new town council once the arrivals from Prescott had settled in, but all of that had vanished when Abraham took control. The unexpected proposal from Beth had caught them both off guard, but they were eager to put their political savvy to use for the betterment of Abraham's community. While Zach appeared more than willing to take on this task, Pat seemed slightly less enthusiastic and hesitant. Nevertheless, both of them were determined to help bring Abraham's vision to life. Despite their vastly different political and religious beliefs, they were united in their desire to contribute meaningful work instead of idly watching the world go by. It was a refreshing change from their usual routines, and they revelled in the opportunity to make a lasting impact. As Shauna slid into the Humvee beside Beth, her soft smile contrasted with the tension inside the vehicle. She settled in, her gaze briefly lingering on the bruised marks that marred Beth's neck before looking away, the unspoken words hanging heavy in the confined space. The Humvee's engines rumbled to life, harnessing the dawn's light. The convoy moved out, carrying its cargo of strained alliances and whispered threats down the gravel path, past the overgrown grandeur of the Biltmore Estate, and towards the uncertainty of Kingsport. Shauna's gaze drifted outside the window, taking in the sight of overgrown hedges blurring past. Beth shuffled beside her, adjusting the pack at her feet.

"Haven't seen much of you lately." She remarked.

"Mostly out on supply runs," Shauna replied, her eyes returning to meet Beth's, the calm in her voice was a stark contrast to the undercurrent of tension in the Humvee, "I've scouted most of the southern towns and then east into Charlotte. That's why they wanted me for this trip."

"You'd think we would've crossed paths with Kingsport by now." Beth's brow furrowed.

"Never needed to go this far north before." Shauna shrugged, glancing back at the convoy trailing them. Beth turned her attention to the Humvee behind theirs, its cargo of soldiers in military attire moving with rigid discipline. She craned her neck slightly.

"Where's Mary?" She asked, hoping she had simply missed her friend among the faces.

"Mary," Luis snorted from his seat upfront, sparing a brief glance in the rearview mirror, "she woke up sick." His tone carried an edge of irritation, or perhaps it was satisfaction.

"Abraham wasn't pleased, but he let her stay behind." Shauna added, studying Beth's face as she spoke. A pang of disappointment hit Beth - she had counted on Mary's support and familiar comfort during their expedition. Still, Ben's presence offered silent reassurance, and Shauna's composed figure was not without its comfort. It was Luis who broke the momentary silence that enveloped them.

"Too many women coming along as it is," he muttered distastefully, "shouldn't send a woman to do a man's job." The Humvee rolled forward, tires crunching against the gravel driveway. A heavy quietness settled over them as they left the safety of the estate, the vehicle's suspension rocking gently with each imperfection in the road. Towering trees gave way to the familiar structures of Biltmore Village, their faded facades standing testament to the world that once was. Northward they drove, into the breadth of a landscape reclaimed by nature.

Austin stood rigid, his silhouette etched against the windowpane as the convoy's dust trail blended with the horizon. As the last Humvee vanished from view, he pivoted sharply, his boots silent on the polished wood floors of the estate's second floor. The living hall stretched before him, a vast expanse of history and power juxtaposed with the stark reality of their new world. He cast a lingering gaze at the staircase, then to the corridor where shadows danced in the morning light. His thoughts flitted to the fourth floor, to Chase and Tyler, potentially hidden somewhere within the estate's labyrinthine upper reaches. The guards paced their designated paths, oblivious to Austin's scrutiny, their eyes fixed on the doors to the playroom. Austin crossed the hall, his steps measured and sure. The murmur of soft voices drew his attention to the children's playroom. Through the half-open door, Jennifer's soothing tones mingled with Hannah's gentle laughter and Grace's quiet affirmations. The sounds carried a warmth that contrasted the cool detachment of the guards outside. Turning away, Austin navigated the length of the corridor, skirting the open space above the banquet hall. Below, remnants of breakfast clung to porcelain - scrambled eggs, toasted bread, half-eaten fruit slices. The residents, weary yet resilient, tended to their plates with methodical care, restoring order amidst the chaos of their daily survival. Austin ascended the tight winding back staircase, his hand lightly grazing the cool, coarse texture of the wall. The third floor greeted him with a hush, its hallway stretched like a forgotten whisper. He climbed the narrow stairs leading to the fourth floor, each step deliberate and soundless. The dim light from the small windows did little to chase away the shadows that clung to the corners of the servant rooms. Dust motes danced in the beams of sunlight that dared to pierce the gloom. Austin moved from door to door, pushing each one open with a gentle nudge of his shoulder. Sparse boxes lay scattered across the floors, their contents a mystery left unexplored. At the end of the corridor, the grand servants hall stood tall and imposing, a reminder of bygone days. The once-polished wood of the ancient table now lay covered in a thick layer of dust, its intricate carvings barely visible. The air hung heavy with the musty scent of neglect and disuse, as if time itself had forgotten the top floor of the estate long before the pandemic had engulfed the world. Cobwebs clung to every corner, adding to the eerie atmosphere that filled the room. It was a ghostly relic, frozen in time and shrouded in memories long forgotten. He made his way into the observatory, the highest vantage point of the estate, where the world outside could be seen in panoramic splendour. Squinting against the glare of the morning sun, Austin searched for any sign of the convoy. But the southern horizon revealed only emptiness - the vehicles had disappeared beyond his view, likely threading their way northward by now. The sudden creak of the floorboards echoed in the observatory, a sharp note against the silence. Austin whirled around, muscles tensing as he faced the newcomer. Mary stood there, the dimness of the room softening the lines of her face.

"What are you doing up here?" Her blue eyes searched his, a quiet curiosity within their depths.

"I was sent to gather supplies." Austin stated, his voice steady despite the surprise. Mary's lips curled into a faint smile, a brief flicker of amusement crossing her features.

"There's nothing here that you'd have been sent for." She assured him, her gaze sweeping over the sparse room.

"Then what brings you here?" Austin pressed, narrowing his eyes at her. Her voice dropped to a murmur, as if the walls themselves might eavesdrop.

"I'm looking for someone."

"Is there anyone else up here?" His question hung between them, heavy with unspoken urgency.

"Probably," she shrugged, her shoulders lifting slightly under the fabric of her blouse, "Abraham would only stash your friends in an attic corner, far from prying eyes." Austin's heart skipped a beat. Such candour from Mary was unexpected, and alarming.

"Do you know what he did with Chase and Tyler?" The words left his lips like bullets, pointed and loaded with implications of threat. Mary met his gaze, and in that moment, her usual timidity seemed to dissolve into something harder, more resolved.

"If they're hidden away here, then Abraham has plans we've yet to see." Mary's shoulders lifted in another noncommittal shrug, a gesture Austin was coming to recognise as her shield against the world.

"Mary, if you know something—"

"I really wouldn't know where else they might be." She swept her gaze back towards the shadowed expanse of the servants' hall.

"Then why are you here looking for them?" Austin's words were pointed, an arrow seeking its target.

"I have a proposition," turning to face him again, Mary's features tightened with purpose, "one of them might want to consider it.

It could save a life." Austin studied her, noticing the subtle shift in her demeanour. Before he could question further, the sound of footsteps echoed from the grand staircase, drawing closer. Instinctively, he reached out and guided Mary further into the observatory, their steps silent against the aged floorboards. Behind the ornate fireplace, they huddled close, the heavy scent of soot and time enveloping them. In the near distance, the muffled voices of two men seeped into the hiding space, indecipherable but laced with authority.

"Who is that?" Mary's whisper cut through the stillness, her eyes reflecting the flickering light that filtered in through the dust-caked windows.

"Shh." Austin cautioned, his own breath subdued. He edged forward, peering around the cold stone, but the figures had already retreated, their presence now just an echo down the corridor. Silence settled over the observatory like a thick fog, the tension between Austin and Mary palpable in the still air.

"Did you recognise their voices?" Mary broke the quiet with her hushed inquiry. Austin shook his head, his gaze fixed on the shadowy corridor where the voices had faded. He stood sentinel, muscles tensed, ready to spring into action if necessary. Time trickled by slowly until the men's voices returned, echoing off the walls with stark clarity.

"It's okay, you go on break, I'll go feed the other one." One man said to the other. Their footsteps receded as they descended the staircase, their departure granting Austin and Mary a momentary breath of relief. Once the sound of their steps was well and truly gone, Austin faced Mary squarely.

"What proposition are you talking about?" He asked, his voice low but demanding.

"Do you think they've separated them? Feeding them on different floors?" Mary sidestepped the question, eyes darting towards the stairwell. Austin gave a curt nod, his mind already racing through the implications. With a sense of urgency, he moved towards the corridor the guards had taken, the last unexplored path whispering promises of answers. Mary trailed behind him, a silent shadow in his wake.

"Mary, you should go." He said over his shoulder, his stride purposeful. The echo of his boots against the floor marked their progress through the oppressive gloom of the estate's forgotten halls. Mary's heels clicked against the wooden floor, her steps insistent as she followed Austin.

"I'm not leaving," she stated, "I have my own agenda." Austin pivoted, blocking her path with his broad frame.

"What agenda? What proposition?" He demanded.

"It's none of your business." Mary shot back, a flicker of defiance in her blue eyes. She attempted to sidestep him, but he matched her move, effectively cornering her.

"Listen," Austin said, his voice hardening, "you're not going anywhere until you explain, and if I have to I'll haul you downstairs and tell Adam I followed you up here and found you snooping where you shouldn't."

"You think he'd believe your word over mine?"

"That depends," Austin gave her a slight smirk, "who does he hate more? Black people or women?" With a huff of frustration, Mary grabbed Austin's arm and yanked him towards the nearest room, a small servant's quarters. She slowly clicked the door shut behind them, plunging the space into near darkness, save for the feeble light straining through the grimy window. The dust particles danced in the sparse rays that invaded the gloom, casting long shadows over the sparse furnishings. Austin scanned the room, its walls holding secrets of a bygone era, of quiet servitude and unseen labor. Mary's fingers traced the aged grain of the wooden tabletop, her gaze flickering up to meet Austin's.

"Chase and Tyler," she began, "they were together in the basement, caught by one of Abraham's *loyal followers*." She paused, swallowing hard as if the words themselves were a burden too heavy to bear. Austin's stance stiffened, his muscles coiling like springs wound too tight.

"What do you know?" He pressed.

"Only whispers, rumours that slither through the hallways," Mary replied, "Abraham sees their love as a sin worthy of death. They disappeared not long after." A shiver ran down her spine as she spoke the grim sentence.

"Are you certain they're still alive?" Austin's voice was steady, but under the calm surface swirled an undercurrent of urgency.

"Abraham craves his theatrics so he wouldn't squander the chance for a public lesson," her eyes met his, conveying a truth that needed no further explanation, "he would display their fate for all to witness, yet there has been no spectacle, no warning made example—"

"No public hanging, you mean." Austin finished her thoughts aloud.

"Well he didn't build that platform only for Sabrina."

"Then why spare them?" The question hung heavily in the air between them.

"Potential," Mary said, the word laced with a bitterness that belied her gentle appearance, "to Abraham, every able-bodied man is a soldier for his divine cause. He must believe he can mould them into his image, reshape their desires to fit his vision for the new world." Austin processed this, the gears of his mind turning, piecing together the sinister implications of her revelation. Their breaths mingled in the stillness of the room, two souls momentarily united in a silent vow to defy the tyranny that held them captive.

"And if he can't?"

"Abraham needs to show the community that he is forgiving, when he wants to be," Mary looked up at him, unblinking and devoid of any emotion, "people need to believe that he is just, and has done all that he can to help a lost soul, before they are punished." Austin scanned the dimly lit room, his gaze settling on Mary's figure as she tentatively brushed a strand of hair behind her ear. The silence was punctured by the distant echo of footsteps elsewhere in the vast estate.

"Mould them," he repeated, his voice low but clear "what does that entail?"

"Late at night," Mary began, her eyes darting away momentarily, "I've seen women led up these stairs. They're not volunteers." He felt a chill, his words laced with a mixture of disdain and fear.

"So Chase and Tyler, are they being coerced?"

"They want them broken, reshaped." Mary's shrug was a ripple of unease. Austin's jaw tightened at the thought. He watched as Mary's hand moved to rest gently on her stomach, a protective gesture that spoke volumes. Austin raised an eyebrow, glaring at her hand across her swollen abdomen.

"And your agenda?"

"I have a problem." She confessed.

"A problem." He echoed, his attention now fixed on the slight curve beneath her hand.

"Someone needs to claim this child," she said, her eyes held a mix of fear and determination, "Chase or Tyler could. If they agree, it might spare one of them."

"And Abraham would accept such a thing," Austin glanced at her midsection with skepticism, "a child born out of wedlock?"

"We would be married before the child is born." Mary answered, her voice faltering slightly. Austin raised a questioning eyebrow.

"A child conceived out of wedlock then."

"Abraham has his rules, but survival bends all laws here," the air between them grew heavy as she spoke, laden with the weight of desperate choices, "my child would be a blessing. The father and I would be punished, but our lives would be spared." Austin's stance remained resolute, his mind already racing through the implications of Mary's words. Outside the small window, the light shifted as clouds passed over the sun, casting shadows that danced across the walls of the servant's room. Mary's fingers trembled as she traced the contours of her stomach through the fabric of her dress, her gaze fixed on some distant point beyond the room's confinement. Austin stood motionless, his eyes locked on the subtle movement, an unspoken understanding dawning between them.

"It could be worse," Mary said finally, breaking the silence that had settled like dust in the dimly lit chamber, "if Abraham knew the full truth." Austin's expression hardened, a slight furrow creasing his brow. The air felt thick with secrets, each one more dangerous than the last.

"Truth?" He pressed, the word hanging between them like a sword poised to strike. Mary drew a slow breath, her voice a fragile echo of fear and resolve.

"In the Bible, incest is clearly prohibited, especially in the legal codes of the Old Testament. It is considered a serious sin, and those who commit it face harsh consequences." Her words seemed to linger in the stale air, a testament to the grave reality that underpinned their existence within Abraham's domain, a place where ancient edicts mingled with modern ruthlessness.

"Incest? Mary—"

"These prohibitions," she interrupted, "they reflect the belief in maintaining purity within family relationships and social boundaries. While some instances of incest are described in the Bible, they are never condoned and often lead to negative outcomes or divine disapproval." Outside, the groan of overgrown ivy against stone whispered alongside their clandestine exchange, while the faintest scent of decay from the forest floor seeped through the cracks of the aging estate. They stood, two figures ensnared by the weight of the past and the uncertainty of the future, bound by the sacred and the profane. Mary paced the length of the dimly lit room, her shadow stretching and retracting across the peeling wallpaper as she passed the solitary window where light fought to penetrate the grime. The weight of secrets pulled at her shoulders, a burden she bore with every hesitant step. Her hands fluttered to her stomach, a protective gesture that couldn't shield her from Austin's piercing gaze. His eyes narrowed, a grimace distorting his features as he took in her swollen abdomen.

"That's—"

"Judge not," she snapped, her voice carrying a sharp edge it usually lacked, "do not judge, or you too will be judged. For in the same way you judge others, you will be judged, and with the measure you use, it will be measured to you." She released her hold on her rounded belly, letting her hands fall limp at her sides. Austin's nostrils flared, his jaw clenching.

"Never thought quoting the Bible at someone applied to something the Bible is inherently against."

"Are you without sin then?" Mary's laugh was devoid of humour, a scoff that filled the space between them with its scorn.

"Well I've never fucked my sister." Austin shot back, the words slicing through the air like a blade. Outside, the birdsong seemed to halt, the leaves stilled on their branches, and even the grandeur of the Biltmore Estate fell mute behind the gravity of their exchange. "Survival has its own rules," Mary said, a trace of defiance creeping into her voice, "without Aaron, I'd be just another ghost haunting these halls." Austin's eyes, hard as flint, met hers. The air between them crackled with tension, the musty scent of old wood and neglect pervasive in the silence.

"Was your sin worth your soul?" He asked, his tone edged with something that might have been concern or condemnation.

"Next time you're alone with Beth, ask her the same." Mary shot back. Her blue eyes were steel now, no longer pleading for understanding but demanding it. His anger surged like a wave, then receded just as fast, leaving a cold resolve. Austin relaxed his body, refraining from causing more tension within the already strained and confined space.

"What's your plan then?"

"Chase or Tyler could say it was one of them," she offered, her words measured, "say I was exploring, and bored, and found them up here, and that I was nursing them back to health. That we got close, fell in love, and sinned. Out of lust, not blood."

"And you think Abraham will buy that?" Austin's skepticism laced his question like poison.

"It's a sin he can forgive," Mary shrugged, the gesture heavy with resignation, "no one dies for love."

"And if they don't go along with it?" Austin pressed, already knowing the weight of her answer.

"Then they're on their own." Her gaze didn't waver, a mirror to the harsh reality they faced. He turned, his boots thudding against the grandeur's faded glory. Down the hallway, he moved past portraits whose eyes seemed to follow him, through the whispers of a world left behind. Room after room he searched, the shadows growing longer as the sun rose outside the ivy-draped windows. Finally, at the end of the corridor, in the back servant's quarters, he found what he sought. Chase, rugged and calm despite the handcuffs binding him to the cold metal pipe, ate slowly with his free hand, picking at the meagre offerings he had on the plate before him. His presence was a silent testament to the strength that had always defined him, even now in captivity. Chase's grey-blue eyes widened as the imposing figure of Austin came into view, muscles tensed with purpose beneath his worn shirt. The air in the room grew thicker as Chase's gaze flickered past Austin, landing on the ethereal form of Mary lingering hesitantly behind him. Austin, his movements exuding a silent command, crossed the space between them and knelt, resting a firm hand on the nape of Chase's neck.

"Oh, you're really here," Chase murmured, the warmth from Austin's palm seeping into his skin, "thought I was imagining you." Austin's attempt to refrain from showing his concern for the state of his friend was feeble.

"I'm really here, brother."

"Mary?" Chase's voice held a thread of disbelief as he searched her face for confirmation.

"She's real too." Austin's response was a simple nod. The dust motes danced lazily in a shaft of sunlight that cut through the room's decay, illuminating the trio in its golden hue. Chase shifted, the sound of his movement echoing off the mansion's grand walls, now stripped of their former glory.

"What're you guys doing here?" Chase asked, the question hanging in the stale air. Mary stepped forward, a tentative smile curving her lips.

"They couldn't keep Austin away if they tried." She said, the humour in her words failing to mask the concern etched deeply in her expression. Chase snorted, dismissing the lightness in her tone. He knew too well the gravity of their situation.

"Do you know where Tyler is?" Austin's sharp eyes remained fixed on Chase, searching for a hint of knowing. A shake of the head was Chase's reply, the mere gesture was enough to send a cascade of dried blood flaking from his wrists to the floor.

"I don't think he's on this floor." He said, his voice raw. Austin followed Chase's glance to the crimson-stained bindings. Each mark told a story of struggle, each scab a testament to their dire reality. They all understood the unspoken truth - these were not merely remnants of physical restraints, but symbols of their fight against the oppressive theocracy that sought to bind them all. Chase leaned against the cold stone wall, its peeling wallpaper brushing against his skin as if whispering secrets of escape. He inhaled deeply, the musty scent of decay mingling with the copper tang of his own blood.

"I managed to slip out once, when it was just rope," he began, his voice betraying a hint of pride amidst the weariness, "searched this entire floor for Tyler, but found nothing." His memory wandered through the desolate fourth-floor hallways, their grandeur now just an echo of the past.

"Shit." Austin muttered under his breath, his gaze narrowing on the metal cuffs that bit into Chase's flesh. They were cruelly tight, the skin beneath them an angry shade of bruised blue.

"I got as far as the hallway after the stairs on the third floor before I was hit over the back of the head and I woke up here again," Chase winced as he flexed his hand, "can't feel my fingers much." He confessed, shifting his hand in futile defiance against the unyielding steel. Mary approached cautiously, her eyes reflecting the dim light as she reached for his hand. Chase instinctively recoiled, his trust worn thin by the days spent under Abraham's ruthless grip. Austin's hand came to rest reassuringly on Chase's shoulder.

"It's okay," he said, his tone firm yet laced with empathy, "she's here to help, I think." With a roll of her eyes, Mary ignored the men's exchange and focused on the task at hand. Her fingertips probed gently at Chase's swollen wrist, her touch clinical yet not devoid of concern.

"Can you feel this?"

"Barely." Chase grunted, his jaw set against the discomfort.

"He's going to lose his hand if those handcuffs don't come off soon." Mary declared with an urgency that brooked no argument. Her assessment was clear - the deep cuts on his wrist were more than just wounds, they were a harbinger of infection, the skin starting to rot and blister alarmingly. Austin's resolve hardened at the sight, the leader within him already calculating the next move. They couldn't allow disease to claim another ally, not when so much depended on their unity, their shared will to resist Abraham's iron-fisted rule. Chase's admission hung heavy in the stale air of the room.

"I've been sick. Worse than just the pain." His voice trailed off, echoing the dull throbbing that seemed to pulse through his entire being. Mary's eyes narrowed with clinical concern as she examined him.

"The infection's likely spread to your bloodstream," she said, her voice low but steady, "you need antibiotics." He let out a humourless laugh and leaned back against the cold wall, the fight draining from him.

"Seems like this room will be the end of me after all." He muttered, almost to himself. Austin crouched down beside him, gripping Chase's shoulder with a pained intensity.

"Don't talk like that," he commanded, his gaze locking onto Chase's resigned eyes, "we're getting you out of here."

"How?" The skepticism in Chase's voice was palpable as he looked up, meeting Austin's unwavering stare. Mary glanced away for a moment, her gaze settling on the dust motes dancing in a shaft of light before she faced them again.

"There might be a way," she said, her words deliberate, hinting at her plan formed behind her sombre expression, "and you're not going to like it, but I don't think you have a choice."

CHAPTER 17

The Humvee's engine growled softly as it navigated the cracked and overgrown East Center Street, a relic of a world long gone. Faded signs loomed like spectres above, the once-bustling Bank of Tennessee looming silent and desolated to their left. The vehicle came to an abrupt stop a block before a makeshift barricade cobbled together from rusting metal and rotting wood. In the watchtower overhead, armed men loomed ominously, their guns trained on the newcomers with unwavering precision.

"Shauna, Beth, out." Abraham's voice crackled through the radio.

"Go on." Luis smirked as Ben glanced at Beth, his eyes mirroring a storm of unspoken worries. She returned the look with a minute shake of her head, a silent pledge of compliance, before her hand reached for the door handle. Dust kicked up under their boots as Beth and Shauna joined Abraham, Zach, and Pat on the sun-scorched tarmac. They advanced down the block, hands raised in uneasy truce, the sun glaring down upon them with oppressive heat. Abraham's shadow stretched long and dark on the cracked pavement as he walked ahead, his figure a stark contrast against the brightness that bathed the town in relentless light.

"Friends," Abraham called up to the watchtower, "we bring only peace with us."

"What do you want?" A voice boomed down, authoritative and cold.

"I wish to speak with whomever is in charge," Abraham called out, shielding the sun from his eyes as he gazed upward, "my name is Abraham Bishop, leader of a community to the south. We desire nothing but to talk." His voice was steady as a drumbeat. Murmurs floated down from the guards, their speculative gazes never leaving the group.

"Don't move!" A voice called down. Bathed in the harsh daylight, every line of Abraham's face was chiseled with the certainty of purpose, his stature embodying the resolve of a man who would not be easily turned away. The tension among the group became palpable as the guard atop the watchtower turned away, conferring briefly with another before the latter disappeared from sight. Abraham and his party stood still beneath the relentless sun, squinting upwards. The glare of the midday light reflected off the lenses of the sniper scope, a constant reminder of the precariousness of their situation.

"More military than I expected." Abraham murmured to Zach under his breath, his voice barely more than a rustle of dry leaves. Zach's nod was subtle, his eyes never leaving the now solitary figure above them. Time stretched on, the only sound the distant cawing of birds and the soft ruffle of wind through the deserted streets. Then, with a groan of hinges burdened by disuse, the doors across from the barricade began to move. Slowly, deliberately, they opened to reveal two figures emerging into the sunlight, followed closely by more armed men. Abraham's tensed muscles slowly relaxed, his arms dropping to his sides as he signalled for the others to follow suit. The newcomers approached with cautious steps, their eyes scanning the surroundings warily. The man, distinguished by his silver hair shimmering in the sunlight, took a step forward with open gestures, inviting them closer. Beside him, the woman's smile was hesitant but not unkind, conveying a sense of cautious warmth.

"Kevin," the man announced, his voice seasoned with years yet firm, "and this is my wife, Jocelyn."

"Abraham Bishop." He responded with a new friendliness that Beth had not yet heard come from him, yet still displaying his usual authority. Jocelyn smiled cautiously, her eyes darting between Abraham and Beth.

"Forgive our caution. We don't often get visitors."

"Can't be too cautious these days. My wife, Beth," Abraham gestured to her with a sense of pride and possession, then to the rest of his companions, "and this is Shauna, and our council members, Zachary and Patricia." Beth's gaze darted between Abraham and the strangers, frustrated by the brief display of confusion and dissatisfaction at his fraudulent tone. But it was fleeting, and she smoothed her expression into one of neutrality as quickly as it had appeared.

"Welcome." Jocelyn said, her cautious optimism hanging in the air between them. Her eyes scanned their faces, taking the measure of each person with an educator's thoroughness. The exchange of pleasantries did little to dispel the unease, but it marked the beginning of a dialogue, one that carried with it the weight of futures yet unwritten. Beth's smile, genuine and open, bridged the distance as she stepped forward, hand outstretched in a gesture of peace. But the sudden jerk of rifles being hoisted into ready arms shattered the moment. Her hand retracted instinctively, a startled shiver running through her body.

"Lower your weapons." Kevin's voice cut through the tension, firm yet not unkind. The guards complied, muscles relaxing, guns lowering. Beth's smile returned, though now tinged with caution as she withdrew to the safety of her companions. Jocelyn moved closer, her hand gentle on Beth's arm, a silent reassurance that echoed in her eyes.

"Please, come inside," Jocelyn invited them warmly, "but leave your vehicles here, and your weapons with them." Abraham's protest was immediate, his gaze shifting to Kevin.

"We've invested much to modify these Humvee's with solar power," his pride in their ingenuity was evident, even as he appealed for understanding, "can we park them just within your gates?"

"Your cars may enter," Jocelyn considered the request, her head tilted in thought as she nodded once, decisively, "but keep your weapons inside them." Kevin watched the exchange silently, giving no sign of objection or agreement. Abraham, his features set in a stoic mask, gave a curt nod of assent. Abraham's eyes lingered on Kevin, a silent question hanging between them as Jocelyn unilaterally made her decision. He gave a stiff nod before turning away, his thoughts cloaked behind a careful mask. The gates yawned wider, an invitation laced with the underlying tension of the unknown. The group's collective breath seemed to release, a subtle relaxation as the threat of conflict receded like shadows at dawn. They would abide by the terms, their path forward now under the watchful eye of both friend and sentinel. Jocelyn's grip was firm on Beth's arm as they moved together through the threshold. The warmth of the sun touched their faces, and Beth allowed the sense of camaraderie to ease her nerves. Around them, the hum of the convoy engines died down as the vehicles edged into the designated area, an echo of civilisation in the still air. Aaron brought the Humvee to rest beside the others, and the doors clanked shut, sealing away their arsenal. One by one, the military personnel stepped out, their movements deliberate under the watchful gaze of their hosts. The pat-down was thorough, hands searching for hidden threats, and the sound of metal on metal rang out as weapons found a new home in the back seats.

"Lock it up." Aaron instructed, his voice a low growl that didn't quite hide the edge of unease. Beth, now within the safety of the compound, glanced up at Jocelyn, her curiosity piqued by the dynamics at play.

"You and your husband, do you both make the decisions here?" She asked, her voice carrying a note of genuine intrigue. Jocelyn's lips quirked upward, her eyes holding a glint of authority that needed no confirmation.

"Sometimes," she said simply, "but I'm the one in charge." The town hall loomed ahead, its presence both grand and sombre against the sky. They walked towards it, boots crunching on gravel, the air rich with the scent of earth and growth.

As dusk fell, the dining hall of Biltmore buzzed with an unusual vibrancy. Austin sat back in his chair, his meal half-forgotten as he observed the shift in atmosphere. With Abraham gone, the rigid hierarchy had softened, conversations flowing more freely among those left behind, even after such a short time. Eve slid into the seat across from him, her dinner plate a splash of colour against the wooden table. She met his gaze, her own unreadable. Austin continued his slow chewing, the rhythm unchanged despite the company. Footsteps approached and retreated, guards meandering past with less urgency than before. The clinking of cutlery mingled with laughter, a rare sound that spoke volumes of the change in air. Austin took it all in, the corner of his mouth twitching upwards ever so slightly. Eve broke the silence between them, her voice quiet but clear.

"It seems we've found a brief reprieve." She said, her eyes flitting to the empty stairwell posts.

"Seems so." Austin nodded as he reached for his glass, the cool water a contrast to the warmth filling the room. Eve watched him, her own meal untouched as she waited for the evening to unfold. She leaned forward, placing her elbows on the table gently.

"Any luck today?" Her tone was casual, but her gaze held an edge of urgency.

"We can talk later." Austin kept his focus on the food before him, methodically chewing a mouthful of roasted vegetables.

"Mary mentioned that you found Chase." Eve continued, spearing a potato with her fork and placing it into her mouth. She chewed thoughtfully, eyes drifting away from Austin's intense stare. At the mention of Chase, Austin's jaw stilled mid-chew. His eyes locked onto Eve, seeking an explanation in her nonchalant demeanour.

"What exactly did Mary say?" He turned his head slightly, scanning the dining hall until his gaze settled on Mary. She sat isolated, her shoulders hunched over her plate. He caught her attention with a subtle nod, motioning her to join them. After a moment's hesitation, Mary glanced at the guards stationed around the room, then shook her head, her eyes returning to the safety of her meal. Eve shrugged, a silent acknowledgment of their precarious situation.

"It's probably for the best," she murmured, "we can't be seen together too much, especially not with Mary all of a sudden. Who knows what people would say if we were all suddenly friends." Austin resumed eating, the rhythm of his meal unbroken. The aroma of fresh herbs wafted up from his plate, a reminder of the new crops flourishing outside.

"Friends? No one would assume we're suddenly friends with Mary—"

"I have to hand it to you," Eve interrupted, taking another bite, "you've done well. The garden's really coming along." He nodded again, his dark eyes meeting hers across the small distance of the table. Austin took another bite, savouring the crisp texture of the vegetables. Silence fell between them once more, punctuated only by the sounds of their shared meal. Austin slid his empty plate away, the clatter of ceramic against the wooden table punctuating the end of his meal. He clasped his hands together, resting his forearms on the table's edge, and fixed his gaze on Eve.

"Yes, the black guy has done a great job tending to the crops so that everyone else can eat." He remarked, his voice carrying a bitter edge. Eve paused mid-chew, her fork suspended in air. She set it down and met his eyes, a flush creeping up her neck.

"I didn't mean—"

"I know," Austin cut in, his tone even but firm, "but it grinds me that Abraham can't see past his prejudices. I should be out there with Beth and Ben, not stuck behind these walls."

"Maybe so," Eve conceded, "but if you were, Chase would still be missing. You found him, not them." Austin's posture relaxed slightly as he leaned back, his muscles easing from their taut state.

"Only because I went looking. They would have found him eventually."

"Any clue where Tyler might be?" She asked, her voice low. He shook his head, the line of his jaw hardening.

"Nothing."

"Austin," Eve glanced around the room before leaning forward, "I think I might have an idea where Tyler might be." Interest sparked in Austin's eyes, the prior indifference evaporating.

"Where?"

"Not here," she replied, standing and collecting her plate, "meet me in the gallery tomorrow morning, while everyone else is at breakfast." She strode away with purpose, leaving Austin to ponder the implications of her cryptic message.

The aroma of freshly brewed coffee filled the town hall as Jocelyn placed a steaming carafe on the table. She settled into her chair opposite Abraham, Beth, Zach, and Pat with Kevin by her side. The late afternoon light streamed in through the tall windows, casting a golden hue over the clean surfaces and polished wood.

"Thank you." Beth murmured, accepting a large mug from Jocelyn. She took a cautious sip, the bitter warmth spreading through her. Her gaze wandered over the room's meticulous order, contrasting the haphazard efficiency she had grown accustomed to under Henry's watch.

"So, what brings you folks to our neck of the woods?" Jocelyn leaned back in her chair, her eyes resting on the visitors before her. Abraham cleared his throat, his fingers tightening around his own cup.

"We're not here to waste your time," he began, his voice resonating with a calm certainty, "I've come to extend an olive branch to communities within our reach."

"Sounds noble." Jocelyn replied, the steam from her coffee curling up between them.

"Well there are so few of us left. It's only fitting that we should be friends."

"Friends," Jocelyn mused, "tell me about this community of yours."

"We offer sanctuary," Abraham said, stretching his legs beneath the table," a place where people can find solace, nourishment, and peace. I lead with fairness and justice. My wife here can attest to the tranquility we've cultivated." He continued casually. Jocelyn's gaze shifted to Beth, the question clear in her eyes. Beth spoke slowly, her eyes fixed on Jocelyn but watching Abraham in her periphery.

"Being the leader's wife has its responsibilities—"

"She thrives in her role. Guiding our people in their daily lives, setting an example of devotion and grace." His statement hung in the air, leaving an unspoken certainty of who held the power in their union. Abraham gestured to Beth with an open palm, a practiced move that drew the room's attention.

"I try—"

"Beth is exemplary," he continued, his voice carrying the weight of his pride, "she leads our social gatherings and bible studies, a paragon for our community." At the table, Kevin shifted his gaze between the couple, a thoughtful expression on his face.

"It's invigorating, being married to a leader," he admitted, "I contribute my thoughts, yes, but Jocelyn has a knack for politics. She ensures our safety, steers us clear of danger." A brief silence followed, filled only by the clink of coffee cups set back onto saucers. Abraham nodded, acknowledging Kevin's sentiment with a curt smile.

"Beth sets the standard high, yet when it comes to governance, the decisions rest with me and my kin," he paused, scanning the faces before him, "my cousin Aaron is part of our convoy, while my brother Adam remains at Biltmore, safeguarding our home."

"Ah, Biltmore," Kevin interjected, warmth entering his tone as if recalling a fond memory, "what a beautiful place to settle. We visited once. The grounds, the architecture, it's truly remarkable."

"Yes," Jocelyn chimed in, her nod slow and reflective, "we took the kids there on a field trip once. I was the principal at Dobyns-Bennett High School, just down the road. Well, once upon a time."

"Our home is well hidden," Beth said, her voice steady and mechanical, "with its resilient walls and strategic design. It has offered us a sanctuary, a place where leadership finds strength. It's hard for someone to sneak in." Or out, she thought.

"I understand. Our defences were a challenge to raise," a light laugh escaped Jocelyn, laced with an undercurrent of strain, "we nearly abandoned this place for somewhere more secure, but then some survivors rolled through town. One was an engineer. Imagine the luck." She mused with a shake of her head. The conversation moved like a gentle breeze through an open window, bringing with it the scent of fresh coffee and echoes of a world both lost and found. Sunlight streamed through the tall windows of Kingsport's town hall, casting long shadows across the room where Abraham and his contingent sat with their hosts. The air hummed with the tension of new alliances as Jocelyn leaned back in her chair, her eyes dancing over the faces before her. Abraham held his tongue, a flash of regret passing over his features as he recalled the slip about Biltmore. Beside him, Beth sensed his unease - her touch was light upon his knee, reassuring without a word.

"Your names carry quite the legacy," Jocelyn observed, breaking the momentary stillness, "Abraham, Adam, Aaron. Biblical giants, each with their own destiny." The weight of history seemed to press down on the conversation, demanding recognition. Turning away from the scrutiny, Beth faced their hosts with composure. A sly smile crept across Abraham's lips.

"I'd say our names are quite fitting."

"Abraham, Father of many, a key figure in the Bible, known for his faith in God's promises, the patriarch. Adam, formed from the dust of the earth, his name reflecting his connection to the ground. Aaron, reflecting a position of honour and elevation, he played a crucial role in helping Moses lead the Israelites out of Egypt," Jocelyn leaned forward in her chair, resting her elbows on her knees, "tell me, Abraham, do you and your brother and your cousin reflect the true identities of your namesakes?"

"Of course," Beth interjected, sensing the strain within Abraham as the muscle under her hand grew tense, "my husband and our family are commendable examples. They all reflect their callings with pride." The afternoon sun began its descent, stretching the shadows further, as if trying to reach out and connect the two groups, each wary yet bound by the necessity of survival. As the afternoon light waned, casting a golden hue over the town hall's interior as the silence stretched thin. Kevin cleared his throat, his voice breaking through like a pebble into still water.

"Perhaps it's time we discussed accommodations," he suggested, his gaze shifting between the wary faces, "I'll show you where you can wash up before dinner." Jocelyn nodded, her eyes settling on Abraham and Beth.

"You two will stay with us," she declared, her tone warm yet commanding, "and your guards, if you insist." Her laughter was a bright chime in the quiet room, dispelling some of the tension. Abraham, ever vigilant, responded without hesitation.

"Shauna and Aaron," he said, nodding towards them in the other room, "they're integral to our security."

"We pride ourselves on our safety, and our Southern hospitality,"

Jocelyn chimed in, her smile unwavering, "but of course, we have room for six if you need."

"Zachery and Patricia too." Abraham added, glancing at his council members before their eyes returned to their hosts. Jocelyn turned to Kevin, her voice carrying a motherly authority.

"Ensure the others are settled with Amelia," she turned back to Abraham and Beth, "my daughter and her wife live next door, so you'll all be close." With a dutiful nod, Kevin gestured for Beth and the others to follow him out, leaving a trail of footsteps echoing against the polished floor. Once alone with Abraham, Jocelyn's gaze softened as she regarded Beth.

"Beth is beautiful," she mused, a hint of admiration touching her words, "dutiful and, I'd wager, quite clever. Did you meet her before or after?"

"After," Abraham stated, his tone even but firm, "her past is behind her now. My wife has renounced any failings and stands true, to me and to God." His words hung in the air, mingling with the scent of coffee and the subtle shift of shadows as the day ebbed into evening. Jocelyn leaned forward slightly, her hands clasping the warm ceramic mug.

"I'm a woman of faith myself," she began, her voice steady but betraying no particular conviction, "but I don't believe it dictates how we live our lives here." Abraham's gaze remained unflinching as he responded, the blue of his eyes almost piercing in their intensity.

"Faith is our compass in this new world," he asserted, "the apocalypse was not chaos but cleansing, divine intervention to give God's true believers a chance to rebuild."

"Rebuild?" Jocelyn prompted, her eyebrows arching just so.

"Indeed," Abraham said with a nod, "and Beth will soon bless me with a son, a child destined to save what remains of humanity." A brief flicker of surprise crossed Jocelyn's features before she smoothed it into a practiced expression of understanding.

"Have you and Beth been married long?"

"Selection brought us together," Abraham replied, his tone suggesting reverence for the process, "from many eligible women, Beth emerged chosen, tested and true, to stand by my side and bring forth the next bearer of our legacy. We were married only earlier this week."

"Is that the way for all in your community?" The question carried a hint of probing beneath the polite curiosity.

"Those who are with us share our loyalty to the cause, to the divine order." He answered, his words leaving little room for doubt about the allegiance he commanded. Jocelyn set down her coffee, the clink of china on wood punctuating the moment. Her gaze lingered on Abraham, contemplating the man before her, a leader shrouded equally in devotion and dogma. Abraham stood, his tall frame casting a long shadow across the dimly lit room where Jocelyn sat. The air was still, heavy with anticipation. She watched him with cautious eyes as he paced slowly before her, hands clasped behind his back.

"Tell me about your people," Abraham finally broke the silence, his deep voice resonating in the sparse space between them, "what are they like?" Jocelyn hesitated for a moment, assessing the man who towered over her.

"They're happy," she began measuredly, "the kids attend school. We have movie nights and game nights. Everyone is free to do as they please, so long as they contribute and don't harm anyone."

Abraham nodded, the motion deliberate and slow.

"And do they follow the word of the Lord?" His inquiry hung in the air, a test laid bare.

"Some attend church on Sundays," Jocelyn answered, her tone guarded, "religion is a choice in Kingsport, not an obligation." A flicker of something unreadable crossed Abraham's stern features. He turned his piercing blue gaze upon her once more, contemplative.

"Your daughter," he pressed on, "she is married to another woman?" Jocelyn leaned back in her chair, her posture relaxed but her mind alert.

"Yes, and they've built a very happy life here." She replied, ensuring her response bore no trace of defensiveness.

"*Your* daughter," he repeated, "and not Kevin's?"

"From my first marriage." She maintained her casual facade. Abraham considered her words, nodding again with a certain respect veiled beneath his stoic exterior.

"I see."

"Abraham," after a pause, Jocelyn ventured a question of her own, "have you come to ask us to join you at Biltmore?" His reaction was sudden - a laugh, short and startling in its rarity. Jocelyn flinched subtly, unprepared for the abrupt sound from such a solemn man.

"No," Abraham said, the smile fleeting from his lips as quickly as it had appeared, "I merely wanted to meet my neighbours. You know, in case I ever need a cup of sugar." The tension in the room eased fractionally, though Jocelyn remained vigilant in the presence of the enigmatic leader before her. Abraham's words, simple as they were, carried a weight that lingered in the air, rich with unspoken implications.

"Sugar," a light laugh escaped Jocelyn, uneasy and tentative, "that's a luxury we hardly have to spare."

"That's unfortunate," Abraham's own laughter was rich and brief, the sound like a bell toll in silence, "perhaps we could engage in trade, then. I'm sure we have some sugar to spare, among other things. My people are well-armed, highly trained, and well-educated. We have plenty of food, medicine—" The word 'medicine' snagged Jocelyn's attention as surely as a hook. Abraham, ever observant, noted the subtle shift in her demeanour.

"Go on." She encouraged.

"Indeed," he continued, voice smooth as he painted a picture of abundance, "we have doctors, nurses, and our scavenging teams have been rather successful in acquiring medical supplies." A protective wall around Jocelyn seemed to crumble, brick by invisible brick.

"We do have a need," she conceded, her voice softening with the admission, "something quite specific." Abraham arched an eyebrow, interest piqued.

"Yes?"

"Chemotherapy pills," Jocelyn said, the words carrying a weight of personal importance, "for my daughter." Retreating into his chair, Abraham steepled his fingers together, his blue eyes narrowing thoughtfully under the weight of this new information.

Kevin and Beth ambled along Broad Street. The air carried the scent of asphalt warmed by the sun, its rays casting long shadows from the figures moving through Church Circle. Their steps were unhurried but purposeful as they rounded the roundabout and ventured further away from Kingsport's heart. Beth observed children playing in the street, their laughter piercing through the mundane quietness until watchful parents called them inside.

"Your husband sure has a way with words," Kevin remarked suddenly, a hint of curiosity in his tone, "barely lets anyone get a word in." Beth turned her gaze from the retreating children back to Kevin.

"Abraham is our leader," Beth responded, her tone neutral, the words rehearsed, "it's his role to handle such political matters." Kevin nodded, though skepticism played at the corners of his eyes. They continued on, footsteps synchronising with the distant echo of a world trying to mend itself. The sun dipped lower in the sky, casting a golden hue over the desolate landscape as Kevin and Beth continued their journey down Broad Street. The road was cracked and littered with remnants of a world long gone, yet nature crept in, softening the edges with stubborn weeds that refused to yield.

"Abraham," Kevin started, breaking the silence, "he seems more like a dictator than a leader." A smirk danced briefly on Beth's lips, a flicker of amusement she quickly buried beneath a mask of indifference. They walked in silence for a few moments, each lost in their own thoughts. The sun had almost set, casting long shadows over the once bustling city. Beth could feel Kevin's gaze on her, waiting for a physical response to his comment, a telltale sign of her disbelief in Abraham's vision. Finally, she let out a sigh and turned to face him.

"I wouldn't say he's a dictator," she said carefully, feigning a sincere defence of her husband, "but he does have a strong personality and vision for our community." Kevin raised an eyebrow in response.

"A strong personality," he echoed skeptically, "seems more like he's drunk on power."

"A leader needs to be strong." Beth countered, her tone becoming defensive, more so than she had meant to.

"Power corrupts," Kevin said with a shrug, "it's human nature."

"He cares about our community and its people." She said firmly.

"Is he your husband by choice?" Kevin's question hung in the air, tinged with the weight of unspoken stories. Beth's gaze met his, probing for signs of ulterior motives, but found none. In his eyes lay an ocean of empathy, undiluted and clear. She exhaled, the confession slipping past her lips like a secret long held.

"I am a small, insignificant person playing a very dangerous game to survive," Beth confessed quietly, an unintentional anger in her tone she had intended to conceal, "what do you think?" Kevin fell silent, the rhythm of their footsteps filling the void between them. He glanced over his shoulder at the group they had left behind, each member carrying the burden of survival with silent resignation.

"Can we trust Abraham?" His voice was low, barely rising above the whisper of leaves skittering across the pavement. Beth's eyes followed his gaze, landing on Aaron, Shauna, Ben, Luis, and the others who trailed at a distance, their faces imprinted with the weariness of the day.

"Have a five-minute conversation alone with that man," she leaned closer to Kevin, her words a hushed breath against his ear, "I'm sure you're smart enough to draw your own conclusions." They walked on, their shadows stretching long and thin as the last light of day fought against the encroaching darkness, the truth of Beth's words settling like a stone in the pit of Kevin's stomach. They rounded the corner onto West Wenola Avenue, the sun's dying light casting long shadows over the cracked pavement. The air was thick with the scent of wildflowers fighting through the urban decay. Beth followed, her footsteps measured and soft against the whisper of the breeze. A quick glance over her shoulder revealed Ben trailing closer behind them, his arms burdened with both sets of bags. His face was set in grim determination, a silent testament to the day's weariness etched into the lines of his forehead.

"Your honesty is refreshing," Kevin said, breaking the evening hush, "most people tiptoe around words these days." Beth looked at him, her expression unreadable for a moment before a small, wry smile played on her lips.

"You're smart enough not to try and lead every dance," she replied, "you let your wife have that space. It makes you a better man than some. At the very least it makes you a better man than Abraham."

"You don't know me at all." Kevin protested slightly, concern evident in his tone.

"Then my testimony against my husband should speak volumes." Beth countered. The subtle dig hung between them as Abraham's towering figure loomed in their minds, a stark contrast to the gentle egalitarianism that Kevin practiced in his own marriage.

"Why are you telling me this?"

"I have nothing to lose," she whispered, "I'm just trying to help you keep your community safe. Entertain his principles, but be cautious." They stopped short of a beautiful green-coloured house laced with white trim. Beth turned suddenly to Kevin, before the others could catch up to them.

"Beth—"

"Ben is the only one you can trust," she whispered quickly, almost pleadingly, "and I hope you understand the danger I've put myself in by telling you everything. I hope it means you know you can trust me." Confusion swept over Kevin's face.

"Danger?"

"What a beautiful house!" Beth exclaimed loudly, loud enough for everyone else's benefit. As she tilted her head imperceptibly, allowing her shirt to slide off her shoulder ever so slightly, Kevin noticed the light bruising on her collarbone. With a nod, he escorted Beth and the others into his home.

The flickering candlelight cast a warm glow across the room as Jocelyn folded the worn quilt at the foot of their bed. Kevin sat on the edge, unlacing his boots with methodical patience. The silence between them felt heavy, laden with unspoken thoughts.

"Tell me what you're thinking." Jocelyn said, her voice breaking the stillness. She watched him carefully, noting the tension in his jaw as he set his boots aside. His gaze lifted to meet hers.

"We need to be careful around Abraham." His words were measured, carefully selected.

"Why?" She perched beside him, the concern etching deeper into her features.

"Beth confided in me," he said, his voice lowering, "she's not with him by choice. She said he's a dangerous man."

"I gathered that," a shiver ran down her spine, despite the warmth of the room, "he said some things, things that set my teeth on edge." Kevin turned to her, his expression urging her to continue.

"What things?"

"About Amelia," she replied, her eyes clouding over, "he didn't seem to approve of her marriage." A knowing look crossed Kevin's face.

"Something you struggled to come to terms with, if I remember correctly." He pointed out. Jocelyn nodded, her lips pressed into a thin line.

"It took me some time, I'll admit," her hands clenched into fists on her lap, a protective fierceness rising within her, "but I love the girls. They're my family, no matter what." Jocelyn crawled into bed, her muscles aching with exhaustion. She reached for the well-loved blanket, pulling it up to her chin and relishing in its softness, a small comfort against the ever-present chill of uncertainty. The meagre light from their lantern cast long shadows across the room, dancing like ghosts on the walls. Kevin remained sitting on the edge of the bed, his broad shoulders hunched in worry as he surveyed Jocelyn's tired face. His expression was tense, lines etched deep into his forehead as he struggled to find words to ease her fears.

"Did Abraham make any trade offers? I assumed that's why they were here." His voice carried a weight that seemed to press upon the walls of the room. She exhaled slowly, the air whispering through her lips.

"He listed what they had at Biltmore. Tools, weapons, food, and—" Jocelyn's fingers fidgeted with the blanket's edge as she paused, "and medicine, plus well trained doctors and nurses. I couldn't help it, I reacted when he mentioned it. It was like he had anticipated my desperation." The muscles in Kevin's jaw tightened, his question barely more than a whisper.

"Medicine for Amelia?"

"Chemotherapy pills." She confirmed, her voice catching on the last word. Kevin rose from the bed and paced the small space between the dresser and the window, his footsteps muffled by the threadbare rug.

"What does he want in return?"

"There is nothing we have that he doesn't have already," Jocelyn watched him move, her heart sinking, "except, perhaps, our lives at

Biltmore, under his rule."

"Dammit, Joss," he stopped and faced her, hands clenched at his sides, "you know we can't do that. Not even for the treatment." A nod, slow and heavy, was her only response. Her eyes traced the lines of worry etching deeper into his face with each passing moment.

"And I know Amelia wouldn't accept it, if she knew the cost" Jocelyn's heart sank even lower, creating a hollow feeling in her chest.

"No," Kevin agreed diplomatically, "Amelia and Laura would die before allowing you to give up our home for the sake of a treatment that might not work. We can keep searching. There must be untouched hospitals we haven't scavenged yet. Besides, she's been doing okay."

"She's getting sicker and you know it," her voice was flat, resignation seeping through, "Abraham's probably picked the surrounding areas clean by now."

"Then we'll have to extend our search area," Kevin's determination sliced through the despair, "we'll find what we need, we always have."

"I know." Jocelyn let out a breath she hadn't realised she'd been holding, the tension between them hanging in the stale air. Kevin turned from the window, where the moonlight cast long shadows across the floor, and faced Jocelyn. His eyes met hers, reflecting a resolve born of countless nights wrestling with uncertainty.

"We can't trust Abraham," he said, his voice laced with an unmistakable edge, "an alliance with him? It's not worth our freedom. Beth said we should entertain him, but to be careful." The dim light in their humble room seemed to flicker in agreement. Jocelyn pressed her lips together, a silent acknowledgment of the grim truth. She rose from the bed, the mattress creaking under the shift of weight. The cool air of the room embraced her as she stepped towards Kevin, the distance between them charged with unspoken fears and the weight of decisions made in desperation.

"Then that's what we'll do," she began, her words deliberate as she reached for his hand, feeling the rough calluses earned through years of survival, "tomorrow, I'll thank them for their visit. But I'll make it clear. We have nothing to trade, and they should leave." Her grip tightened, seeking strength in the unity of their intertwined fingers. Kevin's hand responded with an affirming squeeze. Their shared glance was a silent pact, one of mutual protection against the encroaching darkness both beyond their walls, and now lurking within.

CHAPTER 18

Eve's gaze lingered on the faded photographs lining the gallery walls, each a silent testament to a world long crumbled. Her fingers traced the edges of display books and shuffled papers in an absent-minded dance of anticipation. The scent of mildew and dust clung to the air, mingling with the faint floral fragrance that seeped in through the cracks of the Biltmore's decaying grandeur. Without warning, Austin materialised beside her, his entrance as stealthy as a whisper.

"What did you need to show me?" He asked, voice low and urgent. "Over here." Eve beckoned, urgency lacing her words as she glanced towards the library's sealed door. She cherished the stillness that Abraham's absence afforded them, no prying eyes to question their clandestine meeting. She tugged Austin by the sleeve, drawing him towards a large parchment sprawled across a mahogany table – the Biltmore floor plans.

"What?" He leaned in, dark eyes scanning the intricate lines and notations.

"Look closer." Eve insisted, her fingertip resting on a particular section of the third floor.

"We don't have time for puzzles," Austin muttered, the muscle in his jaw twitching, "tell me what I'm looking for."

"There," she said, pressing her point, "a hidden section, reachable only through one winding staircase above the banquet hall void on the second floor." Her breath brushed against his ear, carrying the weight of their secret discovery. Austin's gaze narrowed, his eyes tracing the lines of the floor plan with an intensity that belied his usual calm.

"Tyler has to be here," he declared, the possibility igniting a fire within him, "this is the only place we haven't checked." Eve nodded, her own expression mirroring his resolve.

"We could wait for nightfall to explore." She suggested, her voice soft. But Austin was already shaking his head, his whole body tensed like a coiled spring.

"The way this place creaks and echoes, not a chance," he said sharply, "we go now." Before waiting for a reply, he turned on his heel and strode out of the gallery, his movements swift and sure. Behind him, Eve let out an exasperated huff, her frustration at his impetuousness clear in the set of her shoulders as she followed him out, her footsteps echoing against the gallery's timeworn floors.

In the dim light of dawn, Beth's eyes fluttered open, the early morning stillness of the room punctuated by Abraham's deep, rhythmic snoring beside her. She lay there for a moment, staring at his oblivious form, before memories of the previous evening crept into her thoughts. She recalled how Abraham had spoken words of prayer, his voice laden with expectation for their yet-to-be-conceived child. The memory twisted in her gut. She remembered how she had pushed back against his advances, invoking the need for discretion given the proximity of their hosts and the thinness of the walls. His acquiescence had been grudging, and soon after, his snores filled the room, a rumbling testament to his reluctant obedience. Beth rose silently, the rustle of fabric barely audible as she dressed. Her fingers fumbled with the button of her jeans, the cool metal a stark contrast to the warmth of her skin. With deft movements, she pulled on her shirt, the fabric whispering against her. She cast one last glance at Abraham's sleeping figure before slipping out of the room, her movements quiet as she made her way down the corridor. The front living room greeted her with the aroma of fresh coffee and the muted morning light filtering through the curtains. Jocelyn and Kevin sat at the dining table, their mugs sending up delicate tendrils of steam. Jocelyn's smile was soft as she gestured to the empty chair beside her.

"You're quite the early bird." She said, her voice as warm as the beverage she cradled.

"I don't sleep much these days," Beth replied, the weight of the unfamiliar ceiling above her still pressing in her memory, "but I suppose we'd all have trouble sleeping, given the unfamiliar territory." Kevin's nod was one of understanding, his hands wrapping around his mug for comfort.

"Please, sit." Jocelyn poured another cup, the dark liquid cascading into the white porcelain with a gentle sound. Beth took a seat, the chair creaking slightly under her weight, her eyes roving over the daylight-kissed details of the room.

"Thanks for your hospitality." She murmured, her gaze lingering on a chink in the wooden floorboards, a testament to the age and stories held within these walls.

"Would you like to go for a walk?" Jocelyn asked suddenly, her eyes holding an invitation. Beth's heart skipped a beat, her mind racing for an excuse.

"Abraham wouldn't like me going on a casual walk alone." She managed, her voice betraying a hint of the trepidation that clawed at her insides.

"But you won't be alone." Kevin insisted.

"Without him, I mean." Beth interjected quickly, her eyes darting between Jocelyn and Kevin. Across the table, a silent exchange passed between the two, heralding an unspoken understanding.

"Kevin would like to have a conversation with Abraham," Jocelyn insisted, her tone gentle yet firm, "as per your proficient suggestion." Beth's muscles tensed, the request wrapping around her like a cold shroud as she acknowledged the necessity of their plan. Beth's fingers tightened around the mug, its warmth seeping into her skin as Kevin's assurance floated through the air.

"I've kept quiet about things that don't concern the community," he said, his voice a low thrum of sincerity, "I told Joss some things we spoke about yesterday, but only what she needed to know." Beth gave a subtle nod, her mind racing with the implications of their whispered strategies.

"Are you afraid of him?" Jocelyn's question pierced the room's calm like a shard of ice. Beth rose, her movements deliberate, and headed for the door with determination etched in every step.

"We can't talk here." She stated flatly, a hint of urgency underlying her words. Jocelyn followed suit, their footsteps merging into a rhythmic escape from the confines of the house. Outside, the town's grandeur unfolded under the morning sun, rays filtering through the overgrown trees which lined the streets, shadows dancing upon the road and footpath. Beth looked down, her eyes tracing the cracks between the asphalt, while Jocelyn's gaze lifted to embrace the azure sky.

"It's a beautiful day." Jocelyn remarked, a note of wonder in her voice.

"Mmm." Beth provided an obligatory sound, though her thoughts were shrouded like the fog that clung to the distant mountain peaks. Jocelyn halted.

"Why are you so scared of saying the wrong thing?" Her question hung between them, an unspoken challenge. Beth paused, her back still to Jocelyn, the weight of the inquiry settling on her shoulders. "Abraham wouldn't approve of me being out here, alone with you." She replied, the words heavy with a burden unsaid. She began to retreat towards the relative safety of the house. Jocelyn's hand reached out, fingers wrapping around Beth's arm with gentle insistence. Their eyes met, a silent exchange fraught with the gravity of unsaid truths. Beth's fingers trembled as Jocelyn released her grip slightly.

"Beth—"

"What is it you want from me?" Beth asked, her voice a fragile whisper carried away by the breeze.

"The truth," Jocelyn stepped closer, the resolve in her eyes softening to concern, "that's all I'm asking for." Beth glanced back at the house, its windows like watching eyes, and a shiver ran down her spine despite the warmth of the sun.

"You understand," she started, her words measured and slow, "that Abraham is not a kind man." A nod from Jocelyn acknowledged the shared understanding, her face clouding as she relayed fragments of their previous night's exchange.

"Abraham mentioned what kind of community you all have at Biltmore," Jocelyn started, her face a blank expression, giving away nothing of her thoughts, "and that you all follow his teachings with pride."

"Pride," Beth snorted involuntarily, "we don't have a choice."

"You can't just leave?" Jocelyn queried as a mere whisper, her face softening as she spoke.

"No, we can't *just leave*," Beth said, looking down at the ground, "we can't escape. Under Abraham's rule, your daughter and daughter-in-law would be expected to renounce their marriage and turn to a relationship fit for the eyes of God, and if they don't—" Beth's heart clenched when she hinted at the potential fate of Jocelyn's daughter under Abraham's rule - a love nullified, and lives threatened. Shock was too mild a word for the expression that crossed Jocelyn's features, it was as if the ground beneath her had shifted, leaving her unsteady. Beth took a deep breath before speaking again, each word laden with the grim reality they faced.

"Abraham didn't come here for alliances, or trade. He isn't that kind of man. He seeks power, power in numbers, and he believes his son will be humanity's saviour."

"Oh, my dear," Jocelyn's eyes searched Beth's, a question forming on her lips, "why would you agree to marry him? There's disdain in your voice, clear as day."

"I didn't choose this," the corner of Beth's mouth twitched, a bitter semblance of a smile, "it wasn't a choice given to me." She looked off into the distance, where the sky kissed the mountain tops, seeking reprieve in their stoic beauty.

"Abraham mentioned there were other candidates." Jocelyn said, her voice steady but her hands betraying a slight tremor as she clasped them together. Beth exhaled, a gust of resignation that fluttered the leaves around them. They stood in silence for a moment, two women bound by circumstance and the heavy cloak of fear that Abraham's name draped over the world. Beth's gaze lingered on a pair of butterflies, twirling in an erratic dance above the untamed bushes which lined the nature strips. The fluttering wings were a stark contrast to the weight of her revelation. She turned back to Jocelyn, the morning sun casting a soft glow on her features.

"There were a few favourites," she confessed, her voice carried away by the breeze, "one would have been tyrannical, making life unbearable for everyone had she been chosen. So I had to overshadow her by matching her enthusiasm." Jocelyn's eyes widened slightly, reflecting the gravity of Beth's words.

"And another?" She prodded gently.

"Devout," Beth continued, plucking at the frayed hem of her shirt, "but she's gay, and she could never match the enthusiasm he wanted. Abraham doesn't know, and he'd kill her if he did. So she begged me to make myself as desirable as possible by accepting God so that she was out of the running."

"You two must be close," Jocelyn smiled, "if you did that for her."

"Yes," she hesitated, her next words hanging precariously on the edge of her lips, "between my enthusiasm, newfound devoutness, and intelligence he sought in a wife, I was the overall favourite. I didn't want to be chosen, but I had one goal in mind. I needed to get close to him." She paused, considering her next words carefully. Beth locked eyes with Jocelyn, the vulnerability in her own gaze giving away the words she was about to speak. But she remained silent, the unspoken confession hanging heavy in the air between them like a gaping chasm. Jocelyn's kind and welcoming appearance radiated warmth, and her eyes held a gentle sincerity that made Beth feel safe and understood.

"Your tone, your words, they change when he's not around."

"I have to watch what I say when I'm with him. I think my words sound so rehearsed and I'm afraid that if I say the wrong thing—" Beth paused, shaking her head, "why do I trust you?"

She murmured, more to herself than to Jocelyn. It was Jocelyn's unwavering stance, the set of her shoulders beneath the burden of truth, which convinced Beth to heed her instincts. She had finally conceded to herself that while she couldn't trust anyone, she could at least have confidence in what her gut was telling her. She knew instinctively that Jocelyn was someone she could rely on.

"Because I understand," Jocelyn responded softly, meeting Beth's gaze with a gentle smile, "I know what it's like to be manipulated and forced into situations you never wanted." Beth nodded, tears prickling at the corners of her eyes. There was a kinship between them now, a bond forged by shared experiences and secrets.

"I never wanted any of this," Beth said shakily, feeling a wave of vulnerability wash over her, "but I had to do whatever it took to get close to him." A sudden rustle in the nearby bushes snapped Beth out of the moment. She stepped back, distancing herself from Jocelyn's touch.

"I can't trust anyone." She stated, her voice steadier than she felt. A cardinal burst from the foliage, its crimson feathers a stark splash against the greenery.

"What were you going to say? About getting close to Abraham?" Jocelyn asked, concern threading her tone.

"Abraham believes he's purifying the world," Beth squared her shoulders as if bracing against an invisible force, compelling herself to tell Jocelyn what she needed to know to save her community, "the good people are those left behind, who will live under his divine rule." Jocelyn's brows knitted together as she took in the implication.

"His rule?"

"Men are heirs to this new world," Beth explained, her gaze drifting over the sprawling grounds where nature reclaimed what was once meticulously curated, "and women, we're merely vessels in his grand scheme to repopulate." Jocelyn's jaw clenched at the revelation, and they shared a look that conveyed a mutual understanding of the stakes. Together, they turned towards the house, its grandeur now overshadowed by the dark truths that lay within its walls.

"You can stay, Beth," Jocelyn offered suddenly, "you don't have to go back with him." Beth let out a low laugh, shaking her head at the idea of escape. Jocelyn's offer hovered in the air, a lifeline that Beth could not afford to grasp.

"I appreciate it," she said, her voice a low murmur as she shook her head, "but if Abraham thought you were keeping me here, against my will or otherwise, he would burn this place to the ground to find me and then drag me kicking and screaming through your gates." She cast a glance back towards the south, as if she could see the grand walls of Biltmore just beyond the trees, where her friends and would-be family remained under the yoke of Abraham's rule.

"It sounds like he'd do that anyway," Jocelyn sighed, "once we tell him we're not interested in joining his mission."

"Even if I wanted to stay, I couldn't," Beth paused, turning back to face her, "I *won't* abandon my friends, the ones who would be left behind to suffer in that aftermath." Understanding flashed across Jocelyn's features, and she gave a solemn nod. With a gentle tug, she linked arms with Beth, guiding her back to the sanctuary of the house.

"Well, if you ever find a way to escape, then you know where to run." The comforting weight of Jocelyn's arm felt like an anchor in the storm of Beth's thoughts. They walked back to the house and stepped through the threshold, leaving the sharp clarity of the morning light for the muted glow within. The distant echo of banging and crashing from a room beyond jolted Beth's nerves.

"I had words with Abraham," Kevin explained, noting Beth's alarmed expression, "and informed him that your time here has come to an end." Beth's breath caught in her chest, and she turned to Kevin, who stood with his back to them, hands braced against the mantelpiece.

"You told him we're leaving today?" She pressed, her voice taut with a mixture of disbelief and fear. Kevin shifted, turning to face her.

"Yes," he confirmed, his tone flat but resolute, "after your talk last night, Jocelyn and I discussed it. I confronted Abraham myself. It didn't take long to see the truth of things." Beth absorbed the weight of his words, feeling the room tilt slightly as she processed the gravity of their decision. The thought of leaving the oppressive shadow of Abraham's influence, at Jocelyn's proposition, sent a shiver down her spine, but also kindled a faint spark of hope. Without another word, she rose from her seat, her movements stiff as she prepared herself for whatever lay ahead. Abraham burst through the door, the thud of Beth's bag being dropped to the floor punctuating his arrival. He then let his bag fall to the floor with a heavy clunk, the sound reverberating against the high ceilings of the living room. His eyes, sharp as ice picks, landed on Beth and scanned the room for an explanation.

"Where were you?" His voice carried the subtle tremor of barely contained anger. Beth's muscles tensed, her body freezing in place, the air seeming to constrict around her. Before she could muster a response, Jocelyn stepped forward, her voice smooth as silk but edged with steel.

"She wasn't feeling well," Jocelyn said, placing a protective hand on Beth's shoulder, "I took her out for some air."

"We didn't go far," Beth added quickly, her throat tight, "just by the front door." Abraham's gaze shifted between the two women, then to Kevin, who stood silent, his stance firm and unyielding.

"It is regrettable that you have decided against joining our cause," a moment passed before Abraham spoke again, his disappointment clear but his tone controlled, "but I pray that you find wisdom in the future." Jocelyn met his gaze evenly.

"I'll inform the rest of your party to gather their things." She declared, turning to leave the space charged with tension, headed to the house next door.

"Guards will escort you to the gates." Kevin added, his voice devoid of any warmth as he headed to another room, presumably for a radio. Once the others had left, Abraham fixed his gaze on Beth, the air in the room growing heavier as silence stretched between them. He took a few deliberate steps towards her, his frame casting a shadow that seemed to engulf the light from the windows.

"What did you say to them?" He demanded, his words like stones thrown with precision.

"Nothing." Beth replied, her voice a whisper trying to be heard over a storm. Abraham's blue eyes narrowed, searching her face for any sign of deceit.

"I am a wise leader and great political strategist," he said coldly, "and after the progress made last night, it seems clear that the only conclusion to draw is that you've spoken against me." Beth maintained her stance, holding onto the last shred of composure as Abraham's towering figure loomed over her. The scent of old wood and dust filled her senses, the house itself a silent witness to the unfolding confrontation. Beth's heart thudded against her ribcage, the echo of Abraham's accusation reverberating in her ears.

"I love you, husband," she asserted, her voice laced with a desperate sincerity, "I would never do anything to jeopardise your plans."

Her plea hung in the air, a fragile thread of hope. Abraham's hand moved with a speed that belied his size, the crack of the slap resonating through the room as Beth stumbled backward, her body colliding with the coffee table. The impact sent a jarring ache through her spine, and for a moment, the world tilted on its axis. The sound of rushing footsteps filled the silence, and Kevin burst into the room, his eyes taking in the scene.

"Abraham, you've overstayed your welcome," he declared, his tone firm, "you will be escorted out at once." The tension thickened as they made their way to the convoy waiting outside. The Kingsport guards stood at attention, their weapons a silent testament to the seriousness of the situation. Beth found herself seated beside Shauna once again, the familiar faces of Ben and Luis providing cold comfort.

"Beth, what happened back there?" Ben's voice was low, concerned. Beth could only manage a shrug, her expression haunted, betraying the fear that clawed at her insides. As the engines roared to life, the vehicles began their slow procession away from the town. Ben's hand stealthily slipped behind the seat, the gap closest to the door so that no one else would notice, an unspoken offer of solace. Beth leaned forward, her fingers intertwining with his, the pressure of their clasp a lifeline amidst the chaos. The landscape rolled by, a blur of greenery and sunlight, but Beth saw none of it, her gaze fixed on the floor of the Humvee. Her tight grip on Ben's hand did not waver, each mile bringing them closer to an uncertain future at Biltmore.

The staircase creaked under their hurried steps, the once grand Biltmore mansion now a labyrinth of shadows and secrets. Austin's hand brushed against the cool stone wall for balance as they ascended the tight spiral, Eve close behind, her breaths measured and silent. Light from outside danced across the walls, catching on the dust particles that floated in the stale air. They emerged onto the third floor, a narrow hallway stretched out before them, lined with doors on either side. Austin led the way, his movements deliberate, checking each room methodically. The fourth door groaned open to reveal a back chamber, a sight so grotesque that it drew an involuntary curse from his lips.

"What the fuck—" Austin's voice echoed off the walls, filled with horror and disbelief.

"I never imagined something like this." Eve stepped beside him, her gaze skimming across the obscene collage adorning the space. Tyler, bound to a chair in the centre of the room, stared ahead, eyes forcibly kept open by small metal speculums, eyelids red and strained. A TV flickered quietly opposite him, the screen a cascade of explicit images, a generator humming softly in the corner providing the power. Eve's eyes darted between the TV and Tyler, her face paled at the twisted scene. Austin moved closer to Tyler, his friend's eyes reflecting a mix of agony and desperation.

"Hey, Tyler." He said, reaching for the cruel instruments clamped upon Tyler's eyelids. As his fingers grazed the cold metal, Tyler flinched, a shiver running through his frame.

"Stop," Eve's voice cut through the tension, "don't touch them." Her tone was urgent, her hands held out in a halt. Austin's hand hovered, his instinct to free Tyler warring with the practicality of their situation.

"Why the fuck not?"

"They'll know someone was here," Eve explained, her voice strained, "so if you remove them you'll have to put them back. It will only hurt him more." She locked eyes with Austin, her own filled with a pained resignation. Austin's heart pounded against his chest, the sickening reality sinking into his gut. He withdrew his hand, the speculums remaining untouched. A wave of nausea hit him, but he swallowed it down, turning away to hide the bile rising in his throat. Austin knelt beside Tyler, the tremble in his friend's body echoing through the stale air of the room. With a steady hand, he rested his palm on Tyler's knee, offering a silent anchor in the storm of torment.

"We found Chase." He murmured, the words thick with the little comfort he could offer.

"Thank you." Tyler breathed out, the vibration of relief barely audible. It was as if those two words carried the weight of their fractured world, a fleeting touch of something akin to hope. Eve's gaze shifted between the two men, her eyes reflecting the harrowing tableau before her.

"We should go," she said, her voice a low whisper carrying the urgency of their plight, "now that we know where he is. There's nothing we can do for him right now." Austin's eyes lingered on Tyler, the bond between them transcending the horrors of their reality.

"We'll come back for you." He vowed, a quiet determination setting into the lines of his face. As Austin retreated, a rustle of movement caught his ear. He paused, watching as Tyler strained against his restraints, a futile attempt at a nod. A whisper escaped Tyler's lips, too faint to grasp. Pivoting on his heel, Austin closed the distance once more, crouching to bring himself level with Tyler's gaze.

"Austin," Eve whispered, "we have to go—"

"What did you say?" He asked, leaning in closer to Tyler.

"I was brave," Tyler repeated, his voice hoarse, "I want you to know that I didn't give in. Tell Chase, tell him—" The confession struck a chord within Austin, the raw truth of it threatening to breach his composed exterior. Tyler winced, his face contorting with the pain as tears welled up in his eyes.

"I know," Austin brushed some loose hair off his forehead, "it's okay. I know it hurts. You don't have to talk anymore." He fought back the surge of emotion, the welling tears a luxury he could not afford. Tyler's voice was a hoarse whisper, barely audible above the soft drone of the television.

"I know you all think I was the weaker one, and that Chase was my strength," Tyler murmured, his green eyes gleaming with an intensity that defied his bound state, disdain tinged his words as he continued, "but I want you to know that I said no to them, and I wouldn't let them change me. That's why I'm here, and Chase isn't." Austin's grip on Tyler's hand tightened, the muscles in his jaw working silently as he processed Tyler's courage. He gave a firm nod, acknowledging the unspoken pact between them.

"We will get you out of here, brother," Austin repeated, his voice low and resolute, "I promise."

"Go." Tyler urged, his gaze locked onto Austin's, imparting a plea for haste. With a final squeeze of Tyler's hand, Austin rose swiftly, casting one last glance at the obscene tableau surrounding his friend. He turned on his heel and strode towards the door, Eve's footsteps echoing his own as they left the chamber. The sound of their retreat faded down the hallway, leaving only the flicker of the muted screen to disturb the oppressive stillness. Together, he and Eve slipped away, leaving the chamber of nightmares behind, the echo of Tyler's bravery haunting their retreat. Austin's descent was a tempest, each heavy footfall on the staircase echoing through the grand halls of the estate. Eve's lighter steps tapped in urgency behind him, her brow creased. They spilled out onto the gravel pathway, past the makeshift gallows outside, the stones crunching beneath their frantic pace. The estate loomed behind them, its ivy-draped facade a silent witness to the turmoil within. Austin couldn't stop himself from getting as far away as possible from their prison, his mind racing with a flurry of thoughts and emotions. Tyler's words replayed in his head, a constant reminder of the bravery and defiance he had shown in the face of danger. But Austin also felt the heavy weight of guilt on his shoulders, knowing that if they had only escaped together, things could have been different. His fists clenched, torn between the heat of anger towards their captors and the regret for not taking action sooner. He hurried through the Azalea Garden, the vibrant colours a stark contrast to the storm brewing inside Austin. His muscular frame moved with purpose, betraying the sharpness of his eyes, which were now clouded with an inner chaos. He reached the Bass Pond Boathouse, the structure worn by time and neglect. Without ceremony, he doubled over the railing and emptied his stomach into the still water below. Eve, panting from the chase, came to a halt just as the last of his convulsions subsided.

"Are you okay?" She asked, her voice laced with genuine worry. In response, Austin turned his fury on the boathouse itself, his fists raining down on the wooden posts.

"Fuck! Of course I'm not okay," he wailed in agony as he cursed, each expletive tore from his throat raw and unfiltered as his flesh split against the splintering wood, "fuck!" Blood stained his knuckles, dark against the pale decay.

"Stop," Eve rushed to his side, reaching for his injured hand with a tentative touch, "you're hurting yourself!" He jerked away, spinning to face the pond once more. A primal scream erupted from him, scattering birds perched nearby and rippling across the water's surface. He inhaled sharply, the sound of his ragged breathing mingling with the distant melody of birdsong. The silence following his outburst was deafening, creating an uneasy void in the atmosphere. Eve looked around nervously, half expecting to see someone lurking in the shadows, their eyes trained on them. But there was nothing except the rustling of leaves and the distant chirping of birds. As she turned back to face Austin, she noticed that his body had gone completely still. He stood at the railing of the boathouse, his knuckles still raw and bloody from his violent outburst. His gaze was fixed on something in the distance, something that only he could see. Eve approached him cautiously, her heart aching for him. She knew that he needed a release for all the pent up emotions within him and she couldn't blame him for losing control. She reached out to touch his arm, hoping to offer some comfort. But as soon as her fingers grazed his skin, he flinched away from her touch as if her mere presence caused him pain. She withdrew her hand immediately, her own hurt mingling with confusion.

"Austin—" She started softly, but he cut her off with a sharp gesture of his hand.

"Don't," he said through gritted teeth, still not looking at her, "just, don't." Eve bit back the words she wanted to say in response and instead chose to give him some space. She leaned against one of the posts of the boathouse and watched him silently, giving him time to process everything that had happened. Minutes passed like hours before Austin finally moved again. He turned away from the railing and looked at Eve with weary eyes.

"Are you okay?"

"I'm sorry." He said simply before slumping down onto one of the benches. Eve joined him on the bench, careful not to invade his personal space any further than necessary. They sat in silence for a while longer before she finally spoke up again.

"Do you feel better?" Eve's question hung in the air, delicate yet probing. Silence was his only reply as he fought to rein in his breath, to calm the tide of adrenaline that had carried him here. Slowly, the rise and fall of his chest steadied, returning to its normal rhythm.

"A bit."

"Is this why you ran out here," Eve's voice cut through the quietude, her figure unmoving as she observed him, "to scream where no one could hear?" Austin turned slightly, his gaze now softened but not meeting hers. The remnants of his anger hung palpably between them, an unspoken testament to the fragility of their existence amidst the opulence turned wild around them. Austin stood suddenly, pacing in front of her, looking back towards the estate. With a turn sharp and sudden, Austin faced Eve, his eyes locking onto hers with an intensity that seemed to carve out the silence from the cacophony of their ragged world.

"As soon as Ben and Beth are back," he said, his voice a low rumble, "we're ending this." Eve bit her lip, the fragility in her stance belying the resolve in her voice.

"We need more time, Austin. Beth isn't ready." She implored, yet her plea was swept away by his vehement response.

"No," the harsh objection was a thunderclap bursting from him, "there's no more time." His formidable frame, usually so steadfast, started to shudder, the cracks in his composure widening until they could no longer hold. Eve stood, closing the distance between them, wrapping her arms around him in a grip that anchored him against the storm of his emotions. As tears began their quiet descent down his cheeks, he buried his face into the sanctuary of her shoulder, the tremors of his cry just another whisper among the rustling leaves.

"It's okay to let go," Eve murmured into his ear, her voice steady like the distant hills that cradled the estate, "it's okay." Austin pulled away, just enough to meet her gaze, his brown eyes swimming with vulnerability.

"I don't do this," he insisted, wiping his eyes, trying to restore the walls within himself, "I'm meant to be the rational one."

"Even the strong have hearts, Austin," she replied, her hand brushing against his arm in comfort, "feelings don't make you weak." He nodded, a slow inhale steadying his breath.

"Do you still have those pills?" Austin queried suddenly. Eve nodded, her eyebrows furrowing.

"Yes, they're well hidden."

"Chase," he continued steadily, "I need some of those pills for him."

"Why?"

"You didn't see him, Eve," Austin pressed, "his hand's a mess. If I can't do anything else, it's the least I can do to relieve a little pain. Maybe one for Tyler too."

"Turn around." She instructed, and though his brow creased in confusion, he complied, turning his back to her as he faced the pond once more. Eve reached discreetly beneath her underwear, withdrawing the small bottle concealed inside her. A quick swipe of her cardigan removed the sticky residue before she uncapped it and presented two pills to Austin. He accepted them, his expression a complex tapestry of disgust and respect.

"You'd really go that far?" He asked, pocketing the medicine.

"Better safe than sorry," she said with a shrug, her hazel eyes meeting his briefly before she turned away from him and returned the bottle to its secret niche, "if they search my room, I can't afford to leave anything to chance." The late spring wind curled around Austin and Eve as they stood in silence, the weight of their previous moment lingering between them.

"And if they strip searched you?" Austin broke the quiet, his voice low but tinged with concern. Eve's shoulders lifted in a nonchalant shrug, her hazel eyes hard with resolve.

"Then I'd have no regrets being punished," she replied, her tone matter-of-fact, betraying none of the fear that such a prospect warranted, "knowing I did all that I could to hide them. Let's head back." She said, a subtle urgency threading through her words. Their exchange complete, they both knew it was time to return, to step back into the roles that survival demanded of them. They departed from the boathouse, leaving behind the echo of their vulnerability amidst the overgrown splendour of Bass Pond. They made their way through the overgrown Azalea Garden, where the scent of soil and decaying leaves marked their path. The distant roar of engines grew louder, and soon enough, a convoy of solar-powered Humvee's came into view, disrupting the estate's deceptive tranquility. They kept their distance, hiding within the tree line as they watched the unexpected arrival unfold. Abraham emerged from the lead vehicle, his door slamming shut with a resounding thud that echoed the anger on his face. He strode purposefully to the second car, yanking open the door to drag Beth out from the back seat.

"Something's wrong," Austin observed, his voice quiet though his stature remained poised for action, "they're back too soon."

"And Abraham doesn't look too pleased about it." Eve nodded, her worry evident as she watched Abraham's furious motions.

Without another word, Austin reached for her arm, pulling her aside to avoid the commotion.

"Come on," he urged, directing them towards the relative safety of the side of the estate, entering through the Kitchen Court Yard with haste, "we can find Ben and figure out what the fuck is going on." Their retreat was silent but swift, each step carrying them further from the unfolding drama and closer to the heart of their own trials within the oppressive walls of Biltmore.

CHAPTER 19

Ben's silhouette flickered under the sterile glow of the kitchen lights, moving with a haste that betrayed his usual calm. Austin, muscles taut beneath his utilitarian garb, raised his voice to cut through the quiet.

"Ben!" The man in question whirled around, his eyes wide, yet composed. Eve's petite frame tensed, her gaze darting between the two men like a sparrow caught in a storm.

"Austin." Ben exclaimed, embracing him in an unexpected hug.

"Talk to me." Austin demanded, his voice a low rumble. Without a word, Ben gestured urgently, ushering them into the shadows of a nearby storeroom. He glanced over his shoulder, ensuring they were alone before he faced them, the door clicking shut behind them.

"The Kingsport leader, Jocelyn, said we had to leave town immediately. There were guards everywhere, and Abraham was furious." He paused, swallowing hard. Eve's hands twisted the hem of her shirt, a silent testament to her worry. Austin's jaw clenched as he processed the scene painted before him.

"Why?"

"I have no idea what happened. Abraham was so mad, it looks like he'd hit Beth," Ben's eyes darkened, "she gripped my hand so tight on the drive back—" A heavy silence enveloped the trio. The air felt thick with unspoken fears until Austin broke it with a revelation.

"I know where Chase and Tyler are."

"Are they—" Ben started, but Austin's sombre look halted him.

"You don't want the details," Austin's tone left no room for argument, "but we need to act tonight. None of them can endure any more of this."

"We're not ready," Eve's hesitation hung palpable in the stale air, "we need more time—"

"Abraham has lost control," Ben interjected, a note of urgency sharpening his words, "as far as we know, he's never hit Beth before. Not across the face. His anger is reaching new heights."

"Then I'll get the pills to Beth now," understanding flickered in Eve's hazel eyes, and she nodded, "if tonight is the night." Their whispered strategising ground to a halt as boots thudded against the corridor floors outside. Voices grew louder, carrying the command that sent a chill through them all.

"Abraham wants everyone gathered outside. Now!" One of the guards barked down the corridor. Tension rose like a wave as the three exchanged solemn looks, knowing the reckoning approached with each passing second.

The bedroom door slammed against the wall as Abraham's grip on Beth's arm propelled her into the room. She stumbled forward, her hands seeking purchase on the plush carpet before she collapsed onto the floor. She gasped, her voice strained with the effort to convince him.

"I swear on my life, Abraham. Kingsport wasn't my doing."

"Then whose fault is it?" He bellowed, his eyes dark pools of rage.

His boot connected with her midsection, a brutal punctuation to his accusation. Beth folded inward, a silent scream etched into her expression. Abraham marched towards the sideboard, his fingers wrapping around the decanter. The golden liquid splashed into the glass, shimmering briefly before he downed it in one gulp, then another. Beth clutched at her stomach, the pain a white-hot brand, while he drank and refilled, over and over. With each breath, she pushed against the agony, rising to her feet. Her back found the support of the bedpost, her gaze steady on Abraham. He observed her through narrowed eyes with an unsettling mix of scorn and admiration. He stepped towards her again with every indication that he was going to afford her another harsh blow.

"Please," she raised her hands, "what if I'm pregnant? You can't—"

"Look at you, so defiant." He murmured, advancing towards her. A slap cracked through the air, his hand leaving a stinging imprint on her cheek. She caught herself against the baseboard, and without hesitation, her hand flew back, striking him across the face with equal force.

"Fuck you—"

"Disappointing," he sneered, his smile chilling as he traced her jawline with a gentleness that belied his simmering anger, "I thought I chose a dutiful wife." Beth recoiled from his touch, standing taller.

"Must be exhausting," she retorted, the smirk on her lips cold and unforgiving, "your righteous path leads nowhere, and yet you trample on, rejected by those who thrive without your God." His hands fell to his sides, the smile wiped clean from his face.

"You think you understand my path?"

"Your child will save no one, Abraham," she said, her voice a low, defiant hum, "you are nothing." In the silence that followed, only the rhythm of their breathing filled the opulent chamber, a testament to the battle lines drawn within the decaying walls. Abraham's hand shoved Beth towards the bed, her body colliding with the softness of the mattress. Her heart hammered against her ribs, each beat screaming a warning of his possible intentions. But then, with a sudden pivot, he stormed to the door, yanking it open with such force that it banged against the wall.

"She stays here until I say otherwise." He barked at Jacob, who stood rigid in the hallway. The guard's eyes flicked to Beth, taking in the crimson trickle from her lip, before he nodded stiffly and turned away. Beth drew herself up, using the bedpost for support, her gaze lingering on Jacob's retreating back. Her mind raced through the possibilities of what lay ahead, the weight of concern pulling her brows together as she peered into the dim corridor beyond.

Outside, the air was thick with tension, a sombre procession making its way through the grounds. Austin and Ben moved as one entity, their steps deliberate, staying within arm's reach. Eve, a silent shadow, kept pace just behind them, her presence a silent pillar of strength.

"Any idea what's happening?" Reece materialised amidst the shuffle, his voice barely audible over the murmur of the crowd. Ben and Austin exchanged a glance, a silent conversation passing between them, and shook their heads in unison. The assembly gathered under the looming gallows, the structure's stark silhouette a dark blot against the grey sky. Rain began to spatter down, droplets pattering against leaves and fabric alike. Abraham appeared on the stage, his figure commanding even from a distance. He swept his gaze across the sea of faces, pausing to signal his guards. In moments, Ben, Austin, Eve, Reece, and Val found themselves ushered forward, the guards' firm grips guiding them through the crowd. They joined Jennifer, who stood stoically as they took their place at the forefront of the expectant throng. As the rain intensified, drops streaked down faces and dripped from soaked hair, the heavens weeping for the unfolding drama below.

"Did you know that Abraham was originally named Abram, which means 'exalted father'?" His voice boomed across the open space as he emerged from the front door, the rain drumming against the gravel. He let the weight of his namesake ripple through the congregation as he marched. Each syllable hung in the damp air, an echo of divine providence entwined with a thread of menace.

"What's happening?" Jennifer whispered to no one in particular. Abraham stood tall upon the platform, his broad shoulders squared to his audience. Water dripped from the hem of his dark coat, pooling around his boots like a spilled secret.

"God changed his name to Abraham as part of His covenant, signifying that Abraham would become the father of many nations. In Genesis, chapter 17 verse five, God said 'No longer will you be called Abram, your name will be Abraham, for I have made you a father of many nations.' Abraham is a key figure in the Bible, known for his faith in God's promises. He is the patriarch of many nations, as I am yours." His eyes were cerulean flames under the brooding sky, searing through the mist with fervent conviction. The silence was palpable, the only sound the relentless patter of rain and the laboured breaths of the gathered flock. With a slight nod, Abraham dismissed one of his guards. The man turned on his heel, his departure a silent command, vanishing into the grandeur of the estate with purpose. Raindrops drummed against the earth, a cacophony that mirrored the confusion in the crowd. Whispers cut through the air, some tinged with concern at Abraham's slurred speech, others merely puzzled murmurs. Mary, her eyes wide and fearful, sought out Adam and Aaron. The brothers stood like shadows beside the gallows, their presence meek but unmistakable. Beth emerged, flanked by guards who marched her to stand before the assembly. Her steps were steady despite the rough handling, her stance defiant as she faced the structure of death. Abraham's gaze found hers, and for a moment, the world seemed to hold its breath.

"It seems that my leadership has been in question lately," he declared, his voice booming above the patter of rain, "by none more so than my own *wife*." The accusation hung in the air, thick with tension. Beth returned his glare unflinchingly. Rain plastered strands of hair to her cheeks, but her spirit remained untamed, even as the droplets traced pathways of defiance down her skin.

"Fuck you." She mouthed, her lips curling into a deranged smirk, a silent rebellion etched into the gesture. Abraham scowled back down at her.

"Today, she struck me," Abraham continued, pointing an accusatory finger, "such insolence might demand the noose."

"What the fuck did she do?" Austin whispered, exchanging worried glances with Ben and Eve. Beth locked eyes with Abraham again, challenging him without words. His lips twisted, and he resumed his sermon.

"The Bible's teachings on leadership emphasise righteousness, humility, integrity, service, and wisdom. Leaders are called to serve others, maintain high moral standards, manage their households well, and lead with justice and compassion. These passages offer guidance on the qualities that make a leader fit to serve in both religious and secular roles. Justice tells me that my wife should be hanged for her insolence, but compassion tells me that I could not do that on this day, not when she could very well be carrying my son at this given moment." Beth's scoff was barely audible over the rain, yet it carried the weight of her scorn as Abraham wove his narrative of compassion sparing her from the fate of the gallows. The rain intensified, every drop an accusation against the soil, as if nature itself sought to cleanse the stains of the day's events.

"If he's not hanging Beth, then why are we here?" Ben looked through the crowd, trying to catch Beth's eye. Abraham raised his arms, beckoning the heavens to witness his decree, and in that moment, he seemed larger than life - a patriarch presiding over his conflicted domain. The crowd held its breath as Abraham's voice boomed, his words slicing through the murmur of raindrops.

"But apparently I must prove my ability as a leader, and as I must serve you all well and maintain my high moral standards, I feel I am forced to prove a point. I will not be questioned, I will not be judged, and I most certainly will not be seen as weak," his gaze swept over the huddled masses before he gestured sharply towards a guard at the door, "in Paul's Letter to the Romans, he writes 'because of this, God gave them over to shameful lusts. Even their women exchanged natural sexual relations for unnatural ones. In the same way the men also abandoned natural relations with women and were inflamed with lust for one another. Men committed shameful acts with other men, and received in themselves the due penalty for their error.'" Austin's jaw clenched, muscles taut with a silent fury that matched the tempest above.

"No—" Eve's eyes flickered with fear, reflecting the storm's chaos as she stood beside him. Ben turned, his expression hardening as he caught the glance between Austin and Eve. A hush fell upon the crowd as a figure was led down the gravel path, a bag obscuring his identity. Beth's eyes widened, darting from face to face, the pace of her heart mirroring the rapid drumming of rain on leaves. Austin diverted his gaze to the sodden earth, a barrier against the sorrow that threatened to spill over. The droplets collected on his lashes, mingling with the unshed tears born of helplessness and dread. Abraham raised his voice once more, proclamations lost to the roar of the heavens, as the assembly braced for the storm's crescendo. The sky wept relentless torrents as Abraham's voice echoed through the rain, his words slicing the air with the sharpness of a blade.

"We have tried and tried again to put our brother on a righteous path, but he refused to see the ways of God." He intoned, his presence casting a shadow over the drenched assembly. A guard's hands, firm and unyielding, tore the bag from the man's head, discarding it onto the mud-slicked platform where it lay, sodden and limp. Tyler's gaze, once clear and determined, was now clouded by the remnants of tears and the redness of fury and fear. His lip trembled, betraying the struggle within, but his stature remained unbroken despite the shackles that bound him. In the crowd, Austin's eyes locked onto his friend's, his lips parting in silent communion.

"*You were very brave.*" He mouthed, the message cutting through the downpour like a promise. Tyler's chin lifted ever so slightly, the nod that followed an act of quiet defiance against the fate that awaited him. The guard looped the noose around Tyler's neck, the hemp rough against his skin, the finality of its embrace undeniable. Each movement was precise, the preparation for death executed with a chilling routine. Beth, mere feet below him, forced her eyes to meet Tyler's. The apology shaping her lips was a whisper against the storm. In response, Tyler offered a smile, faint yet filled with a courage that belied his circumstance. It was a fleeting exchange, a moment of shared grief and unspoken understanding. The trapdoor released with a violent clatter, sending Tyler into an abrupt descent. A snap, grotesque in its clarity, reverberated through the rain, as if the water carried it for all to hear. Beth's gaze remained fixed on the twitching legs before her, the slow, haunting rotation of Tyler's body a grim ballet orchestrated by death's unseen hand.

"I am your *leader*," Abraham proclaimed, his gaze sweeping across the faces upturned in horror, "and my word is final." But Beth hardly registered the words - the sight of Tyler's stillness consumed her every sense, leaving a void where only shock and nausea churned. Amidst the chaos, Eve crouched low behind Austin as the people around her gazed upward, retrieving the bottle from inside. She pushed through the crowd, her movements swift and purposeful as she darted towards Beth.

"Tonight." Eve breathed out, the directive clear even amidst chaos as she pressed the bottle into Beth's palm. She watched as Eve faded back into the sea of bodies, the pill bottle now a burden heavy with implication. Desperation mingled with resolve as she clutched the container, the shape of it pressing against her flesh, a tangible symbol of the rebellion that simmered beneath the surface. Abraham descended the steps, his figure retreating from the gallows. The rain hammered down without respite, washing away all traces of mercy from the day. Beth's heart pounded as she watched Abraham's towering form cut a path towards her through the dissolving crowd. Panic and resolve twisted inside her, urging her feet into motion. She spun on her heel, weaving through the dispersing throng of followers, her damp hair clinging to her cheeks. The grand hallways loomed before her, once a symbol of opulence, now pathways of her living nightmare. Her breaths came in short gasps as she ascended the staircase, the echoes of her footfalls swallowed by the mansion's ancient walls. She darted into their bedroom, the door closing with a hush behind her. With swift movements, Beth slid the pill bottle beneath the pillow, its plastic body a secret promise against the plush fabric. Abraham stormed in, his presence filling the chamber like a dark cloud rolling over the mountains. His eyes, sharp blue and unyielding, fixed on Beth as she stood defiantly. Water dripped from his clothes, pooling on the wooden floor, and Beth could see the muscle in his jaw clench. "You're insane." Beth accused, her voice firm despite the shiver that ran down her spine.

"Perhaps," Abraham retorted, his tone edged with a chilling calm, "but insanity is a matter of perspective, and I needed to prove a point." Beth moved for the door, a desperate attempt at escape. But Abraham's grip was iron as he seized her arm, dragging her back with a force that sent her tumbling onto the bed. The impact jolted through her, a sharp contrast to the softness of the sheets. At that moment, Adam appeared at the threshold, his eyes wide as they took in the scene.

"Forgive me—" He began, only to be silenced by Abraham's thunderous voice.

"Speak!" Abraham demanded, his gaze never leaving Beth's.

"Kingsport," Adam said, urgency lacing his words, "they're talking about us on the radios." Abraham's response was nothing more than a grunt, an animalistic sound filled with annoyance. He released Beth, his stare lingering with an intensity that promised this wasn't over. He strode to the door, turning the key in the lock with a finality that echoed in the hollow space. Alone now, Beth remained on the bed, the sound of the key a grim melody amidst the storm's relentless symphony.

Austin bounded up the worn steps of Biltmore's grand staircase, the echo of his heavy boots reverberating through the hollow corridors. Water dripped from his jacket, forming a transient trail behind him as Ben followed suit, equally drenched. They arrived at the fourth floor, Austin shouldering the door open to Chase's dimly-lit room. Chase eyed them warily before his lips curled into a smile upon seeing Ben.

"Why are you guys so wet?"
"Rain's coming down in sheets out there." Ben replied, running a hand through damp hair. Austin approached Chase, a pill pinched between his fingers. Without ceremony, he placed it on Chase's tongue and handed him a bottle of water. Chase swallowed, coughing slightly as the liquid chased down the medicine.
"What was that?"
"Something to take the edge off." Austin said, his tone leaving no room for further questions.
"Did you find Tyler?" Chase's eyes searched Austin's. With a slow nod, Austin exchanged a loaded glance with Ben.
"Listen, we're busting out tonight." Ben cut in, leaning against the wall with determined eyes. Chase let out a laugh that didn't quite reach his eyes.
"I'll believe it when I see it."

"We'll get you out, Chase. I promise." Austin leaned in closer, his presence solid and reassuring. Chase tilted his head down, squinting his eyes at nothing in particular.

"How's Tyler doing?"

"He's hanging in there." Ben's words lingered awkwardly in the air, and his face clouded over as he caught the unintended darkness of his remark. Austin diverted his gaze to the wooden floorboards.

"We have to go now, but we'll come back for you later." He leaned down, planting a kiss on Chase's forehead and wrapping him in an embrace that was both protective and tender, despite its roughness. Chase winced subtly, a shadow of pain crossing his features.

"I'll be right here." He managed to laugh, finding humour in the bleakness. As Austin and Ben left the room and the door clicked shut, they entered the corridor's stale air. Austin glared at Ben.

"Hanging in there? Really?"

"Shit, man. It just slipped out," Ben admitted, his expression pained, "I didn't mean it like that." Austin drew a deep breath, composing himself. Together they descended the stairs, determination setting their jaws and solidarity fuelling their stride.

"Go warn the others. Tell them tonight's the escape." Austin gripped Ben's shoulder, urgency etched in his eyes. Ben registered the gravity of his task with a curt nod. They both turned at the sound of heavy footsteps, witnessing Abraham's rigid form descending the staircase like an angry spectre. The two exchanged a knowing glance and made haste towards his bedroom. The door was an unyielding barrier, but Ben's knock was respectful, almost deferential.

"Beth, it's us."

"I'm locked in here." Beth's response came swiftly, her voice laced with tension, the words muffled by the solid wood between them.

"Anything you can use to open it from your side?" Ben's voice held a thin thread of hope, which snapped with Beth's next words.

"Sorry," her apology was a whisper of despair, "no." Austin's question was barely audible, a conspiratorial murmur.

"Have you got the pills?"

"Yes," Beth affirmed, her resolve steeling, "I'll do what we planned."

"Stay strong," Ben reassured her through the door, "we'll come for you later."

"Hey, guys," Beth called out as they began to turn away, her hand pressed against the door, "if things don't work out tonight—"

"They will." Ben snapped.

"But *if they don't*," she pressed, "I want you to know, I'm grateful."

"What do you mean?" Austin paused, his heart clenching.

"Thank you for getting me this far," she said, her voice steady despite the pounding of her heart, "I love you both." Austin looked to Ben, offering him a heartfelt smile.

"Take a moment with her." He stepped away, rounding a corner to give them privacy.

"Are you still there?" Beth whispered.

"Right here," Ben assured, leaning into the door as if it could dissolve beneath his touch, "I've missed you."

"Never thought I'd find moments of happiness here." She confessed, trying to smile through the dread that clutched her.

"Coming back for you is the only thing that's kept me going." Ben admitted, the raw honesty of his words hanging in the air like a sacred vow. Austin reappeared, the weight of their mission pressing down on him.

"Time to move."

"See you soon." Ben promised Beth one last time before stepping away. Their footsteps receded down the corridor, leaving Beth alone with her heart thudding against her ribcage. She turned to the bed, fingers trembling as she snatched a bottle of pills from beneath the pillow. With swift, deliberate motions, she emptied the contents onto the dresser and covered them with a pillowcase. The wooden top became an impromptu mortar as she crushed the pills into fine dust, the white powder spreading like a ghostly veil. Grabbing the half-empty whiskey bottle, she took a swig, steeling her nerves before tilting the remainder of the pills inside. She moved the bottle gently, watching the powder swirl and dissolve into the amber liquid, disappearing until only faint particles remained.

The dining hall was stagnant with tension, an undercurrent of anxiety pulling at everyone present. Austin sat stiffly across from Ben, his gaze fixed on a spot beyond the gathered occupants, lost in the unspoken fury that gnawed at his insides. Eve slid into the seat next to Ben, her presence marked by a persistent quietude as she picked at her food without appetite. Val and Reece sat at the table next to them, exchanging wordless communication that only they could understand. A nod from Reece met Austin's eyes briefly before both parties diverted their attention back to their sparse meals. Outside, the wind whispered secrets through the ivy, caressing the stone walls of Biltmore with an eerie gentleness that belied the storm brewing within.

"How will we know when it's time?" Eve whispered between mouthfuls. Austin's lips quirked into a wry smile at Eve's question, his eyes glinting with a hint of mischief only those who knew him well could catch.

"It's Beth. Trust me," he said, "the whole estate will know." Ben's laugh was half-hearted as he pushed the remnants of his meal aside, the food had lost its appeal long ago.

"I'm going for a smoke." He rose from his seat, each movement deliberate, a man bracing for the storm to come. The wooden chair scraped softly against the floor, the sound barely registering in the hushed space. He made his way through the other diners, their own conversations muted whispers of worry and weariness. Through the archway of the dining hall, Ben caught sight of Mary's slender figure approaching the library door, her knuckles rapping lightly on the aged wood. It swung open, revealing Abraham seated in the dimly lit room surrounded by Aaron and Adam, their discussion halting abruptly.

"What is it you need?" Abraham's gaze turned to Mary, an eyebrow arching in expectation.

"May we speak alone?" Mary's voice was a soft thread of sound, almost drowned out by the patter of rain. Abraham gave a brief nod, and with that gesture, Aaron and Adam rose from their seats, their movements stiff and formal. Aaron passed by Mary, his gaze sharp and commanding, a silent exchange that spoke volumes. She acknowledged him with a small nod, her posture rigid with tension. Once the door clicked shut behind the departing men, Mary moved across the room, the distance between her and Abraham charged with unspoken words. She took a seat opposite him, her hands folded neatly in her lap, a study in restraint. Abraham leaned forward, his voice cutting through the silence like a knife through cloth.

"I haven't got all evening, Mary."

"Cousin, you must know that I love you dearly," Mary's voice trembled as she spoke, her fingers fidgeting in her lap, "I've walked in faith with you, been a devout follower most of the time—"

"Most?" Abraham interrupted, his deep voice resonating in the high-ceilinged room.

"Yes," she hesitated, then nodded faintly, "I have sinned." With force enough to startle the sombre portraits lining the walls, Abraham's fist came down upon the arm of his chair.

"First my wife, and now my cousin," he growled, his stormy blue eyes narrowing, "how can I lead a community of the righteous if my own family does not follow?" Mary inhaled deeply, bracing herself against the weight of his gaze.

"I was exploring, and I found one of your guards," her voice dropped to little more than a whisper, "locked away in the attic." Abraham rose from his seat, his tall frame casting a long shadow that flickered in the firelight. He strode to the fireplace, his back to her, hands gripping the mantle as if to steady himself.

"And what is this sin you have committed?" He demanded over his shoulder, his tone edged with steel.

"Desire," Mary murmured, her head bowing, "unholy lust." A moment passed, filled only by the crackling of the fire and the soft patter of rain against the windows. Suddenly Abraham spun around, closing the distance between them. His presence loomed over her.

"I can't decide if I'm more excited or disappointed," he confessed, his voice a low rumble, "delighted that Chase might be redeemed, or disgruntled that my own cousin has fallen so far from grace." Tears cascaded down Mary's cheeks, each drop reflecting the dim light of the room as she trembled, her voice choked with remorse.

"Please, Abraham, forgive me." She pleaded, the words barely escaping her lips. Abraham watched her, an eyebrow arched in judgment, before easing himself onto the couch beside her. His presence was like a pillar of certainty amidst her chaos.

"Why confess now? You could have hidden this truth." He said, his tone more curious than accusing. Her hand instinctively cradled her stomach, betraying the secret life within. His gaze softened momentarily, and he overlaid his hand atop hers.

"I thank you for your honesty," Abraham spoke, a fatherly warmth seeping into his voice, "yet it saddens me that you strayed from virtue."

"Let us wed immediately, Chase and I." Mary suggested, her blue eyes seeking approval from his stern face. A contemplative silence hung between them as Abraham considered the proposition.

"Tell me, when did this union begin?" He probed, his eyes locking onto hers.

"Shortly after I found him." Mary lied, hoping the vagueness of time would conceal the true extent of her condition. Mary pondered her gamble, aware of the risk yet desperate for reprieve. Abraham's hand remained on her belly, his touch firm but not unkind.

"For you created my inmost being, you knit me together in my mother's womb. I praise you because I am fearfully and wonderfully made, your works are wonderful, I know that full well." He recited scripture, his voice resonating with conviction.

"And Mary said, 'My soul glorifies the Lord and my spirit rejoices in God my Saviour, for he has been mindful of the humble state of his servant," she joined in the sacred echo, her voice steadier as she clung to her faith, "from now on all generations will call me blessed, for the Mighty One has done great things for me. Holy is his name.'" Abraham's temper flared as he rose, his form casting a long shadow across the room.

"That verse is holy, a testament to divine favour. You bear no saviour." He rebuked, his hands clenching involuntarily. Mary recoiled, the sting of his words sharper than any physical blow. She stood too, her petite figure dwarfed by his towering anger.

"I meant no disrespect—"

"Leave me." Abraham's voice thundered, the walls of Biltmore absorbing his ire. Mary's form retreated swiftly, a spectre of regret fleeting from the room. Abraham's hand found solace in the neck of the decanter, the liquid amber fortifying his resolve as he drank deeply.

The mansion groaned beneath the weight of the storm, each drop an accusation against the pane. With measured steps, Abraham ascended the grand staircase, his shadow elongating with the setting sun that fought to pierce the clouds. His key grated in the lock of the bedroom door, a harsh prelude to the tempest about to unfold. The door swung open with vehemence, slamming against the wall, as Beth's heart climbed into her throat.

"You, *wife*, shall give me a son." Abraham declared, his words a forceful edict amidst the patter of rain.

"No!" Beth's mind raced as she skirted the bed's edge, her escape a dance of desperation. His hand snatched at her ankle, his grip ironclad, but her foot shot out in rebellion, striking true against his jaw. His curse sliced through the air as she watched him stagger back, fury etched upon his features.

"Fucking bitch." He spat, his retreat towards the dresser a momentary ceasefire. He took a swig of his whiskey and spat at the fire, before taking another mouthful to wash down the remaining blood. Beth edged towards the foot of the bed, her gaze locked on Abraham's seething form.

"No." She repeated, firm in her conviction.

"What did I do to deserve such an unpleasant and hateful wife?" His features contorted with indignation as he posed his question, an incredulous sneer marring his lips. Her laughter burst forth, unbidden and sharp, echoing against the walls of her opulent prison.

"Are you serious?" She challenged, her voice laced with disbelief. He turned, fully facing her now, and the scorn in her eyes was a tangible force.

"What—"

"You are evil, Abraham. Hateful and insane," each word was a verbal arrow, aimed to wound, "your very existence is a blight, you should be ashamed. Even God would detest what you are." The roar of his scream melded with the crackling flames as he hurled the whiskey bottle, his rage giving it flight. Glass met fire, shattering with a crescendo that matched the tempest outside. Beth's heart sank as the liquid vanished into the inferno, the Vicodin's promise of reprieve consumed along with it. Abraham's fury carried him towards her, his body a missile of wrath. She rose to meet him, her hands clawing at his face. Their screams intertwined, a cacophony of desperation and anger. He stumbled backward, his head colliding with the side table's unforgiving edge. As he lay moaning, Beth's breaths came in ragged gasps, her eyes darting frantically for a weapon. Drawers slid open with hurried jerks, their contents spilling onto the floor, yet she found nothing useful. Abraham's groans grew louder, his consciousness reasserting itself. She dashed into the closet, her search frenetic among the dark wooden door and walls. Her fingers closed around a cold bottle of rubbing alcohol, its potential clear. With no time to spare, she returned to the bedroom, Abraham's prone figure a beacon of urgency. Grasping his hair, she yanked his head back, exposing his grimacing face. The bottle tipped, and the clear liquid cascaded into his gaping mouth, a baptism not of redemption but of reckoning. Abraham's body convulsed, a violent symphony of coughs and splatters that echoed through the opulent chamber. Beth steadied his head on her lap, pinching his nose, ensuring each bitter swallow passed down his throat. The door burst open, hinges screaming in protest. Luis stood framed in the threshold, his haunted brown eyes locked onto Beth. Without hesitation, he charged, yanking her from Abraham with a force that sent her sprawling. The bottle slipped from her grasp, spilling its contents across the floor.

"What have you done?" His voice was a low growl, more accusation than question. Before she could reply, Luis slammed her to the ground. His hands found her neck, fingers tightening like steel bands. Beth's hands clawed at his grip, gasping for air that would not come. Darkness began to infiltrate her vision, creeping along the edges. Luis's weight lifted as Austin tackled him, pulling him away. She gulped greedily at the air, each breath a raspy battle against the lingering constriction of her throat. Austin faced Luis, who met him with a sneer.

"You think you can save her?" Luis mocked, and swung a fist. Austin dodged, then surged forward, driving Luis back with a fierce determination. They collided with the fireplace, dislodging a burning log that tumbled out and met the spilled liquids, igniting instantly. Undeterred by the inferno, Luis launched himself at Austin, tackling him with the ferocity of desperation. Aaron burst into the room, gun drawn and wild-eyed. He scanned the chaos, his gaze falling on Abraham's prone form. His eyes darted to Beth, still choking, still fighting for breath, as Luis pointed an accusing finger at her. Aaron hesitated only a moment before swivelling the pistol towards her, his intent clear. Austin struggled beneath Luis, shouting objections drowned out by the crackling fire. The sharp report of a gunshot sliced through the tumult, reverberating against the walls, and for a fleeting second, time seemed to suspend. Blood bloomed on Aaron's shirt as he lurched forward, eyes wide with shock. Ben's shadow loomed behind him. The body hit the floor with a thud - Aaron was dead before he could comprehend his fate. The room stilled, silence punctuated only by Beth's ragged coughs and the crackle of the fire. Then the flames, hungry and unrelenting, claimed a chair in their dance, casting flickering shadows across the chaos-strewn room. Luis's wiry frame shoved Austin aside as he bolted for the door. His haunted eyes revealed no intention of looking back, survival the only creed dictating his actions now. Ben wasted no time. He dove towards Beth, his hands reaching out to steady her as she fought to rise, her breathing still laboured from the assault.

"You're okay." He murmured, though his own heart hammered against his ribs. His protective nature demanded no less than to shield her from further harm. Austin, regaining his bearings, snatched up the gun that had fallen from Aaron's grasp. His sharp eyes surveyed the scene, weighing their dwindling options.

"Guess that's our cue to leave." He stated, the leader within asserting control over the chaos. Ben nodded in agreement, supporting Beth as she took a faltering step forward. Together, they made for the door, leaving behind the heat of the inferno and the cold finality of Abraham and Aaron's bodies sprawled upon the floor.

CHAPTER 20

Beth's lungs burned with the acrid smoke as she, Ben, and Austin spilled into the living hall, gasping for the less toxic air. The room behind them was a dichotomy of destruction, one half devoured by fire, the other eerily preserved. Austin's gaze darted towards the ceiling, his thoughts clearly racing to Chase trapped above.

"I need to get Chase before we lose the top floor," Austin said, urgency sharpening his tone, "but I don't have the key for his handcuffs." Ben unclipped his knife and offered it to Austin.

"Take this," the blade gleamed dully in the dim light, a sliver of hope, "maybe you can pry them open."

"Promise me, if you can't get him out before the fire spreads—" Beth's voice cracked, her resolve firm despite the tremble in her words. Austin locked eyes with her, the weight of the promise constricting his chest. He nodded, the motion reluctant but resolute, before turning on his heel and disappearing up the stairs. Ben turned to Beth, his hand finding her arm, gripping tight as if clinging to reality amid chaos.

"Beth—"

"We need to find Val and Reece, and Eve," she said, calculating how many people they had to warn, "and Jennifer and Hannah and—"

"Wait." Ben's voice was a deep growl, causing her to pause in her thoughts. His piercing gaze bore into hers, conveying a sense of urgency that went beyond their current peril.

"Ben, we don't have time—" Her protest was cut short by his sharp, sudden confession.

"I love you, Beth." The words hung between them, raw and unpolished.

"We'll talk later—" Her resistance dissolved as he pulled her closer, insisting on the moment.

"Later might not come, and I need to tell you how I feel, because every time I've hesitated in the past, something's happened and we've spent too long apart," Ben pulled her closer, his eyes burning with conviction, "when you're with me, it all makes sense. Your resilience, that fierce spirit, your relentless heart. Even in despair, you shine as the most courageous soul I've ever met. I thought I was living, but I was just surviving until I met you. I love you, more than anything. More than the air I breathe, more than I've ever loved anyone. I'll burn in that fire before I let you go again." His words cracked through the chaos like a vow. Fierce, unyielding, and honest. Beth blinked, her eyes stinging with tears. Her chest ached with the weight of it - his love, the risk, the moment she had needed in her darkest times of despair.

"Ben—" She swallowed hard, the lump in her throat threatening to break her wide open. From the hallway behind her, Luis charged like a bull, eyes feral, rage carved into every line of his face. He burst from the shadows and tore across the living hall towards them. Before she could process the reality of the situation, Ben pushed her aside just as Luis collided with him, and the two men tumbled over the bannister in a tangle of limbs and screams. Their bodies crashed into the lower level with a sickening thud, the impact echoing through the grand estate like a war drum. Beth's breath hitched, and time slowed. In a trance, she staggered towards the edge, her chest heaving. Her throat, still raw from Luis's grip, throbbed with every shallow gasp. Pain pulsed through her neck and chest, sharp and unrelenting, anchoring her to the present. With trembling hands, she peered down at the fallen figures below. The dim light made it difficult to see who had broken the fall, but it didn't matter. All that mattered was that both bodies, irrespective of which one was which, were both lying there, motionless. A primal scream tore from Beth's throat, a gut-wrenching mix of terror and agony as she watched in slow motion, her body trembling with shock and fear. She could still feel the burning grip of Luis' hands around her neck, leaving her gasping for air after she screamed as she gripped the edge of the bannister, her heart racing with dread. She dug her nails into the wood, hearing one of them snap, but she felt nothing. No pain, no pressure. As she peered down into the darkness below, her vision blurred with tears and her mind numb with disbelief. In that moment, time seemed to stand still as she tried to process what had just happened. In the darkness, there was no way to tell if they were alive or dead, severely injured or surprisingly unscathed. The only certainty was the haunting stillness of their tangled bodies on the ground below, shrouded in the dim light of the void. And in that moment, Beth couldn't help but wonder if this was all just a nightmare from which she would soon wake up from, or if it was the cruel reality she now had to face. She stammered unintelligible words as they dissolved into the thick air, incomplete, her heart thundering against her ribs. She leaned over the railing, straining her eyes to discern the outcome of the fall. Darkness shrouded the details, leaving her to wrestle with the unknown. Movement at Abraham's doorway snagged her attention. Adam, with Abraham's limp body hoisted over his shoulder, moved with haste. They slipped into the back staircase, disappearing from view. Beth's curse was a whisper lost in the growing chaos. Torn between following them or descending to the dining hall to check on Ben, she clenched her jaw and made for the main stairs, urgency propelling her steps.

With a burst of energy, Austin charged through the door into the cramped servants' quarters. His eyes immediately landed on Chase, who greeted him with a sneaky grin and heavily-lidded gaze. He was either stoned from the Vicodin or delirious from the infection, but right now it didn't matter which. The room was suffocating, filled with an air of desperation and hopelessness that seemed to seep into every corner. Austin moved swiftly to Chase's side.

"Time to go."

"Oh man, but I was just getting comfortable," Chase slurred, humour lacing his words despite the gravity of their situation, "I didn't think you'd come back for me so soon." His laughter grated as Austin fumbled with the knife, attempting to pick the handcuffs.

"Things happened a little quicker than expected—"

"Try again tomorrow when you've got keys." Chase muttered, his voice mellow with the drug's influence. Austin exhaled sharply, scanning Chase's face.

"That's not an option." He considered rushing downstairs in search of the keys, but the thought dissipated as quickly as it formed - time was a luxury they didn't have, and the odds of coming across the precise person with the correct key in all of the chaos was minimal. "Why?"

"We're getting out of here," determination set in Austin's features as he turned back to Chase, "one way or another." The cacophony of panic and the crackling of hungry flames reverberated through the corridors. Chase, seemingly becoming more aware of his surroundings, looked up at Austin, confusion etched into his brow.

"What's going on downstairs?"

"There's a fire," Austin looked back at the doorway, listening to the growing bedlam below, "so I can't come back for you tomorrow."

"Are you going to leave me here?" Chase's voice broke, quivering as he spoke. Austin's voice, strained with regret, broke through the chaos.

"I'm sorry, Chase." He murmured, forcing another pill past Chase's dry lips. Chase gagged on the Vicodin, his eyes reflecting betrayal and fear.

"It's okay," he rasped, his voice breaking from emotion, "when you find Tyler, please tell him I love him, and I'm sorry." Austin stood, walking over to the door and standing in the hallway as it began to fill with the smell of smoke.

"You can tell him yourself when you see him." Austin replied, shutting the door and sealing the room with a click. It was a half-truth, he told himself, as Chase would at least get the chance to see Tyler's body before they had to bury it. He could say his goodbye's then. Austin's hands, slick with sweat, fumbled with Chase's belt, wrapping it tight around the injured man's arm. The decaying flesh of Chase's hand lay in stark contrast to the healthy skin, a reminder of the infection that had taken hold. The room was stifling, filled with a palpable tension that seemed to seep into every inch of the space. Austin stood before Chase, knife in hand, his breath ragged as he tried to steady his nerves. Chase's eyes were wide with fear, his breathing shallow and rapid. Austin swallowed hard, his stomach churning with the weight of what he was about to do. He lunged forward, grabbing Chase's wrist and forcing it against the wall. The weak walls groaned under their combined weight, decaying wallpaper tickling at Austin's skin as he pressed against Chase's wrist. He gripped the knife tightly, wincing as the blade sliced through the air.

"What are you—"

"Forgive me for this." Austin pleaded before the knife bit into wrist flesh. Chase's howl pierced the air, a raw soundtrack to the gruesome severing of bone and sinew. With a savage yank, Austin pulled Chase's arm towards him, tearing into muscle and tendon. The injured man screamed again, his voice breaking from pain and terror. Blood spurted from the wound, splattering against the wall and drenching Austin's shirt. Chase's face contorted into a mask of agony as he struggled against his restraints. Austin ignored his own discomfort, focusing instead on the task at hand. He sliced through veins and arteries with brutal efficiency, watching as crimson liquid pooled down the wall and onto the floor. His hands were slick with sweat and blood, but he pressed on relentlessly. Austin's apologies were a litany as he worked, the knife a brutal tool of mercy until after what felt like hours but was likely only minutes, the hand came free with a sickening pop. Chase gasped for air as he lifted the bloody mass from the wall, feeling it squish between his fingers like wet paper mache. Austin quickly removed his shirt and bound the stump with it, staunching the bleeding with desperate pressure. Chase's breathing quickened as shock ran through his system.

"Austin—"

"Keep this upright." He held up the dripping mess and pressed the arm against Chase's chest with a sickening thud that sent shivers down his spine. He looked down at his own hands in horror - they were covered in blood up to his elbows now, but there was no time for regret or revulsion. They had to keep moving if they wanted any chance of survival. Together, they stumbled into the hallway, supporting each other amidst the dense smoke and rising heat. Down the grand staircase they lurched, Chase's feet dragging, an uneven rhythm against the stone steps. As they twisted down the staircase onto the third floor, and then the second, Anne crashed into them as she was ascending the stairs.

"What's going on?" She yelled, a mix of concern and fear in her eyes.

"Help me!" Austin's voice cut through the commotion as she emerged, her face a mask of shock at the sight of blood-soaked Austin and the maimed figure of Chase. Without hesitation, she shouldered part of the burden, the three of them descending deeper to the ground floor. Austin coughed out in explanation, his throat raw from smoke and shouting.

"There's a fire upstairs."

"What happened to Chase's hand?" Anne pressed, her medical instincts taking over even as they reached the safety of the gravel path outside. Austin barely managed to talk between breaths, the weight of his actions heavy in his heart.

"I cut it off."

"Why?"

"To save his life." They collapsed onto the gravel, the night air doing little to ease the burning in their lungs or the dread that clung to them as firmly as the scent of char, the rain cascading down onto them as they lay on the ground breathing heavily. Anne's voice pierced the night, desperate and commanding as she ordered the guards to fetch her father from the inn. They hesitated for a moment, stunned by the urgency in her tone, then sprinted down the path, their boots pounding on the gravel. Austin, his frame slick with sweat and blood, turned away from the chaos. His shadow was elongated on the ground, half-lit by firelight and half-swallowed by shadow, as he darted back into the smouldering estate, determination fuelling his every step.

Inside, the air was thick with the scent of burning, an acrid tang that clawed at the throat. Val's eyes snapped open, heart hammering against her ribs. The distant cries melded with the crackling that now filled her ears.

"Reece," she whispered, her voice hoarse with sleep and rising panic, "something's wrong."
"Probably nothing." Reece mumbled, words slurred by drowsiness, but a cough racked his body as smoke filtered into the room. In her sleepy state, she pressed her hand against her forehead, a headache forming from their evening fuelled with drinking followed by passing out in bed together.
"I feel like I heard a gunshot before, did you hear a gunshot?" She murmured, but Reece lay still, grumbling over his interrupted sleep.
"You probably dreamt it," he whispered softly, feigning reassurance, "now go back to sleep." Val's senses sharpened as she smelled the thick air.
"Smoke," she leapt out of bed, pushing the sheets aside, her movements swift, "wake up! There's a fire!" Her fingers found Reece's shoulder, shaking him with urgency. Reece's training

snapped to the fore as he jolted upright, his instincts cutting through the fog of sleep. His gaze swept the room, taking in the haze that marred the ceiling.

"Fuck." He cursed, voice gravelly as he scrambled to his feet. Together, they moved, their bond a silent strength between them as they faced the inferno inching closer. Val's fingers fumbled with the buttons of her shirt, the fabric sticking to her skin. She shrugged into her clothes with haste, each movement precise despite the tremor in her hands. The door swung open to reveal a monstrous blaze devouring the hallway, orange tongues licking at the walls with insatiable hunger. They hadn't woken to the commotion down the hall, not with how deeply they'd been sleeping. The fire had spread fast. It had found eager fuel in the silks, tapestries, and centuries-old timber, turning history into kindling, crawling through the walls and poisoning the air. Their room was close to Abraham and Beth's - the source of the inferno - but by the time they stirred, it was already too late.

"Reece!—"

"Back!" His voice was a commanding rumble as he pulled her into the safety of his embrace, shielding her from the heat that roared towards them. His arms, firm and reassuring, wrapped around her, a fortress against the encroaching flames.

"Try the window." She muttered, as he released her only to confront the stubborn glass that refused to yield. His shoulder slammed against the pane once, twice, but it held fast, unyielding.

"Here." Reece directed, his tone threaded with urgency as he gestured to the adjoining door which interconnected with another bedroom. They moved together, a dance honed by survival, slipping through rooms that mirrored their own, a twisted reflection marred by smoke and fear. Reece opened the door to the hallway from the adjoining room, but was again met with the same fiery blaze that was outside their own sanctuary.

"We're trapped." She gasped, eyes meeting his. The word hung heavy between them as flames barred the way forward, a fiery gauntlet they could not pass. Reece's response was a silent nod, his face set in grim acceptance. He drew her close again, lips pressing a wordless promise to the crown of her head. The world outside their embrace seemed to waver, the air shuddering with the collapse of timber and plaster. Val's tears were hot trails on her cheeks, her grip on Reece's shirt a lifeline as much as a plea.

"Val, Reece!" Austin called into the inferno.

"We're here!" Their voices lifted, a desperate duet calling out to Austin, confessing their plight. Austin's distant shout barely carried over the chaos, his words a jagged edge of helplessness.

"I can't get to you!"

"It's okay." Val whispered, knowing Austin couldn't hear her.

"Go!" Reece bellowed back through the smoke, his command cutting through despair.

"I won't leave you!" Austin called back.

"Get out! You can't do anything, just get out!" Reece yelled, cradling Val in his arms. Their sanctuary became a pyre, the heat pressing in with suffocating force. Val clung to Reece, her sobs melding with the crackle and roar of destruction, as the estate consumed itself around them. Val's voice, a hushed murmur against the encroaching inferno, carried a heartbreaking acceptance.

"It's okay," she whispered, her gaze distant, reaching for memories of a daughter lost to another life, "I get to see her again." Beside her, Reece's embrace tightened, a futile shield against fate. The estate groaned under the wrath of fire, and with a thunderous crack, the ceiling had begun to surrender to the flames.

"I'll meet you there." Reece whispered, holding her so tightly he might suffocate her before the smoke and flames ever could. Fiery logs, like the vengeful fingers of a scorned deity, rained down upon them. Val and Reece's screams pierced the heat, a symphony of agony and finality that tore through Austin's heart from where he stood, helpless.

"Val! Reece!" Austin's voice was raw, his throat scorched by smoke and desperation. But the cacophony of collapse swallowed his cries, and soon, an eerie silence took residence, punctuated only by the crackling of hungry flames. Austin stared, the muscles in his jaw clenched, as the room that entombed his friends succumbed fully to the blaze. The weight of loss bore down on him, but survival beckoned with urgent whispers. Turning away, he gazed at the chaos, each crack and pop of the groaning building was heavy with the ghost of their final moments, descending back into the maw below.

As she rushed down the stairs to reach Ben, Beth's mind was consumed with a whirlwind of emotions. Fear for his safety, anger towards Luis for his reckless actions, and most of all, overwhelming guilt for not being able to stop any of this from happening. Her feet carried her faster than her thoughts could keep up with as she reached the banquet hall, her entrance a burst of motion amidst the stillness of devastation. Her eyes scanned the wreckage before landing on the entangled bodies atop the table. She moved closer, dread clenching her heart as she reached out to touch Ben's face. His skin was cold and clammy under her fingertips, sending shivers down her spine. Panic set in as she tried to assess his injuries, dazed and disoriented by the chaos unfolding before her. Here they were, Luis' form twisted unnaturally, his final gasp etched into his contorted features, clearly killed by the fall, and Ben, a broken pillar atop the ruin. Beth's hands shook as she reached out, her touch tentative yet necessary on Ben's neck. A pulse, weak but defiant, throbbed under her fingertips. Relief flooded through her, chased quickly by urgency. He twitched, softly, but enough to awaken from the movement.

"Don't move." She pleaded, her voice firm though laced with fear.
"We need to leave." Ben rasped, consciousness clinging to him by a thread. His attempt to shift resulted in a guttural curse that echoed off the high walls.
"Stay still." Beth countered, her hands moving to cradle his head, her eyes darting around for a way to safety. Ben's heft proved insurmountable for her alone. His slide to the floor was jarring, his back arching in response to the sharp pain. She positioned herself behind him, lifting his head gently onto her lap. The warmth of his skin belied the cold grip of the situation, and she brushed a wayward lock of hair from his eyes, her movements betraying a tenderness amidst the turmoil. She looked over him, and bile rose in her throat. Ben lay crumpled in her arms like a discarded rag doll, his body broken in ways no human body should be. His face was a bloodied mask - skin split open at the brow, one eye swollen shut, lips torn and glistening with blood. His nose was bent sideways, possibly shattered, and crimson streamed from both nostrils, pooling beneath his cheek.
His chest rose in shallow, uneven breaths, but even that looked wrong. One side heaved while the other barely moved, suggesting broken ribs, maybe worse. His arm was twisted at a grotesque angle

behind his back, the bone likely snapped mid-fall, and his foot was bent backward at the ankle, like it had been spun the wrong way, tendons exposed through torn skin and sock. A low, wet groan escaped his lips, barely more than a breath, but it was enough to snap her out of her frozen horror. He was alive, somehow. For now. "You should—" he gasped, "you should leave."

"No," Beth cradled Ben's head, her fingers threading through his hair, comforting him as she whispered, "I'll burn in this fire before I let you go again. I love you too." His eyes met hers, a serene acceptance in his gaze before it fluttered shut and he succumbed to unconsciousness. She shook him gently, panic searing through her as his head lolled away from her lap. With trembling hands, she lifted it back, pressing her fingers against his neck. The pulse was faint, a whisper of life that spurred her into action. She tried again to drag him from the banquet hall, with no use. His athletic figure mixed with the dead weight was enough to feel like she was trying to push a car uphill. She screamed as she tugged, desperate to save him from the clutches of death. But her body betrayed her, unable to summon enough strength to pull him even an inch closer to the door. With a strangled cry, her grip slipped from his shoulders and she tumbled backwards, her head slamming against the unforgiving concrete. The pain exploded behind her eyes as she fought to get back up, peering into the void above as she saw flames and smoke billowing on the floors above. She tried to cry out, her voice hoarse and strained from the effort of trying to pull him towards the door, still feeling the effects of Luis' grip on her. She sat up slowly, crawling towards Ben's limp body. Desperate for one last chance at escape, she dug her fingers into his shoulders, but they slipped away like sand. Jacob and Barnett burst into the foyer, urgency etched in their features.

"Help!" Beth screamed again, as they followed her voice and raced into the dining hall to her aid. Without hesitation, they took Ben's limp form, hoisting it onto their shoulders. The house groaned, a lament for its impending demise, as they navigated the debris-strewn path towards salvation. Outside, the night air bit at Beth's lungs, a stark contrast to the inferno's suffocating heat. She scanned the crowd, their faces a tapestry of shock and fear. As she squinted, she noticed a vehicle's tail lights at the end of the driveway, cutting through the darkness, disappearing into the night's embrace. Anne's voice pierced the turmoil, Beth's eyes wide with horror at the sight of Chase's mangled arm.

"Where is he?"

"Who?" Beth coughed, trying to expel the thick fog of smoke from her lungs.

"Austin," Anne cried, "he went back inside!"

"Check over him." Beth implored, motioning to Ben's prone figure on the ground. Anne nodded, taking up the vigil as Beth turned back to the estate. Her footsteps echoed in the foyer, a rhythm of resolve amid the creaks of surrendering wood. She called out for Austin, her voice a beacon in the consuming silence. She came to a halt, her ears straining for any sound in the thick, eerie fog that shrouded the sprawling mansion. It felt as if she had stepped into a horror film or video game, with the heavy mist obscuring her vision and making it difficult to see clearly. As she gazed around, she stood motionless in the centre of the room, her eyes darting back and forth into the darkness above. The musty smell of the rain outside filled her nostrils, adding to the ominous atmosphere. Every creak and whisper seemed amplified in this haunting place, causing her heart to race with fear and anticipation. She couldn't shake off the feeling that she wasn't alone, as if unseen eyes were peering at her from every corner, but if anyone was still inside, they weren't making any noise. Despite the unsettling surroundings, she knew she had to keep moving forward. Somewhere in the dark halls, Austin was still here, and she wouldn't leave him behind. Cautious but determined, Beth ascended the stairs, the smoke a thick veil obscuring her vision. Each door presented a possibility of life or loss, and she left no stone unturned, searching for any souls lingering in the shadow of death. But the second floor lay barren, its rooms empty shells waiting to be claimed by the fire's relentless advance. Smoke coiled around Beth like a constrictor as she ascended the final steps to the third floor. The heat pressed against her skin, an oppressive blanket that threatened to smother. She emerged into chaos, the air filled with the crackle of fire and the scent of burning wood. Austin stood amidst it all, his figure a darkened silhouette against the leaping flames, his voice hoarse from shouting names into the void.

"Val! Reece!" He bellowed, the words tearing from his throat with raw desperation. Beth lunged forward, grasping his arm with urgency.

"Austin, we have to go." She implored, trying to pierce the veil of panic that had descended upon him.

"They're gone—" His voice cracked, and he turned to face her, eyes hollow with loss. A moment passed between them, an unspoken understanding, before she wrapped her arms around him in solace. Her eyes drifted past the licks of orange and red flames, peering into the room beyond. It was now nothing more than a tomb for Reece and Val, ingested by the all-consuming inferno. The walls were charred black, the air thick with smoke and heat that seemed to dance in front of her vision. In every corner, pieces of furniture and belongings glowed with an otherworldly intensity before crumbling into ash. It was a scene from hell itself, and she could only watch as their loved ones were devoured by its fury. A scream cut through the din, snapping their attention to the other side of the sitting room. They stumbled down the smoke-filled hallway, coughing, eyes stinging from the acrid fumes that filled the space. Beth reached a door, thrusting it open to reveal Jennifer's form rising from the tangle of sheets.

"What's happening?" She asked, her voice wavering on the edge of comprehension.

"What are you still doing here?" Austin exclaimed, rushing forward to hurry Jennifer from her bed.

"I took a sleeping pill," Jennifer confessed, "I wanted to sleep after—"

"There's a fire," Beth interjected, "we need to leave, now!" She commanded, urgency propelling her words as Jennifer scrambled to comply, slipping on shoes and a coat with trembling hands as Austin helped her to the door. Once in the hallway, Austin placed a hand on Beth's shoulder.

"Go downstairs with her. I'll check the rest."

"Like hell," Beth spat back, determination steeling her voice, "I started this, I'll finish it. It's my fault. I need to make sure everyone's safe." She met his gaze, adamant. Austin pleaded with her, his eyes searching hers for some sign of concession.

"Beth—"

"Right behind you, I swear." Her promise hung in the air, a tether to hold onto in the midst of despair. With a final nod, Austin turned away, guiding Jennifer down the stairs as Beth faced the inferno alone, her resolve an anchor as she pushed on to search the remaining rooms for any stragglers caught in the flames' merciless embrace. Her eyes scanned each shadowed corner, her breaths ragged as she moved from room to room within the Biltmore Estate. The opulent chambers, once a sanctuary, now echoed with only the memory of those who had sought refuge within its walls, and then the memory of those held imprisoned here. The flickering light from the fires cast ghostly silhouettes, painting an eerie dance across the walls. Satisfied there was no one left behind, she pivoted on her heel, her soot-stained boots leaving marks on the dust-covered floor. As Beth approached the grand staircase, a figure loomed through the smoke.

"Hey," she called out, urgency sharpening her voice, "hey! You need to get downstairs!" The shape came closer, almost gliding as if the footsteps were non-existent, until the figure was close enough that it solidified into Abraham, his tall frame cutting an imposing presence against the backdrop of chaos.

"You've brought ruin upon us." The figure intoned, his voice steady despite the bedlam. His blue eyes bore into her with accusation.

"Abraham, this isn't on me." Beth countered, her tone firm, even as doubt gnawed at her resolve. She wiped at her eyes, smearing ash across her forehead. Both his and her words seemed to echo off the walls, as if they were underwater.

"Val, Reece, Luis, even Tyler—" the figure listed the names like a litany of sins, each one a weight added to her burden, "their blood is on your hands." Beth shook her head again, more vigorously, a futile attempt to dislodge the guilt that clung to her.

"I didn't do this," she whispered softly, circling the figure in front of her, "this was your fault."

"Whoever conceals their sins does not prosper, but the one who confesses and renounces them finds mercy." The figure of Abraham quoted the scripture as if it was second nature to him, even as a figment of Beth's imagination.

"This was *your* fault." Beth repeated mercilessly, tears welling in her eyes, though from emotion or smoke, she was unsure.

"I didn't start the fire," the figure of Abraham pressed, circling around on the spot to meet her gaze, "I didn't pour poison down my throat or shoot my cousin in the back. I created a sanctuary for people to live in peace, and you destroyed it." Beth lunged forward, swinging at the figure's face. Her anger was futile as the figure disappeared into thin air and she fell to the floor, catching herself on her hands. She clutched at her wrists as she coughed, struggling to pull clean air into her lungs, as a hand seized her arm. Her muscles tensed, prepared to resist, but then she was moving, swept along by a force that brooked no argument. The second floor came into sharper focus as the smoke thinned, revealing Eve as her rescuer. Their descent was swift, the staircase groaning under their hurried steps.

"Why are you still in here?" Beth asked, her voice hoarse from the smoke.

"Making sure we're all accounted for," Eve replied, her features set in determination, "who were you talking to?" In the dim light, her hazel eyes reflected the blaze like twin flames. Beth remained silent, asking herself the same question. They emerged into the night, the rain unforgiving, washing over them in torrents. It plastered Beth's brown hair to her face, mingling with the soot and sweat. The cluster of survivors stood huddled together, their faces upturned as they watched the fire consume what remained of the third floor. Windows exploded outward, shards glittering like ice in the firelight before being swallowed by darkness. The rain couldn't drown out the sound of crackling timber or the collective gasp that rose from the group as the estate continued to surrender to the inferno. With every moment that passed, part of their world, a symbol of the divine order they had known, turned to embers and ash. The rain, now heavy on the smouldering mansion, seemed to extinguish some of the inferno as the roof opened up, but not enough to fully put it out. Beth's boots squelched through the sodden grass as she approached Anne, who was kneeling beside Ben. He lay on an improvised stretcher, his face pale against the shadowy backdrop of the night. A splint immobilised his arm, and a blood-stained bandage wrapped around his head hinted at the violence he had endured.

"Anne," Beth's voice barely rose above the sound of the rain pounding the earth, "how is he?"

"Broken arm, maybe a broken rib, shattered ankle, concussion," Anne replied without looking up from her patient, "he's lucky to be alive. There's probably internal bleeding. He's a fucking mess. We need an ultrasound."

"Please tell me that it's down at the inn." Beth pleaded, frustration etched in her voice. The shake of Anne's head was almost imperceptible, yet it set Beth into motion. As she turned back to the burning building, a strong grip fastened onto her arm.

"Beth, it isn't safe." Austin stood there, his brown eyes searching hers in the flickering light of the fire.

"I can't just stand here," she retorted, wrenching her arm free with a decisive jerk, "Ben needs the ultrasound. Anne needs supplies. There's more people than just him who're hurt." Without another word, Austin fell into step behind her. Together, they plunged into the smoke-filled maw of the estate, descending the charred staircase to the depths below. The infirmary was a scene of ordered chaos, shelves toppled, supplies strewn across the floor. Austin went straight for the small portable ultrasound machine, heaving it off the ground, while Beth tore through cupboards. She grabbed a small metal jug and smashed at the locked cupboards, forcing their doors open, prying them with metal clipboards and whatever else she could find to get inside. Bottles of painkillers, gauze, syringes - she grabbed whatever seemed useful and hurled them into empty boxes from the back room.

"We can't carry all of this." Austin grunted as boxes piled up near the door. But then they were no longer alone. Eve, Barnett, and Jacob materialised in the doorway, their silhouettes cut from the smoky haze like figures in a dream.

"We thought you'd need a hand." Eve smiled, grabbing a box from the doorway.

"Take these." Beth commanded, thrusting boxes into Jacob and Barnett's outstretched hands. Each one nodded, the unspoken understanding between them as palpable as the smoke that wafted up from the inferno above. They manoeuvred the precious cargo through the labyrinthine corridors, the urgency of their mission lending speed to their steps. Outside, the coolness of the night air greeted them as a balm. She watched as Ben and Chase were both loaded into the back of vans to be transported to the inn. They didn't stop moving until the medical supplies were safely deposited in the vans, away from the smouldering estate. Only then did Beth allow herself a moment to watch the destruction, the once grand estate now succumbing to ruin under the relentless assault of the fire.

Beth, we need to go now," Anne held the back door of the van open for her as Ben writhed in pain inside, "are you coming?"

"Yes." Beth said decisively, climbing inside and shutting the door behind her. As she took Ben's hand, holding it tightly, she took one final look at the estate through the windows as the van pulled away.

CHAPTER 21

Beth's grip on Ben's hand tightened with each jolt and turn, her knuckles whitening against his skin. The van, commandeered by Barnett, hummed with urgency, its interior packed with the wounded and weary. As The Inn on Biltmore Estate came into view, and relief spread through the vehicle like a whispered prayer.

"Stay with me." Beth murmured to Ben as they halted in front of the inn. Barnett jumped from the driver's seat and ran to the back, ripping the van doors open. He helped with Ben's stretcher, pulling him from the back as he groaned. Others from inside raced out to help.

"I'm going back for the others," he announced, already scanning the estate for those left on foot, "so they don't have to walk far if they're injured." Anne nodded as she followed Ben inside the inn. Beth watched Barnett peel off into the darkness before turning to join them. Chaos held court where diners once indulged in fine cuisine. The clatter of medical equipment and the shuffling of chairs filled the air, mingling with the groans of the injured, including Ben and Chase. Firelight danced on the walls, throwing stark shadows across Ben's contorted face as he was carefully lowered onto the cold floor. Beth turned to Anne, her voice steady despite the whirlwind of activity around them.

"What can I do?"

"Generator," Anne replied with clinical precision, pointing to the corner of the room, "we need power for the ultrasound." Beth set to work, connecting cords with swift movements. She handed the wand to Anne, who accepted it with a nod of thanks. Scissors flashed in Anne's hands, revealing the damaged flesh beneath Ben's shirt. His cry tore at the stillness as the wand made contact. Beth winced, but she knew she couldn't falter now, not when so much hung in the balance. She leaned in closer, waiting to help.

"Tell me what to do."

"Hold his hand, Beth." Anne's voice, steady and sure, cut through the tense air. Without hesitation, Beth clasped Ben's trembling fingers with one hand and gently brushed his clammy forehead with the other.

"It's going to be okay." She whispered fiercely, hoping her words could shield him from the pain. From a corner of the room, Julia watched the intimate tableau unfold, her expression softening. There was no trace of resentment in her gaze, only a quiet resignation, and perhaps the dawning of peace with the bond between Beth and Ben. Julia raced over, placing a reassuring hand on Beth's shoulder. Beth looked up at her, tears in her eyes, nodding in acceptance of her offering of comfort. With practiced hands, Anne manoeuvred the ultrasound wand over Ben's bruised skin. The hum of the machine filled the space between shallow breaths and muted sobs.

"Jesus. I have no idea how but there's no internal bleeding," Anne announced, her relief short-lived as Ben's chest hitched, a desperate fight for air ensuing, "I need Val. Val!" Anne barked, but the urgency faded into silence as Beth shook her head, eyes wide and haunted. Anne's next breath caught in her throat, her distress mirrored on her face before she spun around and called out for her father. Phillip appeared at her side in an instant, his presence a beacon of hope amidst the despair.

"Diagnosis?"

"Tension pneumothorax," Anne said, her tone clinical despite the gravity of the situation, "delayed onset." Phillip dove into the boxes of supplies, rummaging for the necessary tools.

"What's happening?" Julia pressed, more so on Beth's behalf than for her own sake.

"He has a collapsed lung," Anne explained to Beth, checking for her comprehension as Beth's nod was small but determined, "gruesome work ahead." Anne warned, steel in her voice.

"I'm not leaving him." Beth's response came firm and unwavering. With a scalpel procured by Phillip, Anne palpated Ben's ribcage, her movements precise.

"High-risk procedure," she murmured, "we'll improvise but we need to keep things as sterile as possible. Do you understand?"

"Yes." Beth's grip on Ben's hand tightened, her resolve as clear as the affirmation she gave.

"Keep him calm," Anne instructed, looking Beth in the eye, "calm, and *still*." The fire crackled, its heat incongruous to the chill of dread that settled over them. With every ragged breath Ben took, they were reminded of the delicate thread upon which life hung. Anne's fingers traced the path of Ben's ribs with clinical precision, pausing where flesh met bone, her expression taut with focus. She found the spot just below the collarbone, counting the second and third rib as landmarks for her incision. Phillip stood sentinel with a salvaged knife in his grip. Anne accepted the blade, the fabric of her shirt doing little to cleanse it but necessity overruled protocol. The sharp edge pierced skin, parting tissue with a surgeon's care. Ben's groan echoed through the makeshift hospital, mingling with the crackle of the fire. His body tensed, a slight jerk responding to the violation of the scalpel. Blood, minimal but stark against his pale skin, bubbled at the incision site while escaping air hissed its release. Beth, anchored by his side, tightened her hold on Ben's hand.

"It's okay," her voice, a soothing whisper, wove through the tension, "just breathe."

"Steady Ben." Anne murmured, her hands never wavering from their healing task. The urgency of the moment held everyone in a vice, each breath waiting to exhale until they knew if salvation or sorrow awaited them. The din of the makeshift hospital melded with the crackling fire, as other residents of the inn descended the creaking stairs to bear witness to the unfolding drama. They clustered at the edges of the room, some extending tentative hands to comfort the injured, others merely spectating, paralysed by the gravity of the scene. Beth's gaze shifted from Ben to Chase, who was writhing on the floor, clutching his hand close to his chest. Phillip, with a furrowed brow and a steadiness belying his concern, attempted to clean the wound while also aiding Anne in her urgent task.

"Can't manage both." Phillip muttered, a bead of sweat trailing down his temple. Austin stepped closer, his movements betraying neither hesitation nor doubt.

"What do you need?" He asked, voice steady.

"Keep the vodka flowing onto that wound," Phillip directed, nodding towards Chase, "clean it out."

"And pain medication," Anne glanced over her shoulder, her eyes meeting Austin's, "if we have any left."

"He's already had two Vicodin." Austin updated, the weight of each word measured. Phillip's grunt cut through the room's tension.

"When?"

"Earlier today."

"No more for him then," he decided, "he'll have to endure it." With the situation momentarily under control, Anne turned back to Ben, handing the bloodied knife off to Beth.

"Tubing." She whispered urgently. Her fingers brushed Beth's as they exchanged tools, a tacit acknowledgment of their shared purpose. Beth watched as Anne sliced a piece of the plastic tubing, salvaged from times less grim. The tubing, once meant to syphon fuel, now repurposed to preserve life. With deft fingers, Anne widened the incision, delicately guiding the tube between Ben's ribs. A hiss escaped, not unlike air from a punctured tire, marking the release of trapped pressure within. Ben's face, etched with lines of pain, eased fractionally as his breathing stuttered into a rhythm slightly less laboured. His pallor remained, a ghostly hue against the backdrop of flickering flames.

"The water jug." Anne's fingers maintained a steady pressure on the tubing, her gaze locked on the grim task at hand.

"I got it." Julia sprang into motion, her footsteps echoing across the wooden floor as she snatched the jug from its place on the cluttered table. She returned to Anne's side, offering the vessel like a lifeline. Anne filled the jug with water.

"Submerge it, just there." Anne directed, indicating the level of water with a nod. The plastic tubing was guided by Julia's trembling hands into the jug, disappearing beneath the murky surface to form an improvised seal. As Ben exhaled, a chain of bubbles burst forth, betraying the hidden wound's release. They watched, each bubble carrying away the pressure that had been suffocating him from within. Anne's eyes flickered to Ben's face, searching for the subtle shifts of recovery. Though his chest rose and fell with effort, the tightness around his eyes softened. It was a reprieve in their relentless battle against the odds.

"Is he—" Beth's words were strangled with worry, her gaze fixed on Anne for reassurance. Anne didn't break her vigil.

"I don't know," she admitted, the gravity of their situation etched into her voice, "this might just buy us time, but he needs rest." Her eyes finally met Beth's.

"What does he need?" Beth offered, committed to seeing him through.

"We have to watch for infection," concern etched Anne's face, "we're short on antibiotics, and Chase—" The unspoken understanding hung between them - resources were scarce, and choices grimmer still. They would do what they must, but the shadow of consequence loomed over them, relentless as the night. Anne's fingers worked deftly, pulling rags from a box of dwindling supplies. She tore a strip long enough to encircle Ben's chest, the fabric fraying at the edges. With each movement calculated and precise, she secured the tubing in place, knotting the makeshift bandage with a surgeon's efficiency. The blood that marked her hands transferred to the cloth as she wiped them clean on her pants. Silence claimed the room, save for the crackling of the fire and the groans from Chase. Anne leaned back, her spine meeting the wall with a dull thud. Her gaze lingered on Ben, his chest rising and falling unevenly under the dim light. Around her, the others sat motionless, each lost in their own contemplation of the fragile string by which their lives dangled. A cough rattled through the quiet, drawing Anne's attention sharply back to Ben. His eyelids fluttered, revealing a sliver of consciousness before succumbing again to exhaustion. Anne released a measured breath, her eyes tracing the path of the tubing, watching as each exhalation sent tiny bubbles spiralling up through the water.

"Go check the others," Beth moved closer, her voice soft but resolute, "I'll watch him."

"Keep an eye on the bubbles," Anne instructed, her tone leaving no room for doubt, "call me if he stops breathing."

"What else should I watch for?" Beth asked, her eyes never straying from Ben's still form.

"Signs of fever, pain, or if his skin turns pale or blue," Anne continued, her voice threading through the stillness, "and if his chest doesn't rise equally, we'll need to act quickly." Beth nodded once, her fingers tightening around Ben's hand, grounding herself in the responsibility placed upon her. The room settled into a rhythm of vigilance as Anne turned away to tend to the rest, the echo of their collective will to survive hanging in the balance.

Dawn filtered through the broken shutters, spilling a pale light across the makeshift hospital. Beth remained vigilant by Ben's side, her gaze fixed on his chest as it rose and fell with each laboured breath. Anne returned, her footsteps soft against the floor. She paused at Ben's side, observing the steady stream of bubbles before speaking.

"He's holding up," she said, her voice betraying the weariness of a night spent in service, "have you slept?" Beth simply shook her head, her eyes tracing the outline of Ben's face.

"Chase?" Her voice was a husk, worn from hours of silent vigil.

"We're in wait-and-see territory." Anne's response came with a clinical detachment, a shield against hope and despair alike. The room stretched around them, filled with other survivors, each cocooned in their own battle for survival. Beth let her gaze wander, taking in the hushed forms and the quiet strength that bound them.

"Where's Austin?" The question slipped from her lips, a need to touch base with another pillar of their fractured community.

"Down at the mansion," Anne replied, her hands busy feeling Ben's pulse, "checking the damage, seeing what can be salvaged." Beth squeezed Ben's hand, a silent promise woven into the gesture. "I should—"

"If he wakes up I'll tell him you were here all night," Anne interjected, preempting Beth's thoughts, "that you just stepped out for some air." Beth leaned over Ben, her breath a whisper against his ear.

"I love you," she murmured, the words carrying all the weight of her unspoken fears and hopes, "see you later." She held the moment, letting the warmth of her breath mingle with the cool morning air. Rising to her feet, Beth cast one last look at the man she refused to leave behind. His presence was an anchor in a sea of uncertainty, his fight a testament to their shared resolve. With a final brush of her fingertips against his, she turned away, each step carrying her towards a new day fraught with unknowns. Beth's stride was brisk, her boots crunching the gravel beneath them as she navigated the path leading away from the inn. Each step was measured, purposeful, carrying her towards the estate that loomed ahead, a silent sentinel against the morning sky. The remnants of the storm clung to the air, droplets of rain splattering softly around her, and with every breath she tasted the metallic tang of a world washed clean. The 20 minute drive the night prior was unmatched to the

90 minute walk she had found herself performing. The mansion stood defiantly, its ground and basement levels unyielding despite the gutted floors above. Beth paused for a moment at the sight, the resilience of stone and mortar a stark contrast to the fragility of flesh and bone. The third and fourth floors bore the scars of ruin, gaping holes where once there were windows, charred beams exposed to the grey light of dawn. She pushed open the grand doors, their weight insignificant against her resolve as she stepped into the foyer. The banquet hall sprawled before her, shadows clinging to its corners. Luis' body lay in repose on the table, a macabre centrepiece in the grandeur of decay. She circled him warily, half-expecting some trick of the light to animate his still form. The echo of footsteps drew her gaze up, and Austin filled the doorway, his figure cutting through the dimness.

"What happened?" His voice broke the silence, each syllable heavy with concern. Beth's eyes traveled upward, tracing the path of destruction.

"Luis tackled Ben off the third floor," she said, her voice steady despite the tremor that threatened beneath the surface, "they landed there." Her hand gestured to the shattered table, its remnants scattered like the pieces of the life they once knew.

"Jesus." Austin's face contorted with horror as he followed her indication, his eyes lifting to the skeletal remains of the upper floors. The image of devastation spoke volumes, more than words ever could. Beth's gaze lingered on the ruinous tableau, the once grand banquet hall now a theatre of tragedy.

"If it had been the other way around," she turned to Austin, her voice edged with grim certainty, "Ben would have died breaking Luis' fall." Austin nodded solemnly, his posture a bastion against the tides of regret.

"Best not to dwell on 'what-if'." He said, his tone suggesting a hard-won understanding of life's capricious nature.

"Still," Beth continued, the fire of loyalty burning through her words, "if I had come down to find Ben dead and Luis alive, I'd have killed him myself." There was no surprise in Austin's eyes, only the steady acknowledgment of shared hardships.

"I don't doubt that." He replied, his voice a quiet testament to their collective resolve. He approached the motionless form of Luis, crouching beside the fallen man with a reverence that spoke volumes of their tangled past. Carefully, Austin brushed the hair from Luis' brow, closing his eyes with a touch that closed chapters and settled scores.

"So long, brother." He murmured, a phrase heavy with unspoken stories. Rising, Austin met Beth's puzzled gaze, his expression painting a portrait of nostalgia and sorrow.

"We were brothers, once upon a time," he explained, his words bridging the gap between then and now, "been through a lot of shit together." Understanding dawned in Beth's eyes, a silent nod serving as her response. Her gaze drifted upwards, to where Val and Reece had met their own end.

"Have you been up there yet?" She asked, the question hanging between them like the dust in the air. He shook his head, the heaviness of survival pressing down on their shoulders. Austin led the way, his broad shoulders casting a protective shadow over Beth as they ascended the staircase. Each step was tentative, their ears tuned to the groans of the compromised structure around them. The mansion, once a testament to human grandeur, now lay wounded by the flames of desperation and survival. A piece of wood, charred and precariously angled against the wall, caught

Beth's eye. Without thinking, she nudged it with her shoulder, and it gave way easily. A cascade of ash billowed from the dislodged timber, enveloping her in a ghostly shroud. Austin's reflexes kicked in, his hand clamping down on her arm, ready to pull her to safety if the rest of the ceiling decided to follow suit. They shared a glance, the cloud settling around them like a sigh, and resumed their climb, reassured by the stillness that followed. The air grew thicker as they approached the room where Val and Reece had perished. The scent of burnt wood and lost lives hung heavily in the hallway. Beth's breath hitched in her throat, each inhalation laced with the acrid taste of regret.

"Are you okay?" Austin's voice pierced the silence, a low rumble of concern. Beth paused, her gaze fixed on the doorway ahead. Visions of Abraham, his accusatory finger pointing at her, replayed in her mind.

"I did this." She said, her words trembling like the frail light of dawn. Austin surveyed the charred remnants of what was once a sanctuary.

"You did and you didn't," he said, the truth of his statement landing softly between them, "the fire wasn't your fault, but you should've gone to get them like we'd planned." Beth's hands clenched into fists at her sides, the weight of could-haves and should-haves pressing down on her. She exhaled slowly, a gesture that carried little relief but much resolve. Beth's words hung in the stale air.

"If I hadn't gone to Ben, he might be dead," she said, her voice strained with the burden of their reality, "so either way, you'd blame me for someone's death." Austin's shoulders lifted in a shrug, an echo of resignation in the gesture.

"I don't want to argue with you," he replied, his tone even, the leader within him rising above the fray of what-ifs, "you made your choice." Taking a deep breath, Beth steadied herself against the emotional tide. They moved forward, navigating through the hallway fraught with obstacles. The remnants of a once-lavish existence lay scattered around them, reduced to debris by the calamity that had swept through their lives. Austin reached out, his hand resting on a blackened beam jutting into their path. With a firm shove, the charred wood yielded, disintegrating into pieces of charcoal that scattered across the floor. Dust motes danced in the shafts of light that pierced through the broken windows, and the soft sound of crumbling echoed off the walls. They stepped over the remnants of the past, each footfall a testament to their survival. Beth's gaze traced the outline of scorched photographs along the corridor, the faces within them forever frozen in happier times.

"Watch your step." Austin cautioned as they came upon a pile of splintered furniture. He extended a hand to help Beth across, his grasp sure and steady. Their progress was slow, deliberate, as they made their way deeper into the heart of devastation. A tattered curtain fluttered in the breeze from a fractured pane, the fabric whispering secrets of days long gone. Together, they approached the threshold of loss, where echoes of the life they once knew reverberated through the ruins.

"Austin—" Beth's gaze was locked on the room's grim spectacle, where the unmistakable remains of two bodies lay twisted and blackened amongst the rubble. Austin recoiled, his boot catching on a jagged piece of wood, sending him stumbling backward. With quick reflexes, she reached out to steady him, her fingers gripping his arm firmly. The ceiling groaned ominously, expelling another shower of debris. She tugged Austin away from the danger, his limbs scrabbling against the ash-covered floor as they retreated.

"Shit!" Austin spat out the curse as he turned his back on the horrific scene, his movements heavy with an unspoken burden. They descended the stairs in tandem, the once grand, now desolate foyer enveloping them in its eerie silence. Beth watched cautiously, half-expecting the quiet to be shattered by more destruction.

"Are you hurt?" Her voice sliced through the stillness, but Austin paid no heed, his breath coming in ragged bursts. He unleashed his frustration on the wall, his fist connecting with unforgiving plaster.

"Fuck!"

"Austin," Beth stepped closer, her eyes narrowing with concern, "talk to me." He faced her, his chest heaving.

"I was right there," he confessed, "so close, but I couldn't save them." His admission hung heavy in the air between them, a testament to their shared helplessness in the face of relentless calamity. Beth reached for Austin's clenched fists, now smeared with fresh blood against the backdrop of peeling wallpaper and scorched remnants.

"Austin, you can't save everyone." She whispered, her voice a blend of sorrow and pragmatism. He jerked his hands away, eyes aflame with an agony no inferno could match.

"You think I don't know that?" His knuckles cracked against the wall once more, a futile stand against the tide of loss that threatened to engulf him. She caught his wrists, halting another blow.

"What happened to your hands?" Beth demanded, scanning the raw lacerations crisscrossing his skin, wounds not born from this latest outburst.

"I got into a fight with a wooden post yesterday." The words rumbled from Austin's throat, edged with dark humour. Beth released his hands with a gentle shake of her head, the ghost of a smirk tracing her lips despite the gravity that hung between them. "I guess the post won." She turned on her heel, her boots crunching over debris, and made her way towards the library. The room stood as a mausoleum to the days before disaster - books nestled in their shelves, papers strewn across the desk in scholarly disarray, all untouched by flame. It was a capsule of normalcy in a world fractured by chaos.

"I checked the basement," Austin said, trailing behind her, "storerooms and kitchen are still intact." His gaze swept the familiar space, taking solace in its preservation.

"Good, you'll need to get those supplies to the inn." Beth responded, her voice steady as she ran a finger along the spine of a leather-bound tome, dust motes dancing in the air at her touch.

"Me?" He questioned, shaking his head in confusion. Their survival hinged on the careful rationing of what remained, on the hope that even amidst ruins, life persisted. Beth nodded firmly, the weight of responsibility settling on her shoulders as she glanced over at Austin.

"Yes, you should organise that." She said, her voice carrying a hint of command softened by the undercurrent of empathy. Austin's brow furrowed, a silent question in his eyes.

"What do you mean?" He asked, the words barely audible over the stillness of the estate.

"They'll need someone to guide them." Beth explained, stepping closer to place a comforting hand on Austin's shoulder. His muscles tensed beneath her touch, the mantle of leadership an unfamiliar fit for his broad frame. He tried to dismiss the notion with a shake of his head, but Beth persisted.

"You're a natural leader, Austin. You can help people mend," she urged, her gaze holding his steady, "just stay away from leadership styles like Abraham's." A laugh, more out of disbelief than humour, escaped Austin's lips.

"I could never be like him." He admitted, the very thought incongruent with his nature.

"Make friends with the Kingsport group," Beth suggested, her own experiences with Jocelyn and Kevin lending credibility to her advice, "they would appreciate an affiliation with a wise leader, instead of a tyrannical one." Austin's gaze drifted past the library, settling on the den where Adam's radio sat in stoic silence. The device, once a vessel for Abraham's iron rule, now seemed nothing more than a relic. Beth crossed the room, her movement fluid despite the chaos around them. She reached for the radio, her fingers brushing against the cool plastic and metal. Its presence was a reminder of a connection still intact, a line of communication unsevered by fire or fury.

"Kingsport, come in," she said quietly, lifting the radio, "Jocelyn?" Beth's fingers danced across the radio's dials with practiced precision, tuning out the static until a voice sliced through the white noise.

"*Who is this?*" The male inquiry was laced with caution.

"Tell her it's Beth, the former Mrs. Bishop." She responded, her voice even but firm. Austin watched over her shoulder, a faint smile playing on his lips as he admired her calm under pressure. Silence hung in the air for a moment before the crackle returned.

"*Beth? Where's Abraham?*" Jocelyn's voice was sharp, tinged with urgency. Beth held the radio up for Austin to take command, smiling as she gestured for him to take it. Austin took the radio from Beth, his touch gentle against the worn plastic.

"Dead, ma'am." He declared, his tone neutral, respectful, despite his disdain for the man.

"*Who is this?*" Jocelyn pressed further, seeking clarity amidst uncertainty.

"Austin Williams," he said confidently, "United States Army, acting commander of—" Beth's hand shot out, pushing his away from the transmit button to cut him off.

"We don't know who might be listening," she warned, her gaze steady, "don't give away where you are. You couldn't handle an ambush right now." Austin nodded and keyed the mic once more.

"You know where we are," he said cautiously, "best not to give away our position to unknown listeners, not in our current state."

"*Current state,*" Jocelyn's voice crackled back, confused, "*what do you need?*"

"Everything you can spare," Austin exhaled slowly, considering their dire circumstances, "there was a devastating fire. We have injured people who could use a clean environment and a proper hospital bed."

"*Understood,*" Jocelyn replied, her voice now softened with empathy, "*we can provide both.*"

"Then we'll see you this evening." Austin confirmed, relief seeping into his words.

"*Beth,*" a soft hiss of static preceded Jocelyn's voice, concern threading through the airwaves, "*are you okay?*"

"Better than I'll ever be." Beth replied, her voice steady, a stark contrast to the tremors she felt inside.

"*Then I hope to see you tonight,*" Jocelyn said before signing off, "*Kingsport out.*" Beth looked up at Austin, finding solace in his presence.

"Told you," she said, "you're a natural leader." He smiled, the corners of his eyes creasing with the expression, and carefully placed the radio down. They left the communications room, stepping back into the library where the dusty air and the stillness of forgotten words hung heavy around them. The grandeur of the Biltmore Estate library seemed frozen in time, yet it was no refuge for Beth. It was a mausoleum of memories that whispered from every corner. Austin watched her, noticing how her gaze flitted around the room, never settling.

"We."

"Excuse me?"

"You mean *we*, right? Before you said 'you couldn't handle an ambush right now'." His voice was low, carrying the weight of their shared experiences. Beth turned to him, her eyes reflecting the storm within.

"I can't be here." She confessed. Her hands clasped and unclasped at her sides. Austin's brow furrowed in concern. He took a step closer, his posture open, ready to offer support.

"What do you mean?"

"This place haunts me," Beth said, her eyes darting to the shadows that clung to the ornate bookshelves, "memories, they're everywhere." She gestured vaguely, encompassing the vast expanse of the library.

"Beth—"

"Finding Ben locked in that storage room, my jaw," she touched her face reflexively, "the attempt on my own life, Abraham—" Her voice trailed off as if each recollection snatched away a piece of her resolve.

"We'll build new memories," Austin offered, saddened at her pain caused by the walls surrounding her, "I need you here. Whether you like it or not—"

"I was a prisoner here. I've been trapped here for so long. I need to get out. Seeing the faces of Val and Reece and Tyler," the names fell like stones, each one a burden she could no longer bear, "it's too much. The ghosts of them asking me why they're dead, Luis and Abraham and Aaron haunting me too. I can't do it." Austin stood silently for a moment, absorbing her pain. His hand reached out, hovering just inches from her shoulder, an unspoken offer of comfort amidst the ruins of the world they once knew. Austin's gaze shifted to the doorway as if expecting someone to walk through at any moment, but there was only silence.

"What about Ben?" He finally asked, his voice betraying a hint of concern. Beth's shoulders slumped, the weight of guilt bearing down on her.

"I'm no good for Ben," she confessed, "you know it, Austin. I'm no good for anyone." Her eyes met Austin's, pleading for understanding. She took a step back, distancing herself from him and the pain that seemed to seep from the mansion's singed walls.

"I ruined your relationship with Anne, I burned down this beautiful place. People are dead because of me," her hands trembled as she continued, "Chantelle , I should've been there for her. I should've done better." Austin closed the distance between them, his presence solid and reassuring amidst the chaos.

"None of this was your fault." He asserted, his voice steady despite the crackling of cooling embers in the distance. Beth shook her head, a tear sliding down her cheek, leaving a path through the dust and ash that clung to her skin.

"That's a lie," she countered, her voice rising with conviction, "at least some of it is my fault. You can't deny that." Austin let out a slow breath, his own share of the burden evident in the set of his jaw.

"Maybe some of it is my fault too," he conceded as he looked at her, his brown eyes reflecting the stark reality of their world, "everyone has their sins." The word hung heavy in the air, and Beth recoiled.

"Don't use that word." She pleaded, the term resonating with a past they both wished to forget. Austin nodded once, an unspoken apology passing between them.

"I'm sorry." He said, and together they stood among the remnants of a life they could no longer claim as their own. Beth's voice was resolute, slicing through the stillness that blanketed the grandeur of the library.

"I can't stay." She repeated, declaring with finality. Austin's response came with a nod, as if he'd already accepted this inevitability.

"I won't hold you here against your will," he said, his tone more resignation than agreement, "you've been imprisoned for too long. If you feel that you need to leave, I won't try and convince you to stay."

"Thank you," Beth murmured, her gaze falling to the floor before lifting again with a hint of resolve, "could I take some food from the basement?"

"You can take whatever you need." Austin smiled as he stepped aside. Together they navigated the shadowed staircase descending into the cool, musty air below. Austin's hands moved deftly as he packed provisions into a bag, the mundane task belying the gravity of their situation. Emerging into the kitchen courtyard, he heaved the bag into the back of the Humvee. The sound of Beth's laughter broke the tension.

"My bag's still here from when we went to Kingsport." She said, a wry smile playing on her lips. Austin's laughter resonated in the open space.

"Take the Humvee," he suggested, gesturing towards the vehicle equipped with solar panels that gleamed dully beneath the overcast sky, "it'll get you pretty far."

"Thank you." Beth nodded, accepting the keys that jangled with a metallic whisper. Austin pointed to the radio mounted on the dashboard.

"If you need anything, just call me," he instructed, his words firm yet tinged with concern, "and this isn't much, but it's all I have." He then pressed a pistol into her hand, the cold metal kissed by the warmth of his grip, and folded Ben's knife alongside it.

"Thank you." She smiled, looking at her new vehicle with a mix of pride and trepidation.

"Where are you gonna go?" Austin asked, his eyes searching hers for an answer neither of them knew. She looked past him, towards the horizon veiled by the skeletal trees.

"I don't know." Beth confessed, and slid into the driver's seat, the leather unfamiliar beneath her as she adjusted to its contours. With a turn of the key in the ignition, the engine rumbled to life, a growl that reverberated through the cabin and into her bones. Austin leaned against the doorframe, his silhouette etched with concern.

"Are you gonna say goodbye to Ben?" He asked, the words heavy between them. She shook her head, a decisive motion that sent strands of hair across her face.

"If I go back to that inn, I'll never leave." She said, her voice resolute, yet tinged with sorrow.

"Is there anything you want me to tell him?" Austin nodded, understanding colouring his features. Beth met his gaze, her eyes reflecting a storm of emotions.

"He knows," she assured, "I've said all I needed to say."

"Come here." Austin beckoned gently. Beth emerged from the Humvee, stepping into Austin's embrace. Their arms wrapped around each other, a silent exchange of strength and gratitude. She felt the beat of his heart against hers, a rhythm of shared hardships and unspoken bonds.

"I'd be dead if it weren't for you." She murmured, her breath warm against his neck. Austin pulled back slightly, affording her a soft nod.

"I couldn't have done any of this without you." He admitted, affirming their mutual reliance. With a final glance, Beth reclaimed her place behind the wheel. The Humvee lurched forward, tires biting into the gravel, scattering stones in its wake. She navigated out of the courtyard, the estate's grandeur receding in the rearview mirror. The Humvee hugged the curves of Approach Road, the world outside a blur of green and grey. Circling onto the I-40, Beth set her course westward, the compass of her destiny now in her own hands. At the intersection, she paused, a laugh escaping her lips at the absurdity of checking for traffic in a world where vehicles had become ghosts. Merging onto the freeway, she pressed down on the accelerator, the hum of the engine growing into a roar that matched the pounding of her heart. Speed liberated her from the clinging shadows of her past, each mile a step further from the woman she had been forced to become. Laughter bubbled up, a sound foreign and sweet, only to morph into tears that streaked down her cheeks. The emotions tangled within her, joy and sorrow intertwined in a dance as old as time. Freedom enveloped her, an intoxicating rush that fuelled her spirit. And then, a scream tore from her throat, piercing and cathartic, a release of everything she had carried. It was the sound of chains breaking, the song of a soul reborn, speeding along the asphalt ribbon that stretched endlessly before her, surrounded by nothing but emancipation, emptiness and destruction.

DYSTOPIA SERIES

In a world decimated by plague and fractured by power, a group of survivors clings to hope in the face of unrelenting darkness. What begins as a desperate search for safety becomes a relentless battle against tyranny, fanaticism, and the ghosts of their own pasts.

Led by fierce loyalty and fragile trust, they navigate captivity, betrayal, and shifting alliances in a brutal landscape where freedom is a fleeting illusion and survival demands impossible choices. As one woman is thrust into the heart of rising regimes and twisted ideologies, her strength becomes the spark of resistance - and the key to reshaping what remains of humanity.

In this emotionally charged, post-apocalyptic epic, resilience is forged in the fire of adversity, and the greatest battles are waged within.

DEADWEIGHT
BOOK ONE

In a world silenced by plague and ruled by violence, a chance encounter sparks a fragile alliance among those who refuse to give up. As a small band of survivors journeys south in search of sanctuary, their hope is shattered by a brutal regime that thrives on fear and control.

Trapped within a fortress of despair, they face a chilling test of endurance, loyalty, and the will to resist. When escape feels impossible and choices come at devastating cost, each step becomes a fight not just for survival - but for the soul of what's left of humanity.

In this haunting beginning to a gripping post-apocalyptic saga, courage is forged in captivity, and the seeds of rebellion take root in the unlikeliest of places.

DOMINION
BOOK TWO

After a narrow escape from unthinkable captivity, the search for peace leads Beth and her allies to a fragile stronghold deep in the wastelands. But even in a place that promises safety, danger wears many faces - and some threats come not from outside, but from within.

As a deadly force spreads and power shifts into the hands of a rising zealot, tensions boil over into chaos. Bound by loyalty but torn by doubt, Beth must confront the price of survival in a world where faith can become a weapon, and no sanctuary lasts forever.

In this tense continuation of the series, strength is tested, trust is shattered, and the fight for freedom is more treacherous than ever.

DEFEAT
BOOK THREE

In a world ruled by fear and fanaticism, one woman's captivity becomes the crucible of a quiet rebellion. Trapped behind gilded walls, Beth faces a cunning tyrant whose vision for humanity is as seductive as it is brutal. To survive, she must become both a weapon and a whisper of resistance.

As secrets fester beneath a crumbling empire and the line between faith and control blurs, Beth risks everything to reclaim her voice - and her future. But freedom, like truth, comes at a cost.

This harrowing chapter in their journey explores the price of defiance in a world where breaking free is only the beginning.

STILL TO COME

More information can be found at
www.ceshorland.com

www.ingramcontent.com/pod-product-compliance
Lightning Source LLC
Chambersburg PA
CBHW031736180726
48283CB00005B/1532